MW01125262

ABEL

Also by Elizabeth Reyes:

<u>Moreno Brothers Series</u>
Forever Mine
Always Been Mine
Sweet Sophie
Romero
Making You Mine

5th <u>Street Series</u>
Noah
Gio
Hector

<u>Fate Series</u>
Fate
Breaking Brandon (Coming late 2013)

ABEL

(5th Street #4)

Elizabeth Reyes

Abel

(5th Street #4)

Copyright © 2013 Elizabeth Reyes

All Rights Reserved. This book may not be reproduced, scanned, or distributed in any printed or electronic form without permission from the author. Please do not participate in or encourage piracy of copyrighted materials in violation of the author's rights. All characters and storylines are the property of the author and your support and respect is appreciated.

This book is a work of fiction. The characters and events portrayed in this book are fictitious. Any similarity to real persons, living or dead, is coincidental and not intended by the author.

For information on the cover art visit Stephanie Mooney's website at: http://stephaniemooney.blogspot.com.

Editing by Theresa Wegand

I dedicate Abel to my loyal readers who've been waiting "forever" for this one. LOL. I'd like to thank you for your patience. You are the ones who make me so addicted to writing! Thank you for always showing your love and for reaching out! You guys truly make my "job" such a pleasure! I do hope this was worth the wait! Enjoy! <3

PROLOGUE

"I'm game if you're game." Nellie stared at him anxiously. A man's burning urges often ignore all logic. Abel Ayala knew this was all this was. A day of sipping on cocktails and lying around the deck of a cruise ship watching scantily-clad bikini-wearing women giving him go-ahead smiles had done it to him. Now he stood here, staring into the eyes of Nellie Gamboa, a divorcee eight years older than he was. From what he'd heard, she was still carrying a load of emotional baggage and probably still held a torch for her ex as well. She was someone he would not and *should not* be thinking of in terms of releasing some sexual tension. Damn it!

The fact that she'd turned her life around after what had been hailed by Roni, his friend's wife and Nellie's best friend, as one of the most grueling experiences any woman could go through, didn't help. She'd gone and shaped up and did a complete makeover from the mousy woman he once remembered her being. If he hadn't known it, he never would have even guessed that this sexy-as-hell woman would be hitting thirty soon. The sexual tension between them was a living breathing thing and had been going on for months now. Only up until now, he thought he might be imagining her requited feelings of lust.

His twenty-two-year-old ass had no business with a woman her age—no business getting involved with Roni's best friend—especially knowing full well he'd never take a relationship with her seriously. But this changed things. Nellie was telling him that she was all for a no-strings-attached relationship. She was as interested in anything serious as he was. Coming off what she called the divorce from hell, she said she wanted to live it up now. He was glad now for the liquid courage Nellie's wine had provided. If not for it, the offer may've never been voiced. She gone so far as to say that she was all for a fun-and-run experience and that she'd had her eye on him for some time.

It was still a risk, his brain reasoned. Things could sour. This could even cause a rift between him and his good friend's wife if any hurt feelings came from this. But the already throbbing parts of his body said otherwise.

She tilted her head in that sexy way she did so often with curved lips that practically called out for his. To hell with logic! Just pulling her delicate frame against his immediately released some of the pent-up tension that had been building every time he'd been around her lately.

Swallowing hard, he stared at those lips—lips he'd wondered far too many times what they must taste like. "Hell yeah, I'm game," he said as he took her mouth in his. Feeling a desire like none he'd ever felt before, he kissed her deeply, sucking her tongue and her lips. Damn, he wanted to eat her up.

He'd been fighting it—over thinking it—for months. This was just his ever-so-curious body's reaction to finally giving into a longing that had peaked tonight as they'd enjoyed a few friendly dances. That's all it was. But he needed more than just a kiss now. God, he wanted *so* much more, and since she was game . . . He pulled away from her just long enough to catch his breath and take a look around the almost-empty deck.

"I'd invite you back to my room, but Hector and Charlee might—"

She tugged his hand and was already on the move. "Let's go back to mine."

The second the elevator doors closed, Abel pushed her against the wall, pulling her by the waist to him, and his mouth and tongue sucked at every inch of hers. She panted softly, running her fingers through his hair as he moved down to her neck and sucked softly then a little rougher.

As the moving elevator came to a stop, Abel tore himself away. No sooner had the doors opened than they were out in a rush to her room. They turned the corner down the long corridor of rooms.

"How far down?" Abel asked.

"All the way to the end," she replied, taking even longer strides.

Feeling crazed with anticipation, Abel's eyes searched for the ice/vending machine room like the one on his floor. The moment he saw it, he pulled her in it.

He answered her confused expression with a kiss as he closed the door and pushed her against it. "I need to refuel."

All right, he needed to get laid more often. This was ridiculous. Obviously he'd been spending too much time training and not enough socializing, because he'd never felt this kind of urgency. Duly noted—he'd move a few things around in his schedule. She lifted her leg, bringing it around him.

"Careful," he warned, biting her lower lip, "or I may just finish you up right here."

"Do it," was her only response, and he froze.

Pulling back to look in her eyes, he could see she was serious. "Right here?" He asked, his hand already traveling down under her dress.

She nodded as his fingers felt the dampness between her legs and how hot she already was, pushing his heart into overdrive. He squeezed his eyes shut as he leaned his forehead against hers. "Sweetheart, don't play with me."

"I'm not," she assured him breathlessly.

Abel opened his eyes, looking down at her big brown eyes. Up until that moment, he'd never noticed the golden specks that were sprinkled throughout. The desire he saw in them now was as urgent as his own; although, he didn't miss the slightest bit of apprehension. He couldn't blame her.

Anyone could walk in on them. He was certain he'd be able to hold the door closed against the force of any one person or maybe two if they pushed against it—at least until he was sure she was decent. But he didn't want her doing anything she wasn't completely certain about.

"Are you sure about this?" He slipped his finger under her panties, her moisture inviting him in all the way.

She gasped, closing her eyes at his touch, and nodded. "The kiss on the deck . . ." she said, her eyes remaining closed. Abel stared at her lips as she continued to speak a little more breathlessly with every caress of his finger to her silky wet skin. "The elevator . . . This . . . It's exciting. I've never done something so . . ."

Nellie stopped to swallow, licking her lips, and Abel kissed her before she could finish. She didn't have to. Suddenly the need to make this happen for her, make this experience with him be one she'd never forget, took over. It was just an ego thing. That's all it was. What guy didn't like knowing he was a woman's first *anything?*

Abel reached for his wallet, but his lips never left hers. She kissed him back just as urgently, her hands grasping the front of his shirt. She gasped harder at the sound of his zipper opening. So he stopped and looked at her wide eyes. "I'm sure," she said before he could ask again, pulling him to her, and he groaned against her mouth.

Working fast, he got the condom on and reached under her sundress, pulling her panties down. When they hit the floor, he lifted her easily off the ground. "Wrap your legs around me."

She did and he adjusted her, groaning loudly as he entered her. Kissing her harder now as he fucked her against the door, he tried in vain to stifle his moaning, but it felt so damn good to be inside her. He'd been under the assumption that a woman who had been married, especially for several years, wouldn't be this tight. She was tighter than some of the younger women he'd been with, and it felt just too damn good to finally be doing what he could only fantasize about up until now—*so* good it was almost alarming.

With her arms tightly wound around his neck, she began to pant with every thrust, and he went even harder, her panting growing more frantic as he felt her begin to pulsate around him each time he slid into her. Just as her entire body began to tremble with pleasure, he felt her arms tighten around his neck as she pulled her mouth away from him to breathe and cry out. Abel couldn't hold it any longer either. Groaning again, he came in an explosive climax. Sinking deep inside her, he pushed his body against hers, burying his face in her sweet neck. Nellie clung onto him for dear life, gasping for air.

"We're, Nellie started to say before stopping to catch her breath, "still going back to my room, right?"

Abel smiled, squeezing her naked behind and looked up into her somewhat embarrassed eyes. "You bet this hot little ass we are. That was just an appetizer. I hope you have all night, because what I have in mind is gonna take that long."

Her eyes sparkled now with excitement, and she nodded. Hot damn! She was going to be more fun than he'd expected.

CHAPTER 1

To Nellie's surprise, since the cruise had been over a week ago, Abel had come by her place twice already. She hadn't been sure if their fun-and-run agreement on the ship meant he'd be running just as soon as they docked and came back to the real world. Apparently, their agreement extended even into their life off the ship. Still the stipulations stood—no strings attached—no promises, no demands, and no hurt feelings.

With a young stud like Abel—someone Nellie never dreamed would show an interest in her—she most certainly could deal with that, even if her best friend Roni didn't seem to think it was a good idea. She was on the phone with her again as Roni continued to voice her concern about the whole thing.

"You're gonna get hurt," she insisted. "You're not this type of person, Nellie. I know you. You don't do the fuck-buddy thing."

"Need I remind you that I'm no longer the same person I once was?"

Her ex-husband and sister had taken care of that. The old Nellie no longer existed. She'd since discovered taking risks, such as the one she and Abel had taken on the cruise, could be fun—more than fun—absolutely thrilling. She wanted to explore and enjoy this side of herself a little further. She agreed with Roni that, before the hell she'd gone through with her ex, she never would've dreamed of doing what she was now doing with Abel, but she was enjoying it. And since they'd set boundaries, they each understood this was just for fun. What they did when they weren't together and with whom wasn't the other's business. She had no expectations of anything more than a physical relationship.

Besides, it was what she needed right then: to be free to explore this and all the other sides of herself that had been dormant for years while her bastard cheating husband so often neglected her needs. She'd ride Abel literally and figuratively for all he was worth, and when it was over, there'd be no looking back. No regrets. What she didn't want to regret was passing up the opportunity to experience something this tantalizing because of the fear of getting hurt. Nothing could hurt Nellie more than what her ex and her very own sister had done to her.

"You're not gonna stop dating other guys, right?" Roni asked anxiously.

Roni was worried because she knew Abel would be free to fly in and out of Nellie's bed and into others' beds—and he was known for doing plenty of flying around—while Nellie sat around, waiting exclusively for him.

While the offers weren't exactly pouring in, she'd had a few. Nellie assured Roni she wouldn't be turning any down because of Abel. She did leave out the part that, while his visits continued, she wouldn't be sleeping with anyone else until she was ready to cut Abel loose. That is if he didn't cut her loose first. Sleeping around with more than one guy at once was something she wouldn't be exploring. It had nothing to do with being faithful either. She owed Abel as much as he owed her—nothing. It was a morality issue for her. While she wanted to enjoy her newfound freedom, she wanted to feel sexy and reawakened, not dirty. Still, she was sure this would only worry Roni further by confirming that, in fact, she wasn't the fuck-buddy type. So she kept this bit to herself.

Lifting a finger to her assistant, Emily, who peeked in her doorway, she spoke quickly into her cell phone. "Can I call you back?"

"Okay, but you better because I really think you need to think this through a little more. I don't know what makes me more anxious: that even though you won't admit it I think you're still very vulnerable to getting hurt, or the fact that you're doing this with one of Noah's closest friends. I don't wanna hate one of my husband's good friends, Nellie, not to mention business partner, but I *will* if he hurts you." She stopped to sigh dramatically. "Even though you've been extensively warned that this may very well happen, I'd still hate him."

Nellie smiled. "You won't have to hate anyone. Cross my no-longer-breakable heart, and, yes, I will call you back when I'm on the road, which should be fairly soon." She hung up and looked at her assistant. "Did it come through?"

Emily nodded, smiling big. "They want everything that's left."

"Yes!" Nellie clapped her hands together as she stood. "I'll get on this right away. We have signed docs, right?"

"All of them."

"Fantastic." Nellie did a little dancing walk as she reached Emily and hugged her. "I couldn't have done this without you. Thank you so much!"

"All I did was relay the messages and some faxing." Emily pulled back to look at her. "Which reminds me Logan left a very odd message for you while you were on the phone with Roni." Emily's face contorted. "*Slightly Stupid. It's on.* He said that you'd know."

Nellie brought her hand to her forehead. She'd forgotten all about that. "Oh my God, he got the tickets. I didn't think he would, and now I have to go to the concert with him."

"What concert?"

"Slightly Stoopid with two o's no u. They're that band I like. I even have one of their songs as my ringtone. They're playing at The House of Blues this month, but it was sold out last time I checked. He asked if I'd go with him if he could get tickets, and like an idiot thinking there was no way he could get them, I agreed."

The corner of Emily's lips rose. "Logan's pretty hot. I don't see what the problem is."

Nellie walked back to her desk, lifting her chin. "Because he started dropping hints about us going out almost immediately after he was contracted. I know technically I'm not his boss, but it still feels inappropriate. Not to mention I think it'd be awkward to go out with someone you work with."

"Well you're not his boss, so it wouldn't be inappropriate, and you don't really work with him. You said it yourself he's contracted and you only see him once in a while."

This was true, but with the mixer turning into something so much bigger than she'd anticipated, she'd be working a lot closer with Logan now. And Nellie didn't know if hot would be a word she'd use to describe Logan. Abel definitely was, but Logan fell more into the handsome-with-a-hint-of-vulnerably-sexy-thrown-in category. Thinking of Abel and the words hot and sexy all at the same time brought back memories of his last visit.

I wanna take you from behind. Just remembering his words and the way he had followed through with what he wanted had her puddling in places she had no business puddling while she was still at work with her assistant in the same room.

"Why are you blushing?" Emily giggled. "Oh my sweet Jesus, don't tell me you and Logan have already . . ." Emily covered her playful smirk with both hands.

"No! I just told you I've never agreed to go out with him much less just . . . you know. I'm not like that." The hell she wasn't, but she wasn't about to tell sweet little Emily the torrid details of the amazing time she'd been spending in Abel's arms—under his professionally chiseled body—on him, below him, on her back, on her knees, against a door . . . She fanned herself now.

"You're doing it again *and* now you're fanning yourself?" Emily plopped down in the chair across from her. "Okay, what gives? Something has you as red and hot as chili pepper. Spill it."

Emily was right. She *was* hot as a chili pepper. It wasn't something, it was *someone,* and, no, she wasn't about to talk about this here, especially not with all the sordid images and details that were flying at her now. But she'd at least relieve Emily's curious mind about Logan. "There is nothing going on between Logan and me, other than my agreeing to go to a concert with him. I was just thinking of someone else. That's all you're getting. Now scoot. I have a lot of coordinating to do."

Emily stood, frowning. "Fine, but if Logan calls again, I'm grilling him."

Nellie laughed. "Grill all you want. You'll be sorely disappointed."

After putting a few things together and making some calls about the cocktail mixer, one of the biggest she'd coordinated to date, she wrapped it up and left. She'd been so excited she'd forgotten to check her phone. Logan often called her office phone when she didn't answer or respond to her texts. He was persistent that way. Sure enough, she'd missed his call and he'd texted her. She read his text.

Slightly Stoopid, baby. You and me in a couple of weeks. No more excuses!

She refrained from groaning as she picked up her laptop bag and purse. It wasn't that she didn't find him attractive. He actually was attractive and witty, but he'd only been contracted as a project accountant a few weeks ago, and he'd been determined he'd get her to agree to go out with him ever since. Something about that was a slight turnoff. Sure what woman didn't enjoy being pursued by a good-looking man, but he was a bit *too* unrelenting. She didn't want things to get awkward for them when they had to work together.

The Hope for the Youth of ELA charity that she worked for now, in conjunction with the 5th Street Gym, was just getting off the ground, so this mixer that she'd been working on needed all the funding they could get. Now that the Ceja Vineyards had agreed to sponsor what booths were left and were incredibly generous about it, they had the green light to go all out. Nellie would be working even closer with Logan now, making sure all the monies were properly handled and well accounted for. She didn't want anything to mess this up, and that included any awkwardness if things didn't work out.

She hated to admit it even to herself, and she certainly wouldn't to Roni, but as long as Abel was in the picture, she didn't see how anything with Logan or anyone else could work. She just wasn't willing to give up the best sex she'd ever experienced so soon. Her ex-husband, Rick, should be hanged now that she knew how inadequate their sexual life had really been.

This only confirmed that she was so over him. After sex with Abel, it'd be like indulging in a rich strawberry cheesecake dessert with loads of whip cream and the promise of no weight gain then giving it up for a rice cake with a dab of peanut butter. She'd never go back to that again. Abel had even taught her that asking for what she wanted wasn't wrong. It was actually a turn-on to him, and if it was for him, it probably would be for other men as well, unless you were someone like Rick, who would most likely be annoyed because he wouldn't be able to just roll over and snore once he was done.

There were definitely things she'd be keeping to herself and not sharing with Roni because she wasn't about to ruin the best thing that had happened to her in years for the sake of protecting her heart. If anything, this was an eye opener and a learning experience. Unlike what Roni was worried about, once this was over, she wouldn't be sad or hurt. She'd be eternally grateful to Abel for helping awaken a side of her she never even knew she had in her. She even felt years younger and more energetic now.

On her way home, she did as promised and called Roni back. Roni answered on the third ring. "What are you doing tonight?"

"Uh, hello to you too." Nellie laughed. "Nothing, well, working. I got the Palos Verdes cocktail mixer fully funded, more than funded since the Ceja Winery took all the booths left. I have a huge budget to work with now, so I'll have my work cut out for me."

"That's great, Nellie! I'll let Noah know as soon as I'm off the phone." Roni knew how hard Nellie had been working on this, but, still, Nellie felt something was off about Roni's usual very genuine enthusiasm for Nellie and her work.

"Why did you wanna know what I was doing tonight?"

"Because I was hoping you'd say that you had a date with Abel."

"Why? I thought you didn't like me being involved with him?"

"Well, I do if it's going to be an actual relationship. So when Noah mentioned that Abel had a *date* tonight, I thought either you two had decided to make things a little more serious or it's exactly what I'm worried about. He's going on a date while you go straight home *alone*."

Nellie pressed her lips together, glad that she was on the phone with Roni and that she wasn't hearing this in person. She didn't think she could pull off acting as if it didn't matter as she'd been insisting to Roni all along. The thought of Abel rocking another woman's world as he'd done to hers only a few nights ago, slammed through her violently. She knew from the very moment she decided to give into her desires—desires that had been mounting for months—that this reaction was a possibility. Since Abel hadn't made a move prior to the cruise, even though he was obviously unable to hide his attraction to her, Nellie figured it was the age difference or that he simply wasn't looking for anything serious.

Her decision hadn't been on a whim either. Abel had confirmed on that deck as she stared at his lips what she'd been thinking all along. He'd made it perfectly clear that he was very attracted to her but that he didn't want to piss Noah off by messing with his wife's best friend. With his career and this fight looming, he didn't really have time for a social life at all, much less anything serious. Nellie had offered what she'd been considering for months: guilt-free sex with no strings attached. She'd made up her mind long before the cruise that if she ever had the opportunity to put it out there that way she would. So when she had it, she took it. Apparently, Abel had more time than he'd insinuated if he was making time for more than just her.

"If I didn't have so much work, I might not be going straight home tonight."

That wasn't entirely a lie. If she didn't have so much work to get to, she might've stopped to buy more wine to drink at home *alone*. She was getting low, down to less than half a bottle, but she'd let Roni think otherwise.

"Nellie, I'm just going to go on the record and say I *hate* this. When Noah told me about Abel's date, I was seriously pissed for you." Roni hushed her words to a whisper. "Wasn't he just over at your place a few days ago?"

Nellie clenched her teeth for a second, not wanting to think about it. "Yes, he was, but I told you, Roni, that I'm okay with this." She tightened her grip on the wheel then remembered. "And hey, guess who has a date in a couple of weeks and *not* with Abel?"

"You *do*?" Roni wasn't whispering anymore. Nellie wasn't even sure why she had in the first place. It wasn't as if Noah didn't know about her and Abel. "With whom?"

"I told you about Logan, right?"

"The new guy you said was kind of pushy?"

Nellie rolled her eyes. "I'm pretty sure I used the word persistent, but, yeah, him. Emily says she thinks he's hot." She hoped that throwing that in would excite Roni, because Nellie in all honesty didn't exactly agree with Emily. Her idea of hot was now synonymous with only one guy. And Logan didn't even come close in her opinion. "We're gonna go see Slightly Stoopid at the House of Blues."

"You are? I thought you said it was sold out."

Nellie knew Roni would be a bit disappointed. They had talked about going together. Everybody knew it was their favorite band lately, but it'd been sold out. "They were. I don't know how, but he got the tickets. I could ask if he can get more if you want."

"No. We'll go see them together another time. I don't want to crash in on your date. This is a date, right? You called it that. So that's different than with Abel." Nellie could almost picture Roni's furrowed brows as she paused. "Please tell me this is different than with Abel."

Nellie attempted to chuckle, though thoughts of Abel on *his* date tonight made her stomach tighten, and a chuckling mood was the last thing she was in. "It's different, but don't get all excited or anything. I work with the guy. I'm not looking to make things uncomfortable for us. So, yes, I called it a date only because we're going somewhere other than my bed, but don't expect any engagement announcements or anything. I already told you I'm not ready to get into anything serious with *anyone*."

After filling Roni's inquiring mind a little more about Logan, Nellie was off the phone, and her thoughts were immediately on Abel. Except for small talk and a few questions Abel had asked her about the people in the photos in her home, they rarely spoke of their personal lives. The only times he ever really opened up were to talk about his upcoming fight for the heavyweight title. She'd never dream of asking him about his dates with other women. It was none of her business, and she doubted he'd ever ask her about her dates, but mostly because she now knew she'd rather not know about his.

Deciding ignorance was bliss, Nellie drove into her garage, determined to not think about something that didn't matter anyway. Even this wouldn't ruin the breathtakingly little time Abel gave her. She'd meant it when she told Roni she wasn't ready for anything serious anyway.

CHAPTER 2

Making a quick move toward the front door, Abel walked as quietly as he could.

"*Oh,* you look handsome."

Damn. Abel stopped and glanced up at his mother who was looking away from the stove where she was making dinner, while his brother Hector and his girlfriend, Charlee, studied at the kitchen table.

Hector smirked, knowing Abel's cover had been blown. "Another *non*-date with Nellie?"

Abel gave him a look but ignored the question, walking into the kitchen instead of out the door. His mother, on the other hand, as expected, didn't ignore Hector. "Nellie?" She turned to Hector first then back to Abel with a confused expression. "You're dating, Nellie, *Mijo*? Roni's friend?"

"No, Mom, I'm not dating *anyone.*" He shot Hector another warning look. "I already told you I gotta train. I don't have time for dating right now."

His mother was no fool. She threw the dish towel she held over her shoulder and wiped her hands on her apron with a knowing look. "Then where are you going tonight?"

"To hang out with a *friend,*" he said, stabbing a fork into one of the pieces of chicken she had simmering in green sauce and blew on it. He held his hand underneath in case it dripped. "But it's not a date."

His idiot brother was obviously enjoying this. "I'm pretty sure that's what you called it when Noah asked at the gym."

Abel rolled his eyes, biting into the chicken on his fork.

"*Ay*, Abel. So just say it. What's the big deal?" his mom asked as she stirred the beans in the other pot. "Wait, Nellie? Isn't she Roni's age?"

Hector laughed. He knew just as well as Abel that their mother had never been too keen about Noah marrying a girl eight years older. It was no surprise this would be the first thing she'd bring up. Both he and his brother knew their mother would have issues with this—issues he wasn't willing to discuss or get into. It didn't matter—he wasn't dating her.

"It's not a date, and who said I'm seeing Nellie tonight anyway?" Abel set the fork down, kissed his mom's forehead, and looked back at his brother. "I told Noah I had a date. I never said with whom."

His brother gave him a knowing look. Aside from getting together with Nellie in the past few weeks, Abel had been too caught up in his training and everything else leading up to this fight for a social life, period. Hector knew all too well that Nellie had been Abel's only escape from all the fight madness in weeks. And since Abel was notoriously private about his personal life, Hector was also the only one who would know this. Even one girl was too much of a distraction for Abel's anal ass. Juggling more than one at a time like this in his life would be out of the question, so there was no use denying it.

"Okay, so I'm meeting up with her again, but it's not a date," he said as indifferently as he could. "I just said I had a date to Noah to get him off my back. The guy asks too many questions.

"Yeah, well you know why," Hector said just as Abel walked up behind him and squeezed his shoulder so hard that Hector leaned over. "Because he's nosey, that's all. That's *all*," Hector repeated as Abel squeezed harder.

Abel squeezed one last time for good measure. Playful banter or not, he was not getting into this now. The bottom line was Nellie was *exactly* what he needed right now: someone he could spend time with and release all the pent-up stress that was building up because of this fight, without any demands of commitment. And since Nellie was okay with him squeezing in some release time after his training here and there without asking for more, this was the perfect arrangement. God damn it. He'd never needed to release so much in his life.

Coming off that cruise, he told himself he'd keep his distance. As long as she was game, he'd go see her once or twice a month—keep things light—but he hadn't been able to go even a few days before he showed up at her place and they'd gone at it all night.

After that, he promised himself he'd had his fill and didn't need to pay another visit for at least another few weeks, and, son of a bitch, he made a detour on his way home just the other night. Now here he was with every intention of seeing her again, only this time he was going to ask her if she wanted to have dinner first. It was beginning to feel a little rude, his showing up just to get his glorious release and then leave while she slept soundly.

Abel had showered and cleaned up at the gym. Since the bathroom in the pool house behind the house where his mom and brother lived was being remodeled, he'd even taken clothes to change into, all for the sake of avoiding any type of interrogation from his mom. He'd even been willing to endure Noah's questioning instead. Now, because his dumb ass had forgotten his ATM card in the main house, he'd been caught doing both.

Ever since Nellie told Roni about what happened on the cruise, Noah had been all over Abel. In the very beginning, Noah had been angry. Abel remembered that first phone call he'd gotten from Noah the night they got back from the cruise. Obviously Nellie had told Roni everything.

"Are you serious? You're gonna do this with *Nellie*? Do you know the *shit* I'm gonna have to hear once you wipe your hands of her and move on? Hell, I'm already hearing it."

Abel thought he'd silence him when he told him this was *her* idea. But Noah came right back at him.

"Of course it's her idea. She's lonely right now—vulnerable." Abel was still having fun, listening to his paranoid friend fret until his next comment. "Roni knows her better than anyone, and even though Nellie claims she's ready to let loose and make up for lost time, Roni's still worried. She's not a dude, and most important, she's never been like that. Jumping from one bed to another and having meaningless sex with one guy after another will have her feeling like shit in no time. I don't want you, *my* friend, to be caught up in this mess. I'll never hear the end of it."

Abel had been short on words, promising only that he'd keep his distance, only to replay that damn conversation in his head again and again, even as he'd driven to Nellie's place the very next day. He'd make sure he'd work her out long and *hard*, leaving her so exhausted she couldn't possibly think about jumping into anyone else's bed, not for a while anyway. Not that it mattered. It was just a game—a guy thing. It was hard to explain, but the satisfaction he'd felt when he left her sleeping so soundly that she could sleep into next week with no energy to even be thinking about other guys, was damn good. He was enjoying this. That's all it was.

Tonight, Noah had started in on him again, when he saw him getting dressed and not in the usual basketball shorts that he typically changed into just to go home in. But Abel had been quick to shut him up by saying that he had a date. Noah knew Abel didn't refer to his time with Nellie that way. As long as Noah didn't push, he wouldn't have to tell him the truth. Thankfully, Noah hadn't and Abel had left it at that.

He thought the questioning was over from his mom.

"Does Nellie cook?" His mother asked as she sipped from a serving spoon.

"Ma," Abel had to laugh with Hector now. He grabbed his keys. "It doesn't matter."

"What do you mean it doesn't matter?"

"Okay, okay, she cooks, Mom." He turned to her as he reached the door, bouncing his eyebrows. "She cooks *real good.*"

"Ay, *cochino!*" His mother threw the dishtowel at him, but it hit the door as he walked out. "Don't wait up!" he yelled, still laughing as he walked down the concrete stairs.

Abel could hear Hector and Charlee laughing and then his mom scolding Hector for laughing. He shook his head as he reached his car. Suddenly, all thoughts of his mom and Noah's questioning were pushed to the back of his mind, and he thought of something more urgent. He needed to stop and buy more condoms—lots more.

After setting up her laptop on her dining room table, Nellie decided she'd have a glass of wine while she worked. Glad that she had so much work to keep her mind busy and off *other* things, she set her glass of wine on the table. She was about to take a sip when she heard the rumbling of a car engine pull up outside then turn off.

Curious, she stood up and out of her chair. The second she peeked out of her window and saw Abel's car in her driveway, she darted off to her bathroom. Her heart was already pounding, and she felt as silly as a school girl, but she couldn't help it. Luckily, he was sitting in the car still on the phone, so she had a few seconds to freshen up.

Thoughts of his *date* came to mind. Had it fallen through? Was he here for a consolation prize? Is that what she'd now become? "Oh stop!" she said to herself in the mirror as she powdered her nose. "You're being ridiculous," she continued to whisper softly. "This is the perfect setup. Who could ask for more? The guy's body is *unreal!*" Now she pointed at herself menacingly. "Don't you dare let your feelings get involved and ruin this!"

After rinsing with mouthwash and spraying a little perfume on, she hurried to the front door. He'd already knocked once.

"Hey," she said, trying to tone down the huge smile and not look so ecstatic to see him as she opened the door for him.

"Hey," he said with a smile just as big as hers felt then stepped in. Before she could say another word, he pulled her to him. His mouth was on hers instantly, kissing her feverishly.

Nellie fell into his possessive embrace, feeling every inch of his hard body press up against hers. His mouth continued to devour hers as if he hadn't kissed her in months. She held onto him tightly, feeling her legs go weak with every stroke of his tongue, which wrapped around hers. When he finally came up for air, he leaned his forehead against hers and smiled. "You busy?"

Taking a deep breath but still unable to even speak, she shook her head and gulped. His eyes were so dark and full of shine. It had always amazed her how sexy and welcoming his stares could be only to turn into such a contrast when those very same eyes were in the ring, staring down an opponent ominously. They were still sexy as sin either way, but she'd only recently begun to see the smoldering stare—a new one she liked to think he reserved just for her. But she knew better.

Her mind had wandered off to what he would do to her tonight. The very thought unbelievably had her tingling already.

"You wanna go to dinner?"

That shot her right out of her thoughts. "Dinner?"

Abel shrugged, pulling away a bit, and she had to fight the urge to pull him back to her. "Yeah, I figured I owe you that much."

Immediately she shook her head, wondering if Noah or Roni had somehow put him up to this. Maybe Roni had picked up on the dive her mood took over the phone and told Noah to do something about it. "You don't owe me anything, Abel. We went over this in the beginning, and I'm good with the way things are. I really am. In fact, I'm *great* with this arrangement. It's for the best this way. No demands, remember?" She really hoped she sounded convincing, because as much as she hated to admit it, she was more than thrilled to know he was here and not out on his *date,* regardless of why. The last thing she wanted was for him to start thinking that she was expecting more and for his visits to cease.

She noticed his eyes going a bit dark, and he lifted a brow. "Yeah, I remember. I just thought it'd be cool if we went to dinner first." His jaw clenched for a moment then added. "There's a place downtown I think you might find interesting."

Secretly excited that he wanted to do more than their usual but amazing romps, she lifted a shoulder and tried to appear as indifferent as she could. "I guess. I *had* skipped dinner." She nodded in the direction of her dining table with her laptop and a still-full single wine glass. "I was just going to do a little work, but now that you mention it, I am a little hungry."

"Good." His lips spread into a sexy smile. "Then let's go."

She loosened her hand from his so she could go grab her purse from her bedroom, but he grabbed her hand back and pulled her to him again, diving into her neck. Feeling his warm tongue lick her neck then suck it made her tingle in the most private of places, and her entire body trembled in response.

In reaction to her trembling, he sucked harder, moaning against her neck. "God, you taste good."

Unable to hold it in, she gasped as his tongue continued to tease and work its way down to just below her earlobe. She felt him chuckle softly against her ear. "Don't worry," he murmured. "After dinner, I have every intention of coming back here and tasting *every* part of your body."

To her dismay, on those words, he let her go, and she walked away, feeling light-headed, nearly stumbling in the process. His words still lingered even as she grabbed her purse and a light sweater . . . *tasting every part of your body.*

Nellie took one last trembling breath, trying to compose herself before she walked out of her bedroom. No sooner did she reach him in the front room than he took her hand and pulled her to him again. There was a noticeable gentleness about the way he kissed her now. It was still very sensual and very deep, but he toned down the aggressiveness.

"Damn, Nell," he whispered against her lips in a tone that was new to her then inhaled deeply before finally pulling away and leaving her confused.

"What?" She asked, looking into his eyes.

He shook his head, and for a moment, he appeared unnerved as if those last two words had maybe slipped out. "Nothing," he smirked. "You just taste damn good." He kissed her again quickly. "I can hardly wait until later."

She almost got the nerve to suggest that maybe they shouldn't wait. Maybe they could just skip the restaurant and get down to the business of him *tasting* her. But the nerve evaporated quickly as her face heated just from thinking about it.

Without saying it, she *did* want him to know that she was looking forward to later just as much as he was. Biting her tongue, she smiled at him seductively, sending an unspoken message with her eyes. That seemed to do it. His eyes were on her lips immediately as the corner of his mouth lifted. She'd leave it at that and then *show* him later exactly how much her body was yearning for him as well. For now, they were off to dinner.

✳✳✳

They arrived at *The Den*, the place Abel had mentioned would be interesting. It was. While it was obviously a restaurant, it was unusually dark with most of the light coming from the candles that adorned the small intimate tables. And although waiters walked around with trays of food and patrons were enjoying their dinner, the atmosphere was more like a swanky underground club. There were dramatic drapes that covered the walls and matched the linens on the tables and chairs. Throbbing dance music was coming from another room, though their maître d' led them into the dining area.

"My agent told me about this place," Abel whispered in her ear as they walked behind the maître d'. "I have no patience for the paparazzi or overzealous fans. When I signed up for this fight, I knew it would be bad, but I had no idea it'd get this crazy. He pretty much said that I should get used to it, so places like this are best if I wanna keep my social life on the down low."

Social life? She nodded, refusing to comment on that. Did he really consider their booty calls part of his social life? Just then, their waiter lifted the drapes against the wall that actually opened up into a very private booth.

Abel smiled as their eyes met. "I've been here a few times, but this is the first time I requested this much privacy."

Feeling a rush of excitement laced with a bit of sudden nervous energy creep up her spine, Nellie turned back to the waiter and smiled as she slipped into one side of the large booth.

To her surprise, instead of slipping into the seat across from her, Abel slipped in right next to her, immediately taking her hand in his. The waiter took their drink orders then walked away, closing the drapes behind him. They now sat there in complete seclusion from the rest of the restaurant patrons.

Nellie had heard of restaurants like this in Los Angeles for the many celebrities and VIPs who cherished their privacy. She just never would've imagined being at one of these places and sitting next to such an intimidating yet tantalizing specimen of a man.

From the way he'd acted the moment he arrived at her house that evening and being in such an intimate setting, she naturally expected him to start driving her insane with his kisses and tasting her neck the moment the waiter left them alone. To her surprise, he took a sip of his water and sat back. He *did* bring his big arm around the back of the booth, the playful touch of his fingers to her hair alone making her quiver with anticipation.

Regardless of what a small gesture it was compared to how he'd behaved earlier, Nellie's heart sped up anyway. She knew there was no way he'd asked for this much privacy just so he could play with her hair.

She took a sip of her own water, sucking in a small piece of ice in the hopes it would cool her burning insides at least a little.

"So how's the cocktail mixer coming along?" he asked, his fingers still playing with her hair. "Last I heard, Noah said you had some heavy hitters lined up. That's pretty awesome. The last coordinator we had for these things wasn't nearly as successful at getting this kind of stuff together."

Nellie smiled, looking up into those usually very sensual eyes. They now looked genuinely pleased. They'd done little talking during their previous steamy encounters. And of what little they had done, zero of it was personal. Now he seemed ready to chat.

"Are you ready for your drinks?" The waiter asked from the other side of the curtain.

"Yes, we are." Abel replied.

The waiter opened the curtain and set down Nellie's glass of wine first then Abel's rum and Diet Coke. "Are you two ready to order, or would you like some more time?"

Nellie and Abel hadn't even opened their menus. "We're gonna need a little more time," Abel said as his fingertips grazed Nellie's nape ever so softly.

In an effort to conceal her shivering, she reached for the menu that still sat unopened in front of her. It was insane how his touch alone could nearly send her over the edge.

Clearing her throat, she attempted to sound as collected as possible. "Actually, we're all booked and ready to go. A winery from up north decided to take all the booths left, and they were very generous with their donation. Now it's up to me to get it all together, and with the budget we have now, it should be a huge success." She sipped her wine then smiled at him. His eyes hadn't left hers since he'd asked the question. They twinkled with pleasure, and his eyebrows were now raised in reaction. "I'm very excited about it. It's what I was working on when you dropped by today."

Abel smiled big now as she lifted her glass to her lips, making her gulp down the wine harder than she'd anticipated. The man she not too long ago referred to as a boy because of their age difference was absolutely a man in every sense of the word and a beautiful one at that. How in the world had she scored getting this *man* in *her* bed? He was eye candy for crying out loud!

He lifted his glass in the air. "Well, that's awesome," he said as she lifted her own glass again. "I say this is cause for a celebration." They clinked their glasses together and each took a drink. "Does Noah know yet?"

Nellie nodded. "He should. I told Roni about it on my way home today, and she said she would tell him."

Glad that talking about the cocktail mixer was not a personal subject, she filled him on some of the details and plans she had for it. He listened intently, at times unnerving her when his eyes would leave hers and make their way down to her lips, staying there a little too long. He'd smirk every time he noticed that she lost her train of thought because of this but didn't comment.

By the time they'd ordered and their food had arrived, the subject had moved on from the mixer to his upcoming fight. As much as she noticed he tried to downplay it, she knew this was huge. If he won, he'd be up there with such heavyweight greats as Holyfield, Foreman, even Muhammad Ali.

"The guys over at 5th Street and I were talking the other day, and we planned on having this conversation with you together, but I don't see any harm in me bringing it up now."

Nellie tilted her head, stopping her fork just before she brought it to her mouth. They were long past any conversation about the cocktail mixer, but aside from that, she couldn't imagine what else he and the 5th Street guys would want to talk to her about. Roni hadn't mentioned anything either.

There was a moment of what felt like uncomfortable silence on his part, but Nellie waited without saying a word as he wiped his mouth and took another drink of his rum and Diet Coke.

CHAPTER 3

Abel was not about to admit it to anyone, but the idea of having Nellie around 5th Street more often was one that pleased him. Between his intense training, which was getting even more grueling as the fight approached, and all the interviews and appearances he was contractually obligated to do lately, his free time was becoming increasingly non-existent. So when Noah and Gio had brought up the possibility of her not just coordinating events at 5th Street but the ones leading up to his fight, including the ones she'd have to travel out of town with him, he immediately agreed. Her success with the cocktail mixer for their charity foundation further confirmed she'd be a perfect choice.

Nellie was still staring at him, waiting for a response. "Well, we were thinking, since we have a few publicity events coming up for the fight that are gonna take place at 5th Street and a couple out of town, that you could be the one to get it all coordinated."

Abel squeezed her hand when she lifted that sexy eyebrow of hers. He fought the urge to kiss her. It was something he'd been aching to do since they got there, but since he'd come on so strong when he first got to her place, he was trying to tone it down now. She'd made it clear once again that the way things were now between them was for the best. He completely agreed, but he felt so crazed around her that it was beginning to unnerve him. Telling her that she drove him crazy as he almost had at her place earlier might spook her.

Back when her divorce was going on, Noah had talked about her split with her douche bag ex-husband. Abel hadn't really paid attention, but one thing he did get was that it was a *bad* one. It was so bad that the last thing she'd be looking for, for a while, was getting back into any relationships. Abel was more than fine with that, especially because serious relationships were the last thing he had time for anyway and certainly not with a divorced older woman. Saying things like what he almost did might have her backing out of this all-too-perfect set up. He didn't want to blow it now. There was all this sexual tension that had built up between them for months. They'd let it go on for too long, and now he couldn't get his fill, but he was certain it would start waning soon enough.

"Wow," she said, putting her fork down then wiping her mouth with her napkin. "I'm flattered that you think I can handle something this big. I mean the cocktail mixer is turning out bigger than I had expected, but that's because of this last donation. Otherwise, I wasn't planning on this event being so big."

She took another sip of her wine and licked her bottom lip as she'd been doing all night each time she took a drink. That was it. He'd held back long enough. Leaning into her, he kissed her softly, trying to not go overboard as he did earlier. This time he took his time savoring every inch of her delicious mouth. After that much needed and very long satisfying taste of her, he pulled his lips away but just barely. "Of course I think you can handle it," he whispered against her lips.

Abel brought his hand to her face, lifting her chin to him so he could kiss her as deeply as he'd been dying to since they got there. It felt as if he'd never get enough of tasting her mouth, and the taste of her sweet wine only added to his frenzy. As usual, she kissed him back with just as much desire as he was feeling for her. Feeling the craze coming on that he felt every time they kissed like this, he forced himself to back off a little, and he came up for air.

Staring at her soft pink lips as he tried to catch his breath, he spoke again, trying to calm the yearning he was feeling already. "We meet again with the director of PR in charge of this whole fight in a couple of weeks. You think you can be there?"

She nodded as she too obviously struggled to catch her breath. Unable to hold back anymore, he placed his hand on her thigh, thankful that he'd gotten to her house before she'd changed out of her sexy-as-shit skirt suit. His fingers found their way under her skirt and caressed the soft warm inner thigh.

Feeling her quiver made him smile. "What day?" she asked.

"I'm pretty sure Noah said a week from next Friday after closing," his lips were on hers again as soon as she nodded.

She pulled away mid kiss and thought about it for a second. "If that's Friday the 13th, I can't. I have plans that night."

Abel's hand froze on her thigh, and he stared at her for a moment, not sure if he should ask, but he sure as hell wanted to. "Oh?"

"Yeah," she said, nodding, her eyes rushing from his lips to his eyes. "If it were any other night, I could, but that's the only night that I can't. Will you be meeting again with him another time?"

Abel continued to stare at her, hoping she'd shed a little light on what those plans were exactly. When she didn't, he pulled away from her slowly. "I don't know," he said, trying to keep his tone as normal as possible. "Probably, but it'd be best if you were in on everything from here on out since it's getting down to the wire." He reached for his drink, not wanting to have eye contact with her when he asked his next question. "Any chance you can get out of your plans?"

He turned to her when she didn't answer immediately. She was frowning then inhaled thinking about it. "I don't think so. It's a concert, and the tickets have already been paid for." He swallowed down a bigger drink than he had originally planned. Maybe she was going with a girlfriend. "Oh, yeah? Who you gonna go see?"

She smiled suddenly." Slightly Stoopid at the House of Blues."

Feeling the slightest bit of relief and not really understanding why, he remembered Noah recently mentioning that Roni wanted to go see them too, but . . . "I thought Noah said they were sold out."

"They were," she said, taking a sip of her water this time. "At least when Roni and I tried getting tickets they were. Somehow, a co-worker of mine was able to get tickets."

Just moments ago, Abel thought he might need another drink maybe two. Now he was overcome with the urge to kiss her again. "That's cool," he said, leaning into her again. "I know Roni really likes them." With that, his mouth was on hers, and his fingers once again were making their way up her thigh under her skirt. He murmured against her lips, "Ever had sex in public, Nellie?" The thought of taking her right there was already driving him to the brink of madness.

"No!" She gasped, pulling away slightly.

"Shhh! It's okay," he whispered, laughing softly. His hand moved further up in between her legs. Technically, they'd been in a public place on the cruise, but they were behind a closed door. Even though this was a private booth, he understood her apprehension, so he wouldn't push her. "We don't have to do *that*. You said this was exciting on the cruise."

"It was," she said breathlessly. "But—"

"We won't go there. Trust me," he whispered quickly then pulled away to look her in the eyes. "You trust me?"

She nodded, licking her lips, and he dove in again. He kissed her hungrily, feeling her moan in his mouth as he gently pushed her thighs apart.

Not only did she allow it but she adjusted in her seat for him so his hand could travel as far up as he wanted it to. And he wanted it *all* the way up. His fingers reached the damp warm paradise that they sought out. "Nice," he said against her lips then bit her bottom one as his finger pushed her panties aside.

Feeling her gasp again, he kissed her softly. "Relax." He easily slid a finger in her then two more before she could protest. The moment his thumb rubbed that perfect spot, she let her head drop back as her legs spread slowly for him. "That a girl," he whispered as he dove into the open invitation to take her neck and suck as he fucked her with his fingers.

She was beginning to pant and tremble all over as he worked her steadily with his thumb. He brought his mouth back over hers to muffle her moans. Sliding his fingers in and out of her faster now as he felt her getting close to that magic moment, he continued to kiss her deeply mimicking with his tongue what his throbbing erection wanted so fucking badly to be doing to her body.

As her body began that now-familiar trembling, which he thought about too often even when she wasn't around, he slowed his kisses. He wanted to live the moment with her through her mouth. Hearing her struggle to keep her moaning to a minimum, Abel felt something he hadn't felt in years— the panic of feeling that he might mess his pants right there.

Over the years, he'd mastered what he and the guys referred to as not shooting off their load prematurely. This was *way* premature. He hadn't even taken off his clothes yet! What? Was he back in middle school?

Luckily, she pulled her mouth away from his to breathe; her chest heaved up and down as she let her head fall back and rest on the back of the booth. Abel had to literally pry his fingers away from between her legs before he embarrassed the hell out of himself. He squeezed his legs closed. Hearing her continue to breathe heavily as she came down from her climax wasn't helping matters either.

He, too, let his head rest on the back of the booth. The next words out of his mouth flew out without thought. "Your ex-husband ever do that to you?"

The second he heard his own words, he regretted them, not because he didn't want to know but because it was an unspoken rule between them. Though they'd never said it, it was implied loud and clear: no getting into personal stuff, including what they did when they weren't around each other now and in the past. The subject of her failed marriage was one that Noah had made clear was a sore one.

He glanced at her before she could respond. "I'm sorry. Don't answer that. That's none of my business."

Nellie cleared her throat then took a sip of her wine. She turned to him, taking a deep breath as if she were still trying to catch up with her normal breathing. That made him smile despite having asked his stupid question.

"You're right that it's none of your business, but it's not a big deal, so I'll answer anyway. No, he didn't. In fact, we never did *most* of the things you and I have done."

Her smile was one he hadn't seen before; it was bittersweet. He almost regretted having brought up her ex-husband—almost. In the very beginning, he didn't care to know any details of her private life—not the current or the past—but he did now. He chalked it up to curiosity. Of course he was curious. Why wouldn't he be? He'd been around her a few times. They'd had amazing sex in many different positions now. And now here she was telling him she'd *never* had this with her ex-*husband*. How could he not be curious?

Was her ex insane not to take advantage of a woman like Nellie? She was everything a guy could ask for in a sexual partner. She'd been willing and just as eager as he'd been *every* single time. In fact, he'd be willing to bet he might've talked her into letting him take here right there in their booth, but he hadn't wanted to push.

Sure he'd been with girls who were more than willing to do things anywhere anytime, but with Nellie, it felt different. There was an elegance to her. She was sophisticated, smart, and professional, not an immature, squealing, ready-to-party groupie. Even though Noah had mentioned Nellie wanting to let loose—make up for the lost time she'd wasted being married to her ex—there was something about her that made him sure that wasn't the case. Yeah, she was doing it with him, but he couldn't see her jumping from one bed to another as Noah had implied she might. And convincing her to do the things some of the groupies would gladly do in a heartbeat felt like a far more rewarding challenge.

He stared at her, his thoughts suddenly going back to what she'd just said about her ex. "Really? Some of the stuff I've done to you so far," he stopped and smirked, "has been pretty tame by most standards."

Even as she sat there, her panties now soaked after she'd just climaxed at their dinner table, she had the audacity to blush. He had to laugh.

She took another sip of her wine and smiled, her lashes blinking slowly over her wine glass as she licked her lips. Just like that she took the upper hand, wiping the smile instantly off his face.

"Mr. Ayala, are you and Ms. Nellie ready for another drink?" The waiter asked from the other side of the curtain.

"No, but I'll take the check now." Abel responded without taking his eyes off Nellie even for a second, his mind already planning out the all the things he'd do to her tonight.

Nellie hardly had a chance to try and make sense of Abel's interest in her asshole ex-husband, Rick. On the way home from the restaurant, he'd asked a few more questions such as if she still ever saw him and if she ever missed him. She answered both truthfully but kept her answers short: no and *hell* no.

They reached her place and were barely inside when Abel was already all over her. It was crazy how quickly he could have her feeling out of control and breathless. Just as he pinned her to the wall in the front room, already lifting her skirt, her phone rang. Abel slowed for a moment, breathing heavily against her ear. "You wanna get that?"

Like hell she did. She didn't bother to even answer. Instead she turned his chin to hers, needing to feel his lips on hers again already. His tongue stabbed into to her mouth, making her moan in pleasure.

Roni had mentioned how insatiable her young husband was, and Nellie had imagined Abel would be the same, but it was almost embarrassing how easily she'd given into the scandalous things they'd done thus far. The cruise incident had even been *her* idea. And if what he'd done to her in the restaurant had happened during her marriage, it would've been more than enough to keep her happy for the entire next week at the very least. Yet here she was panting—*needing* more *now* as he ripped her panties off.

With her panties off now and her skirt pulled up around her waist, Abel spun her around, bending her gently but quickly over the sofa. "We'll get to the tasting soon enough, sweetheart. But right now I *have* to get inside you."

She heard the rip of a condom pack then his zipper open. Already throbbing for him in anticipation, Nellie squeezed the sofa cushions with both her hands as she waited the few seconds it took him to get the condom on, and then he was inside her. She cried out at the incredible sensation as he slid all the way in.

Just like the last time, he brought his hand around front to massage her as he slammed in and out of her again and again, groaning louder with each thrust. His fingers knew exactly what to do, and Nellie couldn't help moaning in unabashed pleasure. The louder she moaned, the harder he slammed into her. "You like that, baby?"

"Yes," she cried out. "Yes!"

As his fingers hit the perfect rhythm, she knew it was just a matter of seconds before she'd be crying out in ecstasy. With one hand, he continued to build her impending climax while the other one held on to her waist, pulling her back into his thrusts. As erotic as the sound of his body slapping against hers was, it was one she loved thinking about when he wasn't around—when she was lying in bed at night alone. It was the very thing that had made her blush today when Emily called her on it.

Until now, Nellie had no idea sex could be this good. Crying out as the bolts of pleasure raced through her entire body, making her legs weak, she used the support of the sofa to help keep her standing. In the next second, he thrust into her one last time with an enormous groan.

They both stood there, enjoying the contentment with which their sexual encounters always ended. Never before had Nellie felt such satisfaction, and to think she knew this was just the beginning of their evening. He finally pulled out of her and away, turning her around to face him.

The lazy yet sexy haze that draped over his eyes made her smile. He was as satisfied as she felt. "I'd been waiting to do that from the moment I got in my car to come here tonight." He smirked against her lips. "Hell, I've been waiting to do that since the last time I was with you." He kissed her sweetly and softly, unlike the way he'd kissed her most of the night. "You look beautiful tonight by the way." His words were so tender, and he looked so deeply in her eyes in a way she'd never seen him do, that something tugged at her heart. "I love seeing you in your skirt suits." His playful grin teased. "You're insanely sexy." Just when she was beginning to exhale and remind herself to not over think things, he added with the same tenderness as before, "But still beautiful, Nellie, *so* beautiful."

He kissed her longer this time but just as sweetly and softly. She tried concentrating on the sweetness of his kiss—enjoying every heavenly moment of it—but her mind was already fast at work. So he said she was beautiful. He was smooth. How could he not be? The man had probably looked this good his whole life. As young as he was, he'd still had plenty of years to perfect his lines and his delivery. *God,* what a delivery! She'd nearly melted into him from that one compliment alone.

Nellie knew she wasn't beautiful. She never had been. Only just recently had she discovered she could even still be and *feel* attractive but beautiful? No. And nothing reiterated the reality that she was lacking in the way of looks more than the fact that she'd never been enough for her ex-husband. The bastard had cheated on her from the very beginning.

Falling deeper into Abel's embrace, she allowed herself to go with it. Why shouldn't she? She'd take the compliment: this one and any more he wanted to throw her way. One thing she knew he couldn't possibly be faking was that he was as turned on by her as she was by him. Even if it was just a sexual thing, for the first time in a *very* long time she felt sexy again—wanted. He'd reawakened a part of her she thought her ex had destroyed for good. She'd enjoy every unbelievable moment he'd give her, and when this was over, she'd walk away a better, stronger, woman because of it.

CHAPTER 4

The sound coming from Nellie's phone woke them both up. Abel had actually woken up a few hours before when it had beeped a few times. Now it was ringing. He'd almost snuck out earlier while she slept soundly as he had all the other times. She hadn't even stirred from the phone beeping. But he got caught up watching Nellie sleep. He knew now he must've dozed off again, because the last thing he remembered was lying back on the pillow and staring at her.

Not missing the double take she did when she realized he was still in bed with her, Abel smirked, watching her reach for her phone. The second she saw it, she sat up quickly.

"Shit! Is that the right time?"

Abel nodded. "Long exhausting nights will do that to you." He didn't even try to hide the satisfaction that the very thought made him feel. Bringing his hands behind his head in no hurry at all to get going, he smiled smugly. In fact, he couldn't think of anything better than sticking around and going a few more rounds with Nellie. "But it's Saturday, so it's okay to sleep in, right?"

Nellie's phone rang again, and already she was making her way off the bed. "Yeah, but I was supposed to meet someone this morning." Grabbing a robe from the chair next to her bed, she flung the short barely-there thing around her. She held her hand up to Abel, clicking the screen on her phone then bringing it to her ear before he could ask who she was meeting. "Logan? I'm so sorry. I'm running really late, but can I meet you in like forty minutes?"

In direct contrast to how fast he felt his insides warm, Abel sat up slowly, staring at her. He'd had a feeling from day one that, if it ever came down to it he, might be a little bothered to hear about her with someone else. It was to be expected, right? It was human nature. But he hadn't expected to feel what he was feeling now.

"Oh, The Country Kitchen sounds delish. Their breakfasts are huge and I'm starving actually."

He continued staring at her, feeling a bit of curiosity and *something else* as she rummaged through her drawers. This *had* to be business. No way was she jumping out of bed with him to go meet another guy for breakfast. Sure, they had an unspoken understanding, no fucking demands and all that shit, but he'd been certain Nellie had more class than this. Was she really chatting it up with another dude while he was still lying naked in her bed, listening to her?

The rest of her conversation with the guy was even more frustrating. The guy was obviously doing most of the talking because she wasn't saying much more than "uh huh." She wasn't giving Abel much more to go on about who this Logan guy was.

The choice of clothes she laid out on the bed as she continued with her call only made his insides warmer. Instead of business attire like the suits that drove him nuts, she laid out a pair of jeans and a casual knit top. As off-putting as the idea of her wearing a sexy skirt suit to go meet *Logan* at The Country Kitchen was, it would've at least meant that this was for sure a business meeting, not a casual breakfast date with a guy.

He'd gotten out of bed himself now and watched as she brought out the big sexy wedge sandals from her closet. She finally hung up just as he'd finished pulling on his pants. He stared at her as he buttoned his fly, doing his best to keep his cool. If he blew up now, this whole thing could come to an end. He'd known from the beginning that it inevitably had to end, but he didn't know if he was ready to end this just yet.

"I'm sorry," she explained, still rushing around the room. "I don't mean to run out on you like this, but if I'd known you'd still be here this morning, I would've canceled this last night." She paused her rushing for a moment to glance at him a bit uneasily. "I just assumed . . . you know, like all the other times . . ." She looked away before she added the last comment, "That you'd be gone when I woke up."

Swallowing hard, he took a deep breath. No way was he going to blow this. He knew he was walking on a tightrope; one wrong move and he could go down head first or worse. He could do the very thing they'd each said they wouldn't do and the tightrope could snap altogether, leaving no possibility of trying to climb back on. But he had to ask. "Who's Logan?"

She glanced at him for just a second before looking back down into the drawer she was now shuffling through. "He's working on the mixer with me. Now that we have all the funding, we need to sit down and decide what the best way is to go about this and get as much out of the fundraiser as possible."

While Nellie continued to explain how normally she didn't work on weekends, Abel half listened. He was already undoing his fly as he walked around the bed toward her. Knowing that this was, in fact, a business meeting and not something that had nearly set him off, he needed to release some of the tension that had built up so quickly.

A bit startled but immediately smiling as he took her hand and pulled her to him, Nellie kissed him back, as ravished as Abel felt. "I'm already late," she gasped in between kisses.

Lifting her to the bed, Abel smiled. "I'll make this fast."

He opened her robe as he laid her down gently. Exposing her naked body, Abel stared at her, pushing away the possessive mentality that now dangerously began to swallow up any sound thoughts of keeping this fun and uncomplicated. As much as he wanted to spread her legs, drop down to his knees, and pleasure her until she was screaming his name as she had last night, he now wanted to be inside her again—to remind her that she didn't need anyone else as long as he was willing to fuck her into oblivion.

Pulling the condom out of his pocket and ripping it open, he slipped a finger in her to make sure she was ready. Smiling with the confirmation that she was more than ready, he pulled her behind off the edge of the bed, and she wrapped her legs around him. Then he did exactly what he'd wanted to—slammed into her with a purpose, squeezing his eyes shut. Again he was overwhelmed with feelings of wanting to—*needing* to—make to make an unspoken statement here. Her gasping moans as he fucked her faster and deeper with conviction made it all the more pleasurable. This was his secret sinful way of punishing her so good for having made him feel even for a few moments what he'd felt while she'd been on the phone.

Nellie trembled and moaned with pleasure, her bottom in the air now. As Abel grabbed her ass with both hands and plunged into her harder and harder groaning loudly, things were becoming clearer. There was no mistake about it. There was something so much more satisfying about doing this to her now, something more than just the physical ecstasy of it. He could no longer say that this was only about the sex with the certainty and conviction he'd had when they'd first started this—whatever *this* was.

As much as he hated to admit it, and as much as he'd like to think he could keep his feelings under control, he felt firsthand today how easily that self-control could go up in smoke if he ever had to be witness to or even hear about Nellie with someone else. Last night he'd had a couple of other revelations. What he was feeling for her now had surpassed anything he'd thought he'd imagined in the previous times he'd spent time with her. He even thought he saw something in her gaze when he called her beautiful. The sparkle in her eyes when he told her how beautiful he thought she was, almost made him say more than he should. Then the infuriating reminder came hurling at him as it did now.

Nellie might be enjoying this as much as he was, but she'd made one thing perfectly clear last night: She was *great* with this arrangement, and "things were for the best this way." The reminder of her words and the very thought of Noah saying she wanted to let loose had him squeezing her ass a little tighter now—slamming into her even harder. She may be great with this arrangement, but after today, he wasn't so sure he was anymore. Things just may've gotten complicated.

***

Still mulling through the bothersome thoughts of Nellie having breakfast with another guy, even if it was only business, Abel was grateful for the much-needed interruption to his thoughts. It was all he'd thought about all the way home and even as he showered then had breakfast with his mom and brother. Now Andy, his publicist, was talking his ear off as Abel drove to the gym. Abel had an idea of what it would be like going into this fight as far as the appearances and interviews he'd be required to do to make it big out of 5th Street. Felix had filled him in on some of it. In fact, Felix had even hooked him up with his publicist. He said if anyone could get the buzz going, Andy could because he was the best. Abel just hadn't realized how overwhelming this would be. Felix seemed to thrive in the spotlight. Abel hated it, especially when the media aired stories that had little to do with the fight itself and were nothing more than what Andy called sensationalized journalism.

This was what Andy was going on about again today. The press had gotten wind that his opponent, who was now the heavyweight champ, had once trained at 5th Street. This wasn't news to Abel. 5th Street had always been the place to train in East L.A. even back before the gym had become what it was now. Boxers from out of town like this guy were known to come in and not only check out 5th Street but work out there. While Abel had heard about "Hammerhead" McKinley having trained at 5th Street once upon a time, the guy was ten years older than he was. The media was trying to turn this into some kind of grudge match between one of the owners of 5th Street and a former patron of the gym who'd had a falling out. Abel had never even met the dude. It was so stupid.

The problem was that Andy loved the sensationalism. It made the fight a bigger draw for advertisers wanting to sponsor the fight. The bigger the draw, the bigger the sponsors that would come calling for Abel to represent their products. So Andy said no publicity was bad publicity, except for when they crossed the line and could possibly tarnish his image; then sponsors might drop him.

"The media does it for obvious reasons—ratings," Andy explained. "The juicier the story, the more viewers, listeners, and traffic they get to their shows, magazines, and websites. It's all good. Let them make up as much harmless crap as they want, and you neither confirm nor deny that any of it is true, so you don't kill the momentum. But you also have to be mindful of one thing: the other side is watching, listening, and taking notes too. They wanna see what gets to you, and the moment they do, they'll run with it, telling their side of the story, truth or not. They're doing it for other reasons: to get in your head and anything to throw you off your game. So whatever you do, don't give them anything to feed on. If you're cornered into making a statement, keep it vague. This close to the big day, the media starts grasping for anything. They know everyone's watching, and their story has to be better and juicier than their competition's."

"All right, I got it," Abel said as he drove into the gym's driveway.

They'd been through this before. Abel hardly even watched TV, nor did he ever get caught up in the tabloids. Felix had been the first to tell him that it was better if he just didn't read them, especially when he was in training. This, by far, was the biggest fight Abel had ever trained for.

"I'm very serious about this, Ayala. Prepare yourself for not only the media to stop at nothing as the big day approaches but McKinley's camp to pull some kind of stunt just to rattle you. They're getting nervous, and they know this is all new to you. McKinley's been through the whole thing with his alcoholic dad and his younger brother's domestic abuse allegations, but you . . . You haven't had to deal with any of that, and even though you may think it's no big deal now, it is once you start hearing the bullshit over and over. Let me tell you this is why I was calling. It's already starting."

Abel turned off his car but didn't get out. Suddenly Andy had his undivided attention. "What do you mean? What's starting?"

Andy sighed heavily. "I got the call this morning. It could go nowhere, but apparently some bloggers based in Mexico have started some noise about your dad's connection to the Mexican mafia."

"What!" Abel gripped the phone, feeling the very anger Andy had tried to warn him about. "He had no connection to the mafia, and my dad's been dead for over ten years. Who the fuck is digging that far back?"

"It's all bullshit." Andy reminded him urgently. "This is what I've been trying to warn you about. It's all for ratings— viewers—in this case, traffic to their blog. Apparently these bloggers are trying to start something, and if it takes off, it'll be all over, true or not. But you *cannot* react to any of it and give McKinley's camp something to try and bait you with and trip you up. I'm telling you they'd love nothing more than to get into that head of yours. You already have the media dubbing you Aweless Ayala for your indifference to all the hype and your continued ability to stay out of the limelight. Most newcomers eat up the attention. This, I'm sure, is making them nervous. They're wondering why you're so sure of yourself and maybe even wondering if you're hiding something—a secret weapon perhaps. At this stage of the game, paranoia is rampant. So I can guarantee you they're trying figure out just how to get to you and push your buttons."

Abel took a deep breath. *Fucking sensationalism.* He'd always known, even way before he thought he'd have a chance at the title, that he'd hate this part of the process. He'd seen it play out firsthand with his friends, Felix and Gio. "No one's getting in my head," he said with conviction and he meant it.

"Atta boy," Andy said the relief coming through loud and clear. "I'll keep you updated on what you need to know, but in the meantime, you concentrate on training and fuck all this other shit. Avoid making any statements or answering any questions without checking with me first."

"You got it."

Still wearing his earpiece, Abel got out of the car. He had no intention whatsoever of following up on this bullshit story. His conversation with Andy though frustrating had served at least one purpose. It had gotten his mind off his thoughts of Nellie and her breakfast date. That is until Andy mentioned one more thing.

"Listen, I'm not gonna make that 5k run you're doing in San Francisco this week after all. The folks over at the Today Show found out I'll be in New York on Monday and wanted to set up something while I'm out there to see about getting you and Felix on the show together." Abel could already hear the excitement in Andy's voice. He lived for this shit. "I almost said no, but then I got a call from the Letterman show too. I can kill two birds with one stone, and this is huge compared to the run in Frisco. So I'll have to stay in New York a few days longer than I planned. You should be okay.

Still, I don't want you out there alone. You'll have security, of course, but I've got some calls out to a few people who might be able to meet you out there. This way you don't have to worry about coordinating any of the last-minute requests for interviews or signings."

Abel slowed just before entering the gym. "Coordinating?" He couldn't help smiling. "I think I may know someone who'd be perfect for the job."

"You do?"

"Yeah, and I'd feel better because I know this person. I wouldn't be out there with someone I've never met."

"Cool, give me a number and name and I'll get on it."

"Nah," Abel opened the door to gym and started in. "I got this. I'll call you when I know for sure and give you whatever details you need."

✳✳✳

After Abel had worked two hours on his speed, rhythm, and timing on the speed bag, Gio forced him to take a break. "Take fifteen, and then I'll meet you in the ring for some sparring." Gio said, already pulling out his phone.

Abel headed for his locker with one thing in on his mind. Nellie's breakfast date should be over by now. If it wasn't, he was interrupting it. This Logan guy had had her long enough. "Time's up," he muttered as he pulled his own phone out of his locker.

When he asked for her number on the cruise, he played it down, saying he just wanted to be able to give her a heads up before dropping by her place if he ever did. He even threw in a mention of "in case you're not alone" as if that would be a non-issue. At the time, it was the truth. He hadn't wanted her to get the idea that he was anticipating this turning into anything more than what it was—a convenient and uncomplicated arrangement between two consenting adults.

Even after feeling what he had that morning, he still wasn't sure.

He was, however, beginning to understand why Noah had so easily overlooked the age difference with Roni. From the very first time he'd been with Nellie on the cruise—in that vending machine room where he'd taken her against the door—she'd felt just as young as any girl he'd ever been with. And ironically, even though she'd been the only divorcee he'd ever been with, judging by her reaction to some of the things he'd done to her so far, she was far less experienced than most. Sure she was more mature and classier than just about any girl he'd been with, but that was a positive, not a negative.

There was also something about the way she clung to him when he held her. It made her feel so vulnerable; although, her personality and demeanor were just the opposite. Most notably, Abel was surprised that it didn't scare him. He didn't quite understand it, but there was something about it he actually liked. After hearing her reiterate how *great* she was with their arrangement then feeling what he'd felt this morning while she was on the phone, it was almost comforting to know that maybe she was feeling more than she was admitting.

One thing he was sure of was the phone call he was about to make. This was business, and as much as having Nellie to himself for a few days was the biggest motivator here, he also had another reason. This morning was a wakeup call. Noah might've actually been right to worry. If he'd felt what he had from the mere possibility that she was having breakfast with another man, he couldn't imagine how he'd react if he knew she was sleeping with someone else. Shaking his head in frustration, he had to admit that this could pull the plug on what he hoped would last much longer. The last thing he needed was for what Noah was afraid of to happen. He'd snap and everything would change.

This was almost as motivating as being with Nellie for a few days. Almost. He wanted to establish their working relationship. So if he did have to pull the plug on their extracurricular activities, this part of their relationship was set and would remain as it was, regardless.

She answered on the first ring. Abel got right to what he really wanted to know. "Hey, you busy?"

"Uh . . . no, not really. Give me a sec," she said to someone then . . . was that a giggle? And most notably why did it have him clenching his teeth and instantly heating his insides. "I was just hanging out. What's going on?"

Hanging out? Abel took a deep breath, squeezing his eyes shut for a moment, hating to admit now that Noah was *absolutely* right. "Not sure how busy you are this week but I'm in need of some coordinating for an event I'll be doing in San Francisco."

"Oh?"

"Yeah, it's a charity run I'm doing. It's just a 5k, but Andy was supposed to be there with me to make sure everything goes smoothly with the reporters and all that. It's gotten so crazy lately. He'll be stuck in New York for a few days, so he was trying to come up with someone who might take his place, and I figured since you're good at that stuff maybe you could come with me."

She was quiet for a moment then infuriatingly burst into laughter. "I know, honey, just give me a sec."

Honey? "Who are you with?" he asked his tone far more demanding than he'd intended, and the worst part was that, at that moment, he didn't even care.

Next came what sounded like her kissing someone and Abel's frozen insides were completely on *fire* now. "I met with Roni and Little Jack after breakfast at the mall. We're doing some shopping, and Roni's in the dressing room right now. Jack is a handful, let me tell you." She laughed. "But he's also hilarious and adorable." There were more kissing sounds, and then he heard Jack laughing. "And he's just so lovable I wanna squeeze him to death." There were a few more exaggerated kissing sounds until Jack squealed and Nellie laughed again. "I'm sorry, Abel. I was just keeping him busy until Roni was out, but she's done now. So San Francisco, huh? Which days?"

The tension literally draining from his body as Abel's heart still pounded wildly was yet another wake-up call. This was so much worse than he'd thought. He explained about San Francisco and his itinerary, and to his relief, she said it sounded doable but that she'd have to double check and get back to him.

Once off the phone, Abel leaned against the lockers with his hand over his chest. His overworked heart was still beating hard. Closing his eyes, he thought about how he'd nearly slipped off the tightrope *again*. He didn't even want to think about how he might've reacted or what he might've said to her if she'd confirmed it was Logan she was still with while giggling and making those noises.

He squeezed his hand into a tight fist just as Gio walked into the locker room. "You ready?"

Abel nodded, placing his phone back in the locker. This was a little too alarming. He was either going to have to get a grip or end this *arrangement* before stuff like today got the best of him and he snapped with no right to whatsoever. The question now begged to be asked. Was it too late to pull back? As much as he hated to admit it, he had no choice now. The answer to the other alternative was getting pretty obvious. Would he be able to get a grip if he heard about or saw Nellie with someone else? Not a chance in hell.

CHAPTER 5

The redeye flight they'd been booked on was now understandable. Even just after midnight, Abel and Nellie turned heads in the airport. Nellie could only imagine now if they'd taken a day flight. Abel was all about avoiding the media, and so far they'd succeeded in doing so.

"You know," Abel began as they took their seats in first class, "if I'd had more time, I would've driven in a heartbeat."

Nellie smiled. "The drive up the coast *is* beautiful."

"Yeah, it is," he said, slipping his hand into hers. "But I hate flying in general, not so much flying but airports. If it were up to Andy, he'd have me fly everywhere and at the busiest times of the day."

"Why?" she asked curiously.

"He loves the paparazzi. The more they splatter my face and name all over the headlines, the better. He insists I shouldn't care what they say but that as long as I'm in the headlines I'm golden."

"What? How about the hurtful things or blatant lies?" She stared at him, trying to hide her distaste for Andy already.

Bianca had mentioned how much she disliked the guy more than once. Back when Bianca had dated Felix, she felt that Andy was actually trying to sabotage their relationship. He'd insisted that Felix's reputation of a bad-ass womanizer jumping from one famous female's bed to another was far more exciting and newsworthy than what he was actually doing—trying to settle down with one girl for once. She told Nellie that on a few occasions Andy was actually adding fuel the fire in hopes of vamping up the stories of Felix with other women with absolutely no regard to Bianca's feelings.

Abel smirked. "As long as it's not defamation or anything that might hurt my career, he says it's good. I personally don't give a shit what they write about me. I just don't like the cameras in my face and the scenes they tend to make when I'm trying to mind my own business and they're running alongside me, yelling out my name. *That* pisses me off."

Nellie frowned. She'd had a short conversation with Andy already only to go over her duties in San Francisco. He did mention that while Abel was very private Abel didn't understand the importance of staying relevant and becoming a household name. Andy also said that he usually gave the media freedom to ask pretty much whatever they asked but that Abel always insisted on making sure they knew what topics were off limits beforehand.

"I emailed you the list." He'd told her with a chuckle. "But between you and me, I sometimes forget to pass it out to the reporters in time. So it's up to you if you wanna make copies or *forget*."

From that moment on, she'd decided she didn't like the guy, but now that she was beginning to understand just how private Abel really was, it really irked her that his own publicist would ignore his very specific requests.

Abel's squeezing of her hand and then his leaning over and caressing her face before kissing her softly, surprised Nellie. They'd done plenty of kissing in the car that picked them up and drove them to the airport, but the whole time in the airport he hadn't so much as pecked her nor held her hand. She got it and it didn't bother her. He'd actually apologized in advance that her life might get a little annoying after being seen traveling with him because the paparazzi were relentless. So she was certain that keeping any signs of affection that would get tongues wagging was why he'd refrained. But they were technically still in public.

Glancing casually around her surroundings, she could see that first class was half empty and that the only person sitting across the aisle was an older man who was already asleep. But the flight attendant had been just up the aisle when he did this. "Ever been to Oakland?" he asked her curiously, and she was glad they were off the topic of his annoying publicist.

"Yes, I have a few times actually. My ex is kind of a big-time sportscaster. Well he was," she said. "He got tickets to sporting events everywhere, and we went to a few Giants home games whenever they played the Angels." She smiled, trying to ease the sudden hardened look on Abel's face now. "That's how I know the drive is so beautiful."

Nellie had no idea how many details of her divorce Abel knew about. If she had to go by his stern expression, he at least knew it'd been bad. It was so bad that the scandal of her ex not only leaving Nellie but getting her own sister pregnant while they were still married pretty much ruined his career. When the word got out, the network he worked for got so much hate mail demanding that such an offensive man be taken off the air or that people would boycott the shows he broadcasted that it sent the network into a tailspin. It wasn't nearly as big a scandal as say Tiger Woods, because Rick was just a broadcaster, but the show he did was syndicated, so it wasn't just local. He was quickly given paid leave, and his contract that was supposed to have been renewed later that year, wasn't.

The only reason Nellie had even brought up Rick was because of Abel's question. She had every intention of sparing Abel the details. She certainly wouldn't be telling him about how her loathsome ex had had the gall to call her recently and ask if there was any way she could get him an exclusive with Abel. He was now working for a small cable sports show, but an exclusive with Abel just before what was being billed as one of the most anticipated fights of the decade would do wonders to get his career back on track—a career he insinuated might still be intact if she hadn't given that interview right after they separated, letting the world know just what a bastard he really was.

Of course, that call had ended with her hanging up as he started trying to despicably lay the guilt on her, as if somehow he'd been the victim.

"Thinking about him still upsets you."

Abel squeezed her hand. His comment was more of an observation than a question. Nellie hadn't even realized her expression must've gone taut, but Abel was staring at her with a knowing look, brow raised. "I'd say still disgusts me is a better way to phrase it."

That seemed to ease his expression, and then he smirked. "That bad, huh?"

Nellie shrugged and glanced out the window. "I try not to think about him at all, but every now and again, I remember."

"Sorry I trudged up hurtful memories."

She turned back to him. "Not hurtful," she smiled weakly. "I haven't hurt in a long time. In fact, I don't remember ever crying for *him* really. It was . . ." She shook her head, remembering that she was supposed to spare him the details. "Never mind, you don't wanna hear about all that."

This conversation was veering into the off limits. It was personal—*way* too personal—Abel certainly didn't need to hear all this.

Just as their flight took off, Abel leaned into her. "If you'd rather not talk about it, that's cool, but I don't mind hearing about it. We do have over an hour to kill, and I don't know about you," he glanced around, "but I'm too wired to sleep like everyone else on this flight seems to be doing."

Hesitating for a moment, she finally smiled. She supposed she could give him the short version. Since he likely read the sports section, he may've heard about it anyway. "I don't know if Noah told you, but my ex got my sister pregnant while we were still married." By the widening of his eyes, she could tell that this *did* surprise him. She nodded. "They'd been having an affair off and on for years, and supposedly they were going to get married as soon as our divorce was over. *That's* what hurt most. That *she* would do that to me. The fact that Rick cheated wasn't a surprise at all. I'd suspected for some time but was in denial. I'd gotten so comfortable in my established little cocoon of a life I was afraid of what the truth would do to it. But deep inside, I knew I was never enough for him—"

"Did he tell you that you weren't?" Abel's brows pinched now as he searched her eyes.

"No," she admitted. "But from the very beginning, I got the distinct feeling that I wasn't the only one." She lifted and dropped a shoulder. "Woman's intuition, I guess."

"Just because the guy was an asshole who didn't appreciate what he had doesn't mean you weren't good enough for him, Nell." Nellie's attention was brought to his moving Adam's apple as he swallowed hard. "He sounds like a fucking prick. That alone tells me *he* was never good enough for *you*. I'm sorry for what he put you through, but I'm glad he's in your past. He *does not* deserve to spend his life with a woman like you."

As Nellie's insides began to warm and her heart began to swell from hearing the conviction in Abel's voice, she had to remind herself of something. The story of what Rick and her sister had done to her had been enough to have so many people up in arms that Rick had lost his job over it. Abel was one of *the most* intense persons she'd ever met. Of course, the story would piss him off as well.

"Well, thank you," she said, rubbing her hand over his hand, the one that was squeezing hers a bit tighter now. "Overall, the whole experience made me a much stronger person. That's for sure."

"What about your sister? Have you talked to her since then?"

The flight attendant came around and asked if they wanted anything to drink. Nellie asked for iced tea while Abel asked for water.

"Believe it or not," Nellie said, shaking her head. "I offered to let Courtney move in with me." Apparently this surprised Abel more than her husband cheating on her with her sister because he looked stunned. Nellie sighed, nodding. "She'd already sold her condo and was making arrangements to move in with Rick when he left her hanging out to dry. Not only had he changed his mind about the marriage but he also decided that since he was divorced now he wanted to stay single and out of any relationship for a while." A short scoff escaped her just as the flight attendant came over with their drinks. They took their drinks, and Nellie waited for the flight attendant to walk away before continuing. "His no-relationship crap lasted about a month before he moved with another woman in Seattle. Courtney had been staying with our parents and apparently had high hopes that once the baby was born Rick would change his mind. But he moved in with this woman just a few months after my nephew was born."

"So let me get this straight." Abel said, closing the cap on the water he'd just poured into his cup of ice and sliding his hand back into hers. "You offered to not only let your sister, who got knocked up by your ex and had been having an affair with him for years, move in but also her son— you're ex's kid."

"I don't see it that way," Nellie explained. "Gus is my nephew first—not Rick's son. I know technically he is, but that's not Gus's fault. He didn't choose to come into this world under these circumstances. To me, he's just my nephew. He's an innocent baby and a part of my family now. I love him." She sighed, knowing what she would say next would possibly make her sound like the most pathetic and stupidest person on the planet, but it was the truth and she thought Abel, having a brother he was so close to, would understand. "And despite everything that's happened, I still love my sister. Aside from my parents and my brother who's always stationed in some far-out place, she's the only family I have in this country, well, besides Gus now. It's why I offered to let them move in with me."

Abel lifted a skeptical brow. "So why didn't she?"

Nellie glanced away, unable to look at him when she told him this part. "She moved to Seattle to be near Rick. She said that even if they weren't together she still wanted Gus to be around his dad."

She glanced back at him, and Abel looked as disgusted as she thought he would. "She took her son away from the only real family he has to be near a man who tore your family apart and then just walked away? A man she knows is now living with another woman already?"

It got even more complicated than that, and since Abel was already disgusted, he'd be even more so if she went on, so she nodded and left it at that. This time he looked away and cleared his throat. "So are you really never gonna marry again?"

Nellie tilted her head, looking at him. "Is that what Noah told you?"

"Something like that. He said basically the same thing you did on the cruise: that you're not looking to get into anything serious right now and all that. Only Noah said you said possibly *ever*."

Taking a deep breath, Nellie sipped her tea. She needed to be careful here. He could be testing her—making sure they were still in agreement since things had gotten a bit heavier than she'd first anticipated they would. When she'd put it out there for him on the cruise, she wasn't even sure any of this would continue afterward. And even when they did, she thought their booty calls would be maybe once or twice a month if she were lucky.

She also never expected to be sitting here, talking to him about her divorce. But she wouldn't take his interest in it to be anything more than *killing time* as he'd put it, when he said he wouldn't *mind* hearing about it. So she answered very carefully. "First of all, I never say "never." But I married really young and missed out on a lot. I remember hearing my single friends talking about traveling and doing all kinds of exciting things. You know letting loose and really living during that time in their lives between being teens and becoming adults." He was staring at her, focused on her every word now, and it made her nervous. "It's not that I regretted marrying young, but since things worked out the way they did, I figure that this is my chance to make up for it. So jumping into a serious relationship hasn't made my to-do list just yet."

Still staring at her very closely, Abel straightened out a bit before his next question. "What exactly does that mean to you? *Letting loose?*"

This time she cleared her throat for the first time, realizing she didn't even know what she meant when she said that. She'd used the term so loosely, but it was just a figure of speech. Although when she'd told Roni that it was what she was doing with Abel, she knew what she *wanted* Roni to think it meant to her. It was likely what he wanted it to mean as well. She remembered his apprehension on the cruise and the entire months leading up to it when the sexual tension between them had begun to feel unbearable. It wasn't until she'd made it clear what she was game for that he was interested. In case he was asking because maybe she'd begun to give him the impression that perhaps the rules had somehow changed, she played it safe and went with that. "Just enjoying my freedom, I guess. I have no one to answer to now, and I'm taking full advantage of it."

Again that beautiful Adam's apple on his big thick neck distracted her. She'd expected a smile maybe, at the very least a slight show of relief in his eyes. But there was neither. She sensed he had more to say or ask, but he didn't. Instead he finally pulled his penetrating gaze away and sat back, taking a drink of his water.

It seemed he was done killing time with small talk or talk of her divorce. Without letting go of her hand, he laid his head back on his seat and closed his eyes.

They each checked into their respective rooms at the hotel, but Abel had no intention of sleeping alone that night, not for their entire stay for that matter. They would be there for three nights, so it'd be the first time they'd be spending this many days and nights of *letting loose* together. And if Abel got his way, it wouldn't be their last.

The young male attendant behind the counter had recognized Abel immediately, and he was a talker. The last thing Abel wanted was for this guy to go spreading the word about him and Nellie checking into one room only as he would've liked. The press would begin hounding her in no time. So they went through the motions of checking in separately for appearance's sake.

The moment the elevator doors closed, Abel pulled Nellie to him and kissed her. "Stay in my room tonight," he whispered against her lips. "Only reason I had them book two rooms was because of the damn paparazzi; otherwise, I would've just gotten one."

He waited to see if she'd protest in any way about his presumptuous admission. "You sure no one will catch wind of it?" she asked, staring at his lips.

Abel couldn't help smiling. "I honestly don't give a shit for my sake. I just want to avoid *your* life being turned into a circus." Feeling his smile wane a bit, he added, "For as long as I can anyway."

Lifting her gaze from his lips to his eyes, she stared at him momentarily without saying a word. He wanted her to get that this thing they had wasn't going away anytime soon. And while he kept reminding himself that he'd already tasted firsthand his reaction to knowing she might still be *living it up* with other guys, getting her to change her mind about that eventually might be easier than pulling back now. Because with every moment he spent with her now, the likelihood of that happening was beginning to feel impossible.

The anxiety mounted as he waited for a response to his last comment. Would she remind him again of the unspoken rules? Point out that he was starting to sound as if he might be breaking them? Already he'd asked her about her ex more than once. He'd even taken it a step further by asking if she was seriously thinking of never remarrying. She, of course, reaffirmed her desire to make up for what she'd missed out on when she'd been tied down to one guy the first time. What had been the most galling was that serious relationships were not on her to-do list.

"Don't worry about me." She smiled, easing his anxiety a bit. "I've had my share of the press, and I think I can handle them." The elevator came to a stop, and she began pulling away from his embrace. "But I know how private you are and how much you'd prefer to stay out of the headlines, so I think it's best if we're careful."

She started out the elevator doors as soon as they opened, leaving him wondering one thing. "But you're still staying in my room, right?"

Glancing back at him as she pulled her luggage along behind her, she winked. "Try and keep me out."

The huge and very relieved smile was instantly plastered on Abel's face. Then it hit him. "You had your share of the press?" He asked as he took her in from behind. He'd told her to dress comfortably since it was a redeye, and she hadn't disappointed, wearing a very short pair of denim shorts. He somehow got the feeling she hadn't worn them when she was married to her idiot ex-husband.

She turned to him just as they got to the door of one of their rooms. "It's more about my ex, and I'm done talking about him for today. Maybe another time I'll tell you about it."

"Good enough," Abel said, slipping his key in the door.

He was done talking about her ex too. There were obviously not so much as kindling embers left on that torch. The moron had snuffed that out for good. That's all that mattered to Abel anyway. He had better things he wanted to do with his tongue now than stand there and talk about that asshole. He opened the door and held it open for her, already excited about the night ahead of him.

***

It was nice to sleep in for once. Abel thought about the last time he had with a smile. He'd woken up next to Nellie then too. He could certainly get used to long exhausting nights. He could also get used to waking up next to Nellie. At least he had the next two mornings to do just that. The memory of Nellie jumping out of bed to answer Logan's call the last time he woke next to her killed his smile.

They had a free day today since his run wasn't until tomorrow, and he was determined to show her a good time. He'd tell her so as soon as she was back from the bathroom. If she was so hell bent on making up for lost time, maybe he could help her do just that. She wanted to experience all kinds of exciting things? No reason why he couldn't give her a hand there, starting today. Maybe that would be enough for her. *I have no one to answer to now, and I'm taking full advantage.* He didn't even realize he'd been gnashing his teeth until he heard the shower turn on.

Jumping out of bed, he thought about her comment last night. He'd make an extra effort to not make her feel *tied down.* Even though his suggesting that she stay in his room wasn't exactly freeing, she'd accepted happily. She could've told him she'd prefer her own room, but she agreed to spend the night in his. And yet here she was already starting up the shower in his room when she could've easily said she'd go back to hers for that.

He felt even better about it when he saw she'd left the bathroom door half open. If that wasn't an invitation, he didn't know what was. He wasn't even in the door yet, and he was already at full attention.

"Want some company in there?" He paraded his naked ass shamelessly in the already fogging bathroom.

"Absolutely," she murmured with what he'd normally refer to as a sexy smile, but on Nellie it was *beautiful*. "This shower was made for two." She motioned to the second shower head.

Abel glanced at it, but his eyes went immediately back to her. The more he was around her, the more he thought she was the most beautiful thing he'd ever laid eyes on. Even with her hair soaking wet and not an ounce of makeup on, she was absolutely beautiful. It still staggered him that it'd taken him this long to notice.

As soon as he was in the shower with her, his hands were all over her wet body, and he kissed her softly. "You," he said, kissing her bottom lip softly. "Are so," he brought his hands up to her face, cradling it as he kissed her again, "fucking beautiful."

She did that thing she always did when he told her so, closing her eyes for a moment then smiling softly—timidly. "Thank you," she whispered then leaned against his body, making that vulnerability she made every attempt to hide so evident.

He kissed her deeper now, but unlike the first couple of times last night when he'd eaten her up like a starving man— every inch of her—now he wanted to take it slowly. All the times before when he'd told her how beautiful he thought she was, it'd made him nervous—nervous that she might pick up on something he let escape each time—something he apparently had no control over. Now he *wanted* her to pick up on it. He wanted her to know that she may not have to answer to him and he wouldn't ever ask to tie her down if what she wanted was to fly free. But at the very least, as long as she was involved with him, she'd have mercy on his heart. The simple fact that he was thinking of Nellie in terms of what she did to his heart as opposed to other parts of his body, scared him breathless.

What Nellie had told him last night about still loving her sister even after what the selfish little bitch had done to her gave him hope that he'd been right all along about this beautiful woman. She didn't have the kind of heart it would take to spend time that felt this special with one guy and then casually do the same with someone else.

Bringing his hands around her now, he continued to kiss her as he pressed her against the wall, his erection firmly against her hip. He ran his hands up and down her body a little more frantically now as they swept down between her legs. She gasped against his mouth when he slipped two fingers inside her. Her own hand roamed from his shoulders all the way down his arms until they were on his hips, and then she took him in her hand, making him groan.

Instinctively, he began to lift her, wanting her to wrap her legs around him so he could be in her already, but she protested. "We can't in here," she said quickly. "No condom." *Damn,* he hadn't even thought of that. In the next moment, she slid down his body until she was on her knees, and his legs nearly gave out on him as she licked away at what he was certain was already dripping with more than just water. "But there is one thing I can do."

She took him so far and deep in her mouth that he had to hold on to the shower head, certain his legs would give out on him this time. "Oh, *baby!*" He managed to say before his head dropped back in ecstasy as she licked and sucked him harder.

With one hand on the shower head, he ran his fingers through her wet hair. He squeezed his eyes shut, wondering if he'd ever kiss her again without messing his pants. He'd forever be reminded of what her amazing tongue was doing to him now. Normally he could hold out a little longer than this, but already he felt ready to blow. "I'm gonna come, babe," he warned, but she kept on, her tongue going into high gear now. "Jesus!" he said as the first enormous release came and still her tongue went on.

He had to lean against the wall as he continued to explode massively in her mouth. Her hand let go, but her mouth didn't as she continued licking away every drop. "*God*, that's enough, babe, "he pleaded, his legs feeling like noodles now. "I can't take anymore."

She kissed the very sensitive tip before looking up at him with a sly smile. "Just so you know," she said as he helped her up. "I've never done that before." She licked her lips again. "Swallowed. But with you, I *wanted* to." He stared at her, his heart still pounding away as she continued to lick her lips sheepishly and unbelievably a little timidly. "I liked it."

Reaching out, he brought her to him, and she fell into his arms. Maybe it was wishful thinking, but the way she wrapped her arms around him and kissed his chest made it feel as though her little confession, about having done this with only him, gave him hope that it meant more. Maybe this and everything else she'd experienced with him for the first time so far would stay just like that for good—with only him.

CHAPTER 6

"Not on your life, Abel Ayala." Nellie said as she snuck a peek at one of the brochures Abel had taken from the hotel lobby.

"Hey!" Abel smirked, moving it out of her sight. "You're not supposed to be peeking. I told you I wanna surprise you."

"Well, I'll tell you right now." Nellie shook her head defiantly. "St. John will bend a finger the day you or anybody else gets me to bungee jump."

"What!" Abel laughed.

"Yeah." A small smile broke through despite her sudden alarm that Abel might actually try to get her to bungee jump. "My mom says that a lot. Only she usually says it in Spanish. It probably makes more sense that way too."

Abel shook his head, still laughing, and then kissed her softly. "What does that even mean?"

He stared at her bright-eyed, his big gorgeous smile taking her breath away. She felt silly suddenly, though the way he was looking at her made her heart flutter. "You know St. John the Apostle? Most depictions of him have him extending a finger or two up in front of him like this," she lifted her fingers in front of her, feeling so silly about using her parents' outdated saying that she felt her face warm.

Glancing at her fingers then back at what Nellie was sure was now a red face, Abel took her fingers in his hand and kissed them. "You're adorable." First, he kept insisting she was beautiful; now she was adorable? Her heart felt ready to burst. "Say it in Spanish. I'll use that on my mom as soon as I get a chance."

Now she laughed softly as she tried to remember exactly how her mom said it. "*Cuando San Juan se agache el dedo.*"

Abel smiled, staring at her lips. She was beginning to feel a difference in the way he looked at her and spoke to her, but she dare not give it too much thought or get her hopes up. He was so young and had his entire life ahead of him. It would be no ordinary life either. Already he was rich and slowly becoming more and more famous. This fight would be life changing for him, and she completely understood why he'd want to be free to enjoy it as the single wealthy hot celebrity he was quickly becoming—just like Felix Sanchez, the first one of his boxer friends whose fame had reached another level. Felix was all over the magazines with a different starlet or famous female athlete every week.

Abel leaned in, slipping his hand behind her neck, and kissed her, this time a little longer than when he'd called her adorable but just as sweet. "Okay, no bungee jumping," he said, still speaking against her lips. "But you said you wanted to live it up. So we're doing something exciting today."

After ordering room service and having another amazing morning in their room, they explored Fisherman's Wharf. They couldn't leave without trying the famed clam chowder, something Nellie always had when she and Rick would visit, but she'd never enjoyed San Francisco as she had today. And now Abel was telling her the fun had only begun? With her heart hammering away, she wondered how much more excitement it could take.

Instinctively ducking, even though Abel assured her she didn't have to, Nellie thought about another thing she was sure her mom would say if she were ever asked to get on a helicopter. *Ni a patadas.* As nauseated as she was beginning to feel about doing this, she'd already turned down bungee jumping, rock climbing, and paragliding. She'd teased Abel that just because she wanted to try exciting things didn't mean she had a death wish.

A helicopter ride around the bay seemed relatively safe when she'd agreed to it. Now she was seriously having second thoughts about this whole letting-loose-and-really-living thing. Maybe she just didn't have it in her. It took a certain type of person for that kind of lifestyle, and she wasn't feeling it. Just because she'd managed to transform her outer appearance didn't mean she wasn't still the same ole play-it-safe Nellie on the inside. For as much as she talked about wanting to really live and let loose since her divorce, she'd only done a few things out of the ordinary in her free time that diverged from her usual curling up with a good book and a glass of wine on a Friday night. She'd been perfectly content doing so too.

Who was she kidding? Nellie knew it from the very start, but she was even more certain about it now. She wouldn't even consider sleeping with another man while she was still doing so with Abel. The worst part was that, as alarming as it was to admit, it wasn't just for moral reasons anymore. She couldn't even begin to imagine another man touching her now. As much as she was trying to protect her heart and not think it, she was also beginning to get the distinct feeling that Abel wouldn't be so okay with that either.

"You nervous?" Abel asked through the two-way headsets they'd been given before they boarded.

She squeezed his hand and smiled but admitted it. "Yes."

"You'll be fine," he said with the sweetest smile. "I promise."

A few minutes later, they were up in the air and away they went. As the minutes passed and the very friendly pilot narrated the stunning views of the Golden Gate Bridge, Alcatraz Island, Treasure Island, and the entire breathtaking bay, Nellie was able to relax and just enjoy.

To Nellie's delight, the tour included a three-hour dinner cruise after the flight along the bay on a dining yacht. It was supposed to be open to other passengers, but wanting the utmost privacy, Abel had bought out the boat. So it was just the two of them on the cruise being catered to hand and foot. Nellie thought she'd seen enough spectacular views of San Francisco, but seeing them at sunset with Abel holding her was just . . . *magical*. What she'd started with so much apprehension she now didn't want to ever end.

"So you glad you did this?" Abel whispered in her ear as he held her from behind.

She spun around slowly in his arms, pushing away thoughts that this amazing day and what would probably continue into the next few days was only temporary— pretend. Because as wonderful as he'd been to her so far, she knew that once they got back to Los Angeles everything would go back to the way things really were. For now, she'd take what this actually felt like—the real thing. As much as she wanted to deny it, she was falling for this man. It scared her so much, but she wouldn't ruin such an incredible trip, thinking about that. "Yes," she said with as genuine a smile as she could. "I'm so glad I did this, and thank you so much for making me." She tilted her head with a smile. "Maybe someday I'll get the nerve to do some of those other things you suggested."

His brows jumped, and he grinned playfully, pulling her closer. "Bungee jumping?"

"No," she said immediately. "Rock climbing, and dare I say it, paragliding maybe, but bungee jumping *never*."

"Ah," he said with a twinkle in his eyes, "but I distinctly remember you saying that you *never* say never."

He distinctly remembered that? She stared at him for a moment as his expression drifted into the less playful and more serious. Their lighthearted banter took a turn, and once again she felt what she'd thought she'd felt before. Was he trying to tell her something? As tempted as she was to ask— maybe mention how she couldn't remember feeling as alive as she did when she was with him; that her body had never experienced such pleasure; and that for all her talk about wanting to be free, she was more than willing already to give her heart to him if he asked for it—she couldn't. There was no way. What if she was reading too much into the profound way he looked at her so much now? What if he was just this wonderful to all the women he went out with and her suggesting otherwise would ruin this trip, making the rest of their time here unbearably awkward?

As if reading her mind, he searched her eyes now, very seriously. "What are you thinking?"

Did she dare say it? She closed her eyes almost trembling with the fear of what her incorrect assessment might result in. Opening her eyes, she looked up at him, her heart beating harder than ever. "I was just thinking that of all the times I've been to San Francisco this is probably the one I'll remember most fondly." She stared at him, the fear still clutching and suffocating her heart, but she couldn't hold in what she really wanted him to know anymore. "Today was absolutely amazing."

She literally held her breath as she waited for a reaction. She waited to see the disappointment wash over his face that she'd gone *there*—ruined the perfect arrangement. But there was none. The smile that chased away the all-too-serious look on his face just moments ago nearly brought a lump to her throat, and she exhaled slowly.

"I feel the same, sweetheart, and I've been here plenty of times."

Before she could say another word or even respond with so much as a smile, his lips were on hers again. She spent the final glorious twenty minutes of their cruise right there in his arms with him kissing her so sweetly nonstop. She wasn't sure if either of them had actually confessed anything on the top deck of that magical cruise, but by the time they docked, she felt as if she were walking on air.

Neither one of them dared say it, but that night they didn't have sex like all the other times. They made love. Of this, Nellie was sure. No matter what either of them was too reluctant to admit just yet, it was what it sure as hell felt like it was that night, and Nellie was certain that it would feel like that from then on.

If Nellie had been afraid before, she knew fear wouldn't even begin to describe what she'd be feeling from that moment on. Just as her body had never experienced the bliss that only Abel had ever made her feel, she was positive that, even after all her cheating ex had put her through, her heart was yet to endure the pain of eventually having to walk away from this make-believe relationship.

On top of all the other reasons that Abel knew it would be impossible to stop thinking about Nellie now, she blew him away once again. She took complete control of the mini press conference that took place after the 5k run the next day. Andy had already passed along all the information she needed to know to get it all organized along with the list of questions Abel would *not* be entertaining.

Nellie told Abel that Andy had also explained to her how hungry the media was getting for any comments from Abel about all the endless rumors bubbling up everywhere about his personal life and father. After the second time Abel was asked about the allegations that his father was involved in with the Mexican mob, Nellie took charge. She stood up without even a mic, but everyone heard her firm announcement loud and clear. "I've made sure you all received a list of topics Mr. Ayala will not be discussing today. If I missed any of you, I apologize and will be happy to give you one now if you just raise your hand." She glanced around as no one raised his hand. "Great, I didn't miss anyone. Now this is my final reminder. Mr. Ayala was gracious enough and happy to agree to this spontaneous press conference on his tight schedule. But if even one more of those topics he's not here to discuss is brought up again, this conference is over."

Seeing the assertive way she stood up to them without any hesitation was a side of her that Abel hadn't had the pleasure of witnessing before then. She'd worn one of her sexy power skirt suits to boot, making the scene that much hotter. Eyebrows lifted and he saw a few of the reporters take her in from top to bottom as they jotted furiously in their notebooks. A few photographers even snapped a few photos of her. Abel was certain there'd be speculation as to what his relationship with this new, no-nonsense, and not to mention sexy-as-all-hell assistant was. It was something he was actually looking forward to. They might be forced to discuss how exactly they should clarify what their relationship was now. It made him anxious because the conversation they'd had on their flight into San Francisco still nagged at him. *Serious relationships are not on my to-do list.* He might actually be in for a rude awakening. But this trip had gone so well that he was hopeful that if she hadn't already, she'd be changing her mind.

The conversation on the flight back had been much lighter. Their conduct even in front of the flight attendant and other passengers was that of an undeniable couple. Abel wasn't holding anything back now. When they weren't kissing and giggling openly, Nellie rested her head against his chest as he stroked his fingers through her hair, kissing the top of her head every so often. It felt perfect, and he didn't care who saw them or what anyone thought. Then when they reached LAX because their flight had been an earlier one than the redeye they'd caught to San Francisco, the paparazzi were waiting and ready. Nellie turned into the same no-nonsense assistant he'd seen at the mini press conference, walking ahead of him, letting reporters know he wouldn't be doing any unscheduled interviews.

Abel's protective instincts kicked in when he saw the cameras flashing in Nellie's face and the paparazzi not only yelling out his name but for Ms. Gamboa to turn to them. They already knew her name and would no doubt start hounding her if they caught wind of their intimate involvement. He had no choice but to continue to walk behind her and in between his other body guards, who had also been waiting for them at the airport.

For now, he'd go along with what everyone else was assuming: that she was just his assistant and event coordinator and nothing more, but deep inside he felt she was so much more now.

As soon as they were in the comfort of the car waiting for them just outside the terminal and behind the safety of the tinted windows, Abel kissed Nellie as hard as her take charge manner made him. He held her face in his hands and spoke inches away from her lips now. "Do you know what a fucking turn on it is to see you deal with those reporters as effortlessly as you just did?"

She laughed as her bright eyes stared at him. "I actually should've just ignored them, right? Not tell them you weren't available for comments?"

Abel shook his head. "No," he said, kissing her softly this time. "You handled it perfectly." He sat back now but held her hand, playing with her fingers. "In San Francisco, you said you'd handled your share of reporters before. I'm curious now. When and why?"

Her smile went a little flat, and she glanced out the window. "I told you my ex used to be a sportscaster on one of the bigger networks." She shrugged. "He didn't get there overnight. He had to do his share of sleazy reporting before he made it, and being sleazy was something that, in retrospect, came very easy to him. So I already had a taste and knew what reporters were like. Then when we divorced and news began to leak that he'd been unfaithful, the reporters came in droves." She let out a humorless chuckle before continuing. "Even after I gave them a full account of why we'd separated, they were still relentless. They hounded me for weeks—months—wanting more details. I still get requests for interviews wanting to do where-are-they-now type pieces, but I've moved on from that part of my life. I know that, as much as they insist the story would be more about my life now, they'd still ask questions and want me to retell and in essence revive the story and the old me. That's something I have no desire to ever do again. That person is dead and buried. The new me has moved on and is never looking back."

Abel kissed her hand, staring at her somewhat strained expression. "I like the new you," he offered, biting back the urge to use the stronger L word. Unbelievably, after the last few days with her, it was what he really felt like saying now.

CHAPTER 7

Two days. It'd been two days since Abel had seen Nellie. The very next day after getting back from San Francisco, he'd been at her place again. She told him about having pushed a few things aside on her schedule to make time for the unexpected trip and that she had her hands full now, making up for it. With the fight less than two weeks away now, Abel had heavy nonstop training that he had to make up as well. Between that and a few radio interviews he had to tape in the evenings, the last two days had been crazy, leaving no time for visits. He was doing his damnedest to keep his mind off her. Not wanting to blow it with her now that his feelings had changed so dramatically, he had to admit that what Noah had warned him about might happen. It was killing his concentration, and he knew more than anything how something like this could so easily throw his training out of whack.

The last-minute hustle with the major promotional appearances was all lined up as well. He'd do the late show in a few days, and then later that week, he'd be off to New York for the shows Andy had lined up for him and Felix to do together. Felix had just recently announced his next bout. It'd take place next year, but Andy said it was never too early to start promoting.

Of course, Abel's first thoughts were to run it past Nellie. These next couple of weeks he'd be so damn busy training and promoting he knew his time with her would be very limited. Even after the fight, Andy had all kinds of shit lined up for him to do. This was exactly why, before he'd gotten involved with Nellie, he insisted he didn't have time for a relationship—because he *didn't*. But he was determined to make time for Nellie if she asked for it. He'd already asked her to come with him to New York. Unfortunately, she was busy meeting with some of the sponsors of the mixer she was coordinating on the same days he'd be in New York.

Both Gio and Noah had warned him in not so many words that he should shut down his social life from here on until the fight. It was what they all did when a fight was just around the corner, something Abel had always advised as well. Their concentration should be one-hundred percent on training, and they didn't need anything distracting them from it. Noah had even told him to stop reading or even watching any of the tabloid shit. He didn't have to ask Abel twice. He'd stopped reading the bullshit a long time ago. But cut Nellie out for that long? He couldn't even bring himself to stop thinking about her now.

Even on his way to pick up Noah for their run, she was all he could think of. He wasn't sure how much longer he could hide his feelings for her, but until he was sure she was feeling the same way and he was certain he wouldn't be shooting himself in the foot by making her run in the opposite direction, he had to. When Abel had mentioned to Noah as casually as he could that Nellie would be joining him in San Francisco in place of Andy, he hadn't missed the skeptical expression on his nervous friend's face. He didn't entirely buy that Abel had chosen her for her coordinating skills alone.

The very next day after Abel's trip, Noah had annoyingly questioned where he was going. Once again, Abel hadn't slipped into basketball shorts as he normally did when he was headed straight home. Abel knew it was partially concern about his needing to get as much rest as possible now that the fight was so close. But he also knew his questioning had to do with Noah's continual concern over Abel's involvement with Nellie. Abel wasn't about to tell Noah that, after spending the last three nights with Nellie, he was off to her place again, so he referred to a *date* again leaving out who it was with. Noah hadn't asked with whom, but the relief on his face was telling enough that he assumed it was with someone else.

Just as he reached Noah's, he got a call from Andy. As the fight approached rapidly, he hardly went a day without hearing from Andy anymore. But the last couple of days Andy had been so busy in New York that he'd only gotten the few texts from him confirming the dates of his appearances. It was refreshing. Too much of Andy was tiring.

Abel took the call before getting out of his car. "What's up, Andy?"

"I finally got a chance to watch the coverage of Frisco. You looked good, but what the hell's with this Nellie chick?" The humor in his voice made Abel uncomfortable. "They're making her out to be some kind of bad ass. I sort of got that, you know, when I talked to her on the phone. But I thought maybe it was just me. She's the same one I've met before, right? Noah's wife's friend?"

"Yeah, same one," Abel said, offering nothing more.

"I heard what she did at the press conference. Laid the law down for them reporters," he laughed again, making Abel roll his eyes, wondering if there'd be any point to this anytime soon. "Then I saw the photos they got of the two of you at the airport. She looks a lot different than I remember—hot. So are you banging her or what? They're already speculating."

"That's none of your business," Abel said, getting out of the car, feeling even more defensive about this than usual. "Why are you even asking me? You know I don't talk about that kind of shit."

"Because I got the feeling she didn't like me very much. That alone was kind of a turn on, and when I heard what she did at the press conference, I was even more intrigued. So seeing the photos just now," he laughed even louder this time, "I nearly got a hard-on. If you ain't doing her, I'm seriously thinking of giving her a call."

Abel stopped walking and struggled to keep from telling Andy what he really wanted to tell him: that if his scrawny ass even thought about it, Andy would get to feel firsthand what all his opponents who'd hit the canvas face first had felt. But he held back. He had a feeling there was more to this. Andy knew just as well as anyone else that Abel wouldn't be sharing any details of his personal life with anyone. So he knew his sneaky publicist had gone about it a different way.

"She's a friend of mine and for personal reasons not looking to get involved with anyone right now. So as her friend, I'm telling you right now that, other than for business reasons, you stay away from her."

Andy was quiet for a moment. "But you're not involved with her in any other way than just business, and she's a friend."

"Isn't that what I just said?"

"I'm just trying to get it straight in case, you know, she and I hit it off or something—"

"Stay the hell away from her."

Abel's tone was far more lethal this time. He was done with indirect warnings. In case there was any doubt, Andy should know now that if he didn't take the unmistakable warning for it was worth he'd be in a world of pain.

"Got it," Andy said, sounding a little too smug. "As your publicist, you know, we're gonna have to talk about this, though."

"No, we're not." Abel assured him. "I've already told you all you need to know."

Andy exhaled loudly but then chuckled. "Okay, I'll call you later to give you more details about New York. I've got lots to tell you."

As soon as Abel was off the phone with him, he tried to shake off the weird mood Andy had left him in. He also needed to get his mind on something else. Thoughts of Nellie had momentarily ceased when he and Noah began talking strategy and pushing Abel's endurance even harder now. Then Noah brought up the cocktail mixer and what an awesome job Nellie had done getting all the participants together. Irritatingly, she was immediately at the forefront of his thoughts again.

Little Jack, Noah's toddler, scurried into the front room in his pull-up diapers. Roni wasn't far behind, holding his pants. "Get over here, you little stinker," Roni laughed. "I swear," she said, looking at Abel and Noah, "this kid would live in his underpants if I let him."

"So let him," Noah said, grabbing Jack and spinning him upside down. Jack laughed so hard that he squealed. "It's supposed to be a hot one today."

"No, I have to get him fed and ready," Roni insisted. "We're meeting Nellie at the mall again in a few hours."

"That's right. I forgot about that," Noah said, spinning Jack right side up again. "Sorry, little man, looks like you're going shopping with momma. I'd help you out of it and keep you here with me, but I gotta whip uncle Abe's ass here into shape."

Roni immediately shot Noah a look. With a regretful smirk, Noah winced. "I mean butt, son. Whip his butt into shape."

Abel tried but failed at being his "aweless and indifferent" self. Even something as insignificant as this about Nellie had his full attention. He thought of all the times in the past that he'd been around Noah and Roni and heard Roni speak of her friend. He never would've imagined feeling like he did now—hopeful that she'd share more about her best friend. His eyes met Roni's for a moment as she squatted down and helped Jack into his pants. But with a lift of an eyebrow, she brought her attention back to helping Jack, who was struggling to get his leg in the right hole.

"What do you think would be best to wear to a Slightly Stoopid concert? This is Nellie's second attempt to find something for it. Last time we walked out with nothing. She's kind of worried about looking out of place." Roni looked up at them again, and Abel couldn't be sure, but it almost felt as if she were asking him, not Noah. "Concerts at the House of Blues are generally not the dressy kind, right?"

"I've only been there a couple of times," Noah said, standing up. "Both times, I wore jeans and a t-shirt. Most of the guys were dressed just the same. Of course, the ones there to pick up dress a little spiffier. But concert or not, girls typically dress up a little more than guys."

Roni was still looking at Abel curiously. Done helping Jack with this pants, she shrugged and stood up too. "I suppose you could dress up anything, even a pair of jeans if you wear the right shoes and top. I've never been to the House of Blues," she said as she walked away into the kitchen, holding Jack's hand. "Maybe someday *someone* will take me," she smiled playfully at Noah before picking up Jack and sitting him on his high chair.

"Next time, for sure," Noah said. "I'll look into it, and next concert we'll go with her."

It didn't even dawn on Abel until he and Noah were headed out the door. Roni wasn't going to the concert with Nellie. He was anxious to ask Noah about it but knew his interest would spark suspicion. Noah would no doubt start up with one of his perturbing lectures about why getting involved with Nellie in any way right now was a bad idea, so he refrained.

They headed out to Griffith Park, where they usually ran a good four to five miles. Today they'd be doing twice that since they were working on Abel's endurance. Noah filled him in on more of the details of the mixer on their way, giving Abel an excellent excuse to get back to Nellie and her concert Friday. "So that meeting we're having Friday night with the director of PR," he said, avoiding eye contact with

Noah so his question would sound as natural as possible. "I guess Nellie won't make that meeting like we talked about if she's gonna be at a concert Friday night."

"That's right," Noah turned to him, but Abel kept his eyes on the road. "I forgot the meeting was Friday night. Hmm." Noah was quiet for a moment then went on. "If it were anything else, I could probably get Roni to see if Nellie could skip out on her plans or postpone them, but I know she won't for this."

Now Abel turned to him, the curiosity beating out any attempt to not appear too interested in Nellie's plans. "Why's that?"

Noah shrugged. "I guess it's because it's Nellie's first real date in a while. Roni's all excited for her."

Abel gripped the steering wheel, remembering how nonchalant Nellie had been back, when she'd mentioned the concert to him. Sure they had an understanding, but after the incredible time they'd had in San Francisco, it was hard enough to concentrate on anything else right now much less make arrangements to spend *any* of his free time with someone else. All morning he'd already been mentally making room in his busy schedule for when he could see her again. And she was going on a date—a first *real* date? What the hell did that even mean? Had she not mentioned San Francisco to Roni?

Logically, he knew he shouldn't be upset. He'd agreed he'd be "game" to this, and at the time, he had every intention of this being just a fun thing—neither had a right to be upset or ask questions about each other's personal lives. But he'd been certain this trip had been a game changer. He was more than upset, damn it. He was *pissed*.

He was afraid to speak for fear that even one word out of his mouth at that moment would be loaded with indignation so toxic that Noah would be all over it. He parked and got out of his car without saying another word: not about Nellie, not about his training, and not about the meeting Nellie wouldn't be making because of her fucking date. All he wanted to do was run—run the annoying and unreasonable thoughts right out of his head. Visions of her doing what she had been doing with him for weeks after her date inundated him almost throughout the entire galling run.

"You okay?" Noah asked as their run finally came to an end.

Abel took a long swig of his water, still unwilling to speak. Catching his breath after drinking his water, he nodded.

"You didn't overdo it, did you?" Noah's brows were pinched, his eyes full of concern. "Something hurt?"

Yeah, his ego was crushed. But hurt was maybe pushing it—or not. "Nah, I'm good. I had a long night. That's all."

"Another *date*," Noah frowned. "I'm telling you, dude, you're gonna have to cut down on the late nights or all-nighters anyway. This fight is no joke, and your body needs all the time to recoup from the extra training you're doing now."

They started back toward Abel's car, the irritation still weighing heavy. "I'll be fine."

Out of nowhere, Noah chuckled. "Roni was a little pissed at you the other night. I was actually worried she might bring it up today."

Abel turned to him, his forehead pinched now. "Pissed at me? For what?"

"I told her you had a date the night after you got back from San Francisco, and when she confirmed with Nellie that Frisco wasn't *all* business, she was hot."

"Nellie was?" Abel asked, feeling hopeful.

"*No,* Roni was. She still insists that Nellie's gonna get hurt."

Abel frowned, deciding to keep to himself who his date had actually been with that night. Noah would find out soon enough. Abel would spare himself Noah's shrewd expression. "Well, if it pisses her off so much, why did you tell her?"

"Because I want her to get used to it, that's why," Noah said, looking at Abel over the roof of his car. Abel unlocked his door and got in, leaning over to unlock Noah's door. As soon as Noah got in, he continued. "Roni tends to romanticize everything, and even with Nellie telling her she's good with this being a purely physical thing, that she's in no way looking for any kind of relationship, Roni's still worried. Hell, Nellie even assured her again just the other day that she's all about having fun and being a free spirit now with no one to answer to, but Roni still keeps insisting one of you is bound to want more eventually and that you two might sour up things for our little group. So I need to keep reminding her that it's not happening."

Abel didn't think it possible to feel anymore aggravated than he already did. All about being a free spirit? Maybe she *would* be jumping in bed with this guy Friday night. Maybe that was who she really wanted to be now, and what he thought he saw in her eyes, felt in her kisses, despite her saying flat out that serious relationships weren't on her to-do list, was just him being delusional. Maybe he shouldn't give a shit about what she did when he wasn't around, and he should just enjoy the incredible time he had with her. Evidently it was what she was doing.

Swallowing back the irrepressible jealousy, he revved the ignition to a loud start. He now attributed what he was feeling to his overinflated ego. He'd been so sure the extra effort he made to take care of her needs—needs he'd suspected and she'd confirmed had been grossly neglected by her ex—would be enough to keep her from going out and having them be satisfied elsewhere. That and the fact that amidst the most grueling training he'd ever had he was likely in the best shape of his life. His body would probably never get any harder than it was now. He'd been sure she'd be highly appreciative of that and that it would go a long way in keeping her from "letting loose." He didn't admit it then, but now he had no choice because he felt ready to detonate. Only now he welcomed it. Anger was good. As long as it was ego-crushing fury, he could deal with this. Pain was completely different. He had no time to deal with that in his life right now.

"Yeah, well you can keep reminding Roni of that because I'm only in this for one thing. Nellie's *free spirit,*" he said the venom in his words maybe a little too thick, "takes care of what I need without me having to deal with the usual drama of someone demanding more."

The irritation only mounted now because, even as he stared ahead, he could feel Noah's eyes on him. He knew he should've kept his mouth shut. "Good," Noah said as they pulled out of the parking lot. "I'm not gonna lie, man. I was pretty worried about this in the beginning, especially with you making her your own personal assistant. But seeing as how you two seem to have this thing under control, it makes me feel better. You know Roni had this crazy notion that maybe you'd be a little ticked about Nellie going out on a date."

Clenching his jaw, Abel shrugged. "Not at all." As they came to a stop, Abel could see from the corner of his eye that Noah was staring at him again. He refused to look his way because if he didn't know better, Noah was already on to him.

"So did, uh, Nellie mention the *date* to you?"

"Nope," Abel said, staring straight ahead, willing the light to turn green because he had a feeling where Noah might be going with this.

"Hmm, that's kind of odd, no? I mean neither of you is demanding anything from the other, so why wouldn't she mention it?"

The light turned green, and Abel revved up his engine as he took off again. "She *did* mention the concert," he said, turning on the radio. He was ending this right now. "Only she didn't mention who she was going with and I didn't ask." He glanced at Noah for a second. "It's none of my business."

With that, he turned the volume up on the Sublime song on the radio. This conversation was over. It hit Abel now why he hadn't wanted this thing with Nellie to be anything more than what it was from the very beginning. He didn't have time for all the angst he'd felt in the last hour alone. Either he'd stick to what he'd agreed to—take the time he was spending with Nellie for what it was worth and leave any and all feelings out of it—or walk away now before he was in too deep. Only he knew now and he'd known it before he even asked Nellie to come with him to San Francisco that he was already in too deep. The trip had only solidified it. He'd been certain she was feeling the same thing too. But the fact remained she was going on a date—her first *real* date since her divorce—whatever the fuck that meant.

CHAPTER 8

Once again, Nellie gave herself the same speech. This was to be expected. It shouldn't surprise her that it was Thursday and she still hadn't seen nor heard from Abel since the night after they got back from their trip—almost a week ago. He was in training hell, and then he'd gone to New York for a few of those days. It was a trip she'd been invited to, only she didn't realize that not going would mean not hearing from him either. Even a text or two letting her know he'd been thinking about her like she'd been thinking about him all this time would've been nice. But she knew this relationship was different than most. Just because it felt as if things had changed in San Francisco didn't mean he'd suddenly start behaving like a real boyfriend who checked in on a daily basis.

Even still, she'd given in a few days prior and texted him to ask how New York was. His single response, hours later, was "good." She hadn't bothered texting him back, and he hadn't bothered to ask her how she was doing, so it was the only word she'd heard from him since then.

Nellie had heard from Noah and Gio about her coordinating some of the 5th Street events leading up to the fight like Abel had mentioned. Even Hector had called to give her more info on exactly what she'd be in charge of in Vegas the day before and of the fight. It made more sense that Abel would've called her with that info, but again she shouldn't expect anything more from Abel than she had from the beginning.

Maybe this was his way of toning things down after they'd gotten a bit heavy in San Francisco. After hearing from Roni about some speculation about them since they'd been seen traveling together, Nellie thought maybe Abel was trying to save face now with other employees from 5th Street who might've heard about it. Though he never actually asked her to keep it on the down low, he was so private she just naturally assumed that's how he'd prefer it.

There was a knock at her office door, and Nellie looked up in time to see Emily poke her head in the door. "Come in."

Nellie could use the break. Besides, for the last twenty minutes or so she'd done more theorizing about Abel than concentrating on her work.

"Your room is booked for Vegas." Emily handed Nellie the paperwork. "I went ahead and printed out your confirmation for you."

Nellie thanked her, taking the paperwork, slipping her reading glasses back on, and skimming through it. *MGM Grand.* She hadn't been to Vegas in a while. The last time she'd gone, she was still married. She wondered after the stories that had risen because of their San Francisco trip and now his sudden disappearance if this trip would be different. With the hype of the fight and the influx of paparazzi, would Abel would keep things far more professional this time and keep his distance? Certainly he'd have little time to socialize.

"Did you hear what they're saying about Abel's dad?"

Nellie glanced up at her over her glasses then back at the paperwork, feeling a little annoyed. "What now?"

"Well, they're all rumors, and I only noticed because Abel was trending on twitter."

"He was?"

Nellie put the papers down, took her glasses off, and gave Emily her undivided attention. Trending on Twitter was huge. She knew the fight for the heavyweight title was big, and she'd gotten an idea of the kind of excitement his presence alone could garner from the reporters both in San Francisco and LAX, but she had no idea it was *this* big.

She'd heard bits and pieces of the hype here and there, but she'd been so busy with this mixer she hadn't had time to pay attention too closely to the details. And if she had to be honest, she was trying to keep her mind off him, so she was purposely avoiding the stories.

"Yeah, isn't that crazy?"

With a nod, Nellie motioned for Emily to take a seat. Emily quickly made herself comfortable in one of the seats in front of Nellie's desk. "According to the rumors," she began anxiously, "his dad was killed by the Mexican mob. That part of the story seems to be the only part that's fact or at least the part of him being murdered in Mexico when Abel was just a kid. But they're saying he wasn't just involved in the mafia but he was a key player as in one of the leaders of a big time cartel. They're also saying he was a big-time womanizer and well . . ." Emily sat back in her seat, waving her hand in front of her. "If Abel and his brother got their looks from their daddy, I can only imagine the man had it going on too. Supposedly, he had another family in Mexico." Her eyes brightened. "Can you imagine? More yummy Ayala brothers, only these most likely speak the language of love."

Emily made a purring sound before breaking out into laughter.

"You're silly." Nellie put her reading glasses back on, immediately dismissing the rumors. "I can personally vouch for how inaccurate the media can get their stories, and Gio's wife used to date the current welterweight champ, Felix Sanchez. She's also told me all about the tabloids and overzealous reporters. The media were like vultures trying to catch his every move. Every single girl the poor guy's ever been photographed with turns into some made-up story, and the more scandalous, the better. It's ridiculous. I can almost guarantee you that the only truth to Abel's dad's story is that he died on a trip to Mexico. That much I've heard directly from Roni. If there really was so much more to the story, I'm sure she would've mentioned it."

Nellie wasn't sharing yet about her relationship if she could still call it that since he'd seemed to suddenly fall off the planet where she was concerned anyway. So she left out that Abel had told her himself in San Francisco that the stories about his dad were *completely* false.

Exhaling and sounding more than a little deflated, Emily frowned. "Well, unlike Felix, Abel's managed to stay very private. He's yet to even acknowledge the rumors about his dad, and his private life has been much of a mystery. It is pretty obvious the tabloids are digging. I read what they started to wag their tongues about you and him just because of your trip, but I guess after digging enough, they realized you really are just his personal assistant/coordinator. So they moved on to the next girl." That got Nellie's attention instantly, but she refused to even look up as she waited for Emily to continue. "First they took plenty of photos of him and Felix in New York each with one girl after another hanging all over them at some party. They were linking him already with Tammi what's-her-face from that movie *Bloody Hearts* because apparently they left together. But I guess they got some pictures of him having lunch the other day with a local girl who works at 5th Street, who he's actually been linked to before. They're already making him out to be in a," she held up her fingers, air quoting, "very serious relationship with her."

Lifting her eyes away from the paperwork, but making sure her sudden interest wasn't too noticeable, Nellie looked at Emily for a second then back down again. Emily stood up. "I'd sit and chat longer, but I have to get back to work, you slave driver. I'm down to half of that list you gave me of those calls I need to make."

"Good," Nellie said without looking up again.

"And Logan called. He said he's running late, but he'll be here as planned."

Thanking her for the info, Nellie went back to examining her itinerary for Vegas. The second Emily closed the door behind her, Nellie was on her computer. She knew she'd just finished telling Emily that those tabloid stories were ridiculous and made up, but she was still curious. Curious . . . that's all.

Opening her top drawer, she pulled out her inhaler and took a hit. She hated how her asthma was such a dead giveaway that her nerves had been altered. As much as she tried to deny that this was clearly a blow to her heart, the unmistakable wheezing that forced her to pull out her inhaler unwittingly exposed her true emotions.

She typed Abel's name into the search engine, hit enter, and waited. A second later, a ton of stuff about his upcoming fight came up: stats, more stats, fight hype, and commentary. It was endless. Chewing her lower lip, she considered reading about the hype. Even as close as she'd been working with 5th Street and with Abel being up for such a coveted title, boxing was just something she'd never followed. She didn't even know much about Abel's opponent except that they called him Hammerhead something or other and that he'd been the reigning champ for a few years now. Most of this she only knew because she'd heard it from Roni.

A photo of Abel in a suit and tie made her lose her train of thought. Certain that it was because she now saw him so differently than she did say a few months ago, she tried not to inhale too deeply at the photo, but the guy was a dream to look at. Staring at it for a moment, she remembered the very day it was taken. It was last year, the night he announced he was the next contender for the heavyweight title. He smelled as good as he looked, and damn he looked good enough to taste—eat. Okay maybe she was looking at him the same way even back then because she remembered thinking that night when he first walked in the room in that suit the very thing she was thinking now. "Perfection," the whispered word slipped her lips.

"There's someone here to see you," Emily said over the intercom on the desk.

There was something strangely different about her tone and Nellie rolled her eyes. Logan no doubt was standing right in front of her young squirming assistant. Emily obviously had a crush on him. Still staring at the screen, she responded. "Thanks, Emily, send 'im in."

A moment later, the door to her office opened and Nellie's eyes went from the image of Abel on her screen to the glorious sight of him right there in her office. Scrambling and nearly gasping, she clicked the Internet window closed.

"Abel," she said, reaching for her reading glasses and pulling them off.

The expression he wore was an odd one at first, and then he seemed amused. "You look good in glasses. You should wear them more often." The corner of his lip lifted, turning into that sexy smirk she'd seen on him often—usually in bed. "It's all kinds of sexy."

She cleared her voice, standing up, and looked down at the glasses she still held in her hand. It reminded her how she'd avoided using them in San Francisco. Deep inside, a part of her thought maybe it'd be a reminder of their age difference." I only need them to read."

Smiling now, he walked slowly toward her but didn't stop in front of her desk, making her already galloping heartbeat speed up. "I didn't think you could get any sexier." He walked around her desk, sliding his finger over the dark mahogany top. "It completes the look perfectly."

Her insides instantly warmed as he reached her, and she was frozen in place now. His big hand was already on her waist as his eyes went from looking into hers down to her lips. "I missed you," he whispered then licked his lips.

The thought of the reports of him being in a very serious relationship in correlation to his complete disappearance after just having come back from such an amazing trip crossed her mind. She almost didn't say it, but couldn't hold back. "I missed you too."

With a smoldering smile, he leaned in and kissed her, pushing her gently back so her bottom pressed against her desk. As his hand moved down her thigh and under her skirt, Nellie gasped against his mouth, but couldn't summon even an ounce of resistance. Instead, she ran her fingers through his hair, biting down on his lip as he lifted her onto the desk with one hand and began unbuttoning her blouse with the other.

As much as she hated to, she *had* to say something. "The door isn't locked."

He pulled away, breathing heavily with a smirk that made her blush even as she sat there on her desk, her legs already spread for him and his hand up her skirt. "You want me to lock it?"

Still trying to catch her breath as her heart thudded loudly against her chest, she knew what she *should* say. Instead, she unbelievably heard herself breathlessly whisper what she *wanted* to say. "Yes." There'd be no more depriving herself of this kind of pleasure *ever* by playing it safe like the old Nellie would've done. She said this was all she was in this for, and she wouldn't ruin it by letting overwrought emotions get involved now.

Smiling even bigger, Abel groaned, kissing her even deeper. He'd just begun to pull himself away when the intercom went off again. "Nellie," Emily's voice came on, "Logan's here. How long should I tell him you're going to be?"

Abel froze, glancing at the intercom on her desk then back at her. "Not long," Nellie said, exhaling with disappointment.

To Nellie's surprise, Abel didn't move away from her completely as she expected him to. Instead, he moved back closer, taking his place back between her legs again. He stared at her for a moment before leaning in and kissing her then stopped and asked, "Same guy you had breakfast with that one morning?"

"Yeah," she said as Abel leaned his forehead against hers, still staring in her eyes. "For a moment there, I forgot I was expecting him."

Now he smiled. That hardened look in his eye, the same one she thought she saw that very morning she informed him of her breakfast date with Logan, was gone. "For a moment there, I forgot why I came see you."

Suddenly curious, she tilted her head. "Why *are* you here?"

His eyes moved down to her lips. "I wanted to talk to you about Vegas. The weekend of the fight."

She was about to tell him she already knew, that he was the last of the guys to contact her about it, but her words were muffled by his lips. So far, she'd been witness to three sides of Abel. First, there was the hard-ass side in the ring, a side she thought nearly made an appearance the morning he realized she had a breakfast date. Though a few days ago after much theorizing, she'd concluded she'd obviously imagined any possible resentment about her meeting with another guy or even all she thought she felt from him in San Francisco, since she still hadn't heard from him.

Then there was his aggressive insatiable side, the side that made her toes curl and had her tingling all over like when he'd first walked in her office. He'd come there with a purpose, and if it weren't for Logan waiting outside, Nellie had every intention of giving in to him.

But this side of him, when he toned the aggression way down, was what she'd been sure she felt in San Francisco when his kisses became so sweet. It confused her because she could almost feel him trying to express something to her through these kisses. She hadn't wanted to make more of it the first time she felt it last week, but it was impossible to dismiss.

Finishing off the incredible kiss that left her wanting so much more, he took a deep breath before pulling away. "Sorry, what were we talking about?"

She had to think about it for a few seconds before smiling a bit flushed. "You were saying something about Vegas the weekend of your fight."

"Oh, yeah—"

"But I already have all the information. Emily has even booked my room." She smiled. "I'm all set."

"So are you flying?"

That she didn't know. She hadn't even thought about how she'd get there yet. "Hmm, I'm not sure. I'll have to ask Emily if she booked a flight or not."

"That's Emily outside, right?" he motioned to the door. "Your assistant?" Nellie confirmed with a nod. "Then ask her because that's what I was here to talk to you about. You saw how crazy it gets at the airport now. I can't stand all the media, and it's bound to be insane both at LAX and when I arrive in Vegas. I was thinking of driving, but everyone else can't fly out until the day of or even a day before. So I'm looking at driving out by myself. That's almost a four-hour drive. I thought maybe you and I could drive out together."

Nellie stared at him for a moment. The thought of being alone in a car with him for almost four hours now that things may've changed made her nervous but at the same time excited her.

She cleared her throat. "Okay." She hit the button on the intercom, not sure if she should hope her flight was booked or not. "Emily did you book me a flight for Vegas?"

"Not yet, did you need me to?"

Abel shook his head adamantly, smiling, and then kissed her sweetly on the temple, making her heart flutter. It was strange how his sweet kisses made her heart nearly skip a beat versus his aggressive ones that her body enjoyed equally, but there was such a difference in her heart's reaction to them. "No," she said, smiling at Abel. "I'll be driving out. I just wanted to make sure you hadn't booked anything yet."

"No, I haven't," Emily confirmed. "And just an FYI, in case you like your food warm, Logan brought food."

"It's your favorite," Logan's voice came through the speaker now. "From Chente's. I tackled the rush-hour traffic just for you, Nellie. I figured I'd get a few extra points in before our date tomorrow night."

The hard-ass side of Abel was instantly back. The one she'd already dismissed as having imagined before. His unbreakable stare made her squirm against her desk, but he didn't move away. Gulping back the incredible discomfort she was suddenly feeling now that Abel knew tomorrow night was actually a date and apparently this didn't thrill him, she also tried to calm her insides. As uncomfortable as she felt, there was a slow buzz budding inside her. Had her instincts about San Francisco changing everything actually been right? It wasn't a pathetic delusion as she'd begun to think this week.

She pressed the talk button on the intercom, but before she could respond, Abel did for her. "Come on in," Abel said, still staring at Nellie, and her jaw nearly dropped open. "We're done in here."

"What are you doing?" she asked as soon as she let go of the talk button.

For a split second, she saw alarm in his eyes, but then it passed and he smiled. She could see it was a forced smile, but at least he wasn't burning a hole through her with his glare anymore. "I don't want to get in the way of your *work*, and I got what I came here to accomplish—to get you to agree to drive to Vegas with me."

The door opened and any attempt of Nellie's to move out of the compromising position she was still in with Abel standing between her legs against her desk was squashed when he didn't budge. He took in a very surprised-looking Logan from top to bottom as he stood in the open doorway now. "You working late tonight?" Abel asked, still staring at Logan.

"No." Nellie tried in vain to move, feeling completely mortified that here she was on the edge of her desk with this man's thigh between hers as tomorrow night's date stood staring at them.

"Good. I'll come by your place later tonight." Abel kissed her forehead before finally walking away.

"Come on in, Logan," she said, her face completely on fire.

Abel barely nodded at Logan, and he walked past him and out the door. Instead of appearing taken aback by what he'd just witnessed, Logan smiled at her nervously as soon as the door closed behind Abel. "So the rumors about you and Aweless Ayala are really true? Why didn't you tell me?"

"Because there is no Aweless Ayala and me," she said feeling as stupid as she knew that sounded. Clearly they'd been at the very least making out if not more, and then Abel made it a point to mention while looking straight at Logan that he'd be at her house tonight. "We work together now." She cleared her throat. "But besides that, we're just friends."

Logan shook his head. "I'm not sure he'd agree with that. I'm just glad he didn't wipe the floor with me. Should I be worried that he might?"

"No, don't be silly," she said with a laugh in an attempt to make light of it even as she pulled her skirt down casually and sat down. "I've known him for years now. You know because of the work I do with 5th Street. I'm helping with the coordinating of his fight too, so he's around more often. That's all."

Logan eyed her a bit strangely with a smirk as he pulled the food out of the bags he walked in holding. "Are you really? That's so cool. This is one of the biggest and most anticipated fights in a while. So, uh, what's he like?" Crunching on a tortilla chip, he smiled, looking at her a bit too excited. "I mean aside from intense as shit. I got that just from seeing him on TV, but seeing it in real life, I'm not gonna lie. I feared for my life for a minute there."

Nellie smiled but not about to give even Logan any inside information on Abel, especially about her relationship with him, she shrugged. "He's a normal guy. He's just very private. That's all."

"Okay, but c'mon, Nellie. You and him? He made it pretty damn obvious."

Sticking to her guns, she shook her head again. "Nope, we're just friends."

Hearing him exhale heavily, she hoped he was giving up on this. "Well, that's still so cool. Does that mean you get like ringside seats?"

Clicking and opening the mixer file they'd be working on, she stared at it. "I suppose if I asked," she said, glad they were off the subject of her and Abel. "To be honest, as close as I work with 5th Street, I've never really been a big boxing fan. I'm just helping with the coordinating of the events leading up to it that have anything to do with the promotion of the gym. I know the nickname of the guy he's fighting, but if I had to pick him out of a line up, I'd be toast."

Logan eyes widened." Are you serious?"

Looking up at him, she winced. "Pretty bad, huh? I'll do a little homework before the fight, I guess. It just has so little to do with my part of the coordinating, so I didn't think it was a big deal."

"Well yeah," Logan agreed quickly. "I don't follow boxing very closely either. Only reason I even recognized your friend, Abel, is because of all the hype lately, but a few months ago, I'd never even heard of him. I think most people who don't follow boxing are the same. If you're just doing the behind the scenes stuff, it probably isn't important."

Feeling a little relieved and less guilty about her non-interest in Abel's opponent, she was distracted by the food Logan had set out. "Oh my God, you got the *flautas*," she said, suddenly hungry.

"And the salsa with the big chunks of avocado in it."

Nellie rolled her chair away from the computer and got closer to where he'd set the food on her desk.

"Ahem!"

She looked up from the food. Logan motioned to his chest, and it took her a moment to realize that he actually meant *her* chest. Feeling the flush suddenly rush up her face, it suddenly hit her without needing to confirm it. With a jerk of her neck, she looked down at her exposed lacy top of her bra. The three top buttons of her blouse were still undone.

Quickly spinning her chair to take the front of her blouse out of his sight, she buttoned up her blouse quickly. She felt even stupider about saying that she and Abel were nothing more than friends and working together, but still she'd admit to nothing.

When she spun around to face him again, he was chewing with a smirk on his face. She found it a bit odd that this amused him so much when he'd been so persistent about asking her out. It would make sense that he might be a little perturbed by this, not enjoying it so much, but she certainly wasn't complaining. At least she didn't have to feel guilty. "So is it as good as I said it was?" she asked, picking up one of the guacamole-and-sour-cream-smothered *flautas*.

"Yes," he nodded as he covered his mouth with his napkin, but even with his mouth half covered, she could still see that evil little grin on his face.

She refused to give in and ask what was so funny. Logan had been a bit strange almost from the beginning. After she finished one of her *flautas*, she slid back in front of her computer and slipped on her glasses. "All right, we have some ground to cover," she said, already typing.

"Yeah and fast right? Because you gotta get home *early*."

Taking a deep breath, she ignored the undertone. Yes, she did want to get home early, and she was absolutely looking forward to it, but she didn't have to tell Logan about it. Instead, she continued to type, her mind already on what Abel would do to her tonight.

CHAPTER 9

Bam . . . Bam . . . Bam!

The private training room at 5th Street was obviously not private enough. Already there'd been several people with camera phones at the door windows, trying to take pictures of Abel training. As usual, he'd tried to not let it distract him, even when the would-be amateur photographers were asked to leave. What he had a harder time not being distracted by were thoughts of Nellie and her date tomorrow night with Logan.

Bam! Bam! Bam! Bam!

"That a boy," Gio said, holding the bag. "But remember you're not wearing gloves. You don't wanna hurt your knuckles. This is about endurance, not strength, so take it easy."

Abel nodded and slowed a little taking in a breath.

Bam . . . Bam . . . Bam! Bam!

"There you go," Noah said, taking a seat on the stool nearby.

Abel wasn't so sure what was more troubling: the fact that she was going out with this guy she worked with—someone she actually had a relationship not just someone she was planning on just having fun with—or the fact that he cared so much. He'd already made up his mind earlier that day that he had no time for a real relationship. Now was the worst time in his life for that. He had too much going on to be able to give any girl the attention she needed, which was exactly why he thought what he had with Nellie was perfect in the first place. So what if she saw others when he wasn't around?

Bam! Bam! Bam!

"Easy, Abel!" Gio reminded him again about his knuckles.

So what if she might end up sleeping with Logan tomorrow night?

Bam! Bam! Bam! Bam! Bam!

"Dude!" Noah stood up off the stool. "What're you doin'?"

Abel slammed his fist into the bag one last time before backing away and wiping the sweat off his face with the front of his shoulder. "I'm done," he said simply. "I gotta get outta here."

He started to walk away, but Noah stopped him. "What's wrong with you? Everything okay? You've been on edge all week."

Both Gio and Noah stared at him now. "Nah, I'm good," he said, afraid to look Noah in the eyes, so he started undoing the wrap on his hands.

"Give me that," Gio said, reaching out for his hand. Abel reached out and let Gio help him take off the wrap. "Maybe you should take a few days off." Gio offered.

"Nope," Abel said, immediately shaking his head. "I just took time off for New York. I can't take any more off. We're too close now."

"Well you need to relax, man." Gio insisted. "You can't keep having these kinds of workouts where you're either beating the shit outta one of the trainers you're sparring with or your own knuckles. *Someone's* gonna get hurt."

"I'll relax," Abel said then smirked. "I know exactly what I need, and I'll take care of it tonight."

Noah's expression soured, but surprisingly he didn't say anything. Abel had thought about it all damn week. Ever since Noah had told him about Nellie's date, he'd thought that was it. He'd take a break from his visits to Nellie for a while if not for good. The trip to New York had helped. Hanging out with Felix, whom he hadn't hung with in a while, was a much needed distraction. The guy knew how to party, and if Abel wasn't in the middle of such in intense training, he might've partied with him. The time he spent with him still served its purpose. Felix was also a pro at handling the media, telling Abel that if he just stopped and posed for a few photos the paparazzi would be more relenting. The only problem with that was that Felix didn't mind posing with every girl who was all over them. Abel hadn't bothered to check, but he was certain there were plenty of shots with each of them looking as if they'd for sure gotten laid that night. Felix most likely did. Abel had gone back to his room alone and thought about the same damn thing he'd thought about all week—Nellie's date.

He'd been so desperate to just get over it that he'd even gone as far as agreeing to have lunch with Rachel, one of the girls who worked the juice bar at the gym. Knowing from experience that she was good for few rounds of fun and wasn't the clingy type either, he figured that she might do the trick. She was forever dropping hints that she was ready to go at it again whenever he was. Stupidly, or maybe he'd just been naïve, he thought maybe she'd make a nice little stress reliever, just as he'd claimed Nellie was. .

But after spending a whole half hour listening to Rachel's endless drivel and cheap attempts to be sexy with her fluttering lashes and sucking of her own fingers as she ate, he had to pass. There was zero substance, something Nellie had in buckets and something he hadn't realized until now that he wanted. He'd decided that he was being an idiot, and not only could he handle the understanding he had with Nellie but doing so was absolutely worth the reward. He wasn't so sure now. Worse yet, he wasn't sure if maybe he'd blown it today by making his aversion to her date tomorrow so obvious. He could only hope now she wouldn't send him packing tonight when he showed up at her place.

Once done taking off the wrap, Abel made his way back to the private showers. Noah followed. Somehow Abel had a feeling he would. "So is it true?"

Abel walked into one of the open shower stalls and turned on the water. He turned back to Noah who sat down on one of the benches on the other side of the stall's pony wall. It came up past Abel's waist, so he could still see Noah's curious expression. "Is what true?" Abel asked, pulling off his trunks and briefs, and stood under the shower.

"That you and Rachel are *real* serious?"

"*What?*"

Noah laughed. "Roni saw it first and asked me about it, but just last night, I was flipping through the channels, and it was on like two different tabloid shows. They have pictures of you and her earlier this week having sushi and then getting back in your car, so apparently it's real *serious.*"

"It's bullshit. We had lunch. That's all. Andy said they'd do this once we got closer to the fight." Not wanting to look at him now, he stood under the shower for a few seconds, lathering up before asking. "What did you tell Roni?"

"I figured as much. So I told her you'd just bagged the girl a few times in the past and that's probably all this time was too."

Abel squeezed his eyes shut. *Fucking great.* As if he needed to give Nellie more reason to feel free to jump from bed to bed. If *he* was doing it, why shouldn't she?

Noah stood up now. "Is she who you're seeing tonight?"

This wasn't like Noah. He never asked Abel details of his conquests, and he knew better than anyone that Abel wasn't one to be talking about his personal life. The only reason Noah even knew about Rachel was because *she* was the one who told everyone. There could only be one reason Noah was asking now—the same reason he'd ever asked before—so Abel had to ask, but he still wouldn't look at him." Why?"

"Just wondering."

"No, you're not." He turned to him now. The irritation that had mounted all week and that he'd had to fight to keep under control in Nellie's office today had just peaked. "You don't wonder about my personal life, and you know I don't talk about it. *Ever*. So what gives? The little wifey put you up to this?"

"First of all," Noah pointed at him with a murderous glare, "you watch that fucking tone when you talk about Roni. You hear me?"

Abel turned back to the shower, leaning his head under it. He seriously needed to get a grip. He might as well just tell Noah he had no idea how to deal with knowing that Nellie would be on a date tomorrow and that it was making him insane since he was being so damn transparent about it.

"Second," Noah continued, sounding a little calmer. "Roni mentioned Nellie hadn't heard from you since last week, the day I told you about her date this Friday. *I* was just hoping that the tiny little flame I *thought* I saw in your eye that day had finally set something off upstairs and you'd come to your senses. Then after seeing you enjoy your time with Felix and all those girls and watching the Rachel gossip on TV, I thought you'd really moved on. But seeing you walk around here all week with that look on your face, the one you usually reserve for the ring just before you're getting ready to tear someone a new one, it got me thinking." Noah stopped talking and Abel assumed he was waiting for him to look at him, so he took a deep breath and did. Noah lifted a brow. "Please tell me what Roni thought might happen and you assured me wouldn't, isn't already happening." Abel stared at him and Noah shook his head. "Aside from us, Nellie is the only family Roni has. Tell me no matter what happens that we'll be able to sit around the table or be in the same room without the tension becoming so thick it changes everything."

"Nothing's changing," Abel said, turning off the water. He grabbed a towel from the shelf on the wall. "This fight is getting real now. You know I have no patience for the paparazzi, and they've been all over my ass. I've just been wound a little tight." Finished drying up, he tied the towel around his waist then looked up at Noah and hoped he could pull this next part off. "But Nellie and I are cool. Like I said before, her personal life and what she does when I'm not around is none of my business."

Noah let out a heavy breath, looking somewhat relieved. "Good."

Abel started walking away toward his locker then turned and looked back at Noah "And sorry about my *tone* there. You know I love Roni."

"You better be sorry," Noah chuckled. "'Cause I don't care how big you are. Mess with her and I'll come after you."

For what felt like the first time since Abel had first walked into Nellie's office today, he smiled. "Yeah, I know you would."

He'd have to keep in mind how closely Noah was watching him now. He thought it earlier this week, and he was beginning to think it again. Maybe Noah was right. Maybe it wasn't such a good idea to keep this up. If only he could convince his heart of that, the same heart that was already pounding against his chest from just knowing he'd be seeing her real soon.

After getting dressed, Abel picked up his brother's tablet, which sat on the desk in the back office. He'd done everything he could to avoid the tabloids stories ever since he heard the stuff they were saying about his dad. He didn't really care, but it'd pissed him off that his mom had felt it necessary to once again explain his father's death as if he or Hector were in any way buying the bullshit stories.

His dad had been in a bar with his brother in Mexico where a brawl broke out. There were shots, and his dad and uncle were two of several men shot and killed that day. End of story. It was later reported that the fight had originated between two guys arguing over a drug deal gone wrong, but his dad and uncle had just been in the wrong place at the wrong time. They weren't involved in the argument at all. The tabloids however were painting a whole other picture. He could only imagine the shit they were saying about him and Rachel and the girls in New York, especially since a few of them were celebrities. Felix told him not to sweat it. He was a free man. These kinds of photos only became a problem if he was ever involved with someone. Abel could only pray now this wouldn't become a problem because Felix told him to expect the photos to go viral.

Frowning as the photos came up on the screen, he groaned flipping through them. There were *so* many. And of course he looked like he was having the time of his life in most of them. So Felix was fun to hang out with, and he was hilarious when he was drinking. But damn it if they didn't catch every compromising position he'd been in with those girls. Felix had warned him ahead of time that the girls at these clubs were *not* shy. And they were especially touchy-feely when they knew they were being photographed. There was photo after photo of him with one girl or another either wrapped around him or leaning into him, saying something to him extra close to his face since the music had been so damn loud.

"*Fuck,*" he muttered as he came across the photo of him and that actress he'd met getting in a car together. He read the bullshit caption under the photo.

LEAVING HIS BUDDY WELTERWEIGHT CHAMP SANCHEZ BEHIND, BOXING'S HEAVYWEIGHT CONTENDER "AWELESS" AYALA WAS CAUGHT MAKING AN EARLY ESCAPE WITH THE BEAUTIFUL TAMMI FISCHER.

Caught? He walked right out the front door flooded with waiting photographers. Since Felix had made no secret about which hotel they were staying at, Tammi knew they were going the same way. She suggested they share a car so they both could escape the paparazzi faster. What was he supposed to say? *Hell no? They've already taking enough incriminating photos I don't want my non-girlfriend to misinterpret?* Luckily there were more photos of each of them arriving at their different hotels alone. No story there, assholes.

Then he saw the other headline and bigger story.

HAS SOMEONE FINALLY BROKEN THE TOUGH EXTERIOR OF AWELESS AYALA?

Just under the headline were three photos of him sitting with Rachel at the sushi place. He never once noticed photographers that day. In the first two photos, it appeared that he was completely captivated by her conversation. The third one had her feeding him a piece of her sushi. He remembered being annoyed when she'd done that. It was just another attempt to be sexy, and maybe if it'd been someone who didn't try so hard—someone like Nellie—it might've been amusing.

Seeing the photos now, he had to wonder if maybe Rachel had given the photographers a heads up. That day he'd chalked up her overly playful and flirtatious behavior to maybe her getting caught up in the fight hype as well. Now that his name and the fight were all over the TV, radio, and Internet maybe she wanted some of the spotlight on her. She wouldn't be the first to try this, and she'd told him all about her dream of making it as a fitness model. She certainly had the body for it. And after getting to know her a little better, he didn't blame her for trying to make the most of her looks. Like in his first few lustful encounters with Nellie, they'd never done a whole lot of talking, but unlike with Nellie, he'd never been inclined to spend the night at her place or have her stay at his. After only three times, like most of the girls he had fun with, he'd also lost interest. Not once had he felt the undeniable need to be with her again like he was feeling that moment about being with Nellie in just a few minutes.

Unable to get past even the first ridiculous paragraph about how it appeared that without warning his heart had been stolen, he shut the tablet down and thought about the irony of the headline and story. Inadvertently, they were on to something about his heart being stolen. Only just like the stories about his dad, they had their facts all wrong.

*＊＊

Abel was going to use all the restraint he could muster to hold back from giving free rein to his body's needs when he saw Nellie. There was something bigger looming, something too important now he needed to communicate to her. Since he was still too damn scared to ruin things by doing so verbally, he'd be showing her as he thought he had in San Francisco.

He'd only been at her place for a few minutes when he stopped her in the kitchen where he'd followed her. Holding out that long had been a feat in itself. The moment he got the chance, he leaned her against the counter and his lips were on hers. As weak as he felt to have failed so miserably at restraining himself, he *did* kiss her tenderly. It took great effort, but he didn't kiss nearly as hungrily as he really wanted to. Okay, maybe he was going to have to try a little harder. Just like earlier that day in her office, it felt like it had been forever since he last kissed her. As much as he enjoyed kissing her this sweetly and softly, his insides were ready to unleash what they'd missed so intensely this past week. Somehow her mouth tasted even better than he remembered, and she felt so much more perfect in his arms now.

Forcing himself, Abel pulled away then held her face in his hands, smiling. He really should feel a little alarmed about what a struggle it was to not just eat her up, maybe even a little worried he'd start freaking her out. Instead, even as worked up as he'd been all day, all he could do was smile like an idiot as he stared into her beautiful eyes.

"You're all I've thought of since I left your office today."

It was mostly true. She and her fucking date tomorrow had consumed the majority of his agonized thoughts even before he'd gone to her office, but more so after gaining a little more insight about the date. She'd be going with Logan, the same guy she'd jumped out of bed with Abel to be with once already.

The playful way she grinned at him cooled the heat he'd begun to feel just thinking about the nature of her relationship with *Logan*.

"I have to admit I've had a hard time keeping my mind clear of thoughts of you today too." She licked her lips. "Your visit today was a very pleasant surprise. So the disappointment of our interruption is one I knew I wouldn't get over until I saw you again."

She wrapped her arms around his neck and kissed him more ravenously than he'd expected, heightening what his already frenzied insides were trying to restrain. Unable to hold back any more, he moaned against her lips, kissing her even deeper. He brought his hands down and stroked them over her behind a little harder than he'd planned on doing this soon. She rubbed her body up against his, smothering her breasts against his chest.

Abel was done holding back. She was as shamelessly frantic for more as he felt, and it made him insane. He could only hope that meant that, like him, she'd gone without any satisfaction this entire week. She reacted to him squeezing her ass with both hands by bringing her hand down and rubbing him over his jeans. He was so hard now it hurt, and he lifted her onto the counter with a growl.

Tonight was supposed to have been about conveying something deeper to her. Now the only deep thing on his mind was how deeply he wanted to be buried in her.

"You missed me?" he asked roughly against her mouth then bit her bottom lip.

"God, yes!"

He smiled before diving into her mouth again. All right, time for Plan B. It was something that may not be as effective in getting her to feel the very real emotions he felt for her now, but it might work for him in a different way. He'd make love to her so hard and so often tonight and maybe even well into the morning that she couldn't possibly dream of letting or *wanting* another man do this to her so soon and hopefully *ever*.

The concert was so awesome that Nellie actually felt guilty that her first time seeing Slightly Stoopid live hadn't been with Roni. It was Roni who'd actually introduced her to the band in the first place. Her best friend knew she'd always loved Reggae music, and this band was just that, only they added a mixture of blues and folksy funk that made their sound even sexier. It'd been exactly what she needed to listen to and just relax with a glass of wine when she was going through her nightmare divorce. She'd been surprised how much their folksy laid-back rhythms could take the edge off the stress she was feeling, and now she'd heard them live, and they were just as good—and Roni had missed it.

Shaking it off, she felt another kind of guilt seep in, a guilt she knew had no business flustering her. So she was on a date less than twenty-four hours after another mind-blowing night with Abel. It'd been more than mind-blowing, it was *different*. He drove into her like a man on a mission— hungrier than she'd ever felt him—and it made her wild. Then he'd tone it way down, kissing her deeply the entire time they did what felt like making love again, not just having insanely hot sex. More than once he'd stared into her eyes while sliding in and out of her and telling her she was so damn beautiful. Just like all the times he'd told her before, he said it so convincingly and so full of passion that she almost believed it, almost believed that he was there for more than just their lovemaking. In fact, he'd even spent the night again, and they'd had breakfast together. She got the distinct feeling he didn't want to leave either. And now, here she was on a date with someone else.

So what? Yesterday, after Logan had finally left her office, she got a chance to finish looking up what she'd started to look up when Abel had walked in her office. She only meant to do a little homework about his opponent but was quickly distracted with the photos of him and Felix in New York. Nellie knew well enough that stories of him suddenly being involved with the actress he'd been seen leaving with were very likely untrue. She knew how the media worked, and even though he appeared to be having a good time, she'd gotten to know Abel well now. Well enough to observe that while he appeared to be enjoying himself and smiling in many of the photos, they'd also captured a few of his expressions that she recognized all too well: his almost annoyed expressions, some at the most telling moments— like when one of the eager girls draped herself all over him.

The fact that he'd left early without Felix was also telling. Even though the media said he'd been caught ducking out with that celebrity, there was no evidence in any of the *many* photos of the two leaving together that either was trying to be sneaky. The fact that they had zero photos of them arriving at their hotels together was further confirmation that the tabloids were reaching with this rumor. But even if it were all true, he'd gone out and had a fabulous time partying up like the hot celebrity he was now and even left with another hot celebrity. As hard as it was to take, this was his life now. It was only going to get worse. Still somehow, something deep inside held on to the hope that while Felix might enjoy this life Abel had made it clear that he wasn't like Felix.

Seeing the images and reading about him with that young juice girl, however, did worry if not confuse her. Roni had already confirmed that this was someone Abel had, as Noah so eloquently put it, bagged in the past. She was someone more low key than a celebrity and one he'd obviously actually shown some interest in. And why wouldn't he? She was young and a knockout. Worse yet, they had a ton in common because she worked at the gym and from what the stories suggested was an inspiring fitness model. Of course Abel would be attracted to her.

It was far more likely that there was some truth to this story—that he'd prefer a relationship with someone low key versus a high profile relationship with a celebrity—hence the confusion about his blatant reaction to Logan yesterday. Did he really have the nerve to be acting all territorial when he'd very possibly *bagged* this girl just earlier that week?

Feeling the same irritation she'd first felt when she read the story of him and juice girl all over again, Nellie glanced around looking for Logan, who'd brought her to the VIP lounge—the same lounge where band members would later be having drinks. Roni was going to die when she heard about this. Logan had walked out after buying her a drink to take a call. He said they'd be meeting a friend of his there but didn't elaborate. Having the opportunity to sit and watch the band as they relaxed and possibly even jammed in the lounge this close and the fact that Logan had a friend coming were the only reasons she didn't insist on him taking her home right after the concert. She hadn't wanted to spend too much time alone with him, but she couldn't pass this up, and his friend being there would take a little from the intimate feel this might have had otherwise.

Staring at her drink now as she stirred it, her thoughts were back on Abel and her body actually quivered. Their incredible time last night and this morning was the only hope she had that maybe he hadn't been with that girl all week. She kept reminding herself that if she wanted to keep experiencing incredible nights like last night with Abel, what he did when she wasn't around *needed* to remain a non-issue. After going nearly a week without him, her body had welcomed him back as if she were famished. There was nothing she could think of that would be worth ruining things and having his visits end.

After the incident in her office yesterday, there was no doubt he knew about her date tonight, but last night he'd made no mention of it at all. That and his trysts with Rachel that week were a clear reconfirmation of what she'd thought for a moment might be changing but hadn't. Even knowing she'd be out with another guy tonight, he was as content with things as they were as he had been from the beginning, and so she would be too.

It didn't matter that he'd held her a bit tighter all night and whispered in her ear how beautiful she was in such a sweet yet genuine way more than once during the night when he'd thought her asleep. Swallowing back any and all hope that it meant something, she took a big swig of her martini. He may've been doing that since day one, and she'd just missed it because she'd been so soundly asleep. He was just sweet that way, and there was nothing more to it.

"Are you Nellie?" she flinched, looking up into a pair of the clearest blue eyes she'd ever seen. "I'm sorry. I didn't mean to startle you. I'm Sam . . . Smith, Logan's friend." He reached out and shook her hand before taking the seat across from her on the sofa.

"It's okay," she smiled, a bit taken with how uniquely light but very pretty his eyes were. "Yes, I'm Nellie. It's nice to meet you, Sam."

"Logan's outside on the phone," he explained. "I hope everything's okay. Do you know who he's talking to? He seemed worried."

"No," she said, glancing back toward the entrance where Logan had stepped out, feeling a little guilty that she'd been so caught up in thoughts of the concert, Roni, and Abel.

She'd hardly noticed Logan's extended absence. "But he did walk away kind of fast when he got the call."

Sam glanced back at the entrance then stood up again. "I could be wrong, but I thought I heard him say the words "emergency room" as I walked away. Let me go check on him."

Nellie decided that if neither of them were back within a couple of minutes she'd go check on Logan too. She felt terrible that she'd hardly given any thought to his taking a long time. Looking up again, she saw Sam walking toward her. He smiled as their eyes met, and her eyes traveled down to his impressive built. At this point, she knew nothing would ever compare to Abel's body, but surprisingly this guy's came pretty close. "Well, this is kind of awkward, Nellie, but he did say you two are just friends—co-workers. Right?"

She nodded, a bit confused. Yesterday as they worked on the mixer, she'd worked it into the conversation how she'd never get romantically involved with someone she worked with. In a way of reiterating what she'd already told him about her and Abel, she'd made mention that just as with her and Logan, things were strictly platonic. So she could say this with complete certainty. "Yes, we're just friends." She nodded with a smile, still not sure why this had anything to do with Logan not being back yet. "Co-workers." She reaffirmed. "Why?"

"Well," he said, taking a seat next to her this time. "It seems his ex-girlfriend's been in an accident. She's in the hospital and asking to see him."

"Oh, no." Nellie straightened out quickly. "Is it bad?"

Sam shook his head, rolling his eyes. "I know his ex. She's kind of a drama queen, and she's pulled this kind of stunt before, but he's gonna go see her anyway." He waved the waitress down and ordered Nellie another martini and a rum and Coke for himself, immediately bringing thoughts of Abel back to Nellie. "Anyway, I told him he was an idiot for leaving a beautiful woman like yourself hanging, and that's when he mentioned that you're just friends." He smiled, those light eyes once again distracting her. "Since I'm no idiot, I told him there was no sense in wasting the night out and offered to keep you company then give you a ride home, if that's okay with you?"

Speechless for a moment by the sudden turn of events, Nellie stared at him as their drinks arrived. "Um, yeah, it's okay with me," she finally said, taking her drink from the waitress. Just then, she saw two of the band members walk in and take a seat in one of the corner sofa lounging areas. "I wasn't planning on staying too late, but it's not often I get to hang out in a VIP lounge like this."

"Good," he grinned, those blue eyes sparkling and looking very pleased. "If I'd known tonight was going to turn out this way, I would've gotten here earlier." He held his glass out to her. She reached out and tapped it with hers. "To chance meetings," he said with a smile that only accentuated the dark lashes draping over those crystal blue eyes dramatically.

"To chance meetings," she smiled back, shaking off the sliver of guilt she began to feel again.

Coming here tonight she knew there'd be nothing romantic between her and Logan or anything that might make this feel *wrong*. She had no intention of tonight being more than just an innocent night out with a male friend, but the gleam in Sam's playful eyes said he had something more in mind.

Taking a sip of her martini, thoughts of Abel *bagging* Rachel just this past week came to mind. She didn't know a thing about Sam yet, but if she had to go strictly by his looks, staying out a little later than she'd originally planned didn't sound so bad after all.

CHAPTER 10

The meeting with the director of PR last night went well, though Abel had hardly been able to concentrate much. He still hadn't heard a thing about Nellie's *date,* and he had no intention of asking anyone about it, not Nellie, not Noah, *no one*. The only thing he could hope for was that he'd worn her out enough Thursday night so that the last thing she'd be thinking about on her date was ending it literally with a bang.

He slammed the locker closed much harder than he intended, especially after he remembered Noah was still around and watching him too damn closely.

Andy leaned against the wall, reading off his iPad. "So I need to go over a few things with you. I know you don't follow the tabloids, but I just need to keep you up on the big stuff. This way, no reporters catch you off guard."

Abel sat back into the huge full body massage chair, clicking the remote to place it in just the perfect reclining position, and closed his eyes as the massage started. It was just one of the perks from his latest sponsor. He made a cool six figures for doing a thirty-second commercial for one of these, and they threw in a couple of these chairs for his own personal use. The other one was at his home. While the massage was supposed to be state of the art and it had all kinds of gadgets so you could hook it up to your tablet, phone, or iPod, nothing relieved his tense muscles like the one activity he wished he could do tonight.

Once again, he'd barely heard anything of what Andy was saying. His mind had wandered off to thoughts of all the things he'd done to Nellie and everything he still wanted to do.

"You need to remember that McKinley's camp plays dirty when it comes to trash talking and trying to get in your head through the press. They've already started."

Abel opened one eye. Andy had his attention but just vaguely. Abel still didn't give a shit about the tabloid stories. He heard Hector and Gio's voices coming toward them.

"That story about your dad and the Mexican mafia didn't really go anywhere, but McKinley and his camp are still trying to keep it alive by commenting about it every chance they get."

"Oh, I heard about this," Hector said. Both he and Gio were sitting on stools between Andy and Abel. "McKinley was on Howard Stern the other morning talking about how it makes sense now that an amateur boxer and someone so young could afford to own and run a gym of this caliber."

Admittedly that pissed Abel off. Obviously the asshole hadn't done his homework or he'd know how it was possible. But he refused to let this guy get to him. "I'll deal with him in the ring," he said, closing his eyes again.

"His brothers remind me of B-list celebrities with one sibling who has actually made it," Gio laughed. "They ride their famous sibling's coattails, doing reality shows and interviews all over, when no one really gives a shit about them. But man do they love trash talking."

"This is what I'm talking about," Andy said. "They're known for going all out to get in their opponent's head." He chuckled. "I think it's killing them that they haven't been able to get a peep outta *Aweless Ayala*."

"And they're not going to," Abel reminded him.

He clicked the remote and the massage chair began inclining upward. Noah walked in the room. "You guys are all coming down to my place tonight, right?" he said, taking the wrap off his hands.

"Oh, shit," Gio stood up. "That reminds me. I'm supposed to stop and grab some stuff from the market for Bianca. She texted me earlier. She's making chili."

Hector stood up too. "I was gonna pick up Charlee and go grab some pizza, but she'll probably wanna hang out at your place instead. Her friend Drew's been out of town for weeks now, and she misses the girl talk."

Gio laughed, grabbing his phone and wallet off the desk. "You better check your phone, dude. Bianca already mentioned Charlee bringing her chicken pasta salad."

Hector's jaw dropped and he hurried away. Noah smirked, turning to Abel. "You're coming down too, right?" Abel read the apprehension in his face right away. "The featherweight championship is on HBO tonight. It's why I decided to throw a barbeque together. Andy says they'll be airing more of your bio before the fight. And I figured we could all take a small break from this grueling training."

Abel didn't have to ask, but just the fact that Noah was asking instead of just assuming he'd be there like he normally would meant Nellie would be there tonight. This was what both Noah and Roni had been worried about from the very beginning, that Abel and Nellie's involvement would change things. Her having gone out last night and his supposedly "serious relationship" with Rachel would be hanging heavily in the room—the tension Noah had mentioned.

Determined to ease Noah's mind and prove he could deal with this, he nodded. "Yeah, I'll be there."

Who was he kidding? As much as he dreaded being around her while Roni and Noah scrutinized their behavior, a part of him was dying to see Nellie already. He'd just been with her a couple of nights ago. That was a worrisome thought and something he'd have to decide how to deal with—soon.

✳✳✳

The contract Abel signed with HBO specifically stated that he must give them exclusive interviews regarding the fight

and his story of how he got to where he was now. They were
the only interviews he'd done where he'd spoken beyond just
boxing and allowed them access into 5th street, giving them
the background on how Jack, the late owner of the gym, had
taught him everything he knew about the sport.

Andy told Abel that, seeing as how difficult he'd been
about giving exclusive interviews, these short documentary-
like interviews were getting huge ratings. They'd been airing
bits and pieces of the interview for weeks now alongside of
the interviews they also had with McKinley. It was all part of
the hype. Abel had sat and watched similar ones endless
times of all the big fights he grew up watching. So to see
himself being the one featured and the hype being about *his*
fight was a bit surreal.

He didn't purposely set out to be difficult. He'd just
heard too many stories about journalists from Felix. As far as
Felix was concerned, you couldn't trust them for shit. Most
were either too lazy to double check that they got their facts
straight or didn't think the interview or article was juicy
enough, so they purposely misquoted you for an added flair.
It usually stirred up some kind of controversy that didn't sit
too positively in the interviewee's favor. Abel had neither the
time nor the patience for any of that. So he'd sooner turn
down any and all interviews that he wasn't contractually
obligated to do. Hence, the media frenzy was beginning to
build, and the race was on to get *anything* additional on him
out there.

He sat there on Noah's sofa, watching the pre-fight hype
with clips of some of his own and McKinley's fights. There
were a few clips he hadn't seen of McKinley and his brothers
when they were trash talking him. It was to be expected.
Andy said it was actually encouraged. The viewers ate it up.

"That's the younger and louder of his two brothers," Gio
said, pointing at the screen. "I can't stand his ass."

If it wasn't for the guy's light complexion along with all
the other lighter features, Abel might have thought him a

New Jersey grease ball type because of the way he wore his hair and the number of rings on his fingers. The guy wearing a Pistons jersey was pointing at the screen, speaking directly to Abel. "Turn it up," Hector said with a smirk. "This guy's such a joke."

"You don't know about Hammerhead McKinley, *Aweless Ayala!*" The guy taunted him. "And when McKinley is done wiping the canvas with you on *Cinco de Mayo,* you're gonna wish you never came sniffing around the big boys, because you ain't nothing but a *chavala.*" He laughed, eyeing the screen and leaning in closer. "That's right, Ayala. I called you a little girl in your own language because you're always hiding and I know why. You're nothing but an F-Beep!-ing *chavala.*"

Abel took a swig of his beer, completely unmoved by the idiot's performance. "What's this guy's name?" he asked.

"They call him Beefhead." Hector laughed. "More like Meathead. He's the one who does all the celebrity reality and game shows. As you can see," Hector turned back to look at Abel, "he's an attention whore. The other one, his older brother . . . I can't remember his name."

"They call the other one McRage something or other," Gio said, "because supposedly he has a short fuse. Even though McRage has been known to do some trash talking, he's not nearly as loud or as big an attention whore as the douche younger brother is. And unlike Beefhead, he was actually pretty good once upon a time."

"I heard he fucked up his own hand and wrist getting into a drunken brawl," Noah said. "Pretty much ended his career because the dumb ass slammed his fist so hard into a brick wall that it cracked in I don't know how many places."

"Yeah, yeah," Hector said. "I heard about that too. And, yeah, I've watched tape of him. He *was* actually pretty good, probably better than Hammerhead even." He turned to take the bottled water his girlfriend Charlee brought over for him and kissed her. "Thank you, baby."

She smiled at him, running her finger over his brow for a second. It was something Abel had seen her do often. Then she walked back to the dining room with the other girls. The guys continued talking about Hammerhead and his idiot brothers. Abel half-listened, his mind wandering off at times and the knot in his stomach still not easing up as the girls chatted and laughed. Nellie hadn't arrived yet, but it wasn't seeing her that had him tensed up. There was a slight possibility that she wouldn't show up alone. Noah hadn't mentioned a thing about her date, and Abel still wasn't asking, but it was safe to say that if things had gone well Roni very well might've encouraged her to invite *Logan*.

As good as Abel was with his poker face, he wasn't sure he'd be able to pull off being around her and another dude without Noah picking up on his irritation. And feeling irritated was an understatement if there'd ever been one. Just the thought of seeing her walk in with another dude tensed his insides even more. He'd hardly eaten because of it.

"Hey!" Roni stood from the dining room table as Nellie walked in the front door—*alone*. She was carrying a covered tray. "Oh my God, did you make deviled eggs?"

"Yes," Nellie smiled. "That's why I'm late. I got a craving at the last minute and decided to whip up a batch." Roni took the tray from her, smiling, and Nellie turned to the front room now where he sat. "Hi guys!" She waved, smiling beautifully.

Abel had to wonder why he'd never seen the *beauty* until recently. He'd noticed the change in her well enough. She'd gone from Roni's docile quiet friend, who'd been practically invisible to him for the most part, to suddenly this head-turning vixen. He got *that* part. It wasn't unheard of for a scorned woman to want to reinvent herself in a way that made her feel more attractive, better about herself —reborn. It happened often actually. But the beauty he'd never picked up on before was what got him. He'd been attracted to her long enough. It was hell trying to fight the sexual tension between them for as long as they had, but now he was seeing past that, and every time he saw her, he had to fight the urge to overdo telling her how damn beautiful she was.

He didn't even realize he was already smiling when he acknowledged her, taking her in from top to bottom. She wore a simple enough short little black and white patterned cotton summer dress with wedge sandals similar to the ones she'd worn on her breakfast date with Logan. It was a dress he'd probably seen her in before, but somehow now it was cause for sitting up straighter and gulping. He was already having visions of pulling the spaghetti straps down along with the top of the delicate fabric of her dress and taking her beautiful breasts in his mouth. But more than anything, he wondered if he'd make it through this night without cornering her somewhere and kissing her, because it was what he really wanted to do so badly now.

"I'll have to get with you guys in a little bit," she said as Abel continued to take her in, "so you can fill me in on last night's meeting."

Noah began to nod, but before any of them could say anything, Roni tugged at Nellie's arm. "C'mere, you work horse. Forget about that. I wanna hear about last night."

"Yes," Bianca agreed from where she sat. "I haven't heard anything yet. Sit down. I want details."

Nellie laughed as Abel gnashed his teeth then took a bitter swig of his beer. Of course, the second he took his eyes off her and turned to Noah, his friend was already watching him. Neither said anything, and Abel was glad because the way he felt at that moment he'd have no patience for any of Noah's irritating *observations*.

The fight started and Abel tried his damnedest to watch without trying to overhear the conversation going on in the dining room. He overheard bits and pieces. Nellie gushed about the concert being fantastic then about hanging in the VIP lounge with the band members. Somehow, Logan managed to get tickets to a sold-out concert *and* get her into the VIP lounge. Abel wondered about that. Now that he was technically a VIP himself, he'd been experiencing some of that part of this new lifestyle. Typically, you had to be someone big or know someone who could pull some strings to get in, especially if you'd be hanging with band members after their concert.

It could've been his imagination, but it seemed the girls' voices hushed all of a sudden. They were still talking and giggling, but he couldn't make out what they were saying anymore. Maybe it was for the best. It really wasn't any of his business, and hearing the details might be more harmful to his already heightened mental state. Sitting up at the edge of his seat, he decided to give the fight his full attention.

Fuck Nellie's date. The only thing he'd focus on from here on out when it came to Nellie would be when he'd have her under him again. It was all he should care about anyway. Right now he could only hope it would be sometime later tonight. For now, he'd ignore the urgency with which he'd begun to need to be near her—kiss her. It was a sexual urgency. That's all it was.

"I still can't believe Logan just up and left you with another guy. But, okay, you know me," Bianca said, leaning in and lowering her voice. "I'm a sucker for colored eyes and my babe's eyes are probably as good as they get, but I still want details. You said Sam's eyes are super light?"

"Oh my God, yes," Nellie said, thankful that Bianca had lowered her voice.

She knew she had no reason to try to keep this on the down low, but things between her and Sam could be different than with Logan. She'd always said from the moment she started this thing with Abel that if she ever considered sleeping with someone else she'd end things with Abel. Sam was definitely a consideration. "It was so hard to concentrate on what he was saying, because his eyes are so crystal light blue I kept getting caught up in them."

"*Oh!*" Bianca clutched her chest. "I know just the feeling. I felt completely drawn to Gio even way back in high school. It's something about those colored eyes."

The only eyes that Nellie had ever felt completely drawn to were Abel's. She said that Sam's had distracted her, but she'd leave that clarification to herself. Roni looked too pleased at the moment.

"I don't think it's the color but the intensity that gets me," Charlee said, her own big blue eyes sparkling as she smiled, looking lovesick and glancing in Hector's direction.

"I agree," Roni smiled big. "It's what you feel when he looks at you so deeply and profoundly. It's what ultimately did me in with Noah. I'd never felt like that with anyone else." She turned to Nellie, smiling silly. "So was it like that with Sam?"

Glancing quickly in Abel's direction, hoping he hadn't heard anything because Roni wasn't quite as hushed as Bianca, Nellie was relieved to see he was engrossed in the fight. "No, I didn't feel anything like that." Nellie sighed. *Not from him anyway.* "They were just so light. I don't think I've ever seen anything like them." She turned to Charlee. "Your eyes are amazing, but they're deep blue. His were," she stopped to think about it, "almost clear at times. They were so light but still blue."

It was just distracting, but she'd felt nothing. The only thing she could think of was that he'd probably be a good distraction from Abel. He certainly was nice to look at. Roni probed for more as she'd expected, and Nellie told her everything she knew so far about Sam. "He's does news commentary for a cable channel out of Detroit where he's from. He's only out here visiting family for the week."

Roni frowned, crinkling her nose, and Nellie wasn't sure if Roni was disappointed that he wasn't from around here or that his career was too similar to her ex-husband's.

"He said he travels a lot," she said, immediately regretting saying it so loudly as Hector walked up from behind Charlee, placing his hand on her shoulder then kissing her temple.

"Who travels a lot?" he asked, smiling curiously.

"The guy she met last night." Roni grinned widely. "He has sparkling blue eyes, too, that completely captivated Nellie." She continued to grin as she lifted her empty plate from in front of her and stood up. "Who wants cheesecake?" she asked as she walked into the kitchen.

Nellie was nearly caught in Hector's stare as he lifted a brow and his smile virtually vanished. Taking Roni's cue, she stood up, looking away from Hector's prying eyes. Were both Abel and Hector this territorial even over each other's girls? Then she remembered the cruise. It was the only time she'd been around Abel, Hector, and Charlee for that long of a period. On more than one instance when Hector stepped away from Charlee, who was such a head turner with her eye-catching, bright red locks, Abel had stepped up and stood next to her. It was all he had to do. His big, ominous presence next to Charlee was enough to deter even the most courageous admirers. Noah had even teased that Charlee didn't just have a boyfriend she had an entourage.

Abel had played it down, saying he knew his hothead brother and that he was just controlling any sparks before his brother came back and it turned into an all-out blaze. He said he didn't want them all getting kicked off the ship. But Nellie saw more in his eyes than just a protective big brother keeping his little brother out of trouble. It was what she'd seen in Hector's eyes tonight. They were watching out for each other's *property*.

The way Charlee explained it was far more romantic than this theory sounded. Charlee said that she and Hector owned each other's hearts. She'd long ago assured him she was completely his because he so often told her she owned his heart.

Nellie's own heart suddenly skipped a beat. Was it possible that Abel had said something to Hector about his feelings for her? Could Hector be getting all hardnosed about her meeting a guy last night because he was feeling protective over Abel's feelings?

She cleared her throat, glancing back, and making sure Hector was far enough away. Abel was still sitting where he had been when she walked in. Roni turned from the kitchen counter where she was slicing the cheesecake and smiled at her.

"Listen," Nellie said, knowing this might get Roni all riled up, but she had no choice. "Maybe we shouldn't talk about my date last night in front of Hector and Abel." She lifted her hand at the sight of Roni's raised brows. "Not that I'm afraid he'll be upset or anything because I'm absolutely certain he won't. I just don't want him thinking I'm *trying* to rub it in to get a reaction or anything."

Roni stared at her for a moment very straight-faced before licking the cheese cake she'd smeared on her finger and turning back to face the counter. "Maybe I *was* trying to rub it in."

This alarmed Nellie. She *was not* going to start playing those games. "*Why?*"

Roni turned back to her, looking a little worried now. "Okay, you still promise there are no feelings involved and you're not expecting anything more from this except letting your free spirit loose, right?"

"Yes," Nellie said in the most assuring voice she could gather. It was far from the truth now, but she had to keep up the front.

"I guess Noah was beginning to worry like me that maybe Abel was going to start changing his mind and that he might even get upset when he heard about your date, so he asked him straight out, and Abel assured him he's only in this for your free spirit, insisting you take care of his needs and that he doesn't have to worry about any *drama* or *demands*.

And then those photos of him in New York and the stories of him and juice bar girl he's doing just after you got back from that trip were all over the Internet and TV." She stopped and exhaled exasperatingly. "I'm sorry. I know it doesn't bother you, but it pisses *me* off. I love you, and I just want him to know he's not doing you any favors, helping you unload your free spirit. There are plenty of others out there who'd be willing to help out."

Feeling the stab of reality lodge in her stupidly hopeful heart so suddenly, Nellie couldn't help rolling her eyes in reaction. "Geez, Roni," she said, swallowing back the infuriating lump in her throat, "I'm not a charity case."

Roni reached for her arm, and after seeing the apparently undeniable hurt in Nellie's eyes, she hugged her. "No, no, no! I didn't mean it that way." She pulled back to look at her. "I'm so sorry, honey. I know you're not. I just meant that if he's going to openly date other women, knowing full well that it's bound to get back to you, then why the hell should we keep your social life away from him quiet? You're an exquisitely beautiful woman with a ton more class and so much more to offer than any of those girls he goes around *bagging.* I just want him to know that if he doesn't see it others do." She crossed her heart quickly, glancing back toward the front room where Hector had now joined the rest of the guys. "I promise I'll keep my nose out of it from here on, though. You're brilliant, and you seem to have things under control. I need to trust that you know what you're doing. If you'd rather not talk about it in front of him or Hector, then I'll keep my big fat mouth shut."

Nellie smiled, gathering her composure. Roni hadn't said anything to her that she shouldn't already know. Their agreement had been a very simple one, one they'd each accepted. Her hurt feelings were irrational. He'd never promised her anything. She knew betrayal of the worst kind and this wasn't it. This was just her heart getting one step ahead of itself, something she knew better than to let happen.

"It's already out there, so if it's brought up, there's no need to hide it. Let's just not openly flaunt it." She winked at her still-worried-looking friend. "You're right. I do have a ton more class than the girls he's used to banging. Let's keep it that way."

Relief washed across Roni's face. It was so melodramatic it made Nellie laugh. "C'mon that cheesecake looks delicious."

She helped Roni bring the cake plates and utensils out to the front room. Maybe she would take Sam up on his offer to have brunch with him tomorrow. She certainly would need a huge distraction to wean her off Abel. Especially now that she *knew* she wasn't going to be able handle continuing this with Abel if he was going to be bagging other women at the same time. Tonight was proof. Her heart literally ached just before she walked through the door because she dreaded walking in and seeing Abel with Rachel. It was why she'd really been late. Her last-minute deviled-eggs story was bullshit. She'd been so close to calling and canceling but was certain Roni would know she was lying and that things were already changing like she was so afraid of.

Thankfully Abel hadn't brought her, but that could change soon, and just seeing him tonight, trying to contain her delight that Rachel wasn't sitting with him or at the table with the girls was hard enough. Getting the reality check that, in fact, she was alone in crossing the line and thinking there was something more growing between them was further proof that she needed to jump ship soon. She'd never been good at hiding her emotions. Roni would see right through her soon, so she had to seriously consider the real possibility of cutting her losses very soon and making a clean break before things got too painful.

Sticking a fork full of cheesecake in her mouth, she thought about what Roni had said. *She was brilliant and had things under control.* Her wounded heart was proof of how under control she really had things. Shoving more cheesecake in her mouth, she thought about what she'd been trying to convince herself of all this time. She'd be a stronger woman for having done this and all that shit.

CHAPTER 11

Walking out into the night's cool fresh air, Nellie prayed Abel wouldn't follow her, but her heart yearned to hear the door behind her open. As she made her way down Noah and Roni's driveway, she thought of the way Abel's eyes had pierced through her all night and the gentle smiles he offered when their eyes would meet. Each time her heart had fluttered like a butterfly on crack. She was beyond over her head now.

After Roni had let her in on Abel's reconfirmation that this was nothing more than what they'd agreed it would be from the very beginning, she sat there drowning her sorrows in cheesecake. She'd eaten nearly three full slices. Knowing that soon she'd be dealing with a pain she swore she'd never allow herself to get caught up in again, she wasn't even worried about the astronomical amounts of calories she'd inhaled tonight. She was certain that, like every time she'd had to deal with a dark moment in her life, she'd lose weight without even trying.

This shouldn't be so dark. Their relationship was very much physical. It should be easy to move past it soon, but her head reminded her she'd known Abel for a while now. Her attraction to him, not just his body and good looks but *him,* had been growing for some time: The noble and loyal friend he was to Noah and Gio. The overprotective brother he was to Hector and now even Charlee. The way he didn't care that the guys busted his balls for being a momma's boy. The man bowed down to the woman and had no qualms about admitting it. Even being the celebrity he was now, he'd still run over in a heartbeat to help fix your car. She'd seen and heard about him doing just that from Roni so many times. He said he loved working on engines and insisted that taking it to a mechanic was always a rip off.

Add to all that the intensity Charlee talked about in Hector's eyes. Nellie knew exactly what Charlee was talking about because she'd seen the very thing in Abel—felt it in his kisses. It must be an Ayala thing. She was now beginning to understand that utterly mesmerized thing she so often saw on Charlee's face. Charlee admitted it openly and as unabashedly as Hector did. She was madly in love with the guy. If Nellie didn't put an end to this now, she too would be doomed to fall hopelessly in love with Abel, and that could ruin everything because this relationship was completely different than his brother and his girlfriend's exclusive one.

Even now, she felt the boulder in her throat just thinking about the possibility of having to be around him with other women. It would *kill* her. The tightness she felt in her chest all night after Roni had informed her of what Abel had told Noah went even tighter now, and she could feel herself starting to wheeze again. What in the world was she thinking when she started this?

"Nellie?"

Startled, she turned to see Abel walking toward her. She'd been staring into the trunk of her SUV where she'd set her tray down. "You okay? I called your name out twice."

Nodding, she tried blinking away the warm tears that she hadn't even noticed had filled her eyes. "I'm good," she said, leaning into the back of SUV, moving imaginary things around as she blinked wildly in the hopes that the tears would be gone by the time he reached her.

When they weren't, she yawned a bit exaggeratedly in desperation and turned, smiling at him. "I'm sorry. I was lost in thought, I guess."

His smiled waned with that comment. "Did your long night last night wear you out?"

Surprised by his question, she continued to smile even as her insides roiled. The way he was staring at her now only confused her already aching heart. "Yeah, the concert was over pretty late, and then we had some drinks after, so it was a *longish* night."

While his eyes searched hers, he didn't say anything. Instead, he took another step further and kissed her, softly, sweetly, the way that melted her heart every single time. As usual, she couldn't summon even an ounce of resistance. Her previously roiling insides were now doing summersaults. With his big hands cradling her face, he pulled away but still sprinkled kisses around her lips. Closing her eyes, she sighed, giving into him once again. *This* is where she wanted to be forever. Even as her head screamed at her to jump ship and do it *now,* her heart clung to the unspoken emotion she *felt* from him.

She knew it was unwise and dangerous given how she was already feeling, but her instincts were screaming now too, drowning out her head that this wasn't a kiss from a man who wanted nothing more than to relieve his needs. There was so much more to it. There had to be. *Right?*

He finally stopped long enough to stare at her for a moment. "Can I follow you home?" he whispered. "I wanna make love to you *so* badly."

Without even a moment's thought, she nodded. As pathetic as it was to clutch on to something so small, he'd never called it making love before. He'd told her he wanted to fuck her or taste her or needed to be inside her on more than one occasion, but he never said *make love.* "Yes," she whispered back, staring into his eyes. "I want you to make love to me."

He smiled one of the sweetest smiles she'd ever seen on him. "Let's go."

✳✳✳

Determined not to become emotional like she had last night as Abel swayed in and out of her slowly and rhythmically while staring deeply into her eyes and *making love* to her again in the early morning, Nellie decided to just enjoy it. Arching her back, she closed her eyes as she felt the now familiar building of another mind-blowing climax, and she dug her fingers into his big, hard back.

Speeding up, Abel's brows pinched, and he began to moan, driving in deeper and deeper. Grunting now as he rocked into her this time, he was a little rougher than he had been the night before. He pumped her harder than he had the entire night last night, but she loved it. She moaned in reaction and in anticipation of her already throbbing pre-climax.

"Yes! Yes! Yes!" She cried out as she came more intensely each time he slammed into her, until he came to a final loud grunting drive deep into her, lifting her waist up against his body. He remained that way for a few moments until he collapsed atop of her.

"That was amazing," he said breathlessly against her ear. "But then it's always amazing." He kissed her forehead, slipping his hand into hers and squeezing it, keeping his body on hers, exactly where she wanted it.

They lay there, breathing heavily as she ran her fingers through his hair, pushing away the emotion that once again began to creep in. She would *not* do this. How could she? So what if he wasn't hers entirely? As tempted as she was to put it out there—tell him what she was feeling because she was almost positive now he was feeling it too—she just couldn't. What if she were wrong? What if what he'd told Noah was really true? He didn't want drama. That's exactly what this would be because she felt so overwhelmed with emotion that she was certain she'd break down if she opened up to him. It was too big of a risk. He'd run and she'd lose what little he *was* willing to give her.

She was only glad now that it was too dark last night for Abel to see the tears that spilled out just as she came so dramatically when he made love to her the first time. The entire night's mixture of emotions had just mounted until that very moment, and it couldn't be helped. This was now beyond her control. Her heart was in this now, and as much as she wanted to believe she could walk away from this unscathed, she knew better. And yet she still couldn't bring herself to walk away from this man.

What scared her most was that, even as horrendous as her divorce with her ex had been, she feared this might be more painful. She remembered that the pain during her divorce had been more about her sister betraying her than Rick. She'd felt the disconnect between herself and Rick long before she'd even found out that he'd been having an affair with her own sister. The old-fashioned thinking instilled by her mother had told her that divorce was not an option, so she'd turned the other cheek when she suspected something was awry, but she knew the end was near. Even when her delusional heart chose to believe him when he promised he'd change after the first time she caught him cheating, she still knew deep inside what they'd had long ago was gone. She was no longer in love with him either; she was just afraid of having to start over and being alone.

Certainly she'd *never* felt the passion she felt with Abel from her ex. She wouldn't dismiss the entire relationship because she'd admit that she *had* been in love with Rick once upon a time. She'd just never felt that magical thing both Roni and Bianca had described feeling with Noah and Gio. Then sweet little Charlee had spoken of this passion she felt even at her young age—something Nellie had no choice but to admit she'd never experienced . . . until now.

Abel rolled off her but still held her close, facing her. "What are your plans today?"

This was another unspoken rule that he was breaking. They didn't ask each other what the other did on their own time, but she liked that he was breaking rules. Maybe it meant that she could too. "Nothing really. Work on the mixer a little and then figure out what I'll be wearing tomorrow to 5th Street."

His eyes looked at her curiously. "What do you mean what to wear? To work out?"

"No," she laughed. "The representative from that vineyard that donated so much for the mixer will be in town tomorrow. I offered to give her a tour of the gym that started the foundation we're doing the mixer for. I uh . . ." She glanced away for a moment as she'd always done when she wanted to be sure she didn't sound like she was trying hint at anything. "I told Gio and Noah about it last week when you were . . . out of town."

The curiosity in his eyes was replaced with what almost looked like remorse, but it switched quickly and he squeezed her. She felt him inhale deeply and very satisfied against her ear. "That's right. Noah did mention that." He lifted himself onto his elbow suddenly. "What time do you have to be there?"

"She's been here all weekend and decided she'd stay an extra day." His silly expression now made her smile curiously. "But she wants it out of the way early, so we're meeting there around eight." She tilted her head even more curious. "What's that look about?"

"I have an early morning radio interview that I'm doing at the station." His smile was even bigger now. "Come with me. We can ride together to 5th Street because I'll head back to training right afterward. The interview should be done way before eight, so we might even have time to grab breakfast. *And*," he leaned in and kissed her nose, "if you wanna save me some time and having to get up that much earlier to pick you up first, I can just spend the night here again." He lifted a hopeful eyebrow. "I can meet you back here tonight with all the clothes and stuff that I'll need for tomorrow."

She'd begun to hide how excited the thought of him wanting to spend the night *again* and so soon made her, but he was staring at her, looking just as excited as she felt, so she nodded, smiling big. "That sounds good to me."

He hugged her, groaning against her ear with what felt like the same utter bliss she was feeling. She couldn't be imagining all this, could she?

After rolling around in bed a little longer to the point where it felt like they'd be going at it again, Abel shared a better idea. He needed to meet the guys at the gym soon, so he invited her to take a shower with him. Within minutes, they were lathering each other up. As her hand ran over every incredible muscle on his body, he lifted her chin and stared at her for a moment. "You really are beautiful."

She smiled, gulping back the incredible emotion that he made her feel now. Only this time it wasn't bad or the dread of falling too hard. This time it was a delightful emotion that danced inside her. "If you say so." She smiled, kissing him.

"No, I know so," he said, kissing her as sweetly as he had last night when he came out to find her outside of Noah's. There was so much unspoken sentiment. "I can't get enough of you," he said, lifting her against the shower wall.

She wrapped her legs around him like she had in the ice vending room on the cruise, kissing him a bit more frantically, and then gasped with pleasure when she felt him slip inside her. Okay, she'd be insane to walk away from this now.

Andy was at it again about the media. He'd called three times since last night when Abel had decided to turn off his phone and give Nellie his undivided attention. So when Abel turned on his phone as he got in his car, he saw the missed calls. He didn't bother listening to voicemails just hit speed dial as he drove out of Nellie's driveway.

He was going on about a photo shoot and interview that Fitness Magazine wanted to do with him. "Is this part of the fight contract?"

"No, but hear me out. There will probably never be a better time for you to do this kind of layout. Your body is in its prime, and since the fight is right around the corner, they want you on the cover. This would be huge. It would also be great publicity for 5th Street, and I think I might even have another way to add a positive spin to it that you might like for once."

Abel rolled his eyes. There was always something Andy wanted to add to the circus that the media was already making of this. "What's that?"

"We can get a few of the gym's regulars and up-and-coming hopefuls to be featured, so it's more about the gym than you. I figured you'd like that. Not only are you giving some of your people from your own gym the opportunity to get noticed but the spotlight and interview isn't completely about you."

He had to admit that it wasn't a bad idea. "That might work, but I wanna see a list of the questions they'll be asking. I want this interview to be strictly about my training for the fight and the gym. They get *nothing* personal."

"Of course," Andy assured him. "I'm already here at 5th Street, and Noah's given me a rundown of who he thinks might be good to feature. But you'll get the final say."

"Whatever Noah says is fine with me. I trust his judgment."

He got off the phone and called his mom to let her know she wouldn't be seeing him again until later tonight and that was only while he blew in and out to grab his stuff for tomorrow. Between the media crap, training, and now making time for Nellie in between, he'd hardly been home at all lately. And as long as Nellie didn't protest, he planned on spending a lot more nights at her place. Maybe without him having to actually put his feelings out there, his staying would deter Nellie from going out on any more damn dates.

Clenching his jaw as he drove into the 5th Street parking lot, he pushed aside the annoying thoughts of Nellie on any dates with someone else. Before he could even get out of his car, he saw Rachel hurrying toward the car. *Well shit.* He glanced around casually to see if he spotted any paparazzi. They'd long since posted signs all over warning of charges being pressed on any unauthorized photographers or paparazzi who were ever found trespassing anywhere near 5th Street's private property. That included the parking lot, but he knew that that never stopped those vultures. During Gio's mess and even when Felix had visited since then, they'd been known to pay people who lived in the nearby apartment buildings whose windows faced 5th Street to camp out by their window to try and get that perfect shot of *something.*

"Abel!" Rachel raced up to him her hands clasped in front of her face. "Oh my God, I just heard about the Fitness Magazine photo shoot thing." She spoke a mile a minute. "This would be such an enormous opportunity for me. To get featured in a magazine of that caliber would do wonders for me. You know I've been trying to get into fitness modeling, and this could be just the break I need. Andy said you had the final say, and I just wanted to say that I'd be willing to do *anything—*"

He lifted his hand, stopping her right there with a smile. "You're in." Her eyes opened wide, and she brought her hands over her mouth, her eyes instantly swimming in tears. It only made him smile bigger and feel better about doing this. "You're right. This is exactly why we're featuring regulars from the gym. You're a perfect candidate for this. It is an awesome opportunity, and I agree this *could* do wonders for you. They take one look at you and you're golden."

She shook her head, apparently too overwhelmed with emotion to speak, so he pulled her to him and hugged her, chuckling. "You're gonna do great."

Wrapping her arms around him tightly, she jumped up and kissed him, missing his lips by an inch. "Thank you so much! You have no idea how much this means to me."

"I do actually," he said, pulling away from her and realizing that if the media did get any footage of this they'd have a field day. That's the last thing he needed, especially now that he sensed he was making strides with Nellie. Maybe her damn date was just what he already knew—something she'd had planned long before their time in San Francisco. Luckily, it wasn't even eight yet. It was probably too early for the vultures to be lurking. He squeezed her arm. "Let's go tell Andy."

Her eyes opened wide again; only this time she looked alarmed. Grabbing his hand, she tugged him along, laughing, but practically broke out into a sprint. "We gotta hurry. He mentioned that Noah had already made his choice. And even though he said you'd have the final say, I don't want Noah telling any of his choices that they're in and then say that it's too late for me."

Abel hurried along with her, assuring her she was in no matter what. Just as they got to the door, she brought her hands to her face again, her eyes doing the crying thing all over. Then she wrapped her arms around his neck. "I *cannot* thank you enough." She laughed against his neck. "As soon as we talk to Andy and Noah, I'm calling my dad. He's gonna flip!"

Wrapping his arms around her waist, Abel couldn't help smiling. Finally, Andy had an idea that wasn't purely about getting publicity or sponsors. This might actually make the interview and photo shoot worth it.

CHAPTER 12

For the past forty minutes, Nellie had practically pranced around her bedroom, going through her outfits for tomorrow. She'd decided to ignore Sam's text asking if she was going to be able to join him for brunch. Roni would be furious, especially because her decision to ignore him was a direct result of her night and morning with Abel.

There was no question about it now. She was definitely picking up on a vibe from Abel. She wasn't alone with her growing feelings, but she was still too chicken to dare say anything. Their second night in a row together, although she wasn't counting on it, might shine some light on things. She knew there was only so much small talk they could make before delving into personal stuff. Already Abel had broken some of the unspoken rules on more than one occasion.

That reminded her that she still didn't know much about his opponent, and they'd certainly be talking about his fight from here until the big day that was fast approaching. Last night they'd filled her in on their meeting with the director of PR, someone she'd be meeting with in a couple of days.

Since she was in the middle of a load of laundry, she decided to have some coffee and do some homework on this Hammerhead fellow they spoke of last night with such disdain. Apparently he and his camp were all about playing ugly in the media. She'd be handling all the fight-related events at 5th Street leading up to the fight where there would be reporters, cameras, and such present. It was best if she knew a little of what she was getting herself into.

Firing up her laptop on her dining room table, she pulled up a browser and typed in "Abel Ayala's opponent."

Immediately, Nathanial "Hammerhead" McKinley came up. She scrolled through the photos first. There was something very familiar about him. Maybe she *had* been paying more attention than she originally thought because she'd definitely seen this guy before. She read the short bio under one of his photos. He was born and raised in Highland, Michigan, where he and his brothers stayed out of trouble by joining the local boxing gym instead.

That made her smile. As much as the guys spoke so sourly about McKinley and his brothers last night, they had something huge in common with them. They couldn't be too bad, right? And they all agreed that the kind of trash talking that he and his brothers did was all part of the hype. Abel just didn't want any part of that. So he refused to do any.

She skimmed through all the need-to-know stuff about McKinley: how long he'd been the champ, who he beat to win the title, what his weaknesses were, etc. Just a few minutes later, she'd had enough. She figured she didn't have to know *everything* about the guy, just the key things, and she'd covered them all.

With a smirk, she deleted the word opponent, hit enter, and then walked away to pour herself some coffee. She'd rather drool over photos of Abel than read boring boxing stats of someone else any day. Her phone rang, and she frowned when she saw that it was Roni. She had a feeling why she'd be calling this early, but she answered anyway.

"Good morning," she chirped, sounding a little too cheery.

Roni was quiet for a moment before speaking. "Someone's in a good mood. Is it because you're busy getting ready to go on your brunch date?"

Nellie did the Roni thing and crinkled her nose. "Um, I haven't talked to Sam, actually." She picked up her mug, still feeling the little skip in her step as she walked back toward her laptop. "We didn't make *for sure* arrangements, so I figured since I haven't heard from him he changed his mind."

Okay, that was a little white lie, but it was necessary. Roni knew her too well, and if Nellie told her she'd changed her mind, Roni would know exactly why. Already last night she'd cornered her in the kitchen and teased her about her and Abel not being able to keep their eyes off each other. Nellie had assured her they were just flirting, reminding her once again that they were fuck buddies after all. Of course, they'd be flirting. But as always, she'd seen the worry in Roni's eyes. Though to her credit, Roni kept her promise about keeping her nose out of it and let it go.

"Did you and Abel . . . you know . . . last night?"

"Maybe," Nellie said, her smile going flat the moment she sat down in front of her laptop. She didn't even hear what Roni said next as her eyes were glued to the latest headline about Abel and the photos just beneath it.

THINGS HEATING UP BETWEEN AWELESS AYALA AND ASPIRING FITNESS MODEL, RACHEL DELGADILLO.

Never had her mood done such a wild and abrupt about face. She literally felt the air sucked out of her. The wheezing in her breathing was already feeling heavier with every breath she took, and she reached for the inhaler in her purse. Taking a big hit from it, holding it in until she felt the pressure in her lungs ease, she exhaled slowly.

The time on the headline said it was uploaded less than an hour ago. Among the new photos of Abel and the fucking juice girl, there was one of her running out to meet him as he pulled into the 5th Street parking lot. He wore the very tank and basketball shorts he'd pulled out of his trunk just that morning and changed into. She appeared to be very excited to see him. Nellie's heart sank at the sight of Abel, who'd had to practically pry his arms off Nellie just before he'd left, pulling this girl to him with that same sweet smile she'd seen on him so often lately.

Nellie hadn't even realized she gasped at the photo of them embracing until she heard Roni's worried words. "What's wrong?"

Knowing there'd be no way she'd be able to hold a conversation with Roni now without her best friend picking up on her mood change, she said the only thing that might excite Roni more than worry her. "That's Sam on the other line. Let me call you back."

"It is?" Roni asked, not sounding nearly as excited as Nellie thought she'd be. "Oh, okay, well, call me back."

The strangeness in Roni's reaction made Nellie wonder what all she'd missed of Roni's remarks after she'd confirmed that maybe she and Abel had . . . *you know*. But her mind was still completely wrapped around something else to give it too much thought.

With a deep breath, she clicked the photos, her chest tightening with every different one of Abel's sweet encounter with Rachel. "Don't do this," she whispered to herself as her eyes remained glued to the photos. "This is just how the paparazzi work."

Her head argued with her heart that she needed to give him the benefit of the doubt. After the night and morning they'd had, she owed him that much. Each photo she clicked on with him smiling so sweetly at Rachel as he took her in his arms wounded Nellie's fragile heart a little further. Still she held out hope that it was just an innocent exchange—that even though Abel had reached out for her first, the girl was just a touchy-feely bitch who couldn't keep her hands off him, and what was Abel supposed to do? Then she froze at the sight of the photo of them kissing, the ache in her pounding heart unbearable.

Wiping the stupid tears from her eyes because they'd blurred her vision, she was determined to look through every last goddamned photo of him and this girl. As much as it hurt, her delusional heart needed this. Furious with herself now, she clicked on every picture, staring at them even as she swatted tears away. Of course, Nellie had been completely taken by him. The man was beautiful and he said *she* was beautiful. But the worst thing was that she was actually beginning to believe him. Of course, he'd be into fitness models. Why would he settle for anything less? His body was perfection, and he may be the next heavyweight champ. So it made perfect sense that he'd seek out perfection, not some older divorcee whose husband had left her for her own damn sister!

"No!" she stood up with a sudden conviction, her eyes still stuck to the photo of Abel and *Rachel* embracing yet again as they reached the entrance of 5th Street. "I am *not* just a divorcee, and I may not be a fitness model, but I can hold my own!"

Sam was *very* good looking, and she could admit it now without feeling the ridiculous guilt she'd felt last night when she couldn't bring herself to use the word to describe his eyes—they were *beautiful*. And he seemed to have taken a liking to her immediately. In fact, he'd flirted with her outrageously the entire night and then said he'd really hoped to see her again before he left town—tonight.

Picking up her phone, she ignored her shaking hand as she scrolled through her texts. She slammed her laptop closed and started to her room just as she found the text from Sam that morning. Without another thought, because she knew if she even hesitated that she might change her mind, she responded.

> Sorry I slept in. Just now saw this. Does the offer to get together for brunch still stand?

Her phone beeped before it even hit her bed where she'd tossed it. Infuriatingly, the tears were still coming, and she continued to swat them away as she picked up the phone.

> Of course! I was still holding out hope that I'd hear from you and hadn't made plans. You feel like Mexican brunch? The

place I mentioned came highly recommended, and I was told I HAD to try before I leave Cali. It's a couple of hours away in La Jolla. I'm told it's absolutely worth the drive. But you'd be looking at spending most your day with me. Not sure if you're up for that just yet. ;)

Still struggling with the pain of those photos that were now burned in her memory, she swatted more tears away. But they were angry tears now. She just wasn't sure who she was angrier at: Abel for being so good and making her feel so damn special or herself for falling for it so hard. Using the very words she once used on Abel, she responded.

I'm game if you're game. Just give me about thirty minutes to get ready.

Sam told her to just text him her address when she was ready. Nellie knew she'd regret agreeing to do this, and she did almost immediately. What the hell was she thinking? An entire day with this guy? She hardly knew him! But the thought of Abel and his fitness model bitch had her looking for her most provocative outfit that was appropriate for a brunch.

Maybe she wasn't fitness model material or worthy of having such an amazing guy all to herself. While Abel may be outstanding at a lot of things, he couldn't possibly be *this* good of an actor. She did have it in her to turn on even an incredible guy like him. Of that she was positive. There were some things a man couldn't fake. And as much as it hurt how quickly he'd run into another woman's arms even after the amazing night and morning they'd had, a part of her still believed that he thought her beautiful. He'd said it with such sincerity.

She needed this now more than ever—needed to feel sexy, attractive to someone who might not just be saying it out of lust. She was *not* about to fall back into the dark place that she'd spiraled into with Rick. She *refused*. She'd come too far and worked too hard for that. Even her therapist had agreed that she was ready to stop her therapy. At the moment, she yearned to speak with her again—needed to be talked off this ledge—but she held her head high and stared in the mirror at the puffy red-eyed women before her. "You got this, babe," she sniffled. "You've been through so much worse."

But had she really? She'd just established this morning that losing Abel would be a hundred times worse than losing Rick. Hell, who was she kidding? It'd be a *million* times worse. Then again, this didn't have to mean that she was losing Abel. This just changed the game back to how she'd originally agreed to play it. She had zero intentions of sleeping with Sam, but agreeing to go on this date with him was part of what she kept insisting she was doing: letting loose.

Taking another much needed hit from her inhaler, she grabbed one of her one-piece office dresses, the kind that Abel had told her more than once drove him nuts. Her mind was made up. "Time to free that spirit, girl," she muttered as she searched the rest of her closet. "Getting hung up on the first guy you sleep with after your divorce isn't exactly freeing shit."

Studying the dress, she chewed her lip, wondering how to sexy-it-up more. She could un-business-it-up by wearing higher heels than normal, and since it was snug but sleeveless, she usually wore a coat over it. Today she had the perfect thing to wear over it instead: a sexy black bolero that she'd been saving for a special occasion.

As brave as she was suddenly feeling, she'd been privy to the Ayala temper in the past, and though he had no right to be a jerk about this, she remembered his reaction to Logan at her office. Things had changed significantly since then. She knew she wasn't imagining his heightened feelings for her. He just obviously wasn't interested in anything exclusive. He'd played the territorial card then, and since she hadn't protested his behavior, she wasn't sure what he'd do if he was waiting for her when Sam dropped her off. Now that she'd seen those eye-opening pictures, there was no way she'd be keeping her dates from him. She had every right to date whomever she damn well pleased. But she wasn't looking to make a scene just outside her front door, so she wouldn't risk it.

After getting ready, she grabbed her purse and keys, texted Sam Roni's address, and then called Roni to let her in on her plans. Only she told her she was really nervous about her outfit, so she was having him pick her up at Roni's house because she wanted a second opinion.

The knot was still firmly at her throat, but she refused to shed even one more tear for Abel or *any* man. She took a deep breath. No more feeling sorry for herself, ever. She made that promise to herself a while back, and she'd almost broken it today. Never again.

It was too odd that Nellie hadn't responded to any of his texts all day. He'd texted her to tell her he'd be at her place later than he had planned. He had to go home and pack first. Then he told Noah he'd come by and check out his motorcycle. It was his original Ninja, one he refused to get rid of even though he could afford much better now. He said it held too many memories. Abel had laughed when Noah admitted that Roni was refusing to let him ride it until he had it completely overhauled. Doing so would cost him way more than the bike was worth, so Abel told him not to. He'd come by and check it out.

Now he had a very bad feeling in his gut. He'd had it almost the entire day. This was exactly why he hated the fucking media. Before Andy even left the gym that morning, he'd laughed, cheerfully showing Abel the photos of him and Rachel. "You're trending again on Twitter."

Of course, to Andy this was a good thing. He had no idea how much that had sunk Abel's insides. If Nellie saw the photos of him and Rachel just minutes after he'd left her place, he knew she'd be thinking the worst. Given their stupid agreement, he couldn't even try to explain. She'd tell him he didn't have to and maybe even infuriatingly remind him again of how *great* she was with this arrangement.

It was subtle, but when he'd arrived at Noah's, he picked up on Roni's chilly reception. Nellie had obviously told her about the night they'd spent together, and he knew the photos and stories of him and Rachel had already gone viral. Noah telling Roni that Rachel was someone he'd bagged was sure to only make things worse. This made the brick sitting heavily in his gut heavier. He now knew what he feared most. Nellie knew and for all he tried to convey to her last night and when he'd made love to her again this morning— when he told her he couldn't get enough of her—it was probably all down the toilet now. She probably thought him full of shit.

Noah glanced up at the back door as Roni closed it behind her. She'd come out to bring them each bottled waters, but again she'd been a bit on the cold side with Abel. Abel downed half the bottle just before replacing the final sparkplug on the Ninja. He glanced at Noah, not sure if he should address it. He didn't have to because Noah addressed it for him.

"She just hates the whole situation, man. Don't take it too personally. She'll get over it." He shrugged. "Nellie is the only family she had before me—before us. She never had this group thing that we brought into her life. She loves it, and she's terrified that things are gonna change. More than anything, she's afraid of Nellie getting hurt again, but I keep telling her you two are good with the way things are. Hell, Nellie's out on a date again right now. I think with the same guy from Friday night. But even that has her worried."

Abel stared at Noah, feeling every hair on his body go on alert. He was dying to ask, but he knew he shouldn't. It was impossible not to care now. She was out on fucking date again? After last night? This morning? It took everything in him as he stood slowly not to pick up Noah's bike and slam it back down on the ground. Instead, he took another long slow drink, nearly finishing his water bottle.

He didn't dare make eye contact with Noah for fear he'd see the rage in his eyes. They both turned when they saw the Town Car pull up at the end of Noah's driveway. A guy got out of the far side and came around to open the door on the near side. Abel almost looked away until he realized the girl exiting the car in the hot dress and three inch heels was Nellie.

Feeling his insides instantly ablaze, he stared at her hard as she smiled at the guy who helped her out then said something to him. The guy had his back to Abel and Noah, so Abel couldn't see his face, but if he had to guess this wasn't Logan. This guy was way bigger and taller than he remembered Logan being. So this was *another* guy?

And then it happened. She kissed him. It wasn't a long kiss by any means, barely a peck on the lips, but it was enough to have Abel slamming his water bottle in the nearby trashcan not giving a *fuck* what Noah or anyone thought anymore and charging down the driveway.

CHAPTER 13

For a moment, Abel thought the growl he'd heard had come from deep inside him because he sure as hell felt like growling, until Noah leaped in front of him, and he realized it'd come from his friend. Just like Abel, Noah looked ready to spit. "Damn it, Abel!" he said, shoving his chest with both hands. "Don't you fucking do this! You said you had your shit under control." Noah shoved his hand in the air, now pointing toward his house. "My wife has lost sleep over this. And I *knew* it. I knew it. God damn it! I knew it the day I told you about her date, and I knew it this whole past week when you walked around looking ready to detonate."

The only reason Abel didn't shove past Noah was because Nellie had already gone in the house and the guy she'd just kissed was long gone. "I *will not* let you do this." Noah said almost through his teeth. "Do you hear me? Either you talk to her and tell her how you're feeling or you suck it up."

"I *can't* tell her," Abel said, stalking back toward the garage now. "It's not what she wants. Hell, I don't even know what *I* want. I just . . ." He glanced back, grinding his teeth as he felt the image of Nellie kissing someone else literally slapping him.

"You just don't wanna hear about or see her with anyone else?" Noah shook his head. "Well, too fucking bad! You knew what you were getting yourself into when you started this. I warned you that this would happen. And how do you know it's not what she wants?"

"Because she's told me she's *great* with this arrangement more than once," Abel said, still trying to calm his breathing, his twisting insides, but the more he thought about it, the more incensed it made him. "And now this," he said, pointing down the driveway. "This is exactly how she said she wanted things to be. Said it was for the best. How much clearer does she need to be? This is the second guy she's been out with this weekend alone."

Third if he was counting himself. *Fuck!* Running his fingers through his hair roughly, he struggled to remain calm. Had she been with this guy all day? And why the hell was she dressed so damn provocatively? The shoes alone screamed fuck me.

Hearing the girls giggle in the kitchen only ignited him further. Was she filling Roni in on her *fabulous* date?

Gnashing his teeth, he reminded himself he had to think rationally before he blew in that back door and told her off. Noah would never forgive him, and there was no faster way of killing this thing than doing just that. He thought back to what had been bothering him before he found out she'd been on a date today. If it really didn't matter and she was really great with this arrangement, then why the hell would she feel the need to lie to him this morning about her plans for the day? Why wouldn't she have at least mentioned she was meeting a *friend* or something? She specifically said she had *no* plans. She was working on the mixer and doing laundry. Period. So either she didn't want him to know about her date because she already sensed something like this would upset him, or she didn't have plans until she saw the photos of him and Rachel, which meant that she'd been pissed too because she was feeling the same thing he was.

This rationale should calm him, but it didn't, not at all. And there was still a whole lot of giggling coming from the kitchen window. There was no way he was staying at her place now tonight, not the way he was feeling. He needed time to calm down, or he might snap and spill his guts. As angry as this made him, he still couldn't bring himself to say he was through with her for good, and if she found out how he felt, this could be over. He turned to Noah. "Don't tell Roni about this."

"Are you kidding me?" Noah said, lowering his voice. "I don't *want* her to know. She'll be a mess, waiting for things to blow up. And don't tell me they won't, because they almost did today."

"It was just a surprise," Abel insisted, trying to sound convincing. "It caught me off guard. I wasn't expecting that, but now I know."

Noah rolled his eyes, looking completely unimpressed as the back door opened. Roni stuck her head out. "Babe, Jack's napping. Can you keep an eye on him? I have to give Nellie a ride home."

Noah looked confused for a moment. "Didn't she leave her car here this morning?"

This *morning*? She'd been with this guy *all* day?

"Yes, but she's had a little too much to drink. So I don't think she should drive."

"I'm fine!" Nellie said from inside.

"I'll take her," Abel said as his mother's words instantly came to him. *Only three types of people tell the truth: Kids, the drunk, and the angry.* She might say more than he wanted to hear, and as pissed as he was, he might spit out a few truths himself, but at least it'd be out there. They could move ahead or end this because obviously this wasn't going to work anymore. Immediately, he saw the look of resistance on Roni's face. "I was spending the night at her place anyway. We have some business in the morning."

Roni lifted a brow then turned back and said something in a voice too low for him to make out what she was telling or asking Nellie. Then there was an awkward silence and finally Roni asked. "Honey, what's wrong?" Abel and Noah exchanged glances as Roni closed the door, rushing back in."

"God damn it!" Noah muttered, rushing toward the back door.

Abel followed with his heart completely twisted. Was she crying? Upset? About him and Rachel maybe? He followed Noah through the kitchen and up the hallway where Roni stood outside the bathroom door, talking in a hushed voice. She motioned for Noah and Abel to go away when she saw them coming.

They walked back into the front room, Abel's insides tightening at the sight of Nellie's extra-high-heeled shoes on the floor. Both he and Noah turned when they heard Roni's voice just behind them. "She says she thinks it's mixture a few too many mimosas that she had with brunch and car sickness from the long drive back."

"Long drive?" Abel asked, immediately getting a warning stare down from Noah.

"Yeah," Roni said, rushing to the purse next to Nellie's shoes on the floor and dug through in until she pulled out an inhaler. "They went to a restaurant down in the San Diego area. La Jolla, I think."

La Jolla?

Roni headed back toward the bathroom, turning to Abel. "But she will need that ride home, so if you don't mind giving her a few minutes, she'll be out in a little bit."

"We'll be outside," Noah said before Abel could respond. Roni was already down the hall. "Outside." Noah motioned with his head and walked out before Abel.

Abel followed, knowing he was in for one of Noah lectures. Noah just better keep it short because Abel was in no mood for anything lengthy. Noah walked all the way down the porch stairs and onto the sidewalk; obviously, whatever he planned on saying to Abel, he wanted it as far away from Roni's earshot as possible.

As soon as he stopped walking, he turned to Abel with a purpose but spoke in a lowered voice. "First of all, if you think seeing her with other men is something you're gonna get *used to,* let me tell you right now that you're out of your mind. It's only gonna get worse each time. And I don't think

I need to tell you that this couldn't be happening at a worse time. You're in training for the biggest fight of your life, man. You really wanna blow it by having this shit messing with your head?"

"It's not."

Abel didn't even know why he bothered to try to sound convincing. He knew Noah wasn't buying anything from him now.

"Are you kidding me? You don't think I've noticed all week how off your training has been?"

"I told you. The closer the fight gets, the heavier the hype and paparazzi are getting." And again he didn't know why he bothered. The bored look on Noah face said it all. "It's what I've been trying to adjust to. It threw me for a loop this past week, but I'll get back in the swing of things."

"Really?" Noah crossed his arms in front of him. "So if that dude—the one she *kissed,*" Noah emphasized that last word as if it were necessary to have Abel instantly lit again, "comes back here right now and offers to take her home, maybe even to spend the night, and she sends you packing, you'd be cool with that?"

Swallowing hard, Abel glanced away. The thought of Nellie kissing the guy alone was enough to jumpstart his already wounded heart and had his nostrils flaring. Noah was just being an asshole now by taking it a step further and suggesting that maybe Nellie was sleeping with the guy. Abel wouldn't—*couldn't* even pretend he'd be cool with that.

To his relief, noise at Noah's front door got their attention. Roni and Nellie stood by the door, still talking. Nellie held her shoes in her hands and appeared to be reassuring that Roni she was fine.

"Either you come clean and tell her how much this bothers you—try to change things so they're not as casual as she seems to think they are since she's obviously still seeing other guys," Noah warned in a hushed but urgent voice, "or you end this shit now. I don't care what you say, Ayala. This is already making you crazy, and it's gonna fuck everything up, not just any kind of delusional friendship you *think* you might still be able to handle once this is all over but this fight. You could seriously get hurt in that ring if your head's not all there." Noah took a step further as Nellie started down the long porch toward the steps. "Are you listening to—?"

"I heard you!" Abel snapped through his own clenched teeth.

The image of Nellie kissing that guy was already making him breathe hard again. Noah made some excellent points, but he had no idea how *impossible* both his suggestions were. For one, infuriatingly, it was true. Obviously, Nellie was still *great* with this arrangement since after the night and morning they'd had, she got all dressed up to meet with a guy she was on kissing goodbye terms with—more than just an acquaintance. If he did what Noah said he should, tell her how he felt about this, she may suggest they take a step back and slow things down. He may very well be forced to do the other impossible thing Noah had suggested: end this—stay away from her—something he didn't think he was capable of doing anymore.

He turned to Noah just as Nellie made her way down the porch steps. "I'll handle this. Don't worry."

Nellie waited with baited breath as Abel, who didn't look at all thrilled, walked around the car after letting her in the passenger side. She'd forced herself the entire day to look at the photos of him and Rachel on her phone as often as she got the chance. The guilt she felt for being out with Sam was unreasonable. She and Abel had never agreed to anything exclusive, and those photos of him with his juice bar girl were painful reminders of that.

She hadn't even realized that Abel was there until Roni mentioned telling Noah that she was giving Nellie a ride.

Hearing his voice had been enough to choke her up. The alcohol mixed with all the agonizing she'd done all day over those damn photos had really done a number on her. But hearing him say he'd take her home—that he was spending the night at her place—so matter-of-factly, knowing she'd been out all day with another man, had finally done her in. Claiming to be carsick and needing to throw up so she could run out of Roni's sight before the tears really started flowing, had been her only choice.

Now she couldn't be sure, but she sensed that he wasn't as casually okay with this as she first thought. The memory of how he reacted to Logan in her office came to her. Was he really going to have the nerve to go all caveman on her after his sweet morning greeting with the juice girl?

"That wasn't Logan," he said as soon as he got in the car. "Noah thought maybe you were out with the guy from Friday night. I thought you went to the concert with Logan?"

He started up the car but was still staring at her, so she sat up straight, lifting her chin. Not that she owed him any explanations but she wouldn't make a big deal of it. "I did go to the concert with Logan. He had an emergency and had to leave early. His friend offered to take me home and then asked me if I wanted to have brunch today." His already outstretched brow went more severe. "Logan and I are just co-workers, nothing more." Lifting a shoulder, she glanced away from his pressing eyes. "Sam seemed like a nice enough guy, and I had a good time with him Friday, so I figured, why not?"

"This morning you said you had no plans," he reminded her as he pulled out into the street.

"I didn't because I hadn't heard from him yet, and I hadn't confirmed for sure that I'd be going." Nellie wasn't sure what to think of this line of questioning, but one thing was for sure: Abel wasn't even trying to hide the fact that he was irritated about all of this. The giant balls of brass on this guy! "He texted me this morning, so I agreed. He'd told me about this restaurant Friday night. It was as good as he'd heard it was, *totally* worth the two-hour drive."

Nellie continued staring out her window, refusing to look his way. Her mind was made up, even if her heart wasn't quite there yet. This ended *now*. She'd been naïve to think she could actually do this—that the incredible sex and the temporary times she got to pretend he was all hers were worth it.

"So you just met this guy Friday and agreed to let him drive you home that same night and then take a two-hour drive with him today? Kind of dangerous, don't you think?"

"He wasn't a complete stranger," she clarified, the annoyance with his tone growing heavier with each question. "He's a friend of Logan's."

"And how long have you known Logan?"

"What is this? Twenty questions?" she snapped, glancing back at him, sounding more defensive than she'd planned.

Truth was she hadn't known Logan for too long or very well at all. She still thought him a bit peculiar. When she'd spoken with him yesterday morning to ask him about his ex and how she was doing, he'd been vague. She thought maybe he'd been embarrassed since Sam did say his ex was dramatic and that's why he'd changed the subject so abruptly. Oddly, he'd seemed more interested in hearing how things had gone with her and Sam, but not in a prying, questioning way as she would've thought. He sounded genuinely pleased that Sam had called him that morning to tell him they'd really hit it off. He even asked if she'd be seeing him again.

Her sudden snap in mood seemed to have rendered Abel speechless for a moment because he was staring straight ahead, his jaw working, and he hadn't responded. So she was glad for the interruption when her phone buzzed. Her mom had already called her once earlier, and not wanting to be rude to Sam she'd sent it to voicemail, but her mom hadn't left a message. She had a thing about not wanting to take up too much of Nellie's time, so she rarely called twice in one day unless it was important. At that moment, the last thing Nellie was worried about was being rude to Abel, so she answered.

"Hi, Mom, I was gonna call you as soon as I got home."

"I know. I wouldn't have called you again, but your father and I are about to board a plane, so I was going to leave a message."

"Board a plane? Where are you going?"

Her parents were hermits, and if they ever did take a trip, it was planned out and talked about for months in advance. She'd just spoken to her mom the other day. Never once did she mention a trip.

She heard her mom sigh heavily. "It's a long story, honey, but basically, Courtney is in mandatory rehab. I don't know if you knew anything about this."

Nellie straightened abruptly. "No, I didn't. I haven't talked to her in forever. She never answers or returns my calls."

If neither having to run to Roni's bathroom to try and compose herself nor Abel's questioning hadn't sobered her up completely, this did.

Her mother filled her in quickly on Courtney failing to pick up Gus at the daycare center one too many times and custody having been given solely to Rick. As far as Nellie knew, the jerk was a deadbeat dad who didn't do half his part of spending time with Gus as Courtney had hoped. But it'd been so long since she'd actually spoken to her sister that things might've changed.

"Anyway, Courtney's been in rehab for weeks already, and Rick is just now calling to tell us because he says she made him swear he wouldn't. But he says he's been struggling with Gus because his job requires him to go out of town a lot and was hoping to hire a nanny soon, only he can't afford one yet." Her poor mother sounded so worried. All those feelings of hatred toward her sister and Rick that she thought were long behind her came rushing back. "In the midst of the conversation, he mentioned how already he's had to leave him in the care of neighbor for a few days at a time more than once while he goes out of town for work."

"*What?*" Nellie squeezed the phone tighter. "A neighbor? Which neighbor?"

"Those were my first questions, Nellie, especially because Courtney told me just a few months ago that Rick had moved out of his girlfriend's place and gotten his own apartment. If he's only lived there for a few months, how well can he know these neighbors, and he's leaving my grandson with them for days at a time?"

"What did he say?"

"That he's gotta do what he's gotta do."

"That selfish bastard," Nellie muttered. If she didn't already, she now had Abel's full attention.

"He leaves again day after tomorrow for a week."

"And you and daddy are flying out to stay with Gus?"

"No. We're bringing him home to stay with us until Courtney gets out. She only has a few of weeks left to go. When I voiced my concerns about him leaving Gus for a week with near strangers, he said, 'It is what it is.' Then he said if it bothered me so much and we wanted to come get Gus he was all ours. He'd even sign guardianship over to us."

All theirs? That's how much he cared about being near his son? Nellie brought her hand to her mouth, closing her eyes. She felt completely ashamed that she'd once been married to this man.

"Something wrong?" Abel asked, the tension that had filled that car just minutes earlier now replaced with a feeling of urgency.

Nellie nodded but waved at him to give her a second. After her mom gave her all the facts about how long she'd be in Seattle and how and when she'd be back with Gus, Nellie got off the phone. Everything she'd been so worried about all day regarding her love life now seemed so trivial in comparison.

She shamefully explained about her sister in rehab and her asshole ex-husband pawning their son off on her parents. "They're on a plane now to go bring him home until Courtney gets out and she can get custody back."

Abel frowned, looking very genuinely concerned. Any resentment he may've been feeling toward her earlier was completely gone now. "Anything I can do?"

"No, there's nothing." She smiled softly then felt sadness deep in her heart for what she had to say next. "But I think maybe it's best if you don't stay tonight and I skip your radio interview tomorrow. I didn't get the work done that I was supposed to on the mixer today, and now I have a few more things I need to look into for my parents, regarding my sister and Gus."

Abel pulled up into her driveway without even looking at her, and without turning off his car, he nodded, his moving Adam's apple once again catching her attention. "That's fine. You take care of what you have to take care of. If you need to reschedule anything else you have going on with 5th Street or even going on with the fight, that's fine too, Nell. I don't want you stressing over any of that when you have this to worry about now."

Feeling the enormous knot in her throat nearly suffocate her because this totally felt like the beginning of the end, she shook her head. A part of her, that pathetic little part of her heart still held out hope—hope that she could just shut off the hurt of knowing that as with Rick she alone would never be enough for Abel—hope that she could just accept this arrangement for what it was and that she wouldn't have to walk away to save herself from further pain. That same pathetic part of her aching heart had also actually hoped that he might insist on staying. As strong as she was trying to be, she knew with all certainty that if he stayed with her she'd be in his arms all night. Once again, she'd give into him entirely despite the amount of time she'd spent agonizing over those photos today.

Swallowing back the knot that was still lodged in her throat, she fought the urge to take him up on the offer to cancel everything and just stay in bed for the next few weeks instead. Unless she was planning on cutting Abel along with her work with 5th Street completely out of her life, which would kill her best friend, she may as well face the inevitable. "No, they won't be back for a few days. They'll be renting a car and start driving back tomorrow. My mom said she has no desire to be anywhere near Rick for any longer than she absolutely has to be. But we should have everything squared away before the fight and the other things I need to work on."

"They're driving back from Seattle?" Abel asked wide-eyed. "That's a hell of a drive."

Nellie nodded in agreement then explained why. "They think it'll be less dramatic for Gus than taking him through the whole airport and flying experience. And they figured the long drive home would get them better acquainted with him." She opened the car door, her heart aching with every move that she made to end this night with Abel. "They haven't had a vacation in a while. This will probably be it for them for a few years."

"Maybe I'll see you tomorrow at the gym. You said eight, right?" he said as she got out, making no attempt at all to reach out for her and kiss her madly as he normally did.

"Yeah, eight."

With the realization that she was really walking away from Abel for the first time in weeks without so much as a peck goodbye and that he was perfectly fine with it, she couldn't even turn to face him now as she closed the door.

"I'll be on the lookout."

He didn't even wait for her to go in before revving up his car and pulling out in a hurry. Maybe he figured he still had time for a quick one with the fitness model or whoever else he had lined up.

With her vision completely blurred now as she struggled to unlock her front door, she finally got it open and hurried to her room. The second she made it to her bed, she lay down and let out all the pain she'd felt that day. She knew no matter how much she wanted this to keep going that she had to put an end to it. It was just too damn painful to keep insisting that she could do this. She'd been an idiot for bringing him back home last night even after Roni had told her how he still felt about their relationship. Maybe he did enjoy doing romantic things with her like in San Francisco and even the night they had last night then again this morning. But it didn't mean he wanted that for an extended amount of time and exclusively with only one girl.

She sobbed into her pillow, the pain smashing into her heart and stealing the air from her lungs so much so that it alarmed her. Gasping for chunks of air through what felt like a tiny straw, she reached for her inhaler on her nightstand. She forced herself to calm down because she could feel herself getting close to that point of no return—a place she'd dove into far too many times when she was a child but only a handful as an adult. If she didn't calm down now—force herself to take long deep calm breaths—she could end up having another asthma attack that was so bad she'd be in the emergency room all night. That hadn't happened since she was still married. Before that, she hadn't had an episode that felt like this one since high school.

As she sat there, still trying to calm herself, taking long slow breaths, she realized something. She hadn't imagined herself falling so dangerously hard for Abel. This was further proof that she was too far gone to continue with this arrangement.

CHAPTER 14

Something had definitely changed. Last night Abel hadn't wanted to stick around for even another minute. He'd been beyond pissed. One date with this Sam guy, and suddenly Abel was yesterday's news? But once he calmed, he realized there was more to it. Aside from the news that Nellie had just gotten about her sister and nephew, it was blatantly obvious she wasn't in the greatest mood even before the call. He held on to the hope that the goddamn photos of him and Rachel that were still going viral were the reason behind her "twenty questions" retort, because it was so out of character for her. But then again, he wasn't used to asking personal questions, so he wouldn't know exactly how she'd normally respond. Was this just her way of finally saying he'd crossed the line, or could he actually be right and the photos were the cause of her bad mood?

The morning she arrived at 5th Street for her meeting with the winery rep had been weird again. He ran into her in the parking lot of 5th Street. She'd worn one of her business skirt suits, but more than sexy, beautiful was the only way he'd describe her now. As much as he yearned to kiss her, he'd refrained—too afraid she'd reject him. It might confirm what had kept him up most of the night: that maybe she'd changed her mind about this whole thing. Maybe *Sam* had something to do with her decision. There was definitely something different about her demeanor toward him— colder—distant.

They made small talk about her nephew and then about her parents arriving safely in Seattle. She'd avoided eye contact for the most part then excused herself when she got the text from the rep she was meeting, letting her know she was right outside. And that was it. Abel had been quickly caught up in training again. The fight was only two weeks away now. He'd be going into virtual training lockdown and conditioning soon and for sure would have little to no time for a social life.

At first, he thought it was a good thing. With things definitely going in a new direction, he gave into Noah's pleas to concentrate on this fight and nothing else. He'd had every intention of doing just that before becoming involved with Nellie. Of all five of the now owners of 5th Street including their silent partner, Felix, Abel had always been by far the most dedicated. A shot at the title was his lifelong dream, and now he'd put it on the back burner for something that had always irritated him about his friends—a girl. So this awkwardness and sudden distance couldn't have happened at a better time.

But even through the last week of intense training that started in the wee hours of the morning and continued until late in the afternoon, leaving him completely exhausted, thoughts of Nellie still lingered. Mid-week he'd given into temptation and texted her to simply say that he missed her. Her response? She missed him too, but nothing more. He'd followed up to mention that his grueling training schedule was endless and would continue to be, up until he left for Vegas. He hoped it answered the unasked question of why he'd suddenly disappeared.

To his relief, her response to that seemed to convey understanding to the answer of her unasked question. She said that she could only imagine then mentioned that Roni had told her that Noah had hardly been home lately either. But the even bigger relief was that she never once mentioned canceling driving out to Vegas with him. As far as he knew, that was still on, but he was worried. Clearly, the day those photos of him and Rachel went viral, something changed. He only hoped the newer grainy photos that had been leaked of him and Rachel in the gym and her turning on the flirtation again by touching his hair and face weren't going to be the cause of more changes. The only reason he even knew of the photos was because Andy and Noah were pissed that obviously someone in the gym was taking photos with his phone and leaking them to the press.

Dread of giving Nellie the opportunity to cancel driving out to Vegas with him, in case she'd seen the new photos, kept him from giving in to the temptation of calling her all week. It'd been over a week since he'd last spoken with her. It was really beginning to feel like torture. What had she been up to? He hadn't dared to ask Noah about it, and he knew Noah wasn't about to bring it up on his own. If anyone knew better what a distraction this could be, it was Noah. Good or bad, his good friend and trainer was not about to let him in on anything that might wreak havoc on his training. As it was, Abel was trying his damnedest to concentrate, and he still felt off. No doubt Gio and Noah had picked up on it too.

Now he lay there, losing the battle against the temptation to call her and just talk to her for a few minutes—hear her voice one time before he went to bed so he could sleep better. But would he? Or would it keep him up longer?

He sat up and grabbed his phone. Hesitating for just a moment, he hit the dial button and waited as her phone rang. Lying back down on his bed, he held his breath. What if she wasn't alone? Now he squeezed his eyes shut, his insides fully engulfed in flames in an instant.

"Hello?"

Just hearing her voice calmed him enough that he actually smiled. "Hey," he said, sitting up slowly. "You busy?"

"Not really," she said, exhaling heavily. "I was just about to call it a night. The mixer's been a little more work than I expected."

Hearing the hint of stress in her voice, he frowned. "Everything okay?"

"Yeah, yeah, everything's fine. I've just had my hands full. That's all." She paused for a moment before her next question. "And you? Training hard? I hear they've been riding you mercilessly."

"Yeah, well, it's getting down to the wire now. I'm in the gym all day every day." He wanted to make that clear. The gym and this fight had kept him from her, nothing or no one else had as the tabloids might be implying. "Tomorrow, I have a few phone interviews in the morning, but after that, it's back to the grind. How are things with your sister and your nephew?"

"They're going. He's here now with my parents, and my sister should be out soon. She wasn't happy that Rick gave Gus up so easily, but what can she do?" He heard her sigh. "It's just so hard to believe that I could have been so wrong about someone, you know? To think . . ."

She didn't finish, and Abel waited for a few seconds, lying back down on his bed before asking. "To think, what?"

"Never mind. He's not something I want to put any energy into thinking about right now . . . or ever again."

After going quiet for a moment, he heard her typing. "You sure I'm not interrupting your work?"

"No," she said even as the typing continued. "I was also chatting online as I worked, but I'm closing it up now."

Abel glanced at the clock. It was already past eleven. With the question begging to be asked—who the hell was she chatting with this late—she started to make another comment. "Listen, about Vegas—"

"Please don't cancel." Abel was already sitting up again. His suddenly pounding heart and desperate tone surprised him but not more than what flew out of his mouth next. "I *need* you there with me, Nellie."

The line went completely quiet. The typing ceased, and he didn't even hear her breathing anymore until she spoke again. "I . . . I wasn't gonna cancel." Her tone had changed. She sounded a little surprised, stunned maybe. Abel waited, praying he hadn't blown it. "I was just gonna ask for the exact itinerary. What day and time were you planning on driving out?"

Pulling the phone away from him a little so she wouldn't hear the enormous breath of relief he took then exhaled, Abel smiled. He told her what day he wanted to leave, and they went through the motions of deciding what time was best for both of them. Neither mentioned his unexpected declaration, but it was out there, and even though he immediately regretted letting it out that way, he was now glad that he had. Maybe she'd remember that the next time she saw another one of those stupid tabloid photos of him and Rachel.

Nellie had already yawned a couple of times, and she had mentioned she'd be up early the next day, so Abel was getting ready to let her go, but not before he made sure he told her what he'd really called to say. "I miss you, Nell."

Like earlier, she was quiet for moment then cleared her throat. "I miss you too," she whispered.

Neither said anything for a few silent moments, and even as exhausted as he was, if she'd only uttered the words that she wished she could see him, he'd be in his car before she finished her sentence. But she didn't. Instead she said goodnight, and just like that the call was over.

Abel lay there in his bed, staring at the dark ceiling, thinking. He wanted so badly to believe that she was feeling what he was. But there was no denying her words. It wasn't just a mistaken assumption or even her lying. She'd told him herself that serious relationships were not on her agenda. She wanted to be free. Then he saw it with his own eyes.

Punching his mattress, he shook his head in an effort to shake the visual of her kissing her *date a*way. One thing was for damn sure: he'd never admit it out loud, but Noah was right. He was either going to have to suck it up or end this thing because there was *no way* he was going to be able to deal with that. The very idea that he could get used to it with time as he'd tried to insinuate *was* insane. He'd never get used to that. His reaction to seeing her kiss Sam would be exactly the same if he ever saw it again. It made no sense to even try to pretend he'd hold back, because just lying there thinking about it made him feel like kicking someone's ass.

That meant he had an even bigger problem now. Even if he did end things as Noah suggested, it still wouldn't change the way he felt. His reaction to seeing her with someone else, as inevitable as that was, would still be ugly. What Noah and Roni had been so worried about would happen. It hit him just then. It had already happened. If Noah ever had a gathering where Abel was warned upfront that Nellie would be there with someone else, he wouldn't show up. There had to be another alternative than the only two Noah thought would work. Ending things with Nellie would effectively mean ending any social gatherings with one of his best friends. He didn't even want to consider that, but there'd be no way—*no way*—his being around Nellie and another man would *ever* work.

The long day at the zoo with her nephew, her parents, Roni, and little Jack had worn Nellie out. She hadn't even realized how long it'd been since she spent that much quality time with her parents or her best friend. Most notably, she hadn't realized how much she needed to take a break from her busy life and tormented heart. It'd been nice to just relax and think of nothing more than having some good family fun.

She'd been closer to Roni than she'd ever been to her own sister, so she and Jack were just as much family to her as her parents. Nellie wasn't even ashamed to admit she loved Roni more than she did her sister. It was natural. Roni's love for Nellie had always been so selfless—the girl would do anything for Nellie, and betray her? Never. Nellie could tell that Roni still felt terrible about making her feel bad the night she'd told her she'd meant to rub it in to Abel's brother that she'd been on a date. Ever since then, Roni had hardly asked about Abel.

The drive home from the zoo was a quiet one except for when Gus got fussy. "He's tired," her mom explained as he squirmed in his car seat next to her, whining.

Nellie handed Roni her phone. "Find the app on my second screen that looks like a big bouncing ball. He likes playing with that one." She turned back to Gus as she reached the stop light. "You wanna play with auntie's phone, Gus?"

Immediately, he reached his hand out. "Fom!"

She smiled as Roni turned around and handed it to him. "Here you go."

Glancing up in her rearview mirror, she could see that, unlike Gus, Jack wasn't the only one who'd dozed off; so had her dad. Her mom's eyes were beginning to droop as well. She frowned, feeling terrible that she'd been so busy that she'd hardly been able to help them with Gus.

"So Logan just disappeared?" Roni asked as she straightened back out in her seat.

"Yeah," Nellie nodded as the light turned green. "I didn't hear from him for a few days, which was weird because he was supposed to be doing the financials for the mixer and from day one he was all about communication, constantly calling and texting."

"I remember you saying he was kind of pushy even."

"Exactly," Nellie could admit it now. He *was* on the pushy side. "Then suddenly he emails me that he'd finished the work he was supposed to be doing and said he'd gotten an offer out of state and couldn't pass it up." She shrugged. "When I interviewed him initially, he *did* say he'd been in a real financial bind for months. So I guess if he got offered something permanent and with more pay, I can see why he'd just up and leave, but now I'm stuck doing it all alone, and this is a huge project. I've been up to my eyeballs with it."

Roni frowned, shaking her head. "Well, that sucks. Is it too late to get a replacement?"

"No, I've actually interviewed a few more people that the temp agency sent over. I think I finally interviewed one that'll do. She's a retired accountant looking for some temporary work and seems to be real good about what she does."

The monitor on her dash went off, announcing an incoming call. The screen flashed Sam's name and Roni smiled. Nellie was too tired and wasn't about to have a public conversation with him anyhow since her phone was hooked up to her speakers. She'd ignored his earlier calls and was about to do the same when the ignore button on the screen disappeared and now read: Connected to Sam.

Glancing back at her nephew, she figured out the culprit immediately. Even though he too was now dozing off, his little fingers were still hitting the screen on her phone.

"Nellie?" Sam voice came over the speakers.

Roni turned around and took the phone out of Gus's hands, muffling her giggles with her other hand.

"Hi, Sam," she said, scrunching her nose, but one look in her rearview mirror and she could see his voice hadn't woken anyone.

"I've been trying to get a hold of you all day. I'm in town and was hoping we could get together."

"Oh . . . Yeah, I spent the day at the zoo with my family. I'm on my way home now, but I'm exhausted. I think I'm gonna have to pass."

"You sure?" he asked, sounding very disappointed. "After tonight, I'm going back home again. I was really hoping to see you, even if it's just a few minutes. Any chance we can do just coffee maybe, or if you're in the mood to just relax, the hotel I'm staying at is on a private beach. I've stayed there before. The sunset is beautiful. We can chill on the beach, watch the sunset, maybe have a little wine, and then I can take you home."

Nellie thought of Abel's call last night. *I need you there with me. I miss you, Nell.* As much as she wanted to put more weight on those statements, she'd seen the photos of him and the girl at the gym. Her mind had been made up a week ago that this *understanding* with Abel was not going to work. Then she got that one text from him with those three simple words, and that was all it took to have her rethinking things. After seeing more photos of him and Rachel spending time together, she'd gone back to her original thoughts, and then he called her last night.

She had to stop letting a few words from him melt her so completely that she'd be willing to overlook the obvious. He wasn't spending every waking moment working out as he made it sound. He was enjoying his downtime with the touchy-feely little fitness model—someone he had an intimate past with and very likely a present one too. And from what Nellie could tell, he was enjoying it. This entire time she'd been away from him, she'd forced herself to look at the photos, and every day there were new ones. Even today, the day after what felt like a genuinely heartfelt call, there'd been new ones of the two of them spending more time together than she had with him in over a week.

Glancing at Roni, who zipped her lips like a good girl but lifted a very telling brow, she smirked. She knew what Roni must be thinking. Since Abel had gone into workout lockdown, she'd only left her place to work. After taking the entire day off today, she'd be back in the office working long hours to try to get the mixer completely coordinated before she'd have to leave for Vegas. Her social life was on hold again for more than one reason. "Actually, Sam, that sounds nice. It'd be a perfect way to end the only day I've had off in over a week."

"Excellent. Text me when you're ready for me to pick you up, and I'll be there."

Roni smiled when the call ended. "I'm glad you're going. I'll admit I was a little worried when you went out with him the first time. I thought for sure Abel seemed upset the night Sam dropped you off, but it's not fair that Abel gets to date and you stay home, faithfully waiting for his visits. But that's all I'm gonna say about it." She zipped her lips again and smiled. "I promise."

Glad that Roni kept her promise and didn't say much more, Nellie didn't comment any further either. She still wasn't feeling entirely sure that this was a good idea, but her heart needed to start moving on. It felt so impossibly stuck where it was now. Maybe going out and trying to enjoy another man's company would start to dislodge it. At the very least, it could do what her first date with Sam had managed to do: make her feel attractive in more than just a sexual way.

Less than fifteen minutes into her visit with Sam, Nellie was beginning to regret it. For starters, when he'd mentioned the private beach they'd be watching the sunset from, she'd foolishly assumed they'd walk out the back of his lavish hotel through the lobby. Instead they'd gone straight to his room. He explained that his beach-front room had a private patio, which led out into a walkway if she wanted to get closer to the water. But they'd spent some time in his room as he poured them each a glass of chilled wine.

Sam had also taken it upon himself to hold her hand the whole way to their room and again when walking her out onto his patio. It had its own private fire pit and its own private pool and Jacuzzi. Sam turned the fire on as soon as they walked out. The ocean breeze was just picking up, so the warmth of the fire felt perfect. It was a very romantic setting and one she would've definitely enjoyed—with someone else.

Even with her reservations and knowing there'd be only one very specific someone she'd prefer doing this with,

Nellie forced herself to enjoy the time but casually reminded Sam that she couldn't stay long. She'd have a glass or two at most and then she had to head out. The sun was just setting as they sat down on one of the plush patio sofas. She had to admit it was breathtaking.

"This is my favorite hotel to stay at when I'm out here in California," Sam said, staring at the sunset.

He'd sat next to her a bit too closely, but Nellie refrained from moving over, allowing their thighs to touch.

"I request this room specifically because of this patio. I only wish you had more time to help me enjoy it. We could take a dip in the pool. It's heated."

"You always travel alone?" she asked curiously.

Surely a man who looked as good as Sam could find someone else to help him enjoy this room. His eyes alone were really something else. And now seeing him in jeans and t-shirt, she could see she'd been right about his physique the first time she met him. He wasn't nearly as muscular as Abel, but his arms and chest were more than impressive.

"For the most part," he said, sipping his wine glass, "if it's business, I usually do. For pleasure trips, I get together with friends and family. But there are exceptions like next week, for example. I'll be in Vegas partly for business and partly for pleasure, so I'll be meeting with friends."

"Really?" She tilted her head, smiling about the coincidence. "I'll be in Vegas next week too. What kind of business are you doing out there?"

There was a noticeable gleam in his eye that she wasn't sure what to make of, but then he smiled big. "The cable channel I work at used to be just local, but they were recently bought out by a subsidiary of CNN, so my role as a commentator has branched out a bit. I'm now covering stories all over, not just the Detroit area. This is why I'm here now and why I'll be in Vegas next week. Will you be out there just for pleasure?" he asked, eyeing her playfully.

She smiled, feeling a bittersweet emotion wash over her. A few weeks ago she might've said both. How fast things had changed. While she knew all too well that Vegas could be as pleasurable as her times with Abel had always been, ever since the morning she first saw the photos, Nellie knew she was in danger of serious damage to her heart if she continued with their arrangement as is. "Business," she sipped her wine. It went down a bit rougher than she expected.

"Maybe we can get together while you're out there. How long will you be there?"

She was about to explain about the fight and her role in it when his phone rang and he frowned, glancing at the screen. "I'm sorry. This is so rude," he said apologetically, "but I have to take this. Will you give me a few minutes?"

"Take your time," she assured him as he stood up and began walking back into the room.

Her own phone had lit up a few times since she'd been there, so she decided to check it. She had a missed call from her mother and a text from Logan. The text caught her attention. She hadn't heard from him since his email informing her he was resigning. He hadn't once bothered to return her calls, and she'd left him a voicemail over a week ago, asking him to please call her. His departure had been so abrupt, and even though he'd fulfilled the last tasks he'd been asked to do, she still had questions on a few things. She clicked on the little envelope now curiously.

Give me a call when you get a chance, please. I need to talk to you.

The irritation was immediate, especially after she read it a second time to make sure she hadn't misread it. The nerve of him! *Now* he wanted her to call him? First, he just up and left her hanging, knowing how much work this mixer was, then he didn't bother to return her calls, even when she mentioned she needed some things clarified. Did he need a letter of recommendation now or something?

Nellie closed out her texts, rolling her eyes. Well, now he'd wait until *she* felt good and ready to call him. That could be never. The *jerk*!

Sam walked out into the patio again, glancing around and up at the palm trees that surrounded the patio. He then turned and studied the building adjacent to his hotel. "Everything okay?" she asked.

He turned back to her with an instant smile. "Fine," he waved his phone at her. "Work. Always something." He put his phone down on the patio table and reached out his hand. "C'mere, I wanna show you something else about this room."

Glancing back at the patio door, Nellie hesitated to take his hand. She could only hope he wasn't taking her agreement to come back to his room with him to mean more than it was. He must've picked up on what she might be thinking because he motioned out toward the walkway that led around the palm trees. "It's not in the room," he laughed softly, confirming he had picked up on what had crossed her mind. "It's out there."

Feeling silly but very relieved, she smiled, taking his hand as she stood up. They strolled along the small walkway around the trees, and then they were on the sand. It was a wide open beach area but still very vacant.

"This beach is exclusive to the hotel. And my room is literally steps away from it. I've stayed at lot of rooms all over the country, but this is by far my favorite." He smiled, and his incredibly light eyes nearly twinkled. "It's a little pricey but worth every penny, I think."

"Yes," Nellie had to agree. "It's beautiful."

She was caught in his eyes for a moment, and he smiled, pulling her gently to him.

"Nellie, I know I told you this earlier this week on the phone, and I didn't miss how quiet it made you. I hope this doesn't freak you out, considering we've only known each other for a few weeks. But ever since that day I spent with you, I really haven't been able to stop thinking about you. I know you said you're still working on getting over your divorce, and I respect that. It took me some time to get over mine. At the risk of sounding a little pushy, would you please just give something between you and me some consideration?" He held up his hand. "Whenever you're ready, that is. I'll be patient. I just wanna put it out there so that we're clear that it's what I'm hoping for here."

If she hadn't been so caught up checking the photos of Abel and Rachel the day of their brunch, it might've been a very pleasant date. Sam was actually very sweet, attentive, and she'd since established *very* good-looking. And ever since their brunch, not a day had gone by that he hadn't called or texted her. They'd even had a couple nights where they'd chatted online late into the night.

This past week, she'd come to the conclusion that Roni had been right—as usual. She wasn't the fuck-buddy type. She'd fallen for Abel so fast and so hard that she'd like to say that was the only reason why the arrangement that they had hadn't worked out. But she was certain now she'd never be okay dating someone who was also seeing someone else. It was a constant reminder of her inability to be enough for any man. For that reason, she was hesitant to become involved with another good-looking, obviously wealthy guy who did so much traveling.

Even as sweet as he was, and as genuinely as he was looking at her now, Abel was a perfect example of how a man could make you feel so very special as if you were the only one he ever looked at that way, when in fact . . .

"I've been burned really badly, Sam." She shook her head, unable to believe she was addressing this so soon with him. "It might be a while before I'm ready to open up my heart," she paused for a moment, exasperatingly feeling the lump in her throat. "Trust," she whispered.

His hand caressed her cheek, and she fought the urge to pull away. Instead she leaned her face against his hand, closing her eyes. He leaned forward and kissed her forehead then lowered his hand, lifting her chin. There was no missing the alarm in his eyes when he saw the tears, but it was only for instant. Then he hugged her, and she let herself fall into his arms, hugging him back. "I get it, okay? And I promise I'll be patient. When you do feel ready, I'll do everything in my power to prove to you that you can trust me."

As good as his strong arms felt around her and as much as she needed that at that moment, neither his embrace nor his words had anything on how Abel made her feel.

He pulled away, suddenly glancing around. "What's wrong?" she asked.

"Nothing," he frowned, still looking around, but began walking back down the pathway. "Let's go sit down."

Her phone was buzzing on the table where she'd left it next to his. It was her mom again. After reading Logan's text, she'd completely forgotten that she had a missed call from her mom, and now she was calling again. "I gotta get this." She turned to Sam, already feeling alarmed. "My mom only calls if it's urgent."

"Go ahead," he said, looking a bit concerned himself.

"Mom, what is it?"

"I don't want you getting upset, and you don't need to come down to the emergency room or anything—"

"Emergency room?" she asked already upset. "What happened?"

Sam's hand was instantly on her back when he saw her clutch her chest.

"Gus shoved a bean up his nose, but he's gonna be fine. The doctors are working on getting it out. Your father and I tried to at home, and when we couldn't, we decided to drive down here."

"Oh my God, Mom!" A myriad of emotions washed over her. Concern over her nephew was the most prominent, but she couldn't help feeling irritated that her elderly parents had to deal with this instead of her sister or her worthless ex-husband. She, at least, had to be there to help them deal with some of this. While her mom sounded calm enough, Nellie heard it in her shaky words: she was worried. "What hospital are you guys at?"

"Nellie, you have to work in the morning. You don't have to come down here."

"What hospital, Mom?" she asked a little more firmly this time.

Sam had already walked away before she'd even ended the call. As she walked back into the room, she saw him rushing back to her with his keys in hand. "You can tell me about it on the way."

He sounded so resolute that she didn't bother telling him that he didn't have to take her. Obviously, he'd balk at the suggestion that she could take a cab to save him the trouble. Not only did he take her but he hung around, meeting her parents and Gus in the process and then drove her home when it was all over. She'd already explained when he picked her up why her home wasn't the same one he'd picked her up and dropped her off at last time. It was easy. She gave him the same reasoning she'd given Roni that night. She'd wanted Roni's take on her outfit.

It was way past the time she thought she would've been home now, but at least Gus was fine. Sam walked her to her door.

"Interesting night out," he said with a smirk.

"I'm sorry it turned out this way," she said, turning to him with a wince.

"Don't be," he chuckled. "I got to spend more time with you and even got meeting your parents out of the way."

The way he said that as if it were a given—something that was bound to happen—made her feel a little weird. "Thank you so much for everything, Sam."

His smile went serious suddenly, and those crystal blue eyes stared at her now as they stood silently staring at each other. Before she could get her thoughts together or even think of a reason to protest, his lips were on hers, and he kissed her softly. She almost let him go on—let him slip his tongue into her mouth—but she couldn't. The knot was instantly at her throat and she pulled away.

"I'm sorry," he whispered quickly. "I said I'd be patient, but I couldn't help myself. I'll try harder. I promise."

She shook her head, angry with herself. Letting loose? What a joke. She couldn't even bring herself to let another man's tongue in her mouth. Who was she kidding when she talked about wanting to free her spirit? "It's okay," she insisted. "It's just that—"

"Shh," his finger touched her lips. "You don't have to explain. I understand. I get it—baby steps." He took her hand and kissed it. "This is all I get for now, and I can live with that. Whatever it takes."

He smiled, making those amazing eyes sparkle. "Thanks for understanding."

Once inside with Sam out of sight now, she stood there in the middle of her dark living room. She brought both hands to her face and kept them there for a long time as she took in the day's events. For as much as she'd talked down how good-looking Sam was, she couldn't deny it any longer. Sam was *hot,* and she was certain Roni would agree. Her mom had used the word hunk when she'd had a moment alone with her at the hospital and she'd seen the looks from the table full of women at the brunch last week when they'd walked past them. He'd turned a lot of heads that day and even in the emergency room tonight.

Not only was he hot but he was sweet and was asking her to trust him already. Any other woman would jump at the chance. Yet here she was, once again consumed with thoughts of that other hunk in her life—the unattainable one, for what she needed anyway.

She should be grateful that she had such a sweet and gorgeous distraction now. Instead, all she could think of was that in less than a week she'd be in a car with Abel for four hours. Even though she said that they'd be keeping it strictly business, she already knew that the minute she saw him she'd melt, and if he even tried to kiss her, all bets would be off.

CHAPTER 15

It had been just over a week since Abel had last seen Nellie and his insides were going wild with anticipation. The whole way to her place he'd driven over the limit. He still hadn't figured out how he was going to make things work with her, but one thing he was certain of was that he was determined to figure it out. This past week alone had been proof enough that he wanted, no *needed* her in his life. But he damn sure wasn't sharing her with anybody. So he *had* to figure something out.

He honked at the idiot in front of him driving *way* too slow. The way he was feeling now was further confirmation of how crazy he was about her, because he couldn't drive fast enough to be near her.

The moment his car was in her driveway and turned off, he jumped out and rushed to her front door.

"Come in!" she called out from somewhere inside. "I'm just packing some last-minute things."

Hastening his step as he walked through her living room and into her bedroom where her voice had come from, his heart sped up as well. As he came around the corner and into her room, their eyes met and she smiled. *Beautiful*. With three long and quick strides, he was at her side. Fear of rejection or not he went for it.

"God, I missed you," he said, slipping his hand behind her neck and kissing her deeply.

The fact that she allowed it and was even moaning in response then stopping mid-kiss just to say that she missed him too, was all the assurance he needed. This trip wouldn't be what he'd dreaded. "I wanna make love to you," he whispered anxiously against her lips before burying his tongue in her mouth again.

He moved the small suitcase she'd been packing on her bed aside, and immediately Nellie lay back down on the bed. Like a man on a mission, he yanked her shorts and panties right off, pulled her to the edge of the bed, and dropped to his knees. Sucking the inside of her soft thigh until he saw the pleasing hickey that would be there for days, he moved on to what he really wanted to suck. Opening her with two fingers, he went in for his prize. God damn it! He needed to make this his and *only* his.

Instantly, her back arched, and she moaned loudly as he licked and sucked all her juices. There were plenty. Round and round he moved his tongue rhythmically, loving her body's reaction to each one of his strokes. She tasted so damn good that he couldn't get enough.

Every time he thought she was getting close, he'd slow, not wanting to have to stop yet. It'd been too damn long since he'd had this, and he wanted this to last as long as possible. Her entire body quivered more and more with every stroke of his tongue, and she'd cry out with every suckle until he latched on to that perfect little spot, the one he knew would have her screaming his name in seconds.

Her fingers ran furiously through his hair until he heard what he now loved hearing. "Abel! Oh my God, *Abel!*" With her body quivering out of control, she continued to cry out in undeniable pleasure until she was begging for him to stop. "*Please,* I can't take anymore."

Getting one last taste then kissing her one last time, he looked up at her gasping and still squirming in delight. He smiled completely satisfied that she couldn't possibly need another guy in her life.

Abel wasn't beyond begging now if she ever spoke of needing to be free to date others. Right then and there, he decided he wouldn't be bringing it up, but if and when the subject ever arose again, he was going for it.

Nothing, not his pride nor the fear of her running away, would keep him from telling her that he absolutely refused to share her. She was his now, and he'd just staked his claim on her. One way or another, he'd get her to agree.

***

The drive was far more pleasant than what he'd been dreading all week. For most of it, Nellie had snuggled up next to him. As much as he still wanted to know if she'd seen Sam again, he dared not ruin the mood. The drive was too long for any awkward silences, and that's what would happen—either that or him blowing up.

She'd pulled out her tablet earlier to check her emails. She was supposed to meet the director of PR later that evening to go over the 5th Street booth that they'd be setting up in the hotel lobby. Starting tomorrow, the eve of the fight when all the hype really got going, a Los Angeles radio station would be broadcasting from there. They'd be giving away all kinds of free stuff with the 5th Street logo on them. Nellie would be in charge of making sure it all got set up and went smoothly.

He glanced at her, so glad now that he'd made up his mind. It was still a risk, but one he had no choice but to take.

His earpiece beeped. Glancing down at his phone, he saw it was Andy. The guy called him nonstop, now that the fight was this close. The media coverage for the fight was nuts now, exactly why Abel hadn't wanted to fly in. He tapped his earpiece.

"Hello?" Nellie glanced at him at the sound of his voice, and he pointed to his earpiece.

"Hey, you almost there?"

"A little more than halfway."

"Listen, today was supposed to be a free day for you. I figured after the drive you'd be in no mood for work. But would you consider having drinks with some of the reps from

Fitness magazine?" Andy was speaking quickly. Abel had picked up on this habit from him. Since he was so quick to say no to so many of the things Andy wanted him to do, Andy would speak quickly and get it all out before Abel could reject the idea as he already felt like doing. "It'd be twenty—thirty minutes tops. It's just a very informal meeting to get a feel of any specific ideas you have for the photo shoot. What date and time of day works best for you—that type of thing. You'd meet them in a VIP lounge. No paparazzi allowed. So you wouldn't have to worry about dealing with any of that." Andy cleared his voice then laughed. "They get that you're, um, I don't wanna say difficult but that you're not exactly thrilled about being in the spotlight, so they just wanna make sure you're taken care of—happy."

Happy was exactly how Abel was feeling right about then. He glanced back at Nellie, who was still very much engrossed in whatever it was she was reading on her tablet. "What time are you meeting with Reynolds tonight?"

"Six," she said without even looking up.

"How long do you think you'll be?"

Now she looked up at him. "He said about an hour, but you've talked to him, right? He goes on and on and *on*. So it could be a little longer."

"Is that all you have going on tonight?"

He'd meant business-wise, but the look she gave him was a strange one. She couldn't possibly have social plans, could she? She looked away too quickly, making his insides turn, and he swallowed hard. "I'm not sure yet. My friend is supposed to text me when he gets into town."

"Lemme call you back, Andy." Abel hung up on Andy before he could even respond. "What friend?" he asked in the most demanding voice he'd used on Nellie to date. This pissed him *off*.

"Sam," she said, staring at her tablet in a voice so low that he barely heard her, but he did and he was instantly lit up.

He jerked the car off the exit they were about to pass so fast that Nellie gasped.

"*Sam? He's* coming to Vegas to meet with you *this* weekend? Are you kidding me?" Pulling the car off the road, he turned off the ignition and glared at her now startled eyes. "Are you seeing him the way you see me?"

His demanding question was as enraging as it was terrifying. Did he really want to know? Was this something he wanted to be thinking about just before the fight? But there was no turning back now. She was nuts if she thought he'd stand back idly, knowing she was on a date with Sam. He'd hunt them down and the media could finally have what they wanted out of *Aweless Ayala.* It'd be the scene of all scenes—the brawl before the main event.

"I've seen him twice since I met him, and, no, I'm not sleeping with him if that's what you're asking, but would it matter?"

Her question wasn't an angry one or resentful that he was being demanding like he'd been expecting. It sounded hopeful, but there was a trace of something else.

"Of course it matters," he said, taking down his lethal tone a notch, and took her hand in his. Only then did he realize how his own hand practically shook with tension. "I can't do this anymore, Nell. I know you're not looking for a serious relationship, but I can't fucking stand the thought of you with someone else."

Her eyes went wide, and he saw of hint of a smile then it flattened. "But you and Rachel, the girl from—"

"It's all bullshit. I swear to you." With the hope of her not telling him off yet, he decided to be completely honest. Thanks to Noah she already knew anyway. "She works at the gym, and, yeah, I've gone out with her in the past, but since I've been seeing you, there's been no one else. *No one,*

Nellie. I'm crazy about you, and I don't want to be with anyone else." He couldn't stress it enough. "I want you and *only* you, but I need this to go both ways. I won't push for anything too serious if you're not ready for that, but I do need to know that you're not seeing anyone else."

She stared at him, her eyes still unsure. "The photos of you and her the morning you left my house . . . You two kissed."

He fucking knew it! "*She* kissed *me,* and it wasn't even on the lips. It was close but not quite, only the angle they got made it look as if we did." Now he spoke as quickly as Andy did in the hopes of her not cutting him off before he could finish. "She was just happy about being one of the 5th Street hopefuls being featured in a big fitness magazine that I'll be doing a layout for soon. But I swear to you *none* of what the tabloids are saying is true." He squeezed the steering wheel, knowing there'd been no mistake about what he'd seen the night Sam dropped her off at Noah's. Now she was telling him she'd gone out with him again and the guy was flying out to Vegas to see her? "You and Sam? I saw you kiss him." He cleared his throat, afraid to ask, but he had to know. "You said you haven't slept with him, but have you done more than that kiss I saw?"

The one was seared in his fucking brain now. He stared at her wide eyes as she shook her head. "No."

"You're not still seeing him tonight or this whole weekend, right?" he asked, and once again like when he'd told her he needed her in Vegas with him, the desperation in his own voice surprised him. "Nellie, you'll kill me. I'll go nuts, knowing you're with him."

To his surprise, her face scrunched up and she began to cry. He had several reactions that he was expecting from her. This was *not* one of them. "Baby, what's wrong?"

He leaned in, bringing her to him, and she immediately wrapped her arms around his neck, speaking through her tears against the side of his head. "You have no idea what

I've been going through these last several weeks, fearing the end was near. Hearing about you and Rachel and then seeing those photos nearly killed *me*. After the night and morning we'd had, I thought I felt something different. I thought I felt it in San Francisco." She pulled away and looked at him. Even with her face all red and her makeup smeared, she was still beautiful. "And then those photos . . ." She shook her head again, staring into his eyes. "It's the only reason why I went to that brunch with Sam in the first place."

His gut had been right all along. If only he'd had the balls to act on his instincts sooner. "Is he really flying out here just to meet with you?"

The jealousy consumed him. Even though she was telling him she hadn't slept with Sam, obviously they'd done a lot more kissing than what he'd witnessed. The guy wouldn't be coming all the way down here just to hold her hand. Although the way Abel felt now he'd go to the ends of the earth just to see her now. Sam was probably as taken by Nellie as Abel was. Who could blame him? It still didn't help the burning he was feeling now as he waited for her to answer.

"No, he said it's part work and part pleasure," she said, wiping the corners of her eyes now.

Part pleasure? Yeah, Abel bet. "But you'll cancel any plans you had with him, right?"

She nodded and something tugged at the corner of her lips. He also saw a glint of what might be excitement in her eyes. "Good," he said before kissing her softly, and then he pushed her down on the seat, thankful for the bench seats that his classic car provided. "You're *mine,* Nellie. And now that we've confirmed this, because we have, right?" He needed to be clear on this. He wasn't leaving anything to be misinterpreted. She nodded, chewing on her lower lip with a smile, her eyes still twinkling with unshed tears. It was all his tortured heart needed. He didn't care how busy his life was. Come hell or high water, he'd make time for Nellie no matter what. With a groan, he dove in, kissing her passionately. "But it's not official until . . ." He started pulling her shorts down.

"Abel!" she nudged at his chest, pulling herself up and looking out at the deserted exit in the middle of nowhere. "Are you crazy? We're right off the exit."

"Good point," he said, sitting up and starting the engine again.

He pulled off the side and started further down the deserted road. "If we drive out further, I can take you outside against the car, under the desert sky."

Her jaw dropped, but he saw the excitement mixed with fear in her eyes. "You *can't* be serious."

With a wicked smirk, he turned his attention back to the desolate road. "I've always wanted to do this. Who better to have my first time out on the open road with than the only girl I've ever been in love with."

Staring straight ahead, he dared not look her way. It hadn't exactly slipped, and telling her he was in love with her wasn't on a whim. The whole time that he'd been tormented this past week, he'd considered showing up at her house and just spilling it. If there was ever anything he'd been certain of, it was this.

He finally glanced at Nellie, her silence scaring the hell out of him. She was staring at him with her hand over her mouth. Her eyes completely welled again and her brows pinched. "It's true," he smiled, "not just in love, Nell, but hopeless, there's-no-helping-this-guy kind of in love with you."

The second he stopped the car, she opened the door and jumped out, startling him. He watched her rush around the front of the car as relief and excitement overwhelmed him. Rushing out just in time, he caught her as she jumped in his arms. "I am *so* in love with you too, Abel Ayala," she said, kissed him madly, then stopped and pulled away to look at him. Her expression was torn between a smile and almost breaking down again. "I've been so afraid to admit it even to myself, but I am completely and utterly in love with you."

A part of him almost hated ruining such an incredibly romantic moment with sex. But an even bigger, throbbing part of him now wanted to fuck the hell out of *his* girl. He tugged at her shorts as he let her feet touch the ground. "Pull these down." He spun her around, pinning her against his car, and dove into the side of her neck from behind sucking hard. "*Mine*," he whispered forcefully into her ear as he pulled his zipper down. Her sudden gasp but zero resistance only made him more insane with urgency. "Now let's make this official."

Winston Reynolds was obviously a big fan of his own voice. The man could talk non-stop; often times he repeated what he'd just spent extensive time explaining in a different way. But Nellie had to hand it to him. The man knew his stuff. Unlike Andy, he disagreed that *any* publicity was *good* publicity.

"You don't want to lose the respect of your public," he insisted. "Sure, getting caught up in any kind of scandal will get your name in all the headlines, but what is that doing to your career? Sometimes—and this is more often than not—less is more."

Nellie smiled, nodding. She couldn't agree more. He wouldn't even have to try to convince Abel of that. After he'd *officially* made her *his* earlier that day, Abel had explained in more depth about Rachel. One thing that she'd noticed about Abel even early on was his inability to fake or hide what he was feeling. So often she'd chalked up what she thought she'd felt from him to be nothing more than lust: the way he kissed her with so much passion even from the very start. The way he looked deep into her eyes and held her so possessively every single time had been so telling of what he'd wholly admitted to her now—that just as she'd been, he'd been drawn to her for months before they ever kissed on the cruise and that ever since then he hadn't been able to get her off his mind.

So his annoyed expression when he spoke of the stories about him and Rachel that had gone viral was absolutely genuine. He'd also called himself a fool for waiting so long to come clean, but her constant reminders to him that she was *great* with their agreement had held him back from doing so. Of course, Nellie felt like an idiot now for having done so and so often, but she also explained why she had. They both agreed to be completely honest about their feelings from here on and that the tabloid stories would have zero effect on their relationship. *Their relationship.* Even thinking about it now made her smile silly.

With her meeting finally over and her ears still ringing from all the talking Reynolds had done, she was finally on her way back to her room--*their* room or suite rather. The MGM had, of course, put Abel in a penthouse suite with a much needed and much appreciated private elevator. There was a private entrance and exit that, judging by the amount of media coverage already at the hotel, Nellie had to admit was more of a necessity than a luxury for someone as private as Abel.

She'd felt him tense even as they neared Vegas. They'd driven by huge billboards promoting the "fight of the decade" with the images of him and McKinley every few exits. Then they exited the freeway. Even with all the glitter and bright lights of Vegas, the enormous billboard that took up almost the entire side of the MGM Grand hotel, featuring both McKinley and Ayala facing off, outshined everything else on the strip.

Nellie had to admit that, for a brief moment, even she'd felt rattled. This was the man she was in a relationship with now. The guy was bigger than life at the moment, and his name was already all over every media imaginable. But just as he'd vowed to make time for her, even though she told him not to worry about it because she completely understood, she vowed to not let his fame bring any conflict into their relationship. She saw and *felt* his loyalty to her. She believed him when he promised her that he'd never hurt her. No matter what she read or heard from here on, she'd promised she wouldn't give it so much as a second thought until she got the truth straight from him.

Walking in through the main public entrance of the hotel, she immediately saw the media frenzy already going on. They were everywhere. Reynolds had mentioned that the crew who would be putting up the radio broadcast 5th Street booth overnight should already be there getting ready to set up. She wanted to make sure everything she'd ordered for delivery had arrived. There was another booth being set up not too far from the 5th Street booth. She read the banner going up.

DETROIT'S HOT 107.5 HAS MCKINLEY FOR THE WIN!

HIGHLAND PARK GYM – MAKING CHANGES WITH DETROIT'S YOUTH.

Frowning, she wouldn't let it get to her. Somehow McKinley's camp had gotten wind of the 5th Street gym's promotion and decided to do one of their own. How original to include his hometown gym doing things for their youth as well. She rolled her eyes and continued going through the list on her tablet of the things that should have been delivered that night.

Loud male voices interrupted her concentration on the inventory, but she looked up only to see some guys in suits and others in work clothes over by the McKinley booth, horsing around. She went back to her list, checking things off as she confirmed they'd arrived.

The loud voices once again got her attention. This time they didn't sound as playful. One of the guys sounded heated. Curiously, she looked up as a few of the others setting up the 5th Street booth looked over too. To her absolute surprise, she had to look twice to be sure she saw who she thought she was looking at. Sam was one of the guys in suits who she'd glanced at earlier. Earlier, she'd only had a view of his back. Now he stood arguing with the other guy in a suit. A few flashes from cameras around the area went off.

Nellie looked around. The paparazzi were even more rampant now. While they masqueraded as normal tourists, Nellie could tell who the real tourists were versus the vultures. A few other actual tourists lifted their phones and took photos as well. Could two guys arguing *near* McKinley's camp really be that newsworthy? She shook her head and glanced at Sam again. He was now headed toward her.

"Oh, no," she whispered under her breath.

The last thing she needed was for Abel to get wind of the idea that she was hanging around Sam still. She'd get this over as quickly and painlessly as she could. The guy he'd been arguing with followed him, and Sam stopped when he noticed.

"Back off!" he barked at the guy who resembled him very closely. "I'm done talking to you. I already said *no*."

The other guy grabbed his arm roughly. "This is for Nate, man. Don't forget whose side you're on."

Sam jerked his arm away from the guy and kept walking. In all the times she'd been around Sam, his demeanor had always been upbeat and bright-eyed. She'd never seen the stony-faced Sam who approached her now.

"Hey, babe, we need to talk."

His hand was in hers the second he reached her, and he kept walking. She tried tugging her hand back and protesting, but he held it tight. "I . . . I can't right now. I'm working."

"This won't take long."

"Don't do this, Sam." The other guy was still yelling out. "It'd never work out anyway. You have to know that!"

Considering the scene that he and the other guy were already making that had cameras still flashing, she decided to not do what she really wanted to do and wrestle her hand free in front of the curious crowd. "Where are we going? I can't leave," she asked urgently in a lowered voice so as not to give the nosey people stopping to look at them a more animated show.

They walked toward a door that read "staff only," and he pushed it open. He turned around to face her as soon as the door closed behind them. "Look, I don't have a lot of time. I just need you to know that my feelings for you are real, okay? They may not have been in the beginning, but they are now."

She shook her head. "Sam, I can't—"

"Listen to me," he continued, sounding a bit more anxious with every word. "No matter what you hear, no matter what anyone says," he tapped his heart, "what's in here is real. I mean it."

Searching his eyes, she took in what he was saying. *What anyone says?* She shook her head. "Sam—"

"I'll make it up to you—"

"Sam—"

"If I'd known that I'd feel like this in the beginning—"

"Sam!" she had to stop him before he spilled his guts. Having no idea what he was talking about exactly, Nellie was sure of one thing. He was telling her that he had feelings for her, and the anxiousness in his words was escalating with every word. She had to end this now. "I'm with someone now. I'm sorry." She shook her head. "I wasn't when I went out with you." Feeling stupid, she shook her head even harder now. "I mean I was, but I wasn't." She shrugged, giving up trying to make sense. "It's hard to explain, but the bottom line is that we're exclusive now and I can't go out with you anymore."

Instantly, his anxious eyes went stony again. "You and Ayala?"

That stunned her. "How did you—"

The door swung open, and the guy he'd been arguing with walked in. "Nate's waiting outside. The crowd's gathering fast, man. We gotta go."

The guy's eyes were as blue and as light as Sam's. He glanced at Nellie once then looked back at Sam anxiously.

"You're really with him?" Sam asked, ignoring the guy.

"Dude, what did you think?"

The other guy's overly annoyed tone got her attention. Nellie glanced back at him, confused. How did either of them know? Her phone beeping in her small swing pack purse distracted her for just a moment.

"Let's go!" The guy said even louder to Sam, who finally came unglued from the spot he stood.

"Stay here for a while." He squeezed her arm as he walked past her. "Trust me. The photographers are relentless." He stopped before walking out, his blue eyes almost clear now. "Just remember what I told you." He tapped his chest again. "I mean it."

They both walked out to what sounded like a mob now, and Nellie's heart thudded. *What in the world?* Her phone beeped again, and she pulled it out of her purse. She had two texts. There was one from Logan, which immediately annoyed her, so she ignored it. Did he not get the hint? She wasn't calling him back *ever*, especially not now. The other one was from Abel. It amazed her how just seeing his name made her smile despite the confusing and somewhat disturbing confrontation she'd just had with Sam.

You almost back? I'm done with my meeting and am back at the room. I need to hit the hay early, and I want you with me when I do. Don't worry. The guys made me promise I'd get SOME sleep. =)

Instantly, any thoughts of Sam and certainly Logan were gone, and Nellie smiled giddily. Just as she began to text back, a young girl's voice startled her.

"Ma'am?" With a flinch, she looked up. The girl in a hotel clerk's uniform already wore a regretful and nervous smile. "I'm sorry. I didn't mean to scare you. I just thought you might want to come out this other way. There are a lot of people standing just outside that door now."

Nellie glanced back at the door, still confused why that might be. Obviously, even with all the billboards and the enormous one that covered the entire side of their hotel, she'd underestimated the prying of the media to get *any* story related to the fight. If they were hounding nobodies from both camps, they must be really desperate. She wasn't such a nobody in Abel's life now, but there was no way the media could know that yet. They'd been very discreet when they arrived, taking the VIP entrance through the back and the private elevator to his suite.

Grateful anyway that she could skip whatever was going on outside, she nodded and followed the young girl. Nellie had also missed a call from Roni earlier. She seriously doubted that Abel had told anyone the revelations they'd made on their way to Vegas and that they were now officially an exclusive couple.

God, just thinking about it made her breathe so much easier.

Still, she was going to have to make that call and tell Roni. For some reason, it made her nervous. It was probably because she'd have to admit that Roni had been right all along and that she'd been that close to calling everything off, even an impossible friendship. There was no way she could've dealt with holidays at Roni's with Abel and a date. She was just enormously relieved that Abel felt the same way.

CHAPTER 16

"I'm just saying that Nellie staying in your room during this fight is not such a good idea. Not only is she gonna be a huge distraction . . ." Andy continued as Abel shook his head in disagreement. He'd let him talk for now, but this wasn't something that was up for debate. Andy was just lucky that Abel was in such a great mood or he might've already bitten his head off. "A distraction is the *last* thing you need right now. Your mind needs to be one-hundred percent on the fight right now. Nothing else. But also you have to think about this: if the media gets a hint of this, it'll be all over, good and *bad.*" He emphasized that last word. "They'll scrutinize everything about her, right down to how much older she is than you—"

"I don't give a shit what they say, Andy," Abel suddenly snapped.

Hearing Andy chuckle only made him angrier. "*Really?* You're not making a very good argument for yourself here, *Aweless* Ayala."

"If they say anything that upsets her, I want names." Abel said through his teeth. "That'll be your job. You get me their names, and they go on my shit list: a list of reporters who I will *never* give an exclusive to. She's staying with me this whole weekend and any other fights I have. I'm done discussing this."

Wisely, Andy didn't argue much more, giving in with a heavy sigh. "Okay, I'll see you then tomorrow."

Minutes after that call, he got another from Felix. He'd just finished reading Nellie's text letting him know she was on her way up, so he was in a much better mood when he took this call. "Hey, you here already?"

"No, but I'm there first thing tomorrow. I may not get to hang with you too much until after the fight," Felix sounded upbeat. "I'll be working. I'm covering your fight, man, on HBO." Abel could hear the smile in Felix's voice. "So how you feeling?"

"Good, I didn't do any training today, but this past week was brutal, so both Gio and Noah agreed a day off would be good."

"Was the airport crazy?"

"I wouldn't know. I drove."

"You *drove*? Why?"

"Because of just that." Abel explained. "I'm not trying to walk through no crazy-ass mob at the airport. I drove here with Nellie, and we came up the back way through the private entrance."

Felix was quiet for a moment, and then Abel heard what sounded like a soft chuckle. "You and Nellie? Noah mentioned that last time I was out there. But it's just a fun thing and business, right? That's what Noah said anyway."

Annoyed that Noah was telling anyone his business, Abel frowned, sitting down in the big lounger in the front room of his suite. But he wasn't keeping this a secret from anyone. "Yeah, she's here with me, but, no, it's not just business or a fun thing anymore. It's official. I'm sure you'll be hearing more about it after this weekend."

Felix made a low whistling sound before speaking. "*Damn,* it's like that, really?" Then he laughed. "What did Andy have to say about this?"

"Andy's my publicist." It annoyed him that Felix would even ask. "My personal life isn't his business."

"Are you kidding me? "Felix laughed even louder. "Everything about your life is Andy's business *because* he's your publicist. And let me tell you that he doesn't much care for the wholesome tied-down-to-just-one-chick image for the fighters he represents, especially not the ones that are supposed to be bad asses like you and me. He says wholesome is boring and boring doesn't make headlines. The more girls you're seen with, the better."

Abel thought about Andy's comment last week: how he might want to be spotted with more than just one girl from the gym. Andy said since it was all bullshit anyway it would make it more exciting if he were seen with someone else besides Rachel. Abel hadn't even bothered to respond to that, and he hoped that was answer enough on what he thought about that kind of publicity.

"Yeah, well, funny you'd bring him up. I just now got off the phone with him, and he did try to suggest that Nellie staying in the same room with me was not a good idea, but I made it clear what I thought of his suggestion, and that was that."

He heard Felix take a drink of something then laugh again. "Well, a word of warning. Like the media, Andy is equally relentless. Don't expect him to give up so easily."

"I don't have the patience you do, man." Abel said, not at all worried that Andy would try to convince him of anything. "He should know that by now. So he better not expect me to put up with that bullshit."

Thankfully, they moved on to another subject: Abel's training and strategy for the fight. Felix gave him some pointers on things to ignore and things to pay attention to during a fight of this magnitude. "Whatever you do," Felix warned, "do not let anything wreck the plan of action you've had for so long. You've never walked into a crowd this size, never seen those front rows filled with A-list celebrities and former champs—your heroes—there . . . watching *you*. The key is to concentrate. Don't get too excited or let anything get in your head. Slow and steady. Fight smarter, not harder."

Halfway through Felix's call, Nellie walked in the room. She motioned that she'd was getting in the shower, something he'd already done, so he stayed on the phone with

Felix a little longer. When he was finally off, he walked into the bedroom. Nellie was in her robe, looking through her suitcase with a towel still on her head. She glanced up, and he expected a smile; instead, she appeared nervous. That instantly alarmed him. "Something wrong?"

She shrugged but glanced back down into her suitcase in an obvious attempt to avoid eye contact. He started toward her slowly. "I ran into Sam downstairs."

Abel stopped walking and waited for her to look up, but she didn't. "How'd he know you were here?" The fact that she seemed to be stalling, possibly trying to come up with an acceptable answer and that she was still staring into her suitcase moving things around was beginning to worry him. "Look at me, Nellie." She did, and he had to swallow hard to avoid snapping. "How does he know where you're staying?"

"I told him."

"Why?" Abel cleared his throat and tried to say that a bit calmer. "Why'd you tell him where you're staying?"

"This was back when we'd discussed us both being in Vegas this weekend. It's a common question. Really?" She went into character. "I'll be there too. Where are you staying? So I told him."

They'd talked about trust earlier and not jumping to conclusions or letting anything stupid come between them, so Abel struggled but managed to stay calm. "He came here looking for you?"

"No, I didn't even know he was here yet. I just happened to run into him downstairs."

Abel refrained holding back his sarcastic remarks about what a fucking coincidence that happened to be. Was she really that naïve? Out of all the hotels in Vegas, he just so happened to be lurking around hers? "So what happened?"

"Nothing. It was just a little awkward. He said some stuff I wasn't expecting to hear, but I told him about us. I made it clear that I'm in a relationship and won't be seeing him anymore."

She went back to looking into her suitcase, and Abel was positive she was just moving things around aimlessly. He trusted her. Even as the infuriating visual of her kissing this guy began to flash in his head again, he took cautious steps toward her along with deep breaths.

"What kind of things did he say?" he asked as he reached her, taking her hand in his. When she still didn't look at him, he took another deep breath. "Baby, look at me." She turned to him slowly, and they were face to face now, their lips inches apart, so he leaned in and kissed her. "Tell me."

"He started to tell me that he had real feelings for me," she shrugged. "It was just weird. I was at the 5th Street booth when he pulled me away and—"

"He pulled you away?" Abel backed up, still searching her too nervous eyes. "Why? And where to?"

"It was getting really crowded. The McKinley booth wasn't too far away, and there were a lot of people taking photos, so I guess he wanted more privacy."

Privacy? Abel clenched his teeth for a second. "And you went with him? Where?"

She explained to him about a staff-only room and how they were only in there for a few minutes before he got called away. Feeling her hand against his tense chest calmed him a bit. "It was just weird. That's all. I wasn't expecting to see him. Then he pulled me away before I knew what was even happening. Then he started pouring out his heart, and I had to stomp on it, and . . ." She shrugged. "I just hate awkward situations, but the good news is that he knows now and that I crossed that bridge sooner than I'd expected."

Slipping his arm around her waist, he pulled her to him. "Please tell me that that's the last I have to hear about you being around Sam."

"As far as I'm concerned, yes, it is." She scrunched her nose. "But like today, I can't predict running into him again." His face must have looked as irritated as that comment made him because she added quickly, "I mean just this weekend.

He's not even from Los Angeles. He lives out of state, so I can safely promise that after this weekend I won't be running into him *at all*."

He kissed her again with one thought in mind. He'd make sure Nellie would be with him for the rest of this weekend. This fucker knew now that she was spoken for, so if he still came sniffing around anyway, he'd have Abel to answer to. If he didn't know who Nellie's boyfriend was, he'd sure as hell know soon. Abel didn't give a shit what Andy thought was a good idea or not. The whole world would know soon that Nellie was all *his*.

Kissing her a little longer and harder now, he undid the belt tied around her robe and pushed her suitcase aside. "You're not gonna need anything in there tonight."

The second her robe fell off her, she wrapped her warm naked body around his and kissed him back just as frantically. "I love you," she gasped against his lips.

Jesus Christ! He could hear that from her over and over and never get enough.

"I love you, too, baby," he said, laying her down on the bed.

They'd already made love romantically when they first arrived at their room earlier. He wanted frantic sex now because that's how he felt. Her telling him she'd run into Sam downstairs then hearing that he'd pulled her away for more privacy had gotten his adrenaline pumping, and he needed to let the rush out *now*.

He'd already been shirtless before she even got to the room, and he would've been in his boxer briefs still, too, if it hadn't been for room service. He'd slipped his jeans back on when he had to get the door. Not wanting to slow enough to even pull them off, he rushed over to the small table with his wallet on it and grabbed a condom out of it.

Seeing his beautiful Nellie sprawled out naked on the bed took his breath away for a moment. Rushing back, he unzipped his pants. Pulling himself out of his briefs, he stared at her as he slipped on the condom. "You know what happens to bad girls who let any guy, aside from their boyfriend, pull them into another room for more privacy?"

Her smile flattened and she shook her head. "But I didn't—"

The soft slap he gave her on the ass as he pulled her to the edge of the bed shut her up suddenly, and she stared at him. His evil smirk made her smile. "What? What happens to them?"

He drove into her hard, and she'd been so ready for him. Abel knew it would take great effort not to finish too fast. Hearing her gasp in delight only made that struggle more difficult, but he was determined to make her scream in ecstasy like she had out in the open desert. It drove him insane. "They get fucked so hard until they're begging for forgiveness."

Slamming into her again, he went deeper and harder than the first time. Seeing her moan and lift her hips higher nearly did him in. She loved it. *God,* he'd never felt so completely taken by someone. He continued to slam into her again and again, feeling his climax build, so he slowed a little.

"Please!" she begged, fisting the sheets on either side of her.

Abel couldn't help smiling. His sweet Nellie was going to beg for forgiveness, not that she had anything to be sorry about, but he was glad she was going along with his game and not pissed about it.

He began to speed up again. "Please what?" he grunted, trying to hold out longer.

"*Please!*" she said again, lifting her hips even higher.

Squeezing his eyes shut, he went in deeper. "Say it, baby. Please what?"

"Please, fuck me harder!"

He slowed for a moment, stunned, opening his eyes. She was squirming and moving her hips, and her entire body was beginning to quiver. Driving into her a few more times as hard as he could, he felt her begin to throb around him. Hearing her say that and feeling her dripping juices as he slammed into her, he knew that he was a goner.

One last time he thrust into her, burying himself deep inside with a loud groan. Words couldn't even describe the incredible bliss of knowing he'd never have to worry about anyone else enjoying his Nellie the way only he would from now on.

Just like every time he'd taken her while standing, his legs felt limp as noodles now. He lay down next to her and kissed her still-gasping lips. Working his way down to her ear, he whispered what he'd already made sure she knew several times that day. "Mine."

She turned her head and smiled at him. "*All* yours."

"Hell, yeah," he smiled big, pulling her against his body.

Nellie was perfect in every way. She even went along with the idea of him *owning* her. Even though it was a hypothetical, he meant it in so many ways, and he knew some chicks would get all bent about that. Not his Nellie. He didn't care what anyone thought or said now, not even the one person he'd been a little worried about—his mom. She'd just have to accept the fact that Nellie was older than he was, because Nellie didn't just belong to him now. She owned him in every way, and nobody and nothing would be changing how he felt about her: not Andy, not his career, and not even his mother.

"So what does that mean? *It's official?*" Roni asked as excited as Nellie knew she'd be.

Nellie walked away from the busy 5th Street booth and put her hand over her mouth as she responded to Roni as hushed as she could. "It means we're no longer fuck buddies." The very phrase made her wince now. How could she have ever thought she'd be okay with that? "We're exclusive."

She heard Roni squeal and she laughed. "I knew it! I knew it! I knew you two wouldn't be able to do this without one of you developing feelings. I'm just so glad it was both of you and not just one. I was *so* scared that that might happen, and to be honest, I saw it in his face the night Sam dropped you off. Saw it in the way he looked at you the night you were both over for the fight. I was so damn worried, Nell! Oh my God!" She laughed." I need a drink now. I've been all tense over this for weeks."

"*You* have?" Nellie gasped. "You don't even know what I've been going through these past few weeks."

"Nellie Gamboa, I am going to kick your butt when I get there today!" Roni scolded. "I can't believe you didn't tell me all this time."

"How could I? You would've flipped, and you were already so mad about him with that other girl, even though I was insisting I was fine with it."

"About that," Roni went from sounding excited and playful to angry. "What's up with him and that little bitch?"

Nellie couldn't help laughing. She explained about Rachel and everything Abel had promised her and why she believed him, and then she dropped the big one on her. "He told me he's in love with me."

The line went silent momentarily, and then Roni spoke her voice a little high pitched. "He did?"

Instantly, Nellie was choked up, and she wished Roni was there so she could hug her. "And he said not just in love, Roni, but hopelessly this-guy-can't-be-helped in love with me."

She'd barely been able to squeal out the last few words, and she heard Roni sniffling. "Okay, I'm really gonna kick your butt now," Roni said, openly crying but still laughed. "You're making me cry like a baby here. But I'm so, *so* happy for you two."

Nellie chatted for a few more minutes with her best friend, confessing how hopelessly in love she was now too. Of course, Roni was as delighted to hear it as she was to hear about Abel being in love with Nellie. They spoke for a few more minutes before hanging up. She noticed a missed call from Logan, and she had a voicemail. But she refused to listen to it or call him back. Her life was too perfect now, and she didn't need to muddle it up or get Abel worked up by calling Logan back.

Instead, she called her parents to check on them and Gus. Her sister would be out in a few days and coming to stay with her parents until she cut through all the red tape it was going to take for her to get custody of Gus back. The good thing was that Rick wasn't fighting or protesting her trying to get custody back. To Nellie's surprise, her mom told her that since Courtney had lost her job she was considering staying in Los Angeles for good. Rick obviously had no intention of taking part in Gus's life. Her sister had finally accepted that it was a lost cause to try and stay near him in the hopes of him somehow having a change of heart. Nellie couldn't decide if this was good or bad news. Being near her sister could go either way. But having her nephew in her life again was the silver lining.

Abel would be in last-minute training most of the day then doing the public weigh-in. He'd warned her that it would be a spectacle that at times could get ugly, so he didn't want her there but promised they'd watch it together on TV when he got back to the room. Nellie wasn't even sure that she wanted to watch. The reality of what he was about to do was really setting in. In less than twenty-four hours, he'd be in the ring with the heavyweight champ of the world, fighting the fight of his life. She'd never tell him, but she was nervous for him.

Finally done for the day at the 5th Street booth, she headed back toward the private elevator. Things had quieted down when the weighing was about to begin, and everyone left to watch it somewhere live. She had no idea how she was going to make it through the fight tomorrow. Just hearing the hype about Abel and McKinley facing off now had her stomach in knots. Unlike everyone else, she wasn't headed to a television. She was headed straight to her room where she'd take a long calming shower instead.

Just as she pulled her phone out of her purse when she got in the elevator, she accidently hit her text log and it opened to Logan's last text.

> Okay I get it. You're still pissed at me for blowing off the job like I did. I know you don't want to talk to me, but I really wish you'd give me just a few minutes. It's about Sam. Call me, please.

Nellie frowned. Whatever he had to tell her about Sam didn't matter anymore. She was as done with Sam as she was with Logan. She was certain now, especially given how often Abel made it a point to remind her that she was his, that he wouldn't be thrilled if he ever found out she was calling Logan to talk about Sam. Closing out the text log, she checked her emails instead. She had quite a few, all work-related.

She sighed as she walked out of the elevator. Her hands would be full once she was back in Los Angeles. That long calming shower sounded even better now.

CHAPTER 17

There was no way that big time celebrities didn't have sight problems. The cameras flashing away even before Abel stepped into the room where they'd be doing the prefight conference already had him seeing stars. The weigh-in had been earlier, and even that had been a circus. Now it was time for the last-minute prefight hype. He'd thought Andy and Felix were being ridiculous with the size of the entourage they'd surrounded him with as they left the gym where he'd showered and changed into a suit. But as soon as they were in a public area, if it hadn't been for that enormous entourage, he would've been mobbed.

He thought he'd had his taste of paparazzi when he'd done his Hollywood and New York appearances. This was insanity. It wasn't even the fight yet, and the crowd leading up to the conference was huge and loud.

Trying to drown it out, he mentally went over everything Felix and Andy had warned him about. The weigh-ins had been mandatory, but this press conference was just a few questions to rile the fighters up, usually all show and hype. With McKinley, Abel was warned to expect more than just the usual hype.

"Expect him to get in your face and trash talk, trying to get a public reaction out of you," Felix had stressed. "Give him one by talking back if you wanna do your part of putting on a show, but do not fall for anything he says. He may even talk about your momma."

That had gotten enough reaction out of Abel to make Felix nervous.

"Dude," he'd assured him, "it's all part of the act, and they want nothing more than to get in your head. They've tried all this time and got nothing. Don't let a little 'yo momma' comment break you. What do they know about your mom? It's all about getting in here." Felix pointed at Abel's forehead. "Don't let it happen, man."

"Yeah," Hector had agreed with a laugh. "If he says anything about Mom, hold it in until you're in the ring tomorrow, and then let him have it."

Abel had seen plenty of these pre-fight conferences go south when things got too personal. He'd even seen McKinley get swung at a few times because he talked so much shit. He wasn't the least bit worried about losing it today. He'd seen plenty of this idiot on television. It was obvious that this guy ate up the attention he got for being obnoxious. He just wanted this over with so he could get back to his room and Nellie.

After today, he had strict orders to just relax and take in as much of the weight-gaining protein drinks as he possibly could. He had every intention of doing just that. From tonight until tomorrow, it'd be all about room service and Nellie. He couldn't think of a better way to spend his time before the fight.

Making their way slowly through the crowd until they were in the room where the conference would take place, Abel was certain that he'd be blind before it was all over. The cameras in the room were worse. He looked down as they kept walking, not wanting anymore flashes in his face.

They'd barely walked in the room, and he could already hear someone running his mouth. "That's the younger of his two brothers," Hector whispered, leaning into Abel. Abel glanced up to see the same grease-ball-looking guy he'd seen on TV trash talking him. Only this time, instead of a Pistons jersey, he was suited up like everyone else. "He's the worst of the two." He saw Hector stretch his neck around. "I don't see the other one."

They got the formalities out of the way, and even the press conference with reporters trying to get a rise out of them went well. Abel kept his cool and answered all their questions without much of a reaction. Then came the photo ops for the press. This was what everyone was waiting for, to see Abel and McKinley nose to nose. Abel's plan was simple. He'd stare him down hard and let him talk all the trash he wanted. As long as the guy didn't touch him, he wouldn't lose his cool, no matter what he said.

The cameras went crazy, flashing away as they stood there facing off. To his surprise, McKinley didn't say anything at first, just stared him down. But his brother who stood just behind him was still running his mouth—a bunch of shit about Abel going down and how he was a *chavala* who'd be calling the fight in two rounds, three tops. Abel focused on McKinley's freakishly light blue eyes.

"Just like your dirty gangsta daddy, you going down Ayala." McKinley's brother kept on, and it got the room buzzing.

"Be cool," Gio whispered just behind Abel. "It's almost over."

Abel swallowed hard as the guy's mouth kept running. This little fucker wouldn't break him. He focused on drowning out his words. He was almost out of here. Soon he'd be exactly where he wanted to be, and tomorrow it was on.

". . . show Nellie what it's like to be with a real man, not some punk-ass kid."

That broke his focus, and he glanced away from McKinley for a second to glare at his annoying ass brother. Did he just say what he'd thought he'd heard him say, or was Abel so focused on getting back to Nellie that he thought he heard her name?

Bringing his eyes back to McKinley to continue the stare down, he noticed the smirk tugging at the corner of McKinley's mouth. "I heard she's a good fuck." McKinley said smugly, but in a voice so low that Abel was sure only he heard in the already buzzing room.

For a moment, Abel wondered if this guy was stupid enough to follow up, clarifying that by she, McKinley meant his mom. As much as Abel had insisted he'd keep his cool, he wasn't sure now he would if that were the case. Still he continued staring him down, refusing to give him the reaction he knew McKinley was digging for.

"I heard she sucks dick like a pro."

Abel couldn't help pinching his brows and clenching his teeth. He'd also started breathing a little harder through his nose. He'd been warned enough about this guy, but this kind of trash talking had to be crossing the line. McKinley smirked even bigger now.

"I heard Nellie spreads her—"

"What did you say?" Abel grabbed him by his vest, and instantly everyone around them rushed in to break it up, the cameras going even crazier. As much as they tried to separate them, Abel had a death grip on McKinley's vest. "What the fuck did you say, asshole?"

"She's a freak in the sheets," McKinley's brother said, stupidly moving in close enough to Abel's face.

It was the only thing that made Abel let go of McKinley and swing at his brother instead. The guy went down instantly, and suddenly there were punches being thrown from every direction. Instinctively, Abel turned and looked for Hector in the brawl. He was holding his own, throwing a few impressive punches himself. Andy had moved out of the way and was the only one in his entourage not involved.

Microphones, tables, and cameras went down as the brawl moved around and bodies continued to fall, thankfully none from Abel's side. It took a while, but when they finally broke it up, they told both sides they were free to leave. Since McKinley's people were still yelling obscenities, security hurried Abel and his entourage out before another brawl broke out.

Still burning from McKinley and his brother's comments, he wondered how the hell they got the news of him and Nellie so fast. As satisfying as it had been to knock McKinley's obnoxious brother the fuck out, he was still pissed at himself for having let them get to him. Now after the fact, he knew it had been their sole intention. For months, they'd tried everything to make him snap, and now they knew the one thing that would.

Noah, of course, read his mind. "It happened one day before the fight. They can't do much now. It's a little late to get in your head now, right?"

"Just keep away from the TV, radio, and Internet from now until tomorrow." Gio said, clapping him on the shoulder as they made their way down the corridor that led to his private elevator.

"Absolutely," Andy agreed. "That brawl is gonna be shown over and over until tomorrow and even after— guaranteed. It's probably already been uploaded to YouTube. The promoters will be milking that shit for every penny-sucking minute of it they can. People who don't usually watch fights will be paying to watch it tomorrow after the video of that brawl goes viral." Andy glanced down at his phone screen. "It hasn't even been ten minutes, and the headlines are already quoting McKinley's reaction. I won't tell you what he's saying because it doesn't even matter. Just do yourself a favor and do not turn on your TV or anything where you'll get even a glimpse of the hype."

Abel cursed himself for having given them what they wanted. Well, he sure as fuck wasn't giving them the satisfaction of hearing them trash talk him anymore. He hadn't read any of the stories about himself since the Rachel ones broke out. Ever since then, he'd avoided all the bullshit, and he wasn't about to go back to hearing about it now. He'd handle that asshole in the ring. For now, a good long dose of Nellie was all he needed to feel better.

He frowned when he realized everyone seemed to be coming back to his suite with him. All of them, with the exception of Noah who'd stopped to take a call, were walking with him to the elevator. Pulling his own phone out, he texted Nellie to let her know he wasn't coming back to the room alone. No way was he chancing her opening the door in something sexy and giving the whole gang a show.

To his relief, everyone except Gio and Hector said their goodbyes at the elevator. Andy reminded him to avoid all headlines and any hype. "You need to go in that ring clearheaded," he said, tapping his own temple. "Is Nellie staying with you tonight?"

"You already know the answer to that." Abel pushed the button for the elevator, annoyed and not bothering to look at Andy.

"I'm just saying—"

"Well, don't 'cause I'm done listening."

Sighing a bit exaggeratedly, Andy once again did the right thing and shut up about it, saying goodbye instead.

Abel was only glad the girls were supposed to be arriving soon so these guys would be gone soon too. He wanted nothing more than to be alone with Nellie until the fight. It was all the relaxation he needed and then some. He'd happily shut the rest of the world off and concentrate on just her.

Glancing down at his phone again, he checked the other text he had from his mom.

15Mijjjo. La telvisson ? Que? Paso? Bien?

Groaning, he showed Hector the text. "She's getting better at it." Hector laughed.

That's not what Abel had been groaning about. Obviously his mom had seen the brawl on TV. He'd now have to spend time on the phone, explaining to her what happened, which also meant telling her about Nellie sooner than he'd anticipated. The only reason she probably hadn't called already was because she most likely assumed he was still in the conference.

That wasn't a call he wanted to make in his room with Nellie within earshot, but he was certain that his mother would be calling soon enough, so he'd get this over with now.

"Let me make this call before we go up," he told all three guys, now that Noah was there too.

Taking a few steps away from them, he called his mom. As expected, she sounded alarmed about the brawl. "That happens a lot actually, Ma," he assured her, still irritated that he'd been so certain it wouldn't happen to him.

"But what did he say that made you so angry? You're usually so composed. Your *Tia* Guillermina says that's all for show, but I know you, *Mijo*. You don't do show. So what did that *desgraciado* say to you?"

Abel pinched the rim of his nose and took a deep breath. "He said some disrespectful things about Nellie."

His mom was quiet for a moment. "Nellie? Roni's friend?"

"Yes, Roni's friend," he said, walking away even further from the guys since his brother was already laughing.

"I don't understand. What do they know about Nellie and . . ." That's the moment he knew it hit her. "How would they know it would make you so angry? *Why* did it make you so angry? You told me you were not dating her."

"I am now, and I have no idea how they know about her. I hadn't told anyone."

"*Mijo*, isn't she Roni's age?"

"Yeah, she is." he said very firmly. "She's twenty-nine, but I don't care about that."

"She's divorced too, no?"

"Yep," he said, turning back to Hector, who was obviously still within hearing range, because he was getting a kick out of his conversation. "She's divorced, Mom. And again, I don't give a shit about that either."

"*Grosero*! Don't use that language when you're talking to me."

After apologizing and getting through the rest of her inquisition, his mom finally finished her questioning about Nellie or so he thought. She'd be watching the fight from home because she never watched any of their fights at all. She was only watching this one because it was such a big deal and because she could change the channel or turn the TV off if she got too nervous, but she still refused to watch her son's fight in person.

"We'll talk more about Nellie when you get home. Call me tomorrow before the fight."

Great, this wasn't over. At the very least, he'd made it clear that while he'd respect her opinion his mind was made up. With Nellie back on his mind, he hurried back toward the elevator.

"So are you grounded?" Hector asked.

"Shut up," Abel said as he slid his room card then pushed the elevator button but couldn't help smirking. His brother was such an ass. He was loving this shit.

Gio and Noah each said they were out. They'd only stuck around to give him a few more last-minute tips on what to and not to eat or do before the fight tomorrow. Hector stuck around after Gio and Noah left, but it wasn't until then that he let Abel know that he was going back to his room too. "Curious," he peered at Abel. "It takes a lot for you to lose it. What exactly did he say to you? Was his brother talking about Nellie when he said that she's a freak in the sheets?"

Abel nodded. "And McKinley said some real nasty shit too. I mean I knew he was big on trash talking, but this stuff was just *dirty*." Abel shook his head, frowning. "I wasn't even sure who he was referring to at first, and then he said her name and I lost it."

"She's staying with you all weekend?" Nodding again, Abel leaned against the wall since his brother didn't seem to be going anywhere anytime soon. The elevator had come and gone long ago. "And you're still seeing her, but not really?"

"No, I'm seeing her for real now."

Abel figured that since he'd already told his mom and soon the world would know he may as well tell Hector. He smirked when he saw Hector's brow jump. Of course, he'd be surprised since all this time Abel had been so adamant that it wasn't anything serious.

"Really?" Hector cracked a smile. "Well, I'm only surprised you're finally admitting it, because, dude, your poker face sucks when you're around her. You're so obviously whipped. I've known you had a thing for her since *way* before the cruise." Hector looked at him strangely. "How long has it been *for real*?"

"On the way up here, we finally talked about it and got it straight."

"Ah," Hector nodded satisfied. "No wonder. So this is as recent as yesterday."

"Yeah," Abel pushed away from the wall since Hector began to back away. "What do you mean no wonder?"

"Nothing really. It's just that a few weeks back at Noah's she was talking about some dude with the girls when I walked up to Charlee and it got my attention. Roni said Nellie had met some guy the night before with eyes that captivated Nellie or some shit like that."

Working his jaw, Abel thought back to how tortured he'd felt that night and every time he thought of her on her dates. *Eyes that captivated her?* No matter how long ago that was, it was still grating to hear about it.

Hector said he had a live chat to get on with his girl, who was at a chess tournament in Canada, and took off. Finally, Abel would get to where he'd been dying to be all day—his room with Nellie.

Shocked didn't even begin to describe how Nellie felt when Abel told her that McKinley and his detestable people not only already knew about their relationship but were using it to bait him. She hated that she'd been the cause of Abel losing it. He refused to tell her the ugly things they'd said. He only said that it made him even more anxious to get the asshole in the ring. Of course, that only made her more nervous. But she was glad that he wanted to avoid the media hype completely. The thought of them saying more things about her or their relationship to upset him made her even more uneasy. She'd be doing the same thing. Seeing her name in any of the headlines for whatever reason would have her hyperventilating for certain.

It was the day of the fight. As much as she was trying to enjoy their day alone in Abel's suite, Nellie was having the hardest time relaxing. Ever since last night when Abel got back to the room and told her about the brawl and the reason for it, she'd had a knot in her stomach. Then that morning she'd gotten another text from Logan, which she planned on ignoring. The last thing she wanted was to have any sort of discussion that might upset Abel. He had strict instructions to relax all day and keep his head clear. She knew bringing up the fact that Logan was still texting her about Sam would ruin the relaxing aura he was supposed to be having today. Even their lovemaking had been just that. Any strenuous or mind-blowing acts like so many of the hot and sweaty ones she'd experienced with him so far—the fun and dirty kind where they both came to loud moaning and breathtaking climaxes—were axed today. Instead their lovemaking had been slow, deep, drawn out, and *beautiful*. Nellie wasn't sure now which she preferred more.

Still lying there with her head against Abel's chest, basking in the glow of the incredible climax she was just coming down from, her phone buzzed on the nightstand. Abel reached for it, and she flinched, so he stopped and looked at her. "What's wrong?"

"Nothing," she said, caressing his incredible chest with her fingers.

"You want your phone?"

She nodded, already mad at herself for being so jumpy, but she had such a bad feeling in her gut. She wasn't sure what to expect. Now she could only pray that it wasn't Logan again and that Abel wouldn't see his name on her screen.

Letting out a slow breath when she saw the text was from Emily, she smiled at Abel and showed him. "Emily, my assistant."

He smiled back, moving a strand of hair away from her face. "The mixer still all good?"

"It was the last time I talked to Emily and the new accountant," she said, hitting the envelope with Emily's text, hoping everything was still fine. She'd told her to text her if anything came up. "Her sister is getting married this weekend."

I'm about to board a plane, but I've been sitting here at the airport, glued to the monitors with all the gossip and even news channels going on and on nonstop about you and Sam. OMFG! They've been talking about that more than the fight of the decade! I'll be turning off my phone now, but as soon as I get to Phoenix, I'll turn it on. Call me if you need to vent, cry, scream! Holy shit! *hugs* Sweetie! <3

Nellie sat up, suddenly needing her inhaler. *Going on and on about her and Sam?* Feeling the wheezing start, she thought of the argument Sam had been in with that guy that first night she arrived in Vegas and all the people taking pictures. Had they photographed her going into that staff only room with him? *They've been talking about that more than the fight of the decade?* What in the world were they saying?

Call me if you need to vent, cry, scream? What would upset her so much?

"You okay?" Abel sat up, staring at her, looking very concerned.

Nellie wheezed in loudly. She hadn't realized she was having such a hard time breathing.

"Baby, what's wrong?" Abel was immediately on his knees, holding her by the shoulders.

She waved her hands in front of her frantically, the air she breathed in barely trickling into her lungs, but it wasn't enough. Scrambling, she jumped out of bed recklessly, grabbed her purse, spilling all its contents, and dropped to her knees, wheezing loudly as she fumbled through everything, searching for her inhaler.

"What is it? What's wrong with you?" Abel asked, already on his knees too then suddenly jumping to grab his phone. "I'm calling 911!"

"No!" she gasped as she found the inhaler, bringing it to her mouth, inhaling deeply, but she knew that she was near that too-far-gone stage—the one where she usually had to make a visit to the emergency room—somewhere she hadn't been in so long.

Abel stared at her, his expression as terrified as she felt. The second hit she took and held in did more to expand her lungs, bringing some instant relief.

"What do you need?" Abel asked, back on his knees in front of her, staring at her, the horror still in his eyes. "Tell me what to do, babe."

She reached her hand out to his and shook her head. "I'm okay now," she managed to say. "It's just my asthma."

Her worked and worn-out lungs heaved up and down, but the oxygen was flowing in smoothly now. Suddenly completely exhausted, she began to lie down on the floor, but in seconds, she was in Abel's arms as he lifted her, cradling her in his arms. He walked her over to the bed. "Do you need to go to the hospital?" he asked, lifting the sheet over her.

"No," she shook her head, smiling weakly. "No, I'm fine really. This just happens sometimes. But I'm fine now." She touched the side of his worried face and smiled. "I promise. I'm good now. I'm sorry. I didn't mean to scare you. I just panicked."

He crawled in next to her, spooning her from behind. "Don't be sorry, Nellie," he said, kissing the side of her face then breathed in deeply, holding her tight. "Just tell me. How often does this happen?"

"Not often. I swear," she said, turning to look at him.

He kissed her softly and frowned. "It wouldn't matter to me if it happens often, sweetheart. I just wanna be prepared and not feel so helpless. Is it always this spontaneous? Or is there anything specific that triggers it."

She turned her head back and laid it down against the pillow, glad that he hadn't picked up on the fact that the text from Emily had triggered it. Her mind raced and she remembered the text from Logan earlier that morning. She wouldn't dare read it now in front of Abel, but she would definitely be reading it as soon as she got the chance.

Explaining briefly that she'd suffered her whole life from asthma but for the most part it was under control, she made sure he knew it hadn't been an issue in years. Glad she wasn't facing him, she squeezed her eyes shut, praying that whatever they were saying about her and Sam wouldn't get back to Abel at least until after the fight.

If it were really that bad, Roni would've called already, right? Maybe Emily was just being her dramatic self. She did tend to get overly excited about everything.

Nellie waited until she knew Abel was asleep. After their lunch and extra-long lovemaking session, she normally would've been sound asleep right there next to him, but there was no way she was sleeping now. Inching her way off the bed, careful not to wake him, she tiptoed to her purse's spilled contents still on the floor. She gathered them up quietly, including her phone that was now flashing with another text. This one was from Sam and she braced herself.

"You okay?"

The sound of Abel's voice startled her, and she nearly dropped her phone. "Yes," she said, looking up at him. He was sitting up on the bed now, his face once again full of concern. "I was just picking up the mess I made," she assured him. "But I'm fine."

"Don't worry about that, babe." He stretched his arm. "Come back to bed."

"I will," she smiled. "I just need to use the bathroom first."

He nodded, watching as she threw a few more things in her purse, including her phone. Slowly she got back on her feet and headed to the bathroom, clutching her purse tightly. Almost terrified to read Sam's text, she forced herself.

I know you must hate me right now, but I swear to you I did everything I could to stop it. I admit I was all for it in the beginning, and I feel like an asshole about that now. But like I told you Thursday, my feelings for you now are real. I'm so sorry about all this. I truly am.

Hearing movement outside the bathroom door, Nellie knew Abel was up and she had to hurry. She wouldn't have time to listen to Logan's voicemail still sitting in her inbox, but with her heart at her throat now, she clicked quickly to read his text from earlier this morning.

If I'd had any idea that this is what they were planning, I swear to you I never would've had anything to do with it. Forgive me!

"They?" she whispered, bringing her hand to her mouth.

Sam and someone else planned something, and Logan had something to do with it? Nellie grabbed her inhaler and took a hit as her mind sped back to the night she met Sam.

Had Logan's sudden departure that night and his ex-girlfriend being in the hospital leaving her alone with Sam all been a ploy?

Feeling her chest tighten, she breathed in deeply, trying to calm herself. She felt as if she were going to have another full-blown asthma attack that would very likely have her in the emergency room. Her heart was going a mile a minute now, but she still didn't understand it. Not just that but if something was going on that warranted this much remorse and apologies from both Logan and Sam and was apparently all over the news, why in the world had Worry Wart Roni not called her yet to check on her? Both her and Abel's phones might as well be turned off for as much as they were ringing. She assumed after Abel's reaction yesterday at the conference that Noah and the rest of the guys would be worried about Abel's reaction to whatever it was going on now. And whatever it was, it sounded *bad*.

There was a knock on the door and then Abel's voice. "You still good, babe?"

"Yes," she responded in as calm a voice as she could manage, but her insides were a hot mess now. "I'm fine. I'll be out in a sec."

"Take your time. I'm just making sure you're okay."

As tempted as she was to listen to Logan's message, she knew better. She'd already had to take several hits of her inhaler. She had no choice now but to wait until Abel left to get prepped for his fight in a few hours. After washing her hands, she walked out and into the arms of her waiting and worried-looking but beautiful boyfriend.

"Are you sure you're gonna be okay alone here when I leave? Maybe you should come with me."

She shook her head, smiling. "I'm fine, really. It was just one asthma attack. I've been dealing with this my whole life. Besides," she reminded him, "you need to warm up and all that. I don't wanna be in the way."

"You won't be," he insisted.

"No, you need that time to concentrate on warming up and the last-minute strategy talk you told me about." She touched his face. "But I promise I'll be there before you walk out then right there ringside the entire fight."

Looking less than complacent, he finally nodded. "Okay, I'll be waiting because, Nell," he leaned his forehead against hers, "I meant it when I said that I *need* you there."

"I'll be there," she promised then kissed him.

CHAPTER 18

Normally Nellie's time with Abel seemed to fly. But knowing there was a voicemail waiting on her phone that could shed some light on the mystery going on outside their sheltered media-free suite had her checking the time often. She still didn't understand why no one else had contacted her or Abel if something this big had her name all over the news more than the impending fight of the decade like Emily had said.

Her parents were a given. They were television snobs. They both said they'd take gardening, cooking, reading, and even taking a stroll over sitting in front of the television, wasting mindless hours. She didn't even know why they owned a television. Even poor Gus was having to deal with the no television—or very limited in his case—rule in their house. But Roni? Nellie was certain that Roni would've called by now. It was the only hope she had that things weren't so bad. Still she couldn't ignore the fact that both Logan and Sam had apologized so profusely.

She walked into the bedroom quietly, literally tiptoeing across the room, making sure she didn't make any noise because Abel was on the phone with his mom. Abel frowned when he saw her, waving a hand at her. It was his way of telling her that she didn't have to be quiet, but Nellie knew better. From all the stories she'd heard about how close he was to his mom, this was not a part of their relationship that she was looking forward to dealing with. Bianca had once let it slip that she'd heard Abel mention his mom not exactly being a fan of the age difference between Roni and Noah. At the time, Bianca had no idea that Nellie had any interest in

Abel, and she'd also mentioned that Abel seemed to agree with his mom that such an age difference would never work. This was one of the reasons she was so surprised that his feelings for her were as strong as he'd confessed them to be.

As far as she knew, his mom knew she and Roni were the same age. So Nellie was certain she'd have her hands full trying to win over Mrs. Ayala.

She didn't miss the way Abel raised a somewhat annoyed brow when he saw her tiptoeing into the room again as she walked out of the bathroom. "Nellie, babe, will you hand me my pants, please?"

Her jaw dropped and he laughed. Not only would his mother know now she was in his room with him but that he was sitting there without pants.

"Nellie says hi, Mom," he said into his phone with a smirk. Nellie threw a pillow at him, missing him when he dodged it, which only made him laugh more. "Nothing," he said into the phone with a huge grin. "Nellie was just tickling me. She can't keep her hands off me." Gasping, Nellie picked up another pillow and threw it at him, this time nailing him, but it only made him laugh more. "I gotta go, Mom. Nellie's out of control. *Claro que si, Madre. Siempre.*"

Still laughing, Nellie jumped on the bed and attacked him. "I can't believe you said that to her!" She squealed then laughed when he started tickling her. "Oh my God," she screeched between laughs. "What did she say?"

"She told me to use protection."

Completely mortified but unable to stop laughing because he was still tickling her, she continued to hopelessly fight him off her. Within seconds, he had her pinned down and on top of her. "Be a good girl or I'll have to call my mom back and tell her how wild you are," he teased before kissing her softly.

"How am I supposed to face her now? That's *so* embarrassing."

"What," Abel smiled, trailing kisses down her neck. "We're both adults. It's not," he stopped to suck her neck making her squirm, "like she doesn't know you've been married. And," he sucked her neck a little longer, sending shivers all the way down to her toes. "She knows your mine now."

That really got Nellie's attention. "You told her?"

He stopped sucking her neck and looked up at her. "Well, not in those exact words, but, yeah, I told her we're together now."

Almost afraid to ask, she licked her lips. This entire morning she'd had been one big knot in her stomach and now this. But hearing him say that they were together so matter-of-factly and that he was so serious about it that he'd even told his mom about them, gave her *something* to smile about. "What did she say?"

"I told you," he grinned, swaying his hips and rubbing his already full-blown erection against her. "She told me to use protection."

"Not about that," she laughed then closed her eyes, the mortification inundating her again. "I *cannot* believe you did that." She opened her eyes, loving the way he was looking at her in that profound way he did so often. "I meant about us being together."

"I love the way that sounds," he said, kissing her softly. "She's already making plans to have you over for dinner. And," he looked at her a little apprehensively, suddenly finally letting her hands loose. He rolled off lying next to her instead but picked up her hand and brought it to his mouth kissing it. "I was gonna talk to you about something once we were back home, but as long as we're on the subject of my mom, I figure now's as good a time as any."

Nellie stared at him curiously, her eyes going from his intense eyes to his lips on her hand. "I promised my mom after all this was over I'd either take her on a cruise of the Mexican Riviera or I'd send her on one with my aunt—her sister who's also widowed and alone. But I was thinking, since things have changed now, any vacation I take you're coming with me."

Nellie smiled, and the reality of this was finally starting to sink in. This incredible man was hers now—it was almost impossible to wrap her head around that.

"So I wanted to ask you. Would you be willing to do a cruise with my mom? Hector and Charlee would be there too. Or," he said quickly, as if she would really protest, "I could send her on one with my aunt by themselves, and we could go on one alone if you prefer. It doesn't even have to be the Mexican Riviera or even a cruise. That's just what she wanted to do."

Nellie smiled, taken by the adorable way he stared at her now as if he were worried that he'd just freaked her out or something. "I wouldn't mind your family there as long as you behave and don't say anything like you just did on the phone to embarrass me."

"Oh," he shook his head immediately, "I could never promise you that. Are you kidding me? That's gonna be the best part about having you around my mom."

Her mouth fell open again, but she smiled at him hopefully. "You better be kidding!"

"No way!" He said, pulling her into an embrace and kissing her playfully. "This is gonna be a blast. Hector's been having all the fun, embarrassing sweet little Charlee, whose face goes bright red every time. It's my turn now."

Nellie's eyes went wide, remembering some of the stories Charlee had shared with them. The way Charlee told it, the stories always came across as Hector trying to razz his mom. She never thought of how embarrassing it would be to be on the other end.

Before she could begin to protest, Abel's tongue was doing that wonderful thing it always did to her neck, making her quiver all over. As he moved his mouth up onto hers and his tongue dove into her mouth, Nellie decided that they could discuss his behavior around his mom later. Feeling how ready he was pressed firmly against her, she was already gasping in anticipation.

✳✳✳

"All right," Abel said, slipping on his dark shades on. "Show time. My *entourage* awaits me downstairs."

Pulling his gym bag over his shoulder and slipping his wallet in his back pocket, he opened his arms, welcoming Nellie into them. "You nervous?" she asked, slipping her arms around his hard body and resting her face against his chest.

"Umm," he squeezed her. "Not yet. But I'm sure as the time gets closer I'll get there. That's why I *need* you there, baby. Try to get there early." He stopped and frowned. "You sure you won't reconsider just coming with me now? I'd hate to think of you having another attack and—"

"Stop," she said, kissing him softly. "I'll be fine." His needing her like he said warmed her insides, chasing away some of the anxiety she'd begun to feel again over the texts she'd read that morning. She looked up at him with a reassuring smile. "I'll be out of here in less than hour. I promise."

He kissed her softly at first then a little deeper, backing her up slowly against the wall. The deeper and more passionately he kissed her, the sooner she'd be moaning, which would lead to other things. As much as she felt as though she could kiss him forever, she knew she needed to stop this. The last thing he needed was to exert himself just hours before his big fight. That's exactly where this felt like it was headed, so she pulled away breathlessly. "You need to go," she smiled, chewing her bottom lip.

Groaning, he leaned into her, and she felt the proof of what she'd been afraid this might lead to against her upper thigh. Burying his face in her neck, he kissed it softly. "I can't believe I waited so long to tell you." Inhaling deeply, he kissed her neck again. "I love you, Nellie."

Feeling her heart swell, she smiled big, almost choking up. "I love you, too, Abel."

He pulled away to look at her. "Don't be long."

"I won't," she promised again with what felt like a lovesick smile.

As soon as he was out the door, she hurried to her phone, her heart already pounding. Before hitting the voicemail button, she wondered whether it would be better to listen to it or to turn on the television and see for herself what Emily was talking about. With her stomach suddenly taking a dive, she wondered what would be *worse?*

The moment Abel had gotten out of the elevator he'd been surrounded by what seemed like an even bigger entourage than yesterday. And he'd thought yesterday was ridiculous. "What the hell's all this?" he asked, looking around as they made a human shield around him.

"You stayed away from the hype, right?" Andy asked anxiously in the middle of the shield with him.

"Yeah," Abel peered at him curiously. "I didn't turn anything on or check the Internet at all." Andy seemed more than relieved. Given the added security, as much as Abel hated to, he had to ask. "Why?"

Andy shook his head quickly. "Nothing. McKinley's just been talking all kinds of shit about last night's brawl. It's nothing but crap you don't need to be distracted by, and the media's eating it up like vultures. They're *dying* to get a comment from you. My phone has been ringing nonstop, but I haven't given them shit."

"Good," Abel muttered, already irritated, and they walked slowly to the exit of his sheltered private corridor.

"You'll hear Nellie's name a lot. McKinley told them it was what set you off last night, so, of course, they've turned it into a soap opera. Ignore whatever you hear them yell out at you. You hear me?"

Andy looked at him very seriously, but there was more to it in his eyes. He seemed nervous. "Yeah, I hear you," Abel responded cautiously, his insides already heating up.

The fact that Nellie's world would be turned upside down now that her name was being dragged through this circus and that McKinley was to blame only made him more anxious to get in the ring and *fuck* him up.

The short distance between the corridor and the back VIP entrance to the stadium where he'd be fighting was absolute chaos. Cameras flashed and his name was called out by so many, all at the same time, that he'd barely made out what most were saying. But he did hear Nellie's name more than once like Andy had warned him.

"You're gonna have to send these guys back for Nellie. I don't want her walking out of the hotel by herself."

Andy nodded but said nothing more. As soon as he arrived at his training room, Abel felt the vibe. He saw Noah, Gio, and Hector exchange strange glances with Andy before addressing Abel. He thought maybe they were just all as nervous as he was beginning to feel. Aside from Felix whose welterweight title fights were just as big, this was the biggest most highly promoted boxing match that any of these guys had been so closely involved with.

"How you feeling?" Noah asked as Abel began to shed his clothes.

"Rested," Abel responded simply.

"Good," Noah said. "It'll help you focus and that's key. Stay focused. After last night's exchange with McKinley, I don't want you stepping into that ring with a different plan. Slow and steady. Don't let anger make you sloppy. It's probably what he's hoping you'll do."

Abel nodded as Gio began to wrap his hands. "That Marc guy your Mom loves so much," Gio smiled, "will be doing the national anthem."

Smiling, Abel wondered how much of the fight his mom would actually watch. When he spoke with her earlier, he let her know that he probably wouldn't get a chance to call her again until after the fight—one he assured her he'd be winning because he had every intention of beating the shit out of that obnoxious prick.

He took a deep breath, remembering Noah's instructions. *Don't let anger make you sloppy.* He wouldn't.

They started the warm up with Gio reminding him every now and again to do his jaw stretches. Halfway into it, he glanced at the clock on the wall. Nellie would be there soon.

"Hector," he motioned with his head to his phone on one of the counters. "Check my phone. Nellie should be here any minute. I wanna make sure she didn't have any trouble getting in."

All at once, he saw Hector and the other guys exchange strange glances. Something else he'd noticed since he'd arrived was how quiet Andy had been. Hector walked over to his phone without saying a word.

Tapping Abel's phone a few times, Hector shook his head then turned back to him. "Nothing from her."

Abel turned back to Gio and focused his concentration on his pad drills. Gio held the pads out moving faster, then slower as Abel began to break a sweat. "Don't overdo it," Gio warned. "We're just trying to warm up. This isn't a workout."

Abel nodded and continued. They did the drills for a few more minutes. Abel knew the day of the fight would be a bit nerve wracking for everyone, but the tension in the room was way more suffocating than he'd expected. Still he continued focusing closely on the jabs that Gio threw at him and blocking them.

". . . fucking kidding me with this, right?" Abel paused, turning to Hector's infuriated voice.

Whatever one of the security guys had been doing on his phone was enough to have Hector in his face now, speaking through his teeth.

"Let's go, champ," Gio said, holding the pads up again.

Holding his own glove up, he motioned for Gio to give him a second while he watched as Hector pointed at the other guys around the security guy. He appeared to be warning them about their phones because they all put theirs away as well. "Get that the fuck outta here too," he ordered, pointing at the monitor they'd brought in yesterday to study McKinley's techniques.

When his brother noticed him watching him, he turned back and gave the guys a final warning look before walking toward him.

"What was that about?" Abel asked curiously.

Hector shook his head, forcing a smile as he approached Abel and Gio. "All day, they've been airing McKinley's obnoxious rants, and those idiots . . ." He pointed over his shoulder back in the direction of the guys for whom he'd just ripped a new one. "They know better than to be watching the clips in here on their phones."

Turning back to Gio, Abel smirked. His brother— forever the hothead. "Yeah, so what's McKinley been saying?"

"Don't worry about that," Noah said, walking up to them. "Focus on this."

Noah pointed at Gio then gave Hector an irritated look. He was probably mad that he'd even brought it up. Abel understood all too clearly. He remembered back when Noah was still dating Roni. Hector had some not so good news about her that Abel knew would piss Noah off. They waited until after the fight to tell him because they didn't want it to affect his fight. Then it hit him. Why Hector was so pissed about the guys watching the clips there and what was the tension he'd felt when he first walked in.

"He's not still badmouthing Nellie, is he?"

"No," Noah said a little too quickly. "Now focus here." Noah touched the pad on Gio's hand. "Right here is where your head should be."

Just the thought of that asshole McKinley trashing Nellie on television pissed him off so much that he landed a hard one on Gio's pad—a lot harder than Gio was expecting because it threw him off balance.

"You see?" Noah urged now. "This is why you don't think about any of that shit before the fight. It'll make you sloppy—throw you off your game. It's what they want, Abel. It's their only hope. You *know* this."

"Yeah," Hector quickly agreed, the look on his face a clear indication of the regret he felt now for having even brought up the subject.

With a deep breath, Abel brought his attention back to the pads and started the drills again, this time holding back the rage that his fists wanted to unleash. He'd save it for the ring. He didn't even have to know what that idiot must be saying to know that he already wanted to knock him on his ass, but Noah was right. If he didn't focus, he'd be a mess— forget about his strategy and go in there ready to kill. That would never work. He needed to focus.

To add to the tension he'd felt from the moment he walked in today, he was beginning to worry about Nellie. She should've been there by now. They were minutes from walking out. She wouldn't be taking the walk out to the ring with him, but he wanted her here while he warmed up. He wanted her by his side until the very last moment.

Andy wasn't anywhere around now. Abel could only hope he was out doing what he'd asked him to do earlier—go back and get her from the hotel. He'd hate to think maybe she'd gotten mobbed and that's why it was taking her so long to get there.

Still wearing his gloves, he asked Hector to get Nellie on the phone for him. Again Hector and Noah exchanged glances. "All right, what's going on?" he asked, suspiciously and more irritated now that he might not see her before the fight. "You two know something I don't?"

Both shook their heads, but neither would make eye contact with him. Abel turned to Gio, who quickly glanced away. "This is ridiculous. What is it? Hammerhead laying it on thick about Nellie, and you guys think I can't handle it? I know he's an asshole." He clenched his jaw, remembering the filthy words McKinley had spat at him last night. "How bad can it be?"

Again they were all silent, and the whole room seemed to hush entirely. Abel glanced around at everyone in the room. Not one of them would look him in the eye.

"She's not answering," Hector said, breaking the silence in the room.

"Get the monitor in here," he ordered loudly to no one in particular, but no one moved.

"No," Noah finally spoke. "You don't wanna do that."

"I do." Abel insisted.

"You don't. Trust—"

"The hell I don't!" Abel barked, silencing the room once again.

Turning very specifically this time to one of the newer trainers from 5th Street, who was lucky to be there, he pointed. "Cuen, go get that monitor."

Noah held out his hand to a very wide-eyed Cuen, who stopped at the sight of it. "It's nothing but a bunch of bullshit, Abel," Noah urged. "Nothing but shit that's gonna get you all riled up right before the fight. Watch it after!"

His words pleaded, and Abel nearly gave in until the door opened, getting all their attention. Andy walked in with a stunned expression when he realized everyone was staring at him.

"Where is she?" Abel asked immediately.

"Nellie? I don't know. She didn't answer the door at the hotel. She's not answering her phone. I even called Roni—"

"You called Roni?" Noah asked suddenly.

"Well, yeah," Andy said. "I knew this guy was gonna be worried, so I called to ask her if she'd seen or heard from her."

"What did she say?" Abel asked, taking a few steps forward.

"She hasn't heard from her either." Andy motioned with his hand. "It's almost show time."

Abel turned back Cuen. "Get the monitor."

Something was up. Nellie wouldn't have just disappeared.

"Don't get it," Noah said firmly then turned to Abel. "You'll watch it after."

"Get the fucking monitor," Abel's words exploded, making everyone in the room flinch. "Now!" he followed up and a frozen Cuen began moving again.

Noah shook his head and walked away. "You really should wait until after," Hector said, his voice much calmer than it had been early.

"Don't start with me, Hector," Abel warned, pacing now and looking around at all the guys in this room who refused to make eye contact with him.

What the hell could be so bad? Andy looked paralyzed where he still stood by the door he'd walked through but stopped at the sight of everyone staring at him. There was something else about the uncomfortable expression he wore. Like everyone else, he clearly wasn't looking forward to having to stand there and watch while Abel saw the footage of whatever had everyone so uncomfortable. But there'd been something a bit smug about the way he'd delivered the news that Nellie couldn't be found. The asshole was probably glad he hadn't found her.

Cuen rolled the monitor back in the big room. With his gloves on, Abel wouldn't be able to do anything. "Turn it on, please."

Cuen began to and some of the guys actually walked out of the room. *What the hell?* Swallowing hard, he waited. As long as Nellie was okay, he could take anything. His stomach dropped, remembering the terrifying asthma attack she'd had in the room earlier. What if that's what everyone in the room already knew? That she'd had another one.

"What's taking so long?" he demanded, the alarm full-blown now.

Fumbling with the buttons on the remote, Cuen finally got the monitor on. He switched the channels, and then Abel froze when he saw the images. "Turn it up," he said, his eyes glued to the screen.

The words the reporter spoke were a low buzz getting louder and louder with every word. Abel watched and listened as his insides began to boil. He wasn't even sure if he'd blinked the entire time he watched, but after a few more minutes, he'd had enough. "Turn it off. Take the key to my room, Andy. She's probably still there, afraid to leave. Go get her."

"You really think that's a good idea?" Andy asked, glancing at Noah for help. "She'll be an even bigger distraction now, right? I think the crowd—"

"I don't give a *fuck* what you think, Andy!" Abel was done with Andy's obvious disregard for the importance of his relationship with Nellie. "You take my goddamn key, go to my room, and you bring her here!"

"But—"

"God damn it!" Abel started pulling the strings on his gloves with teeth.

The music for his grand entrance to the ring outside was already starting.

"What are you doing?" Hector asked his voice completely panicked.

"If I have to go look for her myself, I will!"

"Okay, I'll go!" Andy finally conceded.

Abel continued pulling the strings, unconvinced that Andy was actually going. "Stop that, Abel," Noah approached him, grabbing his glove. "Get out of here, Andy," he ordered without even looking at him. "Go get her."

"Don't come back without her," Abel said as Noah began tightening the strings on his gloves again.

"Look at me," Noah said as he roughly retied the strings on Abel's gloves then spoke slowly but very clearly. "You are going to blow this if you don't get your head back in it. Forget everything you just saw on that damn television, and you concentrate on the technique we've put so much time and effort into perfecting. You hear me?"

Abel nodded, his insides burning up and only getting hotter by the second. That mother fucker was going down.

CHAPTER 19

Minutes after Abel walked out of the hotel room, Nellie still stood there, torn between listening to Logan's voicemail and just turning on the television. Knowing full well that the media never had the entire truth as it really was, she decided to listen to his message first. She hit the prompts until it brought her to her unheard message and closed her eyes bracing herself as Logan's message started.

"Since you're obviously not gonna be calling me back, I'm hoping you'll at least listen to this. I know you must be furious with me, and I will admit that I gave in because of the money that was offered in the beginning, but please let me explain. I never imagined it would turn into this. First of all, I didn't even meet Sam until the night of the concert." He cleared his throat and paused as her heart punched against her chest. The reality of how bad this might really be began to sink in. Sam wasn't actually his friend? "The day I interviewed with you for the job, a guy approached me outside your office as I left. He said he was with the press and knew you worked closely in conjunction with 5th Street. He told me there'd be money in it for me if I could get anything out of you about Abel.

"He made it sound harmless, said you might not know anything about him but I'd still get paid for any effort I made to get *something*. The bigger the scoop I got, the more money there was in it for me. At the time, I didn't even know if I had the job yet, so I took his number and told him I'd call him if I got anything. Later, I'd already decided I wasn't gonna do it, but remember I told you how tight money was for me? So I called and told them what little I had, which was really nothing. They pushed me to get closer to you so I could get more from you. They suggested I ask you out—said they'd pay for everything—but you kept turning me down. So after you mentioned that concert you wanted to go to being sold out, I told them and they said that was my chance, and that's how I got not only the tickets but the VIP passes.

"Financially, things were only getting worse for me, so when I walked in on you and Abel that one day, I figured what harm could there be in me letting them know about that? Nellie, I really, *really* needed the money."

He paused again then exhaled sharply, the dread seeping deeper and deeper with every word she heard. Nellie held her palm flat against her chest now as she continued feeling completely betrayed by both Logan and Sam, but the hurt she felt wasn't anywhere near the dread of what this all meant for the tabloids.

"They got real excited when I told them, especially when I mentioned that it appeared that Abel didn't seem the least bit pleased about me being there to see you. I also told them how I'd almost shit my pants because I'd mentioned having a date with you over that intercom and he'd obviously heard. They were very intrigued that you denied being more than just friends, even when Abel had clearly insinuated just the opposite with his body language. A few days later, they offered me an obscene amount of money if I went along with their scheme at the concert. They told me to say that Sam was my friend, and they said that he was just a reporter who would try to get an exclusive out of you. I was actually happy about the way everything turned out at first, until I found out that Sam was McKinley's fucking brother!"

Nellie nearly dropped the phone, immediately wheezing. She didn't even listen to the rest of the rambling, apologetic message. After taking a few much-needed hits of her inhaler, she turned on the television. She didn't have to the flip the channels more than once before finding coverage of her affair with Sam "McRage" McKinley.

"... it's still unclear if the 5th Street coordinator whose been rumored to be romantically linked with the heavyweight contender, Aweless Ayala, was actually involved with his opponent's brother, a former heavyweight fighter himself, Samson "McRage" McKinley, or if this is just a publicity stunt. Coming off the heels of yesterday's conference brawl between the two camps, it's hard to know what is actually the real story or just hype. Neither Ayala nor Ms. Gamboa has been able to be reached for comment, but with the big fight just hours away, it's all the buzz on McKinley's side. While Samson McKinley has yet to be reached for comment either, his brothers have, in fact, confirmed that the romance between Sam and Gamboa is alive and well."

It wasn't just the tabloid channels talking about it. Even the sports channels were putting in their two cents. "I'm not one to comment on the personal lives of athletes." One former heavyweight champ was commentating on ESPN. "It is what it is, you know? We all have our family and personal drama. From what I've been told, this is not Ms. Gamboa's first personal scandal that's played out in the media, but without getting into that, I'm just gonna say this, getting back to tonight's fight that's only minutes away from getting started: Regardless if she is actually romantically involved with Ayala or if she's just his personal assistant," he shook his head. "I hate to be melodramatic, but technically she is sleeping with the enemy. That's gonna play a role in his fighting tonight, no doubt about it. If, in fact, he has been following the story today, he won't be getting in the ring with a clear mind."

Nellie sat frozen on the sofa. She was barely able wrap her brain around the magnitude of this. She watched in horror as she switched the channel and stopped when she saw Abel's opponent being interviewed about the scandal.

"Well, I don't know if their lack of commentary on the subject suggests they're denying it." McKinley said to the reporter as his hands were being wrapped by his trainer. He shrugged. "My brother's personal life is *his* personal life, and I don't wanna piss him off by saying too much. All I can say is that photos don't lie. And what I can say for certain is Mr. Aweless was none too happy about me mentioning it last night. You all saw how that ended."

He laughed, those light blue eyes twinkling into the camera, and now Nellie knew why he'd looked so familiar when she looked him up. "How did I not put it together?" she gasped.

But how could she have? This was outrageous. Abel had mentioned that McKinley's camp was notorious for going above and beyond to get into their opponents' heads, but this?

As if her heart hadn't had enough, it nearly gave out when the reporter explained what photos McKinley was referring to. Then photo after photo of her and Sam flashed on the screen. There were some of the two of them having brunch, holding hands, walking into his hotel room by the beach, and then photos of him caressing her face and the embrace they shared just outside his hotel patio. It dawned on her at that moment that she remembered him acting strangely and asking her to go out onto the more open beach to hug her. *The bastard!* And here she'd thought him so genuine then. They'd even taken photos of him hanging out with her and her parents just outside the emergency room doors and in the parking lot of the hospital the night Gus had stuck a bean in his nose. Then there was another photo of him kissing her goodnight just outside her home.

Nellie stood up in an effort to try and calm herself because her inhaler wasn't quite doing the job anymore, and she was beginning to struggle to steady her breath.

The photos of her and Sam "sneaking away" to be alone in the hotel lobby Thursday were being labeled especially scandalous given the fact that insiders were reporting that Abel and Nellie had arrived together in Vegas. They even reported that she was very likely staying with him in the same suite.

Unable to take it anymore, she changed the channel again, only to see more photos of her and Sam. She switched it again just in time to hear the commentators of TMZ refer to her as the 5th Street Cougar.

"Well, I don't know if cougar is the right nickname for her," one of the guys joked. "Cougars tend to stick to strictly younger guys. McKinley is actually older than she is. How 'bout 'heavyweight punching bag'? They *all* get a jab at her. Eh? Eh?"

Nellie turned the television off, trying desperately to compose herself. The tears were already trailing down her face. This was a disaster. Now she knew why her phone was still silent and Abel's was probably as well. No one wanted to alert them of the stories. Abel had promised to not watch any of the coverage, and they were probably all praying he hadn't heard anything about it. Roni may even be upset with her.

How the hell could she have been so clueless about Sam? Then an even more terrifying thought slammed into her violently. Abel may not have known before he left today, but as with her, it was just a matter of time before he did. Would he possibly believe that she'd known all along who Sam was? That she'd purposely set out to humiliate him like this? Maybe as retaliation for Rachel?

Rushing to the bedroom with her heart in her throat, she knew she had to get to Abel—had to explain it to him before it was too late. The timelines on those photos with her and Sam at his hotel in Los Angeles were all screwed up. The captions suggested she'd spent the entire day with him in his hotel then he took her home late at night when, in fact, they'd stayed out late because of the trip to the emergency room for Gus.

Nellie had a better grip on her breathing now, but she was still wheezing. She *had* to stay calm. With this much drama all at once, her inhaler would be useless if she really lost it.

She'd packed an elegant cocktail dress, and for such a huge occasion, she would've preferred to spend more time getting ready. There was no time, so she did her face quickly and put her hair up in a twist. It would have to do. With her heart still pounding harder than it had been all morning, Nellie grabbed her clutch and ran out.

The elevator door opened, and she nearly ran into a grave-faced Andy, who stood right in front of the doors. "Andy, I have to get to Abel," she said as she stepped out of the elevator.

"Do you now?" he asked, his face still harder than she'd ever seen it. "Haven't you done enough?"

"But I didn't know. If I had known—"

"Look, the damage is done. He's going nuts over all this, but we think he still has a chance at the fight if he could just get his mind clear of this shit. You showing up is not gonna help."

"But I have to explain," she said, barely able to catch her breath, and she began digging in her purse for her inhaler.

"Let me be honest with you, Nellie." Andy stared at her coldly. "He sent me down here to get you. He's furious about this, but I don't think you going down there now is a good idea at all. Neither do any of the guys. I saw the way they all looked at me as I left. They're all hoping I don't find you."

"But he wants me there," she insisted, the emotion of knowing Abel was furious with her now overwhelming her.

"Not for the reasons he may've earlier." Andy snapped back. "He wants to let you have it now. I've never seen him so disgusted."

Feeling the warm tears fill her eyes, she shook her head. "I had no idea and I can explain it all."

"Explain all you want after," Andy stared at her, not even attempting to hide his utter contempt for her. "If you care for him at all, you'll stay away until after the fight. You'll have plenty of time to explain then. Do you really think that his getting into it with you just before the fight and getting himself more riled up than he already is, is a good idea?" He lifted his brow. "He doesn't really want you there, Nellie. He's just too worked up to listen to reason. He's so pissed off that he thinks telling you off will somehow make him feel better."

Taking a hit from her inhaler, which at this point was pretty useless, she stared at him as she felt the warm stream of tears pour down her cheeks and continued to wheeze. "Tell him I'm *so* sorry. I really had no idea." She stopped to inhale a slow trickle of air that flowed through that familiar straw-like opening in her chest. "Tell him I love him."

She wanted to turn and get back in the elevator, but it didn't feel right, not anymore. How could she sit in his luxurious suite, waiting for him after everything Andy had just told her?

"Just wait for him here." Andy said, pushing the button for the elevator.

"No," she shook her head, still struggling to breathe and wheezed loudly. "I can't. Tell him to call me when it's over."

"Wait," Andy touched her arm as she began to walk away. "This way. You'll get mobbed if you go out that way."

Leading her out the back door, the one she and Abel had arrived in that first day, he quickly hailed her a cab. She slid into the back seat, clutching her purse. "Tell him to call me." She urged Andy again.

Andy nodded, closing the door. She had no idea where she was headed. All she knew was she had to get away. Andy stuck his head in the front window and said something to the driver, but she couldn't hear what he said over her wheezing. From the look on the driver's face when he turned to look at her wide-eyed, Andy had told him who she was.

"Where are we going?" The driver asked as soon as his jaw was no longer hanging open.

"Somewhere far—out of this city," she managed to say between wheezing breaths.

"I go as far as the state line to the Primm and Buffalo Bills—"

"No," she shook her head quickly. "I don't wanna go near any casinos."

The driver frowned before offering something else. "I can take you to a small hotel in Henderson. That's about a half hour away. But I'm a Vegas cabby, lady. I can't go further than that."

Nodding, she agreed quickly, laying her head back on the seat as she breathed in deeply, the tears once again flowing.

As the Hispanic singer Abel's mom loved so much finished singing the U.S. National Anthem, Abel paced around the back corridor that led into the giant stadium. According to Hector, it was a full house. He'd also mentioned some of the celebrities sitting near the girls. "Bianca said Stallone and Schwarzenegger are sitting right behind them," Gio said, smiling. "And she heard them saying they both have their money on you."

Without responding, Abel did more of his jaw stretching as he continued to pace, jumping in place every few steps. He turned to Noah, who was doing something on his phone. "Has Roni heard from Nellie?"

Noah frowned, shaking his head. "She thinks maybe Nellie is embarrassed and waiting to talk to you before she speaks with anyone else about this. She says she's certain Nellie didn't know—"

"Of course she didn't know," Abel snapped. "There's no way she knew. Those bastards set her up."

"Well, let it go, then," Noah said firmly. "As long as you both know the truth, don't worry about any of this until after the fight."

Abel glanced around the rest of his entourage, clenching his jaw now instead of stretching it like he should be. Where the *fuck* was Andy? His intro music started, and Noah lifted the hood of Abel's satin robe over his head. "Show time."

They all started moving with Abel in the front, behind only the guy holding the camera in front of him and the guy guiding the cameraman from behind as he walked backwards. The two security guards at either side of him just a few steps in front of him were there to keep the crowd at a distance. The crowd was already going wild, and he hadn't even come into view. The second he came into view, they got even louder.

Abel did what he always did as he made his way into the ring. He jabbed his arms every now and again to keep his arms warm. Concentrating on the song the mariachis in the ring were singing, he closed his eyes momentarily at some of the lyrics.

Traigo la sangre caliente. No me la puedo apagar.

Little did his mom know, when she chose his entrance song, how right on the money she was. To say his blood was so hot he couldn't cool it down was putting it lightly. Every step he took closer to the ring where he'd get to pummel McKinley, he could literally feel the slow boil in his blood beginning to bubble.

By the time he was in the ring, the crowd was out of control. McKinley was the loathsome loudmouth boxer everyone loved to hate, so it didn't surprise Abel that the entire place seemed to be cheering for him to take Hammerhead down. He had to concentrate on that—winning. At the moment he was doing the exact thing the guys had warned him not to do—raging. All he could think of was ripping McKinley's head off.

His music came to an end, and he nodded at the mariachi band members in appreciation. They all smiled at him proudly, but a smile was something he couldn't bring himself to even force, not with the empty seat next to Roni where Nellie was supposed to be sitting. Taking a deep breath, he lifted his glove up to the crowd chanting his last name.

It was perfectly fitting that McKinley's entrance music was some obnoxious rap song with the F-bomb dropped in every other lyric. The crowd once again went crazy; only this time there was also a lot of booing. Abel continued to stretch his jaw, jumping in a place a few times and jabbing his arms in the air.

Watching McKinley and his brother enter the ring was almost more than Abel could bear. He clenched his jaw as he turned in their direction. Sam was noticeably absent, but his other brother, the one sporting a swollen cheek, smiled at him smugly. Swallowing hard, Abel glanced away before he got the urge to charge at him and drop him again like he had the night before.

The announcer finished with all the formalities of crediting the promoters and introducing the ringside judges. He announced the fighters, and once again the crowd went wild when Abel "Aweless" Ayala was introduced. After last night, he wasn't so sure the name was appropriate anymore.

Nathanial "Hammerhead" McKinley was introduced, and the cheers turned into a mixture of cheers and boos. Abel continued to jab in place until the ref brought them both to the center of the ring and explained the rules. Gio placed Abel's mouthpiece in as the ref spoke, and after tapping gloves with McKinley, who he'd stared down the entire time, they were both excused back to their corners.

"You got this," Noah said as he helped Abel out of his robe. "Just stick to what we've been working on all this time. Clear your mind of everything else."

Abel turned to see the empty seat next to Roni again and bit down on his mouthpiece. Noah tapped his chin as Gio spread petroleum jelly on his upper face. "Are you listening to me? Don't worry about that now, man. There's nothing you can do about any of that until this is over. Don't blow this, Abel."

Nodding, Abel jumped to his feet as the bell rang. The guys all got out of the ring. The buzzing in Abel's head drowned out the crowd. The fact that Nellie still wasn't there and this guy standing in the ring with him had everything to do with that blurred everything around him until his entire surroundings were now black. There was no more sound or anything else. All he saw was his fury's prize right in front of him, and he was going for it. The only thing he heard from that moment on was the bell, and he went for it with a vengeance.

Landing the first one, he missed the next couple of jabs, which were literally air jabs. McKinley got a few in on him, and he stumbled back. Then the images in his head started up: the ones of Nellie and Sam entering his hotel room then the one of his lips on hers. They'd set her up and he fucking knew it. He swung hard with everything he had, and if he'd landed it, he was sure he would've taken McKinley's head off. But he missed and he stumbled, nearly going down since he'd swung with so much force.

When the round was over, everything else began coming back into view, and he heard others talking, but not until Noah grabbed his shoulders with both hands and shook him. "Are you listening to me!" Abel finally heard what Noah was saying and he nodded. "You are gonna blow this thing if you keep going out there swinging like that. This is *exactly* what they wanted. Are you gonna let them win? That's their only hope, that you lose your fucking mind and go out there and keep doing that." Noah pointed behind him in the direction of McKinley's corner. "He ain't got shit on you and he knows it. Even with you turning into a madman like you just did, swinging without even thinking, I still think you got that round, but you *cannot* keep doing that!"

"Yeah, Abel," Hector said. "That was ugly. You nearly knocked yourself out in there. If you'd landed it, it would've been beautiful."

"No shit," Gio agreed immediately. "This fight would be over if you'd landed it, but you're not gonna land anything going at it that way. And what's worse is if you keep that up by round three you're gonna be worn out. You got twelve rounds to go, man. Pace yourself."

"Slow and steady," Noah said as the bell rang, and they all jumped out of the ring. "Get your head together!" Noah yelled as Abel stood up again and once again tuned everything and everyone out.

More than a half hour after leaving Abel's suite, Nellie arrived at a small unassuming hotel somewhere in the outskirts of Henderson. She didn't even care where she was, as long as she was away from the big city where Andy had assured her she'd be mobbed.

Her breathing had finally steadied, but Andy's words kept the tears flowing. *I've never seen him so disgusted. He doesn't really want you there, Nellie.* She paid the driver and walked into the hotel lobby, still feeling numb. Even though it was significantly smaller than the giant hotels in Vegas, it still had a small bar off to the side where, of course, the fight was being aired, and they had a good-sized crowd watching.

Nellie didn't take her dark glasses off and hoped to God that no one would recognize her. She'd pay for her room and go lock herself up for the rest of the night. She could only pray that Abel would actually be calling her after the fight.

"He's totally off tonight," another hotel attendant said to the clerk helping Nellie as he joined him behind the counter.

The clerk looked away from the computer screen and back to one of the monitors at the bar that the other attendant was staring at. "You think it's the scandal that has him fighting so sloppily? I've seen him in other fights, and he's always so damn good."

"I dunno." The guy took a seat on a stool behind the counter but still stared in the direction of the fight. "I thought that was all just a publicity stunt, but something's off, that's for sure." He suddenly stood up as the crowd in the bar got loud. "You see! That's the second time he's almost gone down."

The clerk shook his head as Nellie felt the tightening in her chest again. Her wheezing had never completely gone away, but it'd calmed. Now it was getting bad again.

"Name please?" The clerk asked her.

"Nellie," she whispered. "Nellie Godinez."

Thankful that she still had an old I.D with her married name on it, she began digging for it in her purse as the crowd in the bar got even louder.

"Holy shit." The other attendant hurried around the counter to get a better look at the fight again. "Ayala's gonna go down."

Deciding to forget about the ID for a moment, Nellie pulled out her inhaler instead. She was unable to stand it anymore, so she finally turned to watch the monitor. Abel was still up, but he did look sloppy, swinging way too fast and missing a lot while McKinley kept landing his punches. Almost everyone at the bar was on their feet now.

She didn't even realize how bad she was wheezing, until the clerk behind the counter asked her if she was okay. Her inhaler may as well have been empty for all it was helping. Shaking her head, she managed to get across that, no, she wasn't okay, not at all. Her inability to catch her breath now was so bad that it was really beginning to scare her.

Then it happened. Abel went down with an enormous thud, his head bouncing off the canvas. She stared wide-eyed as she clutched her chest gasping for air, but even the straw like trickle of air she'd been able to inhale earlier was gone now. The clerk's alarmed face was the last thing she saw before everything went black.

CHAPTER 20

"Snap the fuck out of it, Ayala, or you're gonna lose this shit!" Noah barked from the sidelines as Abel got back on his feet. "You're better than this. Damn it!"

Staring at McKinley, Abel shook his head, desperately trying to clear it, and worked on his footwork until he got his rhythm back. *Focus, God damn it!* Being dropped for the first time in his career really snapped Abel out of it, and he was almost grateful because he hadn't been thinking straight at all. He was close to losing the fight of his life against this guy—the guy he wanted nothing more than to bury. But he had to be smart because Noah was right: McKinley didn't have a thing on him.

With steady, well-thought-out jabs, he finally landed a couple of good ones. For the first time since he'd left Nellie's side, he actually smirked. The fear he saw in McKinley's eyes suddenly was all it took. No wonder they'd gone to such lengths to get in his head. It was all they could count on.

"Do it again!" McKinley's brother was yelling from the sidelines, sounding a bit too frantic now. "Finish him!"

Nellie had gone out with Sam weeks ago, and they waited to release the photos until the day of the fight? It all made sense now. Their dirty work had almost paid off, but McKinley finishing Abel? Not happening.

Slowly and steadily, Abel worked in a few more jabs, rattling McKinley and his stupid brother, who for once had gone quiet. The bell rang, and they each went back to their corners.

"All right," Noah said, pulling out Abel's mouth piece and spraying some water in his mouth. "So that's what it took to knock some sense into you? Fine, I'll take it. Just don't let it happen again, and keep up what you're doing now. It's just a matter of time, Abel."

"Any word on Nellie?"

Noah frowned, shaking his head. "Maybe, I don't know. I haven't had a chance to ask anyone, and I haven't seen Andy."

Abel looked over at McKinley's corner. His brother wasn't smiling so smugly anymore. The guy had witnessed the power behind Abel's punch firsthand. *Yeah. Be worried, you little pussy, because it's coming.*

The bell rang and both fighters were on their feet again. *Slow and steady.* Just like he'd always fought and won. This time it was McKinley who was swinging and missing the sloppy jabs. Abel easily dodged them, landing a few in between.

McKinley was slowing down—getting tired. Abel was biding his time. Patiently, he waited as McKinley began to wear himself out. Then Abel let him have it with a couple of combinations back to back. The crowd went wild, adding to the adrenaline already pumping through Abel, and then he saw his moment. Abel wailed on him like he'd wanted to all night, landing punch after punch until the perfect one knocked McKinley's lights out. He fell back, both gloves in the air. His eyes rolled back and it was over.

The place got so loud that he couldn't even hear the ref counting down, but McKinley was *out*. There was no doubt about it. Within seconds, Abel was surrounded by the guys, and two of his bigger security guys picked him up. The entire place was going crazy as Abel was handed the belt. He lifted it over his head, overwhelmed with emotion.

It was a bittersweet moment for Abel. As much as he wanted to revel in it, thoughts of Nellie inundated him. Luckily, with Felix doing the ringside commentary on the fight for HBO and doing the in-ring after-fight interview, Abel had made sure to tell him to keep it short.

Halfway through the interview, Abel noticed that Andy was back, so the moment he was done with the interview, he went straight to him. "Did you find her?"

"Yeah, but I got there just in time to see her jump in a cab," Andy shook his head. "I tried calling her, but it went straight to her voicemail. My guess is she's probably hiding out somewhere from the paparazzi. If they got a hold of her number, and you know how easy that can be, she probably turned it off."

Abel frowned. His only consolation now for the shit McKinley was putting Nellie through was the image of him going down the way he did. For a minute there it looked as if he may have had to be taken out of the ring on a stretcher.

The first thing he checked was his phone when he got back to the locker room, and his heart flipped when he saw a text from her. He clicked on it, instantly hoping she'd tell him where she was and that she wasn't too upset.

I love you, and I'm *so* sorry about all of this. You have to believe me when I say I had no idea. I really didn't. Call me as soon as you can!

Checking the time on the text, he knew that she'd sent it just before the fight started. He hit speed dial immediately, feeling even more irritated with fucking McKinley. Of course, he hadn't questioned it even for a second. But Andy had been right about one thing. His call had gone directly to voicemail, which meant her phone was either dead or she'd turned it off. His money was on the latter, so he left a message, hoping she was checking them periodically.

"Baby, don't worry about all that shit they're saying. You don't need to hide if that's what you're doing, not from me anyway. I don't care about any of it, and I promise you that I didn't believe it. Not even for a moment when I saw the story did I think you knew who he was. Call me as soon as possible. I'll come get you wherever you are."

The celebration in the locker room went on a bit longer than Abel wanted it to. He was itching to get back to the suite to look for any clues. Maybe she'd left a note or something that might hint to where she'd be.

He got a moment alone with Roni and Noah to ask Roni about something that was really beginning to worry him. "How often does Nellie have asthma attacks?"

Roni's forehead pinched. "She hasn't had one in a while, not that I know of anyway. Wait. The day she got back from that brunch she did wheeze a little and asked me to bring her inhaler into the bathroom. But it was nothing compared to some of the attacks she's had in the past. Why?" she began digging in her purse, looking a little worried herself now. "You *still* haven't heard from her?"

"Just a text she sent before the fight, saying she was sorry."

He kept the I-love-you part to himself because like Nellie that was all his, but he waited anxiously for Roni to go through her phone. "I hope you and Noah are not upset with me." Roni covered her mouth after reading the text out loud. "She really thinks we're all mad at her about this. Anxiety triggers her attacks. The last attack she had that was so bad she ended up in the hospital was when she freaked out about something. I was with her. It was *awful*."

Feeling the icy fear race through his veins, Abel remembered her attack that morning. "She had one this morning in my suite. It scared the hell outta me."

Roni's eyes went wide. "Was it because of the scandal?"

Abel began to shake his head then stopped, remembering something. "It was right after she'd read a text from her assistant, Emily."

"Did she say what it was about?" Roni asked, her fingers already tapping on her phone.

"No. I forgot all about it once she started hyperventilating, and she didn't say why, just said her asthma had been acting up."

"You have Emily's number?" Noah asked Roni.

Roni nodded, the phone already at her ear. "Emily, hi, this is Roni, Nellie's friend."

Andy came over just then and began to ask Abel something. Abel slammed a hard hand against Andy's chest to shut him up as he continued to listen to Roni."

"No, no, honey. No one is upset with you. We don't even know if was your text that triggered the attack. She's sort of missing right now. No one's heard from her, and she missed Abel's fight, so we're trying to figure out what's going on. Can you forward me the message you sent her." Roni closed her eyes, pressing her lips together. "I see." She nodded then looked up at Abel with an expression that said she had bad news. "Well, forward it to me anyway, please."

She hung up, frowning. "Emily did message her this morning to let her know that she was watching the coverage of her and Sam and to let her know she could call her if she needed to vent."

Feeling the blow to his bottomed-out stomach, Abel remembered something else that gave him hope that she might not be too upset about this—upset enough to end up in the hospital. "But she was fine after," Abel said, trying to make sense of it all. "Later in the day she was even laughing."

Roni stared at him, looking as lost as he felt. He checked his phone for the millionth time, but there was nothing.

"She was, uh," Andy cleared his throat, "wheezing pretty badly when I talked to her earlier.

Abel narrowed his eyes on Andy, feeling his insides heat. "I thought you said you didn't get a chance to talk to her."

"Shit," Roni said, reading something on her phone, then showed Abel.

He read the text that Emily had forwarded to Roni, and he knew why Roni would be even more worried now. The text didn't make it clear what the story was about, only that it was about her and Sam and all over the news. If that had been enough to trigger such an attack, Abel could only imagine what happened when she saw the real story—when she found out Sam was McKinley's brother.

Grabbing Andy by the shirt, Abel glared at him. "Why the fuck didn't you tell me you talked to her?"

"Because I hardly got to," Andy's eyes bulged wildly as his hand tried hopelessly to undo Abel's tightening grasp on his shirt. "She just said she had to go, but didn't say where. I didn't want to upset you before the fight!"

"You should've said something, Andy!" Roni yelled at him now. "Especially if she didn't look well. Her asthma can get really bad."

"I didn't know!" Andy's voice went high-pitched as Abel's grasp on him moved up closer to his throat. "I figured there was nothing Abel could do at that point, so I didn't want to upset him."

With his other hand, Abel squeezed Andy's throat. "I swear to God, you worthless piece of shit—"

"Abel, calm down!" Noah tugged at Abel's hand, but he only squeezed harder, and then Hector was his other side.

"Dude, you're gonna fucking kill him!" Hector pulled at his hand now, and Abel finally let go, leaving Andy gasping and coughing.

"Where is she!" Abel demanded.

"I don—" Andy coughed, shaking his head. "I don't know. She didn't say. All she said was that she had to go."

Abel pointed to one of his security guys. "Get him the fuck out of here before I do kill him. Call the hospitals," he said to Roni who was already on her phone, looking as frantic as he felt.

"I'm going back to the suite," he said, rushing past everyone.

"I'll go with you," Hector said.

"Take security with you," he heard Noah urge.

Visions of Nellie lying unconscious somewhere assaulted him, and he practically sprinted. His mom's words came to him as he ran down the corridor toward the opening that went out into the casino. With his heart nearly punching at his chest, he cursed his mother's words now. When all of this started happening for him: taking over the gym; winning fight after fight; then ultimately his ultimate dream come true, a chance at the title, she'd sat him down and told him to always remember that the most important things in life couldn't be bought. She told him that while she didn't believe as some people did that money was the root of all evil, she knew it couldn't fix everything either. There were some things that even money couldn't fix.

Did she always have to be right? Feeling the knot at his throat and his eyes begin to blur, he hated that Hector was right behind him. If got bad news about Nellie, he already knew he was going to fucking lose it. She'd nearly gone white that morning. He should've never left her. Damn it! He should've gone with his gut and forced her to leave with him earlier when he'd wanted to.

Kicking the door open, he pushed through the crowd even as some of them called out his name or stared at him, stunned. Within seconds, he was surrounded by his entourage, which he barked at to move faster. He broke out into a sprint again when they got to the private corridor that led to his elevator.

"Wait up," Hector called out, and Abel could hear his brother running behind him.

The damn elevator didn't move fast enough. He explained briefly to Hector what was going on and how he was hoping to find a clue to where she'd gone in his suite. Then he ran out of the elevator as soon as the doors opened. Rushing through every room in his suite, he began to feel like maybe he, too, was going to start hyperventilating any minute now.

"Calm down, dude." Hector said as they both ran into the front room again. "Doesn't look like there's anything here that's gonna help us. She's probably somewhere, hiding out from the press." Abel must've looked as terrified as he felt because Hector stared at him, looking very concerned. "Just relax. Shit." He looked around toward the bar. "Have a shot, Abel. You're freaking out on me."

Normally Abel would say "hell no" to the shot. But the way he felt now, he needed it badly. "Pour me one," he said before double checking the rooms again.

Feeling completely helpless now because he had no idea what to do next, he called Noah. "What happened with the hospitals?"

"She's not been admitted to anything local. Roni's expanding her calls to further hospitals."

Abel took the shot that Hector handed him as he reached the bar area. "Well, she's not here." Both knots in his stomach and throat were growing with every moment that passed. "I don't know what else to do, Noah."

"Maybe she is just hiding out, man. Just give it a couple of hours."

Hours? Was he nuts? He took the shot, wincing as it went down his throat. "Damn," his face soured instantly. "What was that?"

"I don't know," Hector laughed. "It was in one of the fancier bottles at the bar."

Abel told Noah to call him back, and the pacing began. He dared not turn on the television and watch all the stuff that would remind him of what could've triggered another one of Nellie's attacks.

"You want another shot?" Hector offered.

Shaking his head, Abel pulled out his phone to check it again. He felt guilty that he had yet another call from his mom that he'd ignored. He figured this was as good a time as any to call her back. It might take his mind off things, and it would certainly kill some time because she'd for sure keep him on the phone for a while. But mostly, he needed his mom right now. He was so fucking scared that he hoped hearing her voice would somehow soothe the ache in his heart. There was no explaining it, but as much as Noah and Hector seemed certain she was okay, something in his heart feared the worst.

Deep inside, he knew there was something wrong— really wrong. He didn't know what it was, but if he didn't get a grip, he might start slamming his fists into walls in a desperate need to calm himself.

Hector spent his time on the phone with Charlee while Abel talked to their mom. The call was somewhat calming, except for having to explain about the scandal. He hated talking about it, but when he'd told his mom about not knowing where she was and about her asthma attack that morning, he had to leave the room because he thought he might break down, and he didn't want to do it in front of Hector.

"I just have this really bad feeling, Ma . . ." He couldn't go on because he was so choked up.

"Okay, *Mijo,* let's pray," she said, immediately with conviction. "Why not? I've done more praying today than I have my whole life. God and I have a direct line now."

Abel smiled weakly and listened as his mother prayed for Nellie, her future daughter-in-law, to be fine. She assured Abel that everything would be okay and made him promise that he would think positively. "Always positive, Abel. The way I did today, even after you were knocked down. Okay," she admitted, "so I turned off the TV, and for one moment of weakness, I screamed, jumping up and down, clutching my heart, so close to crying, but then I remembered. *Positive.* And I prayed some more and look how everything worked out."

He'd just gotten off the phone with his mom and had splashed some water on his face when he turned off the faucet and heard Noah's voice in the front room. He rushed out, his heart once again beating against his chest. Any ounce of hope that he had good news was gone the moment both Hector and Noah turned to look at him grimly. "She's in a hospital in Henderson. It took this long to track her down because she was under another name. Somehow Roni thought to check under her married name. It suddenly came to her that Nellie might not want to check in under her name because of the scandal."

That gave Abel *some* hope. "So she checked herself in." Already grabbing his keys and wallet, he turned back to Noah. "She wasn't rushed there? How is she?"

Noah shook his head. "Nah, she was rushed. They didn't want to give us a whole lot over the phone. But they did say she was rushed there by ambulance and she's not conscious."

Feeling his heart and stomach sink all at once, he blinked hard, willing the same tears from earlier—tears he hadn't felt since his dad died—to go away. Hector clapped a hand on Abel's shoulder. "Let's go, brother. There's a car downstairs, waiting to take us to the hospital."

It had been a long time ago since the day his mom told him his dad had died, but Abel couldn't remember feeling this agonized in his life, not even then. He was the last one to slide into the limo, but as soon as he got in next to Roni, she hugged him, crying against his shoulder, and he would be eternally grateful for that moment. While his tears were silent compared to hers, he could at least let them out as he hid his face in her hair. "I'm so scared," he whispered in her ear.

"So am I," she whispered back. "She's never been out this long."

He pulled away from her, feeling even more frantic now. "How long has she been out?"

Roni wiped her tears, and he wiped his own with the back of his hand. "She was unconscious when they arrived, and she still was when I called. She's been there for over two hours now."

Abel sat up, throwing his head back against the seat, glad that it was so dark in the car. The tears ran freely down the side of his face, and he was certain of one thing. Never— not in all the fights he'd been in or even the ones Hector had ever been in, which made him more nervous than his own— had he been so terrified in his life.

✳✳✳

Being told that Nellie was in the ICU was an even bigger blow, but Abel held it together. Somewhere on the drive from Vegas to Henderson, he'd gone numb. Nellie had not only listed Roni as one of her emergency contacts but family according to her insurance, so she was the only one allowed to go in to see her. But Roni fought tooth and nail to get Abel in there with her. Abel wasn't sure if he should be grateful for it now because he thought he might be sick as they walked through the ICU ward.

Roni brought her hands to her scrunched face and began to fall apart as soon as they got to the door of Nellie's room and saw her hooked up to all those tubes. The nurse in there, checking her monitors, motioned to let them know they could come in. Once again, he was ever so grateful to have Roni there with him, because he felt ready to fall apart. She took his hand as they walked up to the side of Nellie's bed.

Instantly, everything inside him went from agonized to on fire. "Why does she have a black eye?" he asked the nurse in an all-too-demanding voice, but he didn't give a shit.

The entire side of her cheek was swollen, and in all his years of boxing, he knew a shiner when he saw one. If someone in McKinley's camp had done anything to her, Abel would be in jail for sure before the night was over, because someone would be paying dearly.

The nurse pressed her lips together then looked at Nellie's chart and nodded. "She was checking in at the hotel when she passed out." Wincing, she looked up at Abel. "Her face hit the counter on the way down."

"Oh my God!" Roni gasped.

"But nothing is broken in her face." The nurse assured them as if that would make them feel better. "It's just badly bruised, and there is some swelling."

"She's never been out this long," Roni said to the nurse. "Do they know what's wrong?"

Abel stared at Nellie, feeling numb again. His beautiful girl looked so helpless now, all bruised swollen and full of tubes. He *hated* that he hadn't been there for her. It almost hurt that she hadn't had enough faith that he'd believe she had nothing to do with the obviously staged scandal that she'd been dragged into.

The nurse told them that the doctor would be in to explain exactly what they were doing and to give them an early prognosis. Just like when he'd gotten that vibe from the guys before the fight that they weren't telling him something, he got the distinct feeling from the nervous way she looked at him that she knew more than she was saying.

"In the commotion at the hotel, no one noticed a few things fell out of Nellie's purse. Among them was her phone. They had someone bring it in about a half hour ago." The nurse opened the drawer next to Nellie's bed and pulled it out. "Since you'd already been contacted, we turned it off. It kept ringing."

The nurse handed it to Roni as Abel sat back. "I've notified her parents already," Roni whispered. Abel glanced at the phone when he heard it start up. Roni hit the screen a few times. "All our calls when we were looking for her, and . . . Hmm . . ." Abel noticed an odd change in Roni's tone as she sat up, but he didn't look up at her. He was staring at Nellie again. "Sam's been calling too."

That didn't just get his attention. Abel was immediately glaring at the phone, his insides warming instantly. "When did he call last?"

"A couple of hours ago."

That asshole still had the nerve to be calling her? Did he want to taunt her now? Or were they trying to keep the bullshit story going for the media?

As if she'd read his mind, Roni clicked on the side of Nellie's phone, making the screen go black. She reached over and squeezed his leg, shaking her head. She obviously didn't want him getting worked up over this now, but it was too late. After everything Sam and his fucking brothers had caused, he thought calling her was still going to fly? The very thought had him on his feet because he couldn't sit anymore. He walked out into the hallway and paced. His emotions were being pulled in every direction. Part of him felt like a wild caged animal just waiting for someone to come close enough so he could tear a limb off. Yet another part of him felt so tormented that he'd just as soon curl up in a corner and cry like a child.

He paced until he saw Roni walk out of the room. Turning to her, afraid of what she might be coming to tell him, he held his breath. She shook her head. "I'm just going to go update everyone out in the waiting room that nothing's changed."

Abel nodded, a bit relieved, but at the same time let down that it wasn't good news. Not wanting Nellie to be alone for even a few minutes, he walked back in her room and stood at the side of her bed. His entire chest ached to see her like this. He closed his eyes, trying desperately to keep it together. As soon as he opened his eyes, a blinking light near where he'd been sitting earlier, got his attention. The screen on Nellie's phone lit up, and with it once again, so did his insides.

Walking toward it, he could see that Roni must've left the phone on silent, because it wasn't even buzzing. But there was no doubt a call was coming in, and as he got closer, his suspicion about who it might be was confirmed. The three letters flashed on the screen just below the green incoming call indicator: *Sam.*

Without the slightest hesitation, he picked up the phone and answered. For the sake of not blowing up in Nellie's hospital room, he did his best to remain calm. "What do you want, Sam?"

He walked out of the room and was glad to see Roni on her way back to Nellie's room. She saw him on the phone, but didn't seem to realize that it was Nellie's phone he was on. She didn't comment. She just smiled faintly before walking past him and into Nellie's room.

The silence on the other end went on a bit long until he finally heard Sam's voice. "Is this Ayala?"

"It is. What do you want?" Abel's hands were already fisting, but he wouldn't give this guy the satisfaction of hearing him lose it, so he did his best to remain calm.

"I want to apologize to Nellie," Sam said, clearing his throat. "I won't lie. My intentions going into this were every bit as despicable as I'm sure you both are thinking. It was all about getting to you with no regard for her feelings. But halfway through it, as I got to know her, I had a change of heart. Nellie . . . She's different. I connected with her in a way I never expected."

Abel gripped the phone, breathing deeply. Unbelievably, what Sam was saying now, as unexpected as it was, was worse than what he *had* expected.

"She's one of the sweetest and sincerest women I've ever met, and she's—"

"*Mine,*" Abel informed him very firmly, his calm beginning to unravel as he walked further away from Nellie's room in case Sam said anything that might make him lose it. "She's mine, Sam. So you listen very closely because you only get this warning once. I have not and will not waste even an ounce of energy entertaining the *bullshit* stories you and your brothers are trying to—"

"But that's just it. I didn't—"

"I don't give a shit about your change of heart, asshole!"
Abel pushed the door into the waiting room before he got kicked out of the ICU, because he was done staying calm. If this conversation were taking place in person, Sam would already be on the ground. His friends all looked up at him as he stormed through the waiting room and out the exit.

"And I don't give a *fuck* what kind of connection you think you had with her. She's with me now. You hear that? You blew whatever chance you might've had with her, and now it's me you're gonna have to go through if you want to so have so much as a conversation with her. It's not happening."

"I know I blew it," Sam said, exhaling loudly as if Abel could even for a second feel any sympathy for the guy. "I just want to apologize to her because—"

"Did you hear what I just said," Abel demanded loudly. Then through his teeth he reiterated," It's. Not. Happening."

"Okay." To Abel's surprise that was Sam's only defeated response. But even more surprising was what followed. "Then let me apologize to *you*. It was a shitty thing to do, and at first, I genuinely agreed with my brother and his publicist that this all came with the territory and was part of the game. I was all for it. In hindsight and after the way things went down, I won't ever be a part of anything like that again. I truly am sorry."

Abel took a breath and brought his hand to his forehead. He didn't want to hate Sam, and he knew all about overzealous publicists with only one thing in mind. But knowing Sam and his brothers may very well be responsible for Nellie being in the ICU right now, it was all he felt for him—he loathed them all. But he didn't want to be a total dick about it since the guy was apologizing and did sound sincere. Now that he'd made only thing that mattered clear to this guy, he just wanted to get off the phone and get back to Nellie.

"As long as neither of us *ever* hears from you again, we're straight."

Sam agreed without further argument, and Abel cut the call there. He rushed back to Nellie's room only to find everything exactly as it was. The waiting was torture. Roni had already walked out once to update everyone again that they still knew nothing.

Finally, an older balding doctor walked in and gave them the grim prognosis. "The good news is she wasn't alone when she went into respiratory arrest. The attendant at the hotel she was checking in at called the paramedics immediately. There's a tiny window of five to six minutes in which the brain can be without oxygen before damage begins. The medics arrived in less than four and started administrating rescue procedures."

Looking down at his chart, the doctor paused for a moment before continuing. Abel was already choked up just from hearing the words respiratory arrest and brain damage. Roni was sniffing and wiping tears away again.

"Are you the father?" the doctor glanced up from his chart.

Abel stared at him, confused. "Whose father?"

The doctor pressed his lips together, frowning since both Roni and Abel were staring at him, dumbfounded. "Perhaps she hadn't told anyone yet. She's a few weeks along in her pregnancy."

Exchanging glances, both Abel and Roni shook their heads. "No," Roni brought her hand to her mouth and glanced back at Nellie's lifeless body. "We didn't know, but, yes, he would be the father."

Speechless, Abel was utterly speechless. He knew he should be happy, but this only terrified him more.

"The bad news is that she had to be put into a medically induced coma to force air into the lungs. How long her body will require the tubes to flow oxygen into her lungs is not something we can predict, and they won't be removed until she comes out of it—*if* she comes out."

The doctor looked up at them, and Abel had to sit down before he passed out. Those last four words had made him dizzy.

"Now I say *if* only because I have to make you aware that there is that possibility. She could come out of this in a few hours, a few days, or weeks maybe, but there is that small possibility that she may not *ever*. If she does, it won't be until she's further along that we can do tests to see if the baby suffered any damage from this or not."

Leaning over his legs with his elbows on his knees, Abel dropped his face into his hands, unable to hold it in anymore and cried. Instantly, Roni was at his side, rubbing his back. "She's gonna be okay, Abel," Roni cried. "She *has* to be."

That bad feeling he'd felt was back again, and for as much as he tried to stay positive like his mom had urged, he felt completely broken now. Something else his mom had been known to say on more than one occasion came to him. "You can't have it all."

His mother had insisted that no one had it all. *You might have a lot more of something in your life than others, but there is always something you have a lot less of. God never gives everyone everything.* He knew it was too much to ask for. He was being greedy, but Abel now felt the overwhelming need to have both Nellie and his baby make it. Already, he was bargaining with God. He'd gladly trade all his fame and money—his title—everything if Nellie would just get better and they'd both come out of this unharmed. Then that other saying his mother also said often slammed into him once again. *The most important things in life can't be bought.*

The only choice he had now was to pray, so he did, harder than he'd ever prayed in his life.

CHAPTER 21

"Have you decided?"

Nellie still couldn't see who was asking, but she'd gotten used to it. "I think I have."

There were parts of her life in that other world that were blurry. Some were very clear: she had no children, she was no longer married, and she lived alone. But there were other things equally as clear: her parents, Roni, Gus. They all loved her, but none of them needed her to come back. Her parents had each other. Roni had Noah and Jack now. Gus had his grandparents and Courtney. Yet there was a nagging feeling in her gut. As peaceful and wonderful as it was here, something told her she needed to go back. She'd begun to once already, but the pain in her chest was like fire in that other world, so she'd quickly run back to the peaceful painless world she'd been strolling in for who knew how long.

"I think . . . I'm going to . . . stay here."

"But your baby."

"I don't have a baby."

The voice changed again. She'd heard it before. It sounded so pained that it hurt her heart.

"You're having my baby, our baby, Nellie. Please come back."

Suddenly recognizing the voice, her heart ached even more profoundly, awakening the memory of the only other time when her heart had felt this kind of unbearable pain: Not when she'd found out about Rick and Courtney's betrayal. Not when both her grandparents were killed in a car accident a few years ago. Not even the fire she'd felt in her chest when she'd almost gone back to that other world. A visual came to her out of nowhere, a visual of a man hitting the floor so devastatingly hard that his head bounced. It hurt more than any pain she'd ever experienced in her life because it was her fault he'd gone down, and she needed to get to him now. He was hurting too, and only she could help him.

In the next instant, the pain in her heart was drowned out by the burning in her chest, a burning that got worse with every breath she took as her entire body now bathed in the torturous pain. She couldn't go back to that peaceful place anymore. She had to come back, and now she knew why. There was no question in her mind that this pain was worth it, even if it was spreading. The pain was in her head now too. It was in her throat like scorching lava and seared through every vein in her body. If she had the strength to scream, she'd do it until her voice ran out.

CHAPTER 22

"Come back to me, baby," Abel begged, squeezing Nellie's hand.

Nellie had only been out for two days, but it felt like a lifetime to Abel. The doctors had warned him that the longer she stayed comatose the chances of her coming out of it and the baby's chance of survival, even if Nellie did come out of it, decreased dramatically. She'd given him hope yesterday when she'd begun to react to Abel begging her to come back, but then she gasped and fell right back into it. Ever since then, Abel had refused to leave her side for longer than a few minutes at a time.

Hector had even flown their mom out to be by his side yesterday, because he'd been so concerned. It'd been one of the few times Abel had stepped out of the room since he'd seen some life in her. "You need to eat something, Abel."

"I'm not hungry, Mom."

"Hector says you haven't eaten anything since yesterday. He's very worried about you. Worried about what you'll do if she . . ."

The very suggestion, even if unsaid, had pissed him off. He didn't even want to think it. He wasn't giving up hope, especially seeing that she'd made an effort to come back. Convinced now that even she didn't know she was pregnant or she would've said something to him, he was certain that the effort she'd made to come back was for him and their baby because he'd been whispering it in her ear nonstop.

Her parents and Roni had all sat with her for hours, and none had gotten even the slightest reaction from her. Abel had now become a permanent fixture by her side and would stay there until she opened her eyes.

With his head down as he held her hand, he prayed hard, forcing himself to not do it angrily—bitterly.

"Abel?"

His heart nearly stopped and he jerked his head up. Her voice was hoarse and frail, and her face scrunched, looking as agonized as he'd felt this whole time. "Don't talk, baby."

Glancing up at a stunned-faced Hector who was on his feet suddenly, Abel stood now too. "Get the nurse!"

Hector rushed out of the room as Abel soothed Nellie's hair, completely choked up. "You came back to me," he whispered, the tears already running down his face as he kissed her hand over and over. "You came back to me."

Roni told Nellie that she'd never look at Abel the same way again. Days after coming back to him, as Abel liked to say she did, they were in her hospital room, packing up Nellie's things, and Roni was talking about it again.

"Noah said he'd *never* seen this side of Abel. I don't think even Hector had seen this side of his brother. My God, Nellie, as terrified as I was that you might not make it, I was more scared for him than myself. For someone who's so damn reserved, he held nothing back. Even before we knew you were in the hospital, we all saw the desperation in his eyes, and once we found out, he just fell apart."

It almost hurt Nellie to imagine what he must've gone through. The last thing she remembered before passing out at the hotel was thinking he'd been seriously injured, and that had nearly ripped her heart out. She couldn't even imagine being told he might not make it.

Finding out where she was and why was a big enough shocker, but finding out she was pregnant was a surprise that she still had mixed feelings about. The baby seemed to be doing well as far as the doctors could tell, but it'd be weeks until they found out if it'd suffered any damage. Abel, on the other hand, was ecstatic and very optimistic that the baby would be just fine.

Before Nellie could respond to Roni, Abel was at the door with a big smile. "You ready to go home?"

"Yes," she smiled back. God was she ever.

Roni gave Nellie a quick side look, and Nellie knew what she was thinking: Thank God he hadn't heard her. The nurse had already given her all her take home instructions for the rest of her recovery. One of the biggest things they harped on was rest and no stress. Abel was already making sure of it. The doctor had suggested maybe hiring some in-home care for the first week so that she could stay in bed as much as possible.

Abel wouldn't hear of it. He said he'd wait on her hand and foot himself. Already, he wasn't letting her lift a thing. He reached for the small duffle bag that she was holding.

"Abel, I think I got this."

He gave her a look lifting an eyebrow, and she grudgingly handed it over.

Roni laughed. "Oh, she's a stubborn one, Abel. I think you're gonna have your hands full all week."

"It's what I'm most looking forward to." He winked, moving out of the way so they could exit first.

Hector, who'd flown back to Los Angeles the day Nellie had woken up, was waiting for them at the airport. No one had heard from Abel since the fight. Even Andy didn't know where he was. Abel wasn't over being irritated with Andy just yet. Noah had told Andy the only thing Abel had allowed him to: that he was taking time off and to reschedule any appearances or interviews he had for the next few weeks. As far as he knew, no one but the immediate family had a clue where he and Nellie were or that Nellie had even been in the hospital. He was planning on keeping it that way for a while. The only other person he'd told was Felix when he called to check on Abel. Felix immediately offered his private jet so they wouldn't have to fly commercial and deal with the pain-in-the-ass paparazzi at the bigger airports.

Now that the pool house was fully remodeled, Abel brought Nellie home with him. She'd be recovering there since he lived in a gated community and his home was far more private and secluded than hers. With the scandal still going strong, he was certain the paparazzi were already camped out on her street. He wasn't having it.

They reached his house, and Hector pulled all the way to the back so Nellie wouldn't have to walk far.

"So I never got the story," Hector said to Nellie as he and Abel began unloading the trunk. "What were you doing in Henderson?"

Abel already knew. She'd told him she'd gone there to get away from the media, but they hadn't discussed why she hadn't trusted that he wouldn't be upset with her. He hadn't wanted to go there with her yet. He did have every intention of asking her later, because this media crap wasn't going to go away, especially now that he'd won. He didn't want any more issues arising because of the media attention, so he needed to get a few things straight with her. And once word got out that she was pregnant, they'd be all over it—the disrespectful vultures—no doubt raising the question of whether the baby was his or Sam's.

Even with the photos of her entering Sam's hotel room and of them kissing that night, he never even considered the possibility. He had blind faith in Nellie now. He wouldn't even entertain the idea that this baby was anyone else's but his. The very thought that anyone might suggest so had him grinding his teeth already.

Nellie glanced at Abel for a moment before addressing Hector's question. "I needed to get away. Andy said I'd be mobbed." She turned to Abel, her expression a bit worried. "But even then I was willing to deal with the press, until Andy told me how disgusted you were with me and that you really didn't want me there—"

"He told you that?" Hector and Abel spoke at the same time, and they each sounded equally revolted.

Nellie glanced back and forth from them, looking confused. "Well, yeah, with the scandal being out of control, he said it was best if I stayed away from you."

Feeling his insides go straight to a boiling point, Abel saw red. "That son of a—"

"So all this," Hector asked, pulling out his phone, "might've been avoided—you ending up in the hospital and my brother nearly losing his mind—because this fucker told you to stay away and he said Abel didn't want to see you?"

Nellie stared at Hector, her eyes widening, and Abel remembered the doctor's orders—no stress. "It's cool, babe." He slipped his hand into hers in an attempt to appear calm. "I never said I didn't want to see you, but everything's fine now."

"Andy, where you at?" Hector spoke into his phone a bit deliberately, though Abel could tell he was making an effort to mask his anger. "Yeah, yeah, everything's fine. He's just taking a break. But he wanted me to go over some things with you. Can you meet me at 5th Street right now?" He paused for a second." Cool, see you there in a few."

Hector glanced down at the bags on the floor. "You got this, Abel?"

"Yeah, I got it," Abel said.

Hector kissed Nellie on the cheek. "I'm glad you're better." Then he turned to Abel. "Don't worry about Andy," he said, waving his phone at him, already walking away. "I'll take care of him. You wanted his ass fired anyway, right?"

Abel nodded, a little worried about what exactly his hothead brother had in mind. "Yeah, but hey . . ." Hector turned around to look at him, still walking backwards. "Don't get arrested."

Hector smirked. "I gotta fly out to Maryland with Charlee tomorrow. She'd kill me if I got locked up." He wiggled his fingers in the air. "Might have a few bruised knuckles on our trip, but I won't get arrested."

Nellie turned to Abel. "He's not really gonna fight Andy, is he?"

Despite his insides still being lit, Abel had to laugh. "Are you kidding me? Hector will be lucky if he gets two jabs at Andy before the guy goes down. You *have* seen my brother's left hook, haven't you?" Her beautiful eyes opened wider, and Abel smiled, kissing her. He didn't mean to upset her. "Don't worry, babe. That's why he asked him to meet him at 5th Street. There's an onsite first response guy at all times and a ton of first aid kits. They'll ice Andy and clean him up a little before throwing him out on his ass."

He wouldn't mention that it was a good thing Hector was taking care of this and not him. If it were Abel, Andy's life would be in serious risk. He didn't need to worry her about what he might do to the guy if he ever saw him again.

Once in the house, Abel led her straight to the bedroom where she'd remain for the rest of the week. He fluffed up her pillows and pulled up the comforter. "There you go, princess. That's your place for the rest of the week."

"I can rest on the sofa, too, you know. I don't have to stay in bed all week." Abel lifted a brow, his smile dissolving. "Okay, okay," she said, slipping off her shoes and climbed in. "Mmm," she said as she lay down. "If I'd known how comfortable your bed was, I wouldn't have argued."

Abel covered her and then lay down next to her. "Speaking of my bed," he said, taking her hand, "with a baby on the way now, we need to discuss our living arrangements. I don't want you and the baby living away from me. This place is a good size for a bachelor, but I don't think it's gonna cut it for a family."

"You can move in with me," she offered with a smile.

It amazed Abel that just a week ago he'd been afraid to mention wanting to be exclusive and now they were talking about moving in together—being a family.

"I wouldn't mind your place, but it's way too accessible to the public." He played with her fingers. "It's one thing for them to follow us around and try to get photos. Even that I don't have much patience for. But this is my kid we're talking about now." He touched her belly softly, feeling a knot in his throat already, and he hoped this emotional wussy shit would pass soon, because it was getting ridiculous. "My ass would end up in jail so fast if they messed with this little guy or girl."

There was a knock at the front door, and Abel already knew who it was. He was surprised it took her this long. "That," he laughed, pointing toward the door as he got up, "is another reason why we can't live here." He shook his head. "I love my mom, but she can be a little on the overbearing side. And soon," he lowered his voice, "there will be another one just like her living in that front house. My aunt's moving in next month."

Abel saw her try to smile without reaction, but he didn't miss the way her eyes widened. He'd get his mom in and out ASAP because now that he knew Nellie didn't object to moving in with him, he could really talk to her about his other plans.

Of course, Abel had been right. It was his mom and she came bearing gifts. Freshly made *sopa de fideo* was the first. She said it was easy on the stomach in case her appetite wasn't one-hundred percent yet and she used the pasta shaped as letters. "It was Abel and Hector's favorite when they were kids." She smiled as she set the tray with the bowl of *sopa* in front of Nellie. "But even now Hector still asks for his *sopa*

all the time. Charlee even asked me to show her how to make it. It's very easy." She lifted her brows at Nellie.

Nellie smiled knowingly. "It was one of my favorites growing up, too, Mrs. Ayala. My mom taught me and my siblings early on how to make it."

Mrs. Ayala waved her hand in front of her. "Oh, no, I told you already. It's Carolina, but you can call me Caro."

Smiling, Nellie nodded and glanced up at Abel, who was leaning against the doorway watching them with a cautious smile. Caro sat down on the bed next to Nellie and touched her forehead. "How are you feeling? You look a lot better."

"I feel a lot better." Nellie nodded.

"*Mijo*," Caro looked around then up at Abel, "I meant to bring a box I had for Nellie, but I must've left it on the kitchen counter when I grabbed the *sopa*. If it's not there, then maybe it's in my room on my dresser. Go get it and bring it to me, *por favor*."

Abel started off, and Caro seemed to wait until she heard the front door close. She reached into the front pocket of her apron and pulled out a small box. "He's not gonna find it, but I wanted a moment alone with you." Caro smiled and looked down at the box in her hand. "My late husband had only one brother. Like my sons, they were very close. My husband was the older of the two and also the first to fall in love. My mother-in-law, who's also passed now, sat me down one day after I'd been dating her son for some time and told me she knew I owned her son's heart. She'd waited until she was sure and gave me this."

Caro tugged at the heart-shaped stone pendant hanging around her neck. "It's Fire Agate. I personally don't believe that gemstones have healing powers or promote well-being, but she was one of those people who did, and she said this particular stone was supposed to deflect ill wishing and harm." Caro waved her hand in front of her with a smirk. "But she also said it represented her son's heart. She'd waited until she was certain I owned his completely and wanted me to have it. She said her mother-in-law had done the same with her. She later gave one to my sister-in-law when my brother-in-law fell in love. I really liked the gesture and always said I would do the same one day."

Caro opened the small box with two heart-shaped stone pendants much like hers on chains. She pulled one out and smiled. "I bought these years ago, one for each of my boy's hearts." As their eyes met, Nellie forced herself to hold in the emotion she'd begun to feel. "The only reason I haven't given Charlee hers is because Hector is still so young." She shook her head and laughed. "But I can see now that I've been in denial all this time. That *güerita* owns his heart completely. She has for some time. And you . . ." She smiled, touching Nellie's face. "I'll admit I had my reservations in the beginning." She shrugged. "Noah and Roni are living proof that age has no bearing on true love. And how can I not be pleased that my Abel has found someone who makes him so incredibly happy? It almost scares me how hard he's fallen." She patted then squeezed Nellie's knee over the blankets. "Please, promise me you'll never hurt him."

"Never," Nellie whispered, barely able to speak because she was so choked up.

Shaking her head, Caro exhaled before continuing. "And *please* take care of yourself. My *God,* when you were in the hospital, for the first time in my life, I had no idea how to console my son. I'd never seen him so desperate."

With her heart once again aching for what she'd put Abel through, Nellie nodded and inhaled deeply before speaking. "I promise. My asthma hasn't gotten that bad in a long time. For the most part, I know how to keep it under control. The circumstances this time were just . . ."

"I know." His mom agreed quickly. "I know." She then handed Nellie the pendant. "Take this, *Mija*. His heart is yours forever. I've never been so sure of anything in my life." She laughed, looking down at the box with the other pendant. "Well, that, and who owns *this* one too."

Nellie smiled, taking the pendant. And she had to agree that, as young as Hector and Charlee were, those two were definitely as hopelessly in love as Nellie now felt. She pulled the chain over her neck, feeling the sudden need to wear it. "Thank you, Caro. This means so much to me." She knew now with complete certainty exactly what Charlee had been talking about. "I promise you. Your son owns my heart completely too."

She hadn't even heard the front door open, but Abel walked in just as Nellie and Caro were hugging. "I couldn't find—" He stopped as he walked in, his expression somewhat concerned. "What did I miss here? Everything okay?"

"Everything is perfect," Nellie said as Caro stood from the bed.

"I found it," Caro held up the box to show Abel. "I forgot I slipped it in my apron pocket."

Abel eyed the box suspiciously then looked back at Nellie, who took one big satisfying spoonful of the *sopa* and grinned.

"That's right." Caro said as she began out the door." Eat up so you can get all your strength back. I have to go get dinner started now."

Abel lay down next to Nellie again, careful not to spill her *fideo*. "I told you she'd be taking over."

"If the rest of her food is as good as this," Nellie said as she wiped her mouth with a napkin, "I'm not complaining."

"Oh, no!" Abel's head fell back. "I should've known her cooking would win you over. That woman knows exactly what she's doing. That's how she got Charlee too." Abel lifted his hands and made a buzzing sound as held them up in front of Nellie. "Tractor beam. She's already sucking you in."

Nellie laughed. He didn't know the half of it. But she'd keep her conversation with his mom to herself for now. He'd notice the pendant eventually, and then she'd tell him. Right now, she was still feeling all warm fuzzy about what his mom had said to him. She didn't want him making light of it and taking anything from it. Nellie had seen the look in his mother's eyes—heard the emotion in her voice. This was no ploy to get on Nellie's good side or "suck her in." She'd meant every word she said, and so had Nellie.

"But I do need to eat," she smirked, dipping her spoon into the *fideo*. "You want me to get all my strength back, right?"

That wiped the silly smile off Abel's face, and his eyes widened. "I don't think that's why she said it," he said, already scooting closer and kissing her softly, "but I like how your thinking. Eat up, baby."

Nellie did just as she was told because she was already having visions of breaking in her new bed.

By the end of the week, Nellie insisted that she felt one-hundred percent better from her asthma, but the morning sickness had kicked in pretty bad. Abel wasn't letting her go anywhere.

Abel had been right about Hector being lucky to get two shots in on Andy before the guy went down. It was two shots exactly, one for each eye. Luckily for Andy, both Noah and Gio had been there to tear Hector off him. At first, Abel had laughed at the picture Noah texted him of Andy's eyes swollen shut. But later, he worried Andy would press charges because, even though technically it'd happened in a boxing gym, neither of them had been in the ring and Hector hadn't been wearing gloves.

Andy was going to press charges, but ended up dropping them when Felix threatened to drop him as his agent if he didn't. Felix told Abel that his contract with Andy would be up after his fight anyway. He didn't want to deal with a new agent with such a big fight coming, but once it was over he'd be cutting Andy off and finding another agent. For now, he'd make him think everything between the two of them was still business as usual.

Since Felix was in town, Nellie had assured Abel she'd be fine if he left her side for an hour or so to go have lunch with the guy. Her parents would be over anyway, and she knew that was the only reason he'd agreed to go. Her parents had hung out for a bit but had to go pick up Courtney at the airport. She'd gotten out of rehab today and was moving in with them.

Nellie was surprised to hear from her sister so soon, and she almost didn't answer her call, afraid of what to expect. She hadn't heard from Courtney in months, so she gave in and answered.

"Hey. How are you?"

"Eh, the asthma is better, but now I'm dealing with morning sickness. So, okay, I guess." She sat up on the bed, pulling a strand of hair behind her ear. "And you? How are you doing?"

"Oh my God, so much better." Courtney sounded so upbeat that it surprised her. "You know how they say that it takes you hitting rock bottom to really get you to open your eyes about how fucked up you really are? Well, that was definitely the case with me. Being in rehab opened up my eyes to so much. But forget about me, Nellie. Congrats. I hear you're in love and that now you two have a baby on the way. And holy crap, you and Abel Ayala? Oh my God, you are *so* lucky. I can't tell you how happy I am for you, but Nellie . . . I know right now is not the best time. You're still recovering and you're dealing with morning sickness. So once you're feeling better, we really need to talk. There is a lot I need to say to you."

Curious, but at the same time a bit nervous, Nellie chewed her bottom lip. "I can talk now."

"I don't want to get too heavy on you, and it's a lot to dump on you all at once. Part of it I think you already know.

I have major issues, Nell. Stuff I'm not proud of. I've been so jealous of you my whole life."

They both went silent for a moment. Nellie was speechless. She'd always known her sister was spoiled and, yes, selfish. But she just thought she was one of those people who were never happy no matter how much they had. This was news to her.

"It's true. You were always so complacent and sweet, and I was always such a brat, so deep inside I knew Mom and Dad loved you best."

"Don't say that," Nellie gasped. "That's not true."

"No, it's okay, Nell. I get it. Shit," she laughed suddenly. "If I had two daughters like you and me, I'd love you more too. I was *awful*. But I'm really working on it. The old me would've been seething with jealousy right now that you're with such a gorgeous, rich, and famous man. But, Nellie, I really truly am happy for you. There's a lot more I wanna share with you about what I've learned about myself during this rehab stint, but not now. I know you need to rest, and you do sound a little tired, so I'll let you go now." She paused, and for a moment, there was an odd silence. "Nellie?" her sister's voice squeaked, choking Nellie up again.

"What?"

"Please believe me when I say I love you. I really do, and I know I never really showed it, but there was a reason I was so jealous of you for so long. Because you were all the things I wanted to be: sweet, loving, selfless, and just perfect. I take back what I said about you being lucky. You're not lucky to have Abel, sissy. He's lucky to have you."

Nellie didn't even try to hold them back anymore. Her tears ran freely down her face. "I believe you, Courtney, and I love you too. I never stopped loving you even after everything happened."

They cried together and spoke a little longer before her sister said Nellie needed to rest. Nellie had just gotten off the phone with Courtney when she heard the front door open and heard Abel walking quietly toward the bedroom. As much as she wiped her tears away, she knew she was a mess.

Abel peeked in, and his face was immediately alarmed. "Baby, what's wrong?"

He rushed to her side and took her hand, wiping her tears with his fingertips, searching her eyes.

"Nothing's wrong," she assured him, but his worried eyes still stared at her. "I just got off the phone with my sister. She got out of rehab today."

His worried expression turned to stone. "What did she say to you?"

She smiled at him, touching his rigid face, knowing what he must be thinking. "Everything I didn't even know I've been waiting to hear from her for so long. It was a good call." She sniffed. "I promise."

He stared at her for a moment then hugged her, exhaling. "I found a house." He didn't say anything else for a moment as if he were waiting for her to react. When she didn't, he continued. "As soon as you're feeling better, I'll take you to see it."

She pulled away to look at him. They'd talked about the possibility of buying a house, but they hadn't said it was a sure thing. He stared at her, and she could tell he was waiting for his reaction, so she smiled. "Really?"

"Yeah, really." He laughed. "Hector's dying to move in here already, especially since he knows my aunt's moving in next month. The house is in move-in condition, so if you like it, I'll pay cash and escrow will take a lot less time to close. *And* it's not too far from here, but far enough."

That made Nellie laugh. "Your mom's not so bad."

"She can be, and just wait 'til this baby's here. She's really gonna want to take over. I need to get you out of here *pronto*."

He leaned his forehead against hers as her eyes brightened. "Can we go see it now?

Abel pulled away then seemed to mentally take inventory of her body from top to bottom. "Are you sure you're up to it?"

"Up to what?" She laughed. "Walking through a house? I think I can manage." Truth was she'd been cooped up in the house all week, and she was ready for some fresh air. Abel still stared at her, a bit unsure. "I'll be fine," she assured him as she pulled her legs off the side of the bed.

Finally, he smiled. "Okay. But you promise me you'll tell me the moment you're not feeling so hot."

"I promise," she said, already rushing to her bag so she could change.

It had come as a surprise when Nellie told Abel about the necklace his mom had given her. But even more surprising was what his mom had said the heart represented, not that he disagreed in any way. Nellie didn't just own his heart. She was a part of him now, a part of him that he was certain he couldn't live without anymore. So what his mom had said was spot on. What surprised him about his mom's gesture was that she was so happy and all for this so quickly.

They finished walking through the house. Nellie had been a bit quiet as she took in every room: The huge family room with the massive fireplace in the corner. The granite counter tops in the big open kitchen with the center island and state-of-the-art stainless-steel appliances.

She'd smiled at the double shower heads in the master bedroom shower, and he knew she was remembering San Francisco. When they stepped out into the yard, she nearly gasped.

The intricate cedar play set had taken his breath away as well when he first saw it. It was three parts with slides coming out of both ends. Wooden bridges connected all three parts. One side was shaped like a castle while the other end was in the shape of a ship with a helm and steering wheel.

"It's beautiful," she whispered, her hands at her face.

Abel walked up from behind her, hugging her by the waist, and kissed the side of her face. "So, as a whole you like this house? The location? The inside? This yard? The pool?" He stared out into the spectacular view beyond the play set.

"It's perfect," she said, glancing back at him with a smile then turning back to admire the play set. "When are you planning on telling your mom that we're moving out?"

"I already did," he said, nuzzling her neck.

He felt her stiffen. "Really? What did she say?"

Abel kissed her neck before responding. "She knew it was coming. I'd already mentioned that the back house wouldn't be big enough anymore, and she agreed. I told her I was already looking for the perfect place for my family." His heart sped up a little before asking. "Would you say I found it?"

"Yes," she nodded quickly. "It's absolutely *perfect*."

Smiling, Abel reached into his back pocket with one hand while he caressed her belly with his other then pulled away. "Then only one other thing would make it even more perfect."

She turned just as he got down on his knee.

"What would that—"

Instantly her brows pinched, and her bottom lip began to quiver at the sight of him on his knee, holding out the ring he'd bought earlier that week.

"Make my life *completely* perfect, Nellie. Marry me." He held the ring out to her. "Please?"

Bringing her hand over her quivering lip, she nodded. Abel slipped the ring on her finger and stood, immediately taking her in his arms. Life had never felt sweeter than at that moment.

"I'd love nothing more than to be your wife, Abel, but . . ."

Abel pulled away slowly to look at her. Everything had felt so perfect until that last word. "But what?" he asked, searching her worried eyes.

"It's one thing for us to move into this home and raise this baby together."

Her anxious eyes were making him anxious too. *But what, damn it?*

"Marriage is a whole other challenge than just living together, a challenge I've already failed miserably at once. I just don't . . ." She glanced away and took a breath. "I don't want you thinking we *have* to get married just because I'm pregnant."

"You can't be serious." His brows came together, and he stared at her very intensely. "First of all, *you* didn't fail at anything. That idiot ex-husband of yours failed to see what he had. I *know* what I have, and let me tell you that being married to you will *not* be a challenge. Maybe that's what marriage felt like to you because you married the wrong guy. But I have every intention of making you the happiest woman on earth or die trying. Baby . . ." He softened up what he was sure was too hard of an expression because he wanted to make that anxiousness he still saw in her eyes disappear. He wanted her to look as happy as she made him. "I already feel like the luckiest man alive. I have everything any man could ask for, but I'm gonna be a greedy bastard because I want more. I want it *all*." Finally the apprehension in her eyes gave way to a smile, and it made him smile too. "I'm not asking you to marry me because your pregnant, Nell. I'd wanted this before I even knew you were pregnant. When you didn't show up at my fight and even after I reached what I thought at the time was the ultimate goal in my life, and I was now the champ . . . When I couldn't find you . . . When that doctor said there was a possibility you might not wake up . . ." He swallowed back the overwhelming emotion. "I realized something. Without you in my life, none of that matters. I need you, baby. I need you to make my life complete."

With the tears rolling down her beautiful face, she wrapped her arms around his neck. "I need you too."

He wrapped his arm around her waist tightly. "My beautiful Nellie," he whispered against her ear. "I love you so much."

Sighing deeply, she hugged him tighter. "I'm the luckiest woman alive. I love you too," she whispered, "so much."

EPILOGUE

Two false alarms in one week were enough. Nellie wasn't about to mention her contractions this time until she knew for sure they were coming closer together. A third trip to the emergency room in the same week, only to be sent home again, would be embarrassing now. But she knew being embarrassed was the *last* thing Abel would be worried about. He was already so anxious, and one mention of her contractions would have him herding her out the door immediately as he had the first two times.

Nellie was anxious too. But unlike Abel, she had more than one reason. She hadn't mentioned it in months because so far she'd had a normal pregnancy. There were no complications at all, and the baby was, as far as the doctors could tell, perfectly healthy. But there was still a tiny piece of her heart that feared that maybe her asthma attack so early on in her pregnancy had damaged *something*. She wanted to be nothing more than excited about this baby's arrival, but it was hard to silence that fear completely.

Not only did she not want to embarrass herself with a third false-alarm trip to the emergency room that week but today was Hector and Charlee's engagement party. Nellie wanted Abel to be there for his brother. Earlier that week, she'd been disappointed that perhaps he'd miss out on the party because she might still be in the hospital. She was glad now that Hector had simply wanted to make it official, even if they wouldn't be getting married for several years when they both graduated. Making Charlee Hector's wife was merely a formality because Charlee had moved in that back house with him months ago.

Abel had mentioned how surprised he'd been at his mom's willingness to accept things that years ago she wouldn't have been okay with. He didn't say it and Nellie didn't tell him she knew, but Caro's acceptance of Charlee moving in with Hector even before they were married was probably as surprising to Abel as her welcoming Nellie so quickly.

Roni had explained her theory, which made sense to Nellie. Like Roni had been when all the boys of 5th Street came into her life, Caro was more excited now about her expanding family than she was about old-fashioned traditions and beliefs.

Nellie had made it through the morning and a better part of the afternoon without letting on to anyone that she was experiencing the strongest contractions she'd had all week. But they were still very erratic. At one point, they'd stopped all together, so it'd been a good thing she hadn't said anything.

Now she sat at a table with Roni and Bianca as they watched Hector and Charlee welcome more guests. The party was supposed to have been an intimate one, but Caro had invited a few more people than Charlee and Hector had originally planned.

Roni leaned over and rubbed Nellie's belly just as it contracted. Her big smile immediately fell, and she stared at Nellie. "Wow, that's hard." She lifted a brow. "Are you contracting?"

Nellie shrugged. "Yes, just like I have been all week. But none are significant enough to have me making another trip to the hospital just yet."

She forced a smile, taking a sip of her water as a bitch of a contraction hit harder than any so far and took longer to pass. Glancing down at the time on her phone, she made note of the time. That prior one hit about eight minutes earlier. They were definitely getting closer. Needing to get the attention off her before Roni noticed anything, she turned to

Bianca. "So have you and Gio decided when you two will start with the baby making?"

Bianca grinned playfully but looked away without responding. Nellie and Roni exchanged glances then looked back at Bianca. "Bianca?" Roni's cautious question was laced with the same excitement Nellie was beginning to feel. "What is that grin about?"

Seeing Bianca cover her mouth in obvious pleasure made both Nellie and Roni's eyes shoot open. "I can't say yet," she gushed. "Gio wants to wait until we know for sure." She leaned in after glancing around and whispered. "You can't say anything, okay?" Both Nellie and Roni immediately shook their heads, smiling. "The early pregnancy test I took a few days ago was positive. But it's only been like three days since I missed my period, and we're nervous about making any announcements." Her smile suddenly waned. "I've been off the pill almost as long as you've been pregnant, Nellie. When we found out you and Abel were having a baby, we started talking about when would be a good time for us to start planning for one, and a few weeks later, we decided it'd be a good idea for me to at least get off the pill. I figured it would take a few months for it to get out of my system, but I didn't think it would take *this* long."

Roni and Nellie both spoke at once then laughed. They assured Bianca she was pregnant, especially after she mentioned her overly sensitive breasts and how incredibly tired she'd been lately. "I was beginning to think I was coming down with something. I've been so tired."

"Oh girl," Roni reached over and squeezed Bianca's arm. "You are *so* pregnant."

Bianca smiled giddily. Nellie was about to tell her about stocking up on *fideo* and crackers for the next couple of months because it was the only thing that got her through those first few months when another contraction hit her *hard*.

Holding her hand to her side she wasn't able to refrain from grunting. Roni turned to her, immediately looking concerned. "Honey, are you okay?"

Nellie nodded, unable to say anything as unbelievably the contraction kept on and was brutal. She started the breathing she was taught in Lamaze classes, but either she was doing it wrong or they were full of shit because it wasn't helping. Glancing down at her phone, she saw it'd been only six minutes since the last.

"Nellie, this may be it." Roni said, standing up. "Where's Abel?"

With the contraction finally passing, Nellie looked up and across the yard. Abel was standing with Noah and Gio under the large patio by the backhouse, holding a beer and laughing. He glanced her way and did a double take, his eyes abruptly locking on hers as she still held her side. At that moment, she knew that he knew. It was as if he froze for a moment, and then he moved quickly, so quickly that the guys all turned and watched him rush toward her. Roni waving him over only made him move faster. "Don't make him nervous, Roni," Nellie warned. "He tries to hide it, but he's been a wreck for days."

Nellie almost felt guilty that she'd interrupted a moment where he seemed to be relaxing for the first time in days. Ever since their first trip to the hospital earlier that week, he'd been so jumpy. At any sign of discomfort he noticed she might be having, he was on her, asking if she was okay.

"What happened? What's wrong?" He asked as soon as he reached her and knelt down in front of her.

"Nothing's wrong," Roni said a very reassuring voice. "It just might be time to go to the hospital," she informed him as he continued to search Nellie's face.

"For real this time," Nellie said, forcing a smile because she felt another contraction coming on already.

Well shit. Maybe she shouldn't have waited so long to say something. There was no way it was six minutes from the last one. She moved to her side, squeezing the armrest of the chair in an unsuccessful attempt to ease the discomfort she was now feeling.

She didn't even realize she'd scrunched up her face as the contraction continued to clobber her lower back, until Abel kissed the side of her face. "Breathe, baby," he whispered, massaging her back. "Breathe."

As soon as she took a long breath, she felt it. If Abel's face hadn't been so close, he might not have heard it, but he did—the wheezing. She'd seen the alarm in his eyes earlier that week and saw it when he'd rushed over to her, but now there was something more in them. His eyes widened and she saw the terror. "It's okay," she said, trying to mask the effort it took her to breathe. She hadn't had an asthma attack since . . . "I just need my inhaler. That's all."

Jumping to his feet instantly, he asked. "Where is it?"

"In my purse," she pointed. Abel practically tossed an empty chair aside to get to it. "Please calm down, babe." She tried in vain to stop the wheezing. "I'm fine," she insisted.

She watched, frowning as he rifled through her purse then pulled out her inhaler. He handed it to her, and as soon as she took a hit from it, she felt the instant relief. "You see?" She took a deep breath minus any wheezing. "I'm better now."

Abel exhaled, his already pale face visibly torn between still being terrified and relieved. He held his hand out to her. "Let's go."

"You need me to go get her things from your house?" Roni asked.

"No," Abel shook his head, holding on to Nellie's arm as she stood. "Everything's already in the car. After the second trip this week, I didn't bother to take it out. I figured we were close."

Taking one step, Nellie stopped as she felt another contraction coming. She made every attempt to stay calm and breathe normally. Panicking or getting worked up for any reason could trigger her asthma, and she *was not* going to ruin what should be an exciting and wonderful day for her and Abel.

She noticed Abel making an effort also to appear calmer as he stopped and massaged her lower back. In a very calm voice, he leaned in and whispered. "I love you."

Nellie nodded, unable to respond as she leaned against his big chest. The stupid breathing techniques from Lamaze were not helping with the pain *at all*.

"Do you know how far apart the contractions are?" He asked in that still soothing voice.

As the contraction ceased, she took a long breath, looking up at him, and answered. "About five minutes now."

His brows lifted as his eyes widened, but he quickly caught himself and nodded. "We gotta get you to the hospital."

In the midst of it all, Bianca's stunned face nearly made Nellie laugh. Her big doe eyes said it all. The reality of what being pregnant and eventually having to go into labor really meant, had just sunk in.

Roni assured them she'd let everyone know they were going, including Abel's mom, who must've been inside somewhere because they didn't see her as they rushed out into the driveway. She'd likely be upset that she didn't get a chance to see them off, but at this point, Nellie knew Abel was doing everything in his power to remain focused and keep Nellie calm. The last thing he'd be concerned about was his mother's emotional state.

Ever since what he now referred to as the worst two days of his life, he told her he wanted to be armed with the knowledge of how best to handle her attacks, but even more so how to avoid them.

She'd told him the most important thing was to remain calm whenever she was experiencing trouble breathing. Nothing was more detrimental than freaking out. It only escalated things quickly.

They made it to the hospital without incident, and Abel helped her up the ramp of the back entrance that they were told to use. Being as high profile as Abel was now, nothing would ever be normal for them again. So arriving at the regular emergency room was a thing of the past for Nellie.

The nurse recognized them immediately, not just because of Abel's celebrity but because she'd been there both times this past week when they'd had to be sent home. She took one look at Nellie's body language and nodded. Without even asking, Nellie could already see it in the nurse's eyes. She knew that this time they wouldn't be leaving the hospital without a baby.

Massaging Abel's arm now as she was wheeled into the maternity ward, Nellie smiled. Even as she was hit with another excruciating contraction, she actually felt bad for *him*. He looked absolutely horrified, yet she could still see how hard he attempted to remain calm for her sake.

After changing into her hospital gown and being hooked up to all the monitors, she noticed how somber he suddenly went. "What's wrong," she asked, reaching her hand out to him, feeling a wave of alarm when she noticed his red-rimmed eyes.

"Nothing," he shook his head quickly, took her hand, kissed it, and then shrugged. "All the machines and seeing you in this hospital bed just brought back memories." His brows pinched, and he leaned over and kissed her forehead. "I love you so much," he whispered, just as the nurse walked in again.

The nurse checked the monitors then checked Nellie's progress in dilating. She added more towels under Nellie's behind. "Everything's as it should be. It won't be long now," she said with a smile. "And," she said as she pulled her glove off and dropped it in the waste basket. "You're dilating beautifully. Already close to eight centimeters. It paid off to wait a little longer this time before coming in. If all goes as well as it's going now, we'll be welcoming baby Ayala into the world very soon." The nurse picked up a green stack of folded garments on the counter. "Here you go, Daddy." She handed them to Abel. "It's almost show time—time to get suited up." She winked at Nellie. "You see. If we had kept you here yesterday morning, you would've felt like you'd been in labor for days. Now you can say you came in and handled giving birth like a superstar in under just a couple of hours. I'll go get you some ice chips."

As hard as she wanted to feel as upbeat as the nurse was, Nellie had waited *too* long. It wasn't as safe to get an epidural this far along in her labor, and Nellie refused to take any chances. But she was paying the price in pain by going at this naturally. The contraction she was feeling now had her squeezing the bar on the side of her bed and her lower back felt like her spine was being ripped open. Unable to stand it anymore, she was done feeling sorry for Abel and let out an agonized moan through her clenched teeth.

The nurse made it sound as if they were so close, but the last couple of hours felt like an eternity. Abel wasn't sure if it was because he had to see Nellie in so much pain or if it was because there were so many moments when she really looked like she wanted him dead, even when he was trying really hard to console her. His reassuring her that they were really close and that it would soon be over didn't seem to help at all.

Noah had warned him about how things could get ugly once it was down to the wire. But he really didn't think his sweet little Nellie was capable of turning on him. She'd been a perfect sweetheart, and she was as nervously excited as he was on their first two trips to the maternity ward earlier that week. Then he went to turn on the video camera like he'd done the first two times they'd been there.

"I swear to all that is holy, Abel Ayala," she said through her teeth as she panted through another contraction, "if you turn that thing on, you will lose a hand."

"But, babe, I thought you wanted me to record you in labor?"

Aside from his mother's when he and Hector had been bad as a youngsters, he never thought a woman's glare like the one Nellie gave him just then could be so dangerously vicious. He immediately put the camera down very cautiously and promised it wouldn't get turned back on until the baby was born.

Remembering what his mother had warned him earlier that week on their first false alarm trip to the hospital, he bit his tongue and didn't remind that Nellie recording this whole thing had been her idea in the first place. She'd been the one who asked him to go buy a camera, a camera that had cost him a small fortune, but he figured it was worth every penny if he was going to film the birth of his baby with it. Before he was tempted to say something about it again, Nellie was hit with another contraction that had her crying out in pain.

Feeling completely helpless to do anything for her, he leaned in and let her fist his sweatshirt as hard as she wanted. "Breathe, baby. Do the breathing exercises," he reminded her then demonstrated for her very animatedly as if his own deep breathing might help her.

"I don't wanna do the fucking breathing exercises!" she spat out suddenly, stunning Abel. "I just want this baby out!"

As the contractions passed and she seemed to calm but still whimpered looking so completely spent, his mom's words from earlier that week came to him.

"Nellie has a free pass in that labor room. She can say or do whatever makes her feel better, *Mijo*. Don't take it personally."

Abel wasn't taking it personally, and so far, aside from that last outburst and when she threatened he'd lose a hand, she hadn't said a whole lot. Mostly, she'd groaned, cried, and panted through the contractions. All Abel could do was pray that it would soon be over. She looked and sounded so tortured that he could almost feel her pain, though he knew better than to say that to her at the time.

He was only glad now that he'd been paying such close attention during Lamaze classes, because he at least had a clue what to do. The nurse even said he was a *very* good coach. He'd started to smile about it, until he took one look at Nellie. Apparently, she wasn't as impressed by his coaching skills as the nurse was.

Roni, Nellie's parents, and Courtney had arrived about an hour into the whole ordeal. Her parents and Courtney stayed out in the waiting room with Gus for the most part, coming in for a few minutes at a time. But Abel was once again eternally grateful for Roni. She was *so* much better than he was about saying the right things to Nellie.

Through it all, even with her most lethal glares, Nellie never once let go of Abel's hand. If she were any stronger and if his hands weren't so much bigger than hers, she might've crushed his a few times. But Abel figured what little pain he'd endured when she'd buried her nails almost through his skin was nothing compared to what she was going through.

By the time she was ready to push, Abel was feeling almost as tormented as he had when she'd been in a coma. Seeing her in so much pain was crushing his heart. As anxious as he was to meet his baby, he was more anxious to see Nellie out of pain.

The doctors announced that she could start to push as soon as the next contraction came.

"Almost, baby. You got this," he whispered, wiping her forehead with a towel then kissing it.

Nellie squeezed his hand tighter and tighter, grunting with all her might as the contraction came. Just as the nurse had predicted, Nellie got through it like a champ, and in a matter of a few pushes, his baby girl was born.

The relief of seeing Nellie fall back completely worn-out but finally out of the massive pain she'd just been through, mixed with the reality that he was now a father, was too overwhelming. Abel buried his face into Nellie's neck and let out the emotion. "You did it, Nellie. I'm so proud of you, baby."

"Why isn't she crying?" Nellie asked, anxiously.

"She will in a second," One of the nurses said in an assuring tone.

A few moments passed, and there was still no sound from the baby. Nellie squeezed Abel's hand as his heart once again began to speed up. He glanced over to see the doctor suctioning the baby's nose and mouth and still nothing. Just as he started to feel dread, the squeaky almost meowing sounds came out of his baby's mouth, overwhelming Abel all over again.

For as tiny as she was, the meowing-like noises coming from her sweet little mouth were *loud*. "How does she look?" Nellie asked, stretching her head to see over the towels below her.

"She's beautiful," Abel said, barely able to get the words out.

The doctor called Abel over to do the honors, holding the surgical scissors at his baby's umbilical cord. "Do we have a name yet?" He asked as Abel cut the cord and wiped his tears away.

"Reina," he smiled, looking down at the perfect baby girl that he and Nellie had created.

Abel had agreed early on, that if they had a boy, they'd name him Abel after himself and his father. He didn't remember a whole lot about his dad, but one thing he remembered fondly was hearing his dad often refer to his mom as *mi reina*—his queen. He always said it with so much affection—so much love. So when Abel started looking up baby girl names and saw it pop up several times as an actual name, the decision was instant. His baby girl would be his Reina.

Roni had walked out, just before Nellie started pushing, and as tempted as he was to go out and tell her and everyone else that baby Reina was born, he couldn't bring himself to leave Nellie's side.

As soon as they placed the baby on Nellie's chest, Abel's mind was finally clear enough to remember to pull out the camera. He started filming as Nellie counted all the fingers and toes. He almost laughed at her thorough inspection of the baby.

The nurse noticed, too, because she reassured her that the baby appeared to be perfectly healthy. "And she's big," the nurse added as she started to lift her away from Nellie.

She looked tiny to Abel, but what did he know about baby sizes? The only thing that mattered now was that she was healthy.

The room was soon full with their friends and family. Nellie's family had excused themselves once Gus started getting fussy, saying they'd be by the house in a few days to see Nellie and the baby again. Abel had to get a grip. Every time he held his daughter, he felt choked up again. Then his mom got there, and he was at it again. He was only glad that he was able to suck it up. As far as he could tell, none of the guys had noticed.

After fussing over the baby for a while and giving her all the traditional blessings, his mom went back to the house where they still had a house full of guests. His family members weren't going anywhere. There was still too much booze left, and now they had even more reason to celebrate.

"I told you she'd be fine," Roni gushed, holding the baby in her arms.

"Why?" Abel glanced at Nellie curiously and squeezed her hand. "You were worried she wouldn't be?"

Nellie nodded, looking almost remorseful. "I just couldn't stop thinking about what happened before I even knew I was pregnant. I couldn't help worrying."

"She looks perfectly healthy to me," Hector said then turned to Abel and laughed. "Figures you'd have a toddler-sized baby. Nine and a half pounds?" He turned to Roni. "That's big for a newborn, isn't it?"

Noah laughed, nodding. "They said Jack was a big baby, and he was just shy of nine pounds."

Hector wrapped his arms around Charlee from behind. "You hear that? We 5th Street sluggers make big babies. You better be ready."

Nellie smiled, glancing at Charlee's fire agate heart necklace as her eyes widened and her face went bright red.

"Oh my God! Can you imagine?" Bianca said with a big smile. "You two might have a redheaded baby. How adorable would that be? A little redheaded Ayala."

"I don't care whose hair color our babies get, mine or his," Charlee said. "But I will be hoping for something more along the lines of seven pounds maybe? Gosh, Nellie, I can't even imagine nine and a half pounds!"

"But she did awesome," Roni smiled at Nellie proudly.

"Yeah, she did," Abel· leaned over and kissed Nellie's forehead.

"And I think it's the perfect name," Roni said, nuzzling and leaning over to touch the baby's nose with her own. "Because this little queen is going to have all of you wrapped around her little finger. Aren't you, you beautiful thing?" she asked, making baby noises.

"Yep," Noah agreed, smiling down at the baby. "That's why we're all here instead of partying at your mom's. We *had* to come meet the new little queen. Not one of us was waiting until tomorrow."

That reminded Abel of something. "What about Felix? Did he ever show up?"

Noah frowned, but Hector answered for him." He's fucking up," he said then winced, glancing over at the baby as if she could understand him. He shook his head as Abel waited for him to explain what he meant. "He was supposed to come. He told me he would the other day, but he got into some brawl at a club last night and got arrested."

"Again," Noah added with a frown. "He's getting out of control."

"Again? He's been in more than one brawl? What's wrong with him?" Abel asked, feeling worried for his friend.

"Well, not another brawl," Noah clarified, "but arrested again. Last time it was for disorderly conduct or something equally stupid."

"Isn't he supposed to be in training soon?" Abel asked.

"Soon?" Gio said. "He should've been weeks ago. He's been too busy doing crap like that celebrity dance show and partying like a rock star. He's been all over the TV but for all the wrong reasons."

Abel had missed it all, and it was no surprise. He and Nellie had boycotted any and all tabloid stories or shows. But it was inescapable. Even after all this time, it still inevitably got back to him or Nellie that the stories of her and Sam were still out there.

"I'm sure Andy's eating it all up," Abel said, walking over to Roni. "No publicity is bad publicity, according to that asshole, right?"

Abel outstretched his arms, and Roni handed him his baby girl. Having her in his arms was enough to dispel the annoyance that had begun to build at the very thought of Andy. He was finally getting used to it, and holding her didn't feel quite as terrifying as the first few times. He walked back toward Nellie, and she was already holding her hands out. "Give me a sec with her, will you?" he teased.

Hector and the rest of them hung out for a bit more before heading back to his gathering. Abel and Nellie were finally alone with their baby girl. Sitting back in the recliner,

Abel wouldn't admit that he felt as drained as he was sure Nellie had every right to be. But his wasn't just physical. Emotionally, he'd been put through the wringer ever since the horrific scare Nellie had given him months ago. After that, he'd had to deal with all the doctor visits, planning their intimate but still emotional wedding, and then the last few weeks leading up until today. But staring at his two girls now, as Nellie held his Reina in her arms, it'd been worth every second of the emotional ride.

"She's even more amazing than I thought she'd be," Nellie said, staring down at their baby.

"I couldn't agree more." He smiled, his eyes going from one of his amazing girls to the other. "But. . ." He let his head fall back on the recliner. "Are you sure you wanna do this a few more times?"

In the past few months, as they'd moved in and made that perfect house their home, they'd discussed a few things. With all the extra bedrooms in the house aside from the now decked-out nursery, naturally the question of how many more children each wanted had come up. Nellie told him at least one more. She didn't like the idea of their child growing up without siblings. Abel thought two was good too but that three might be even better. Now he wasn't so sure his heart could take doing all this two more times.

When she didn't respond, he glanced up at her, hoping the question hadn't upset her. To his relief, his beautiful wife didn't look upset. She was still staring at Reina, completely awestruck. Abel couldn't help smiling.

After taking what looked like a very satisfied deep breath, she kissed the baby's nose and looked up at him with a smile so full of adoration that it warmed him. "I'm game if you're game."

ACKNOWLEDGMENTS

As always I need to thank my family first. Thank you for putting up with my countless hours in front of the computer, writing and networking. You've all gotten so much better about at keeping the noise down, and finally you get it when I say I'm working. Mark, Megan, and Marky, you are my world, and I love you!

To my critique partner and good friend, Number One New York Times Bestselling Author, Abbi Glines, having a rock star like you reading and giving me feedback is priceless. I don't know how I got so lucky! And the cherry on top is that I get to read all your blockbuster hits before they're even out! Score!

To my beta readers, Dawn Winter, Judy DeVries, Emily Lamphear, and the newest member of my beta crew, my *commadre* Inez Sandoval, you're all just an amazing group of women, and I feel so blessed to have you all on my team. Aside from always being floored at how quickly you all read the MS and just as quickly have a full report back to me, you have all slowly become very special to me. I really don't know what I'd do without you guys! I look forward to working with you on all my other projects!

To my one-stop superhero beta reader/editor/formatter and listener to all my whiny rants/vents and obsessive worrying Theresa (Eagle Eyes) Wegand, you have truly been God sent, and I'm so, so glad I found you. As always, your work is impeccable, and I can't say enough about it. Thank you so much!

I want to give a special shout out to "my girls," my very special group of incredibly talented and superstar authors. Without you, I think I'd be insane by now. I'm so glad our bond has withstood the test of time. You really are the only ones who truly, *truly* get it. Thank you for the support, love, and *always* being there, ready to say the perfect thing when I need to hear it most. I hope to be including you all in my acknowledgments even when I'm on my 50th book! I love you all!

I'd also like to thank my new cover artist Sarah Hansen of **Okay Creations** for creating the paperback cover of Abel. You're awesome and your work speaks for itself. I'm so excited about working with you on future projects!

And, of course, my incredibly awesome readers! Thank you so much for your continued support, emails, messages, and comments, which always seem to come at the most perfect time, making me smile and sometimes even tear up. I've had the enormous pleasure of meeting and chatting with some of you, and I really hope to meet you all one day! I love you guys, and I can't wait to get the next one out to you!!

ABOUT THE AUTHOR

USA Today Bestselling Author, Elizabeth Reyes, was born and raised in southern California and still lives there with her husband of almost twenty years, her two teens, her Great Dane named Dexter, and one big fat cat named Tyson.

She spends eighty percent of time in front of her computer, writing and keeping up with all the social media, and loves it. She says that there is nothing better than doing what you absolutely love for a living, and she eats, sleeps, and breathes these stories, which are constantly begging to be written.

Representation: Jane Dystel of Dystel & Goderich now handles all questions regarding subsidiary rights for any of Ms. Reyes' work. Please direct inquiries regarding foreign translation and film rights availability to her.

For more information on her upcoming projects and to connect with her (She loves hearing from you all!), here are a few places you can find her:

Blog: authorelizabethreyes.blogspot.com

Facebook fan page: http://www.facebook.com/pages/Elizabeth-Reyes/278724885527554

Twitter: @AuthorElizabeth

Email EliReyesbooks@yahoo.com

Add her books to your Good Reads shelf

She enjoys hearing your feedback and looks forward to reading your reviews and comments on her website and fan page!